A VIEW FROM
My CORNER

A VIEW FROM My CORNER

MARILYN ATYEO

XULON PRESS

Xulon Press
2301 Lucien Way #415
Maitland, FL 32751
407.339.4217
www.xulonpress.com

Paperback ISBN-13: 978-1-66283-604-6
Ebook ISBN-13: 978-1-66283-605-3

PROLOGUE

Farmers, like my dad, woke up and were working soon after the first rooster crow. There were animals to feed, cows to be milked and field machinery to be readied. After all this work, time was needed for relaxation and a good breakfast before heading out to the fields.

In our Kansas home, an old cot served as the resting site for dad while mom prepared a hearty breakfast. He took off shoes and outer clothes and fell onto the cot's mattress. Yes, he usually followed this same routine, before and after, all of the other meals.

The cot sat in the kitchen corner for almost ninety years and listened to the gossip of family members. His story technique is based on that heard by Mr. Ed and his brother. True facts were mixed with half-truths and imagination.

What would be the complete truth is the affection the children and grandchildren had for the principal story characters, Mr. Ed and the Missus. The love, support and guidance of this couple provided direction to their lives and, indirectly, even to the grandchildren of the future.

TABLE OF CONTENTS

Chapter 1

COMING TO THE FARM

The Missus gave my leg a swift kick with the tip of her shoe then whirled around to glare at her husband. "Edward, this cot has to be the ugliest piece of furniture in Kansas. The next time you take a load of junk to the ditch, be sure this monstrosity is placed at the top of the heap!"

The first time I heard the Missus threaten to deliver me to the trenches, I was frightened. Now, after over sixty years, I am aware that the Missus is just talking. I am insulted when called the common name of cot instead of a daybed or a chaise lounge but am aware that she is basically a kind and thoughtful woman. The Missus has done me far more goodness than harm. She always describes my looks as hideous before she gently straightens my wrinkled covers and puffs up my pillows. Deep in her heart the Missus knows I am responsible for Mr. Ed's well being, so she tolerates my disgraceful appearance. She has watched over the years as Ed rested on my mattress a few moments while breakfast biscuits turned a golden brown and, again, as she finished preparation for the noon meal. She

1

*always smiled when, after a long day in the fields, her husband
turned the dial of the radio to the station broadcasting a ball-
game then adjusted his head on top of my pillows.*

The Ancient Daybed

THE LONG JOURNEY

The cot came to the farmhouse in the spring of 1904. It was called to duty when Ed's parents saw its picture and read the description of its attributes in a Montgomery Ward catalog. They recognized what a valuable worth it would be for their household, so quickly completed the purchase form and mailed it back to the company.

The cot's journey on a lumbering freight train started from a factory in Pennsylvania. The loud and noisy engine pulled its boxcars through valleys, climbed around mountains and stopped for at least a few minutes in each and every town along the way. A vacation, so to speak, was spent in St. Louis. The train was pulled off to a side track for several days so that supplies could be loaded and unloaded. At last, the cot's exit from a boxcar was in a remote town in Eastern Kansas named Springville. Until the day arrived when the cot would be transported the final miles to its new home located far out in the countryside, it was stuck at the back of a stuffy freight depot.

A cumbersome spring wagon, pulled by four fine horses, came to a stop in front of the depot. Two burly men jumped off the wagon and identified themselves to the warehouse manager. The older of the two said, "Howdy. My name is Willy Spencer and this young whippersnapper, still wet behind the ears, is Ned Zimmerman. We're here early this mornin' to collect supplies for Mr. Richard. His family owns the Ferndale Farm. It's 'bout a day's journey east of town."

The station manager shook their hands, gave a nod and then searched through a stack of papers piled on his desk. "Yep, boxes destined for that address arrived here 'bout a month ago." As a good Kansan he referred to the weather. "I figured you couldn't make it to town any sooner because all the creeks have been flooded by the spring rains."

The manager glanced at the first paper then pointed over in my direction. "Those two boxes over in the corner are the cot's frame and mattress. That cot is hardy, so don't think any damage could have happened during shipping." He looked at the second set of papers then cautioned, "You might want to take a closer look in these other three boxes stacked by my desk."

Willy took a knife and cut the twine encircling the first box. He peeked in the box and exclaimed, "I'll be danged! Here's a new contraption I once saw a pitcher catalog"

Ned peeked in the opening and viewed an odd-looking wooden box. He shook his head and commented, "I ain't never seen anything lookin' like this. What is it?"

Willy grinned. "Mr. Richard told me he was spectin' something special that he planned to give his wife for her birthday. It's called a phon-e-graph and was created by a man named Edison. Its function is to play music recorded on wax cylinders. Mr. Richard's family has always enjoyed singing and playing musical instruments. Now, they'll also be listening to tunes."

Ned opened the next box. What he found inside looked like a morning glory flower but was black instead of azure blue. "I ain't never viewed any flower this big either. Does it have any use?"

Willy laughed, "That flower is actually an amplifier that will be attached to the phon-e-graph. It helps carry the sound long distances. The phon-e-graph will probably sit in the parlor. Even though it's a fair distance from the barn, do you suppose the cows will enjoy listening to songs when they are being milked?"

The stationmaster asked, "Ain't you goin' to pry open the third box?"

"No Sir," replied Willy. "It's marked 'fragile'. I'm guessing it's filled with wax cylinders that store the songs. I've heard them cylinders break easily. Only Mr. Richard or his wife should be the ones fiddlin' with that box."

Since the cot was large and flat, it was the first to be loaded onto their wagon. The other boxes were carefully roped to the front of the wagon to insure they would not be damaged during the constant joggling during the trip. When all items from the depot were loaded, the men shouted, "Gitty Up," and directed the horses to pull the wagon a short distance before being hitched to a post in front of a store. The large hand painted sign above the door indicated this was Springville General Store. Willy pulled two lists out of his pocket. The longer list had been neatly written by Mr. Richard's wife. "Ned, the mister only wants a few things but his wife made a list a mile long." The men worked quickly and within a short time, several months of sugar, salt, flour, clothes, tools and other supplies were heaped on top of the cot's mattress.

The train trip the cot took across the country was long and cumbersome, but it didn't even compare to the thumps and dips suffered while on the wagon. The fourteen miles to the farm started early in the morning and continued for nearly ten hours. During the long train trip from Pennsylvania, the cot had overheard two hobos talking about the terrain of Kansas, so the cot expected it would be flatter than a pancake. That description certainly was not true for the Eastern portion of the state. It was good the horses were strong because they had to pull the wagon filled with its full cargo up and down steep hills and over several wobbly wooden bridges spanning the larger creeks. They were forced to ford small streams and trudge through steep ditches still muddy from recent rains. The journey was so difficult that several stops were made to let the horses have a drink and nibble green grass and give Ned and Willy a chance to stretch their long legs.

The shadows were dim by the time the wagon reached the final destination of the barnyard. The drivers quickly unhitched the horses then shooed them through the fence into the pasture. Willy groaned, "I'm just too darned worn out to think of unloading supplies tonight. Let's go get some shut-eye. Mr. Richard will be expecting us to be ready for a hard day's work tomorrow."

MEETING YOUNG ED

At the earliest light of dawn, the roosters started crowing which aroused every creature within hearing distance. A cacophony of sounds—moos, squeals, squawks, and growls–soon came from the area down by the big red barn. All the animals on the farm were demanding attention and food.

Awakened by the sounds, the sleepy drivers quickly started unloading the supplies on the wagon bed. They heaved a sigh of relief when the cot, the last item on the wagon, was deposited onto a sea of green grass. Willy flexed his weary muscles and motioned to Ned. "Work is never done on the farm. Mr. Richard needs us to help with the milking. Then we'll be spendin' the remainder of the day at the South Forty field."

Smell was the first sensation the cot had of his new home. The white picket fence nearby was covered with sweet smelling red, pink and white roses. Behind it was a sea of green: a freshly mowed lawn of Kentucky Blue Grass. Pleasant odors such as these were quite sure a change from the coal and grease fumes on the train and the moldy smell in the depot!

The cot's next observation gave a thrill to its springs. A large framed white two-story house stood in the middle of the yard. The shutters surrounding bay windows and trim around the doors were painted an emerald green. Uneven flat stones provided the pathway leading to a large screened porch. Truly, the cot had been blessed. The position of a piece of furniture in this household had to be about as close to heaven as a daybed could get.

Of course, the cot deserved the best! It was truly a handsome piece of furniture. The frame was shiny and black. The sides stayed up when extra resting space was needed. It didn't squeak because the coils of its springs were tight. Its mattress was new and firm. The misshapen appearance with an indentation in the middle of the mattress would not appear until after it had spent many years bearing the weight of a multitude of human bodies.

On that busy morning it wasn't long before folks, as well as animals, were awake and active. In the barnyard men and older boys were busy with chores such as feeding the animals, milking cows, and preparing the tools and machinery needed for the fieldwork which would commence shortly after breakfast.

A constant hum of voices and laughter was coming from inside the house. Womenfolk were gossiping as they prepared a breakfast feast of sausage, eggs, fried potatoes, and biscuits to be served with sweet butter and recently pre-served wild strawberry jam.

Kids of all ages were running around the yard. A young girl with long pigtails was stomping her feet and shaking her fist toward several boys. These brothers and cousins paid no attention to her demands. The young boys in overalls were too busy chasing then trying to jump on the back of a strange looking beast that looked like a colt with big ears. The cot soon heard the name of this odd creature. A buxom gray- haired lady wearing a long white apron slammed the porch door and rushed into the yard. She quickly untied the apron strings then made sweeping motions with the apron over the crea-ture's head. The animal blinked his eyes, swished his tail and twitched his long ears but didn't move. The frustrated lady demanded, "Now boys, you get Anamule out of this lawn area. She belongs in the barnyard."

There was one little fellow a lot younger than the other children. His mama carried him as she walked out of the house and strolled to where supplies had been unloaded from the wagon. She plopped the toddler on the cot's mattress and said, "Stay here Eddie." She then turned to the other children and cautioned, "Boys, keep an eye on your baby brother. Now listen to this rule! Don't be putting little Eddie on the back of that silly mule!"

Eddie seemed to be content to sit quietly on the cot's mattress and watch all the commotion happening in the yard. It was good for the cot to make the acquaintance of this sweet lad. Little did either of them know what would happen in the future! This little fellow and the cot were destined to be lifelong companions. The cot's job would always be to see he had comfort and a place to rest his weary head.

The cot's expectations of status in the new household were set too high. Even though it was to be a part of the household furniture in this grand house standing before it, its designated resting place for more than twenty years would be in one of the second-floor bedrooms. The family had pur-chased it to be the bed for one of the hired hands working at the farm during the summer months. Unfortunately, that meant it bedded a dirty, tired snoring young man each summer. When winter returned, it was stripped of covers and left alone to freeze.

MUSIC TO THE COT'S EARS

The cot was not an eyewitness to all the events happening in the kitchen during the next few years since it resided in a remote bedroom. Fortunately, it was a remarkable piece of furniture, gifted with perception abilities that allowed it to comprehend what was occurring around him. Even from the secluded upstairs bedroom, it did a fair job of keeping up with events happening both in and out of the house.

During the years when all the children were living in the home and Mr. Richard and his wife were healthy, the farm home was the hub of community entertainment. The cot often heard lively music and felt the floors rumble. That meant the carpet in the parlor had been rolled back and folks were dancing. The music box that shared my journey to the farm was in constant use. Each member of this musical family seemed fascinated with the new contraption.

A wooden chest was filled with records that were played on the phonograph. Each cardboard tube storing a cylinder was carefully marked with the name and artist. The cylinders broke easily. The boisterous children were instructed to handle them carefully when taking them out of the chest and to remember to immediately place them back into storage after use. The boys, especially Jack, were careless, so cylinders of musical favorites were often cracked and had to be replaced.

The morning glory shaped amplifier attached to the phonograph easily carried the musical sounds up to the cot's distant space. Had he been able to sing, it would have joined the chorus as they sang, "Camp Town Races," "Sweet Avalon," or "My Old Kentucky Home."

In addition to the phonograph, other sounds of music often flowed from the parlor. The oldest boy squeaked sounds from a clarinet and Jack pounded on drums. The parents sang duets. "When You and I were Young Maggie" and "Tiptoe Through the Tulips" were among their favorites. They must have memorized all the words in the old church songbook. Mr. Richard's deep baritone blended perfectly with his wife's gentle alto when they sang "How Great Thou Art" and "In the Garden." Many evenings they spent practicing because they were frequently asked to perform at church or for special events occurring in nearby communities. Once they were asked to sing at a revival in far off Kansas City.

If the piano was tinkling, it meant that the young girl was practicing her scales. Playing the ivory keys was one of the few times when she was not fussing at her brothers. The cot often heard her scream, "I'm going to tell father what you did! You'll get a good spanking!" The boys constantly got spankings, but seemed to feel that teasing their sister seemed worth any punishment they would receive.

Buggies often brought folks to the farm for a visit. The cousins and nearby neighbors were there so frequently that it was difficult to separate them from those that actually lived in the white house. Some visitors were from long distances, so they arrived with extra blankets and bed rolls so that they could stay overnight, or perhaps even for a long weekend. After consuming a large meal, tradition dictated that everyone gathers around the piano to join in a song fest. Later, furniture was moved to corners or other rooms and the carpet rolled out of the way. The fiddlers tuned their instruments to join with the piano in playing the first notes of, "Turkey in the Straw."

Old Mr. Elmer Simpson yelled, "Young men, don't waste time finding a special partner. We'll start this shindig by dancing the Virginia reel." Hours later, when the musicians took a break, Mr. Richard waved for the men to join him. "Friends, my wife is very strict about the rule that no one smokes in the house. Let's go out to the porch and puff on cigars while we discuss the terrible mistakes of politicians."

It was well beyond the midnight hour before the musicians put away their instruments and dancers complained of sore feet. Only a few neighbors lived close enough to drive home. Most stayed for the night.

This was the first and only time in the cot's existence it was considered as a prize. Mr. Richard pulled a straw from the broom and broke it into varied sized pieces. The young man selecting the longest straw smiled in satisfaction as he pulled off his boots and climbed under the cot's blankets. His friends sighed in regret, put on their heavy coats and headed for the barn's hayloft.

The strange animal the cot met the day of its arrival received a constant amount of negative attention. Anamule refused to accept the fact that she belonged in the barnyard with the other animals. She loitered around the house and frequently caused trouble. The women shouted, "Anamule, you get out of that vegetable garden!" "Anamule, quit eating the lilies." "Boys, you take Little Eddie down from Anamule's back! He is just too young to be riding that foolish mule." "Anamule, you stupid creature, quit trying to pull off those clean shirts drying on the clothesline."

Anamule never received any affection from any of the ladies of the house. Nevertheless, she was the delight of the children. They continuously played with her and frequently provided her with goodies from the pantry.

The boys were responsible for Anamule's addiction to tobacco. In those days tobacco leaves were used for far more than smoking. Dry leaves were crumpled and placed under the carpets to keep away bugs. Even though Ed's mother disliked tobacco scent, she placed leaves in the clothing drawers to fulfill the same purpose. Men weren't the only ones who enjoyed the tobacco's chewy texture and flavor. The older ladies and even children chewed on the leaves. Tobacco leaves were stuffed into the back pockets of overalls. Anamule was most pleased with the smell, so she nudged the boys' behinds to indicate she wanted her share. The boys recognized that her yearning for tobacco was similar to how horses yearned for sugar cubes. They found she could be easily enticed to perform tricks just for a few leaves.

ED AND THE COT CEMENT THEIR FRIENDSHIP

Time passed quickly and the atmosphere around the farm changed. Anamule, now a full-grown beast, assumed her responsibilities of working in the fields and was no longer constantly tormenting the women by loitering around the house. The older children were rarely around between September and May. Living so far from a town made education difficult. Ed's older siblings stayed with their grandmother who lived in a small house in Springville while attending high

school. Until they were married and had their own homes, the farm was only loud and lively during holiday vacations and the brief summer months.

The only child remaining for all the seasons on the farm was young Ed. During the quiet years he and the cot cemented their friendship. Ed loved to read. If he didn't want to be disturbed until he finished a good book, he would climb the stairs, stroll into the back bedroom and plop down on the cot's mattress. He had a tendency to talk to himself about what he was reading, so the cot could tell he was a good thinker. He was particularly fond of books about world geography and would sigh when reading them, "I sure hope it will be possible for this Kansas farm boy to see some of these places."

Only a few years later, the cot's alert listening abilities allowed it to pick up on a conversation between his father and mother. They were seriously considering the future of their youngest child after he graduated from high school.

Mr. Richard remarked to his wife, Emma. "We know that Eddie is really a bright young man. He explained to me that he hopes to attend college next fall."

"Yes, I know. None of our other children expressed any interest in attending college. I agree with you. Eddie needs to have this opportunity. Did you know Eddie has his heart set on becoming an engineer?"

Ed's father nodded in agreement. "We can be sure he would be an asset to that profession. Even when he was just a little lad, he enjoyed figuring out how things worked. He was always the son I turned to when there was a problem with the farm equipment that needed to be solved."

Emma had only praise for her youngest. "Yes, he has been a great help to you, and at the same time, he is my right hand in the house. He was the only one of our boys who noticed that the table was wobbly or the doors on my cabinets weren't shutting properly. When I need to wallpaper, the other children managed to disappear, but he always offers to help."

She smiled with pride and added. "Did you know Eddie is developing a new skill? Old Mr. Barnes is teaching him how to cane chairs."

Mr. Richard pulled the worn ledger off the top shelf of the cabinet. He skimmed the figures with his finger before stating, "The crops have been doing fairly well and we don't have as many mouths to feed now that the other children are on their own. There should be money available to send our youngest off to college."

The following fall, Ed, with his parents blessing, enrolled in the state technical college at Manhattan, Kansas. He was delighted to have this unusual educational opportunity and immediately became immersed in math and engineering classes. His vision of someday becoming an important engineer or perhaps a scientist would be a reality instead of just a dream.

But Ed soon learned that fate is not always kind. Unexpected circumstances dictated that receiving a degree from college was not to be part of his future.

During the 1920's there was a tendency for people to mismanage their money. Chances were taken with poor investments. When the market finally crashed, it was not unusual to read in newspapers about desperate people losing all their money and facing bankruptcy to jump out of windows or step in front of moving trains.

Ed's dad had been a successful landowner and was well off by standards of that time. Unfortunately, he entered into a risky investment project. The scheme did not succeed. He and several of his friends found themselves in big financial trouble. Their loss was so vast that desperate measures had to be taken.

Mr. Richard made the long trip to Manhattan, Kansas, where Ed was attending college. He felt it was necessary to share the grim circumstances face to face with his youngest son. Ed listened with regret as his father explained why he would need to return to the farm immediately and couldn't complete his freshman year. "Son, I had to let all the hired hands go. I can't ask your brothers to assist with the spring field work because they have responsibilities for their new families. I need you back at the farm to lend a hand in cultivating the fields and planting the crops. We'll need to do everything possible to save the farm from bankruptcy."

Fortunately, Ed loved the home place and understood how desperately his father needed his help. He sadly gave up his educational aspirations and accepted his fate as a Kansas farmer.

Chapter 2

MOVING DOWNSTAIRS

Mr. Ed's father suffered a stroke and had other health problems only a few years after asking Ed to abandon higher education and return to the farm. Mr. Richard and his wife decided it was wise to move into Springville to be closer to doctors. Ed was given complete responsibility for operating the farm. He and his new wife lived in a house with many rooms but several were sparsely furnished. Each time one of Ed's older siblings had announced wedding plans, Mr. Ed's parents had generously allowed them to select tables, chairs, beds, vanities and wardrobes considered necessary for their new homes. As might be expected, none of them had any interest in a shabby cot standing alone in the west bedroom.

The Forgotten Cot

MEETING THE MISSUS

As Ed scanned a barren kitchen corner, he had a brilliant idea. He beckoned to his wife, "Honey, come upstairs with me. I think there's a forgotten piece of furniture tucked away in one of the upstairs bedrooms that would be a perfect fit for this corner of the kitchen."

The Missus followed her husband up the stairs and into the west bedroom. She shook her head as her eyes identified the object pointed out by her husband. "Ed, that cot is about as drab as a piece of furniture could be. Did I hear correctly? You want it in the kitchen where we'll see it every day?"

"Careful what you say, honey. This cot has ears, and it's quite sensitive. We two have a special relationship. It is destined to help take care of me and my family."

The Missus was not overly pleased about a ridiculous-looking piece of furniture being a permanent fixture downstairs, but she wanted Mr. Ed to be happy and comfortable. Mr. Ed worked long hours each and every day. The cot would be a good place for him to rest after completing chores.

After years of living in neglect and seclusion, the cot was placed in the kitchen corner. In this spot the cot had the privilege of being the observer, and participated in almost everything that occurred at the farmhouse.

In later years, the cot fondly recalled its first time meeting the Missus. Her sleek dark hair was fashioned in a short-bobbed cut. Her eyes were large and an unusual color of green. Even though she refused to sit on its mattress, it realized she was no bigger than a minute. The Missus was quiet, but when she spoke, her voice was soft and melodious. Mr. Ed often kissed her on the forehead and teased, "You're my special school marm." The pet name fit, because during their courting days, she was teaching about thirty young children at a local primary school.

The Missus was very concerned about the cot's dowdy appearance. She spent evenings and extra minutes during the day cutting and piecing material scraps together to form a Crazy Quilt. The quilt, when completed, was considered too pretty for daily use so it was draped on a rack and only adorned the cot when company was expected.

Daily covers were made from muslin feed sacks. They always looked wrinkled and occasionally had mouse holes. The Missus attempted to make the plain covers look like works of art by patching the holes with geometric shapes and connecting the squares with colorful strips found in her fabric stash. Many years after her children were grown, the Missus decided to order wash and wear covers from a catalog. (Sears of all places!) The cot never appreciated the factory-made covers. The quilts the Missus made to enhance his drab appearance were always preferred.

The Missus often stated, "Cleanness is next to godliness." With this saying in mind, she always had at least two covers ready for quick replacement. If Mr. Ed accidentally brought in some good Kansas dirt from the fields, she pulled off the soiled cover and replaced it with a clean one.

The pillow slips were varied in quality and beauty. The ones adorning the cot when company came to visit were carefully embroidered or crocheted by the swiftly moving fingers of the Missus during the long winter evenings. Like the pretty quilts, the attractive covers rarely replaced the cot's usual ones. The everyday pillow covers were made from leftover cloth pieces after most of the material had been used to make outfits for her little girls. Fabrics for the older girl, Mary Lou, were vivid. Bright greens, reds and yellows matched her dark hair and skin tone and restless personality. Fabrics selected for baby sister, Jane, were pale shades of pink and blue. These colors complimented her curly blond curls and baby blue eyes. In the cot's opinion, this sweet baby looked a lot like her daddy did when he was a toddler.

Even though the cot spent most of his time in the kitchen, there were opportunities to briefly lodge elsewhere. The first transfer of lodging happened in the warm days of summer. The Missus spent the morning slaving with the daunting task of canning green beans. By noon, the temperature in the kitchen was stifling due to the constant use of the stove plus the rising outdoor temperature.

The Missus lovingly gazed at her husband as he rested on the cot after eating lunch. Sweat beads lined his brow and hairline and his shirt looked like he had been caught in a rain storm. The Missus murmured to herself, "It's just too hot for Ed to take his noon nap in this kitchen corner during the summer months. He'll still be exhausted when it's time to go back to the fields. Something needs to be done."

Mr. Ed opened his eyes and brushed his hands over his sweaty face. He complained, "I feel like I've been sleeping in a furnace." After giving his wife a quick kiss on the cheek he groaned, "The weeds are growing by the minute. Guess I need to get back to work in the fields even though I feel drained."

The Missus quickly finished the dishes and tidied up the kitchen so she could devote the rest of the afternoon to facing the challenge of cleaning up the porch. She first attacked the piles of junk strewn in every corner. She did the unthinkable by throwing away old baskets, buckets, worn out boots and even a couple of benches. Clothes and tools not needed until winter were hanging on hooks or tossed in heaps. These she removed and stored in the tool shed.

Finally, enough floor space was cleared and the cot could be exported to its summer site. The Missus hurried into the kitchen and stripped the cot's frame of its pillows, mattress and covers. The cot frame was not too heavy so she had little trouble lugging it to the porch. She gave the mattress a good beating to remove dust before replacing it and the covers on the frame. Giving a sigh of relief, she murmured, "Now Ed can enjoy cool breezes coming through the screens while he takes his siestas."

ON THE PORCH

The covered screen porch was almost as active and interesting as the kitchen. Even after pitching out many objects, it was still a mess. It was cluttered with dirty boots, work clothes, a broken table, tall stools, one chair with only a few strands of straw around the rim of the seat, a rusty pump, and an awkward milk separator.

Shelves built by Mr. Ed to please his wife were covered with plants. The Missus had what folks call a green thumb. Neighbors were aware of her skill and brought her their wilted plants. "Please try your magic. My plant is sick and dying." Her "witchcraft", which included ingredients like shells of eggs, crumpled leaves of tea and sweet talk, helped the ailing plants to once again be healthy and beautiful.

One plant was a constant irritation for the cot. It was hung from a hook directly above the cot, which resulted in spider tendrils dangling within inches of its pillows. The Missus occasionally pruned the airplane plant back, but instead of throwing the spider sprigs away, re-potted them so eventually they could be given as gifts.

Visitors, as well as family members, ignored the attractive front entrance of the house. Everyone chose to park their car in the barnyard and walk up the stone path leading to the back porch. Maybe it was because they knew they would receive a gift of an airplane plant.

Dozens of daily tasks were performed on the porch. This was particularly true during the summer months when the place was a beehive. The Missus sighed with frustration as she finally realized it was impossible to keep it looking neat and clean.

The cot particularly enjoyed mornings and evenings on the porch when Mr. Ed returned from the barn carrying buckets of milk. As milk was separated, the cot listened to Mr. Ed and the Missus outlining another day of hard work and chatting about what had happened during the day. The cot had no fondness for the monstrous- looking contraption used for the separation process of milk and cream. At night, when the only light was glow from the moon, the large tub head, tube neck, spouts and crank, created the illusion of a monster visiting from some faraway planet.

Mr. Ed was gleeful the morning he brought yet another basket of corn and set it down next to four other bushels. "Honey, we are lucky to have one of the biggest and best vegetable gardens in Eastern Kansas."

His pride was justified. Each spring Mr. Ed worked into the soil waste contributions provided by the cows and chickens. Mr. Ed and the Missus followed the directions given by the Farmer's Almanac for the best time to plant seeds. The Missus devoted as much time as possible during the following weeks to keeping the area free from weeds and well watered. By mid-summer, these efforts resulted in an abundance of vegetables, far more than their small family could use. Bushel baskets filled with potatoes, corn, tomatoes, green beans, carrots, green peppers and squash were waiting on the porch, ready to be prepared for canning or shared with anyone who visited.

She tried to give the area a once-over cleaning each morning but it never stayed neat for more than a few hours. Two of the culprits were her daughters. Even when very young, they were expected to help their mama snap beans and shell peas. For them, to reach table height, it was necessary for the Missus to hoist her squirming girls up to sit on high stools. What a mistake! Mary Lou immediately tried to get even higher by standing up and stepping onto the wobbly table. At the same time little sister Jane leaned over too far and started to fall. Both of them were caught just in time by their mother. The Missus abused the cot's pride and sense of dignity by stating, "Girls, instead of the table, you may sit on the old cot to work. You'll be comfortable and safe and can't cause the ugly old thing to look any worse than it already does."

The little girls were extremely sloppy and paid no attention to the messes strewn on the cot's cover. Fine silks from husking corn, a scattering of beans and peas that missed the containers or an occasional escape of a caterpillar were of no concern to them. After they were excused to go play, their mother pulled off the cover, carried it outside and shook it several times. If it was a bit damp, it was hung over the clothesline to dry.

In addition to the food produced in the garden, the family also enjoyed many native foods found in the woodlands and pastures. The cot appreciated the sweet smell of these ripe fruits. The results of labor by careless young children resulted in the cover having a color spectrum resembling a rainbow.

The first stain of the summer which was difficult to remove was from wild strawberries. In years with no late frost, a small section of native prairie located on a southern slope at the far eastern side of their property had an abundance of the fruit. The grasses and flowers growing there had never been disturbed by a plow or hoe and clues of pottery pieces and arrowheads gave evidence that Indians had long ago chosen this place as their home site.

On a warm Sunday afternoon in late April, Mr. Ed said to his eldest, "While I hitch the horses to the wagon, you fetch your sister and mother. Tell them we're going to take a ride and see Mother Nature's Blanket." Mary Lou conjured up a picture of a bed covering similar to one of her mother's beautiful quilts. The idea that someone named Mother Nature was as skilled as her mother in creating colorful covers was of immediate interest, so she quickly ran into the house to announce the adventure.

The wagon ride took them across the creek, up the steep hill, through the walnut grove, then on a rugged lane edging a large wheat field. They were awed at seeing the blanket of beauty bestowed by Mother Nature when the wagon crested the southern slope of their property. A predominate under-lying color was a pale shade of mint green. This background layer was the sprouting prairie grass that, later in the summer, would turn brown and grow to be almost as tall as Mr. Ed. Interspersed throughout the soft grass blanket were patches of blue, yellow, purple and white wildflowers.

Mary Lou shouted, "Daddy, stop the horses and help us off the wagon!" The girls quickly raced down the hill and, while doing so, stopped frequently to pick flowers for a bouquet.

Jane, small and quite low to the ground, was the first to find the elusive small white flowers. She picked several and smiled as she held them up to her daddy. "See the pretty flowers I picked for you?"

Wiser and older Mary Lou protested, "Leave those white flowers alone! If you pick them, we won't have strawberries to eat."

Her daddy smiled. "Don't worry, baby. The hillside is covered with these flowers. If we don't have a late frost, we'll be coming back in a couple of months to fill our buckets with fruit.

In early June, the girls were more than willing to return to the hillside to compete with the land turtles in gathering strawberries. The Missus praised the girls for picking such beautiful berries and instructed them to sit on the cot while removing the stems. The girls were careless as usual. The squashed berries made permanent pale pink stains on the cot's cover.

Later in the summer the oldest child rushed into the kitchen. "Mama, don't you think I'm big enough to climb those trees down by the road? They are loaded with wild plums that you can use to make jelly."

The Missus, who had watched her child's antics for years, agreed. "Mary Lou, you were climbing even before you started walking. Certainly, those trees will be no challenge for you. Get a couple of pails and I'll come with you. If any of the trees are too high, I'll boost you up to the lowest limb."

The plums, when squeezed, squirted juice on the cot's muslin cover, leaving a light pinkish-purple stain. The cot's cover spectrum was further enhanced with a bluish color from elderberries and an almost black stain from grapes. The cot rather enjoyed his rainbow coat but, as you might guess, the Missus was not impressed. At the end of each season, she tossed the summer cover into the trash.

One fruit never added any hint of color to the cot's cover. The sour little marble-like fruit was called a gooseberry. In the last weeks of June during the early morning hours the family donned boots, long sleeved shirts, large hats and gloves then headed toward the woodlands down by the creek. There they battled the brush, weeds, chiggers, and snakes while laboriously yanking off the tiny hard green balls hiding under the leaves and attached to prickly branches. Later in the day, the Missus and girls carefully removed the stems and tails from the miniature fruits. No one ever bit into the gooseberries because before they were cooked with sugar, they were tart and bitter.

Mary Lou speculated, "Daddy is sure going to love a gooseberry pie for supper."

Jane agreed. "Daddy likes the gooseberry jelly mama makes. He puts it on his toast and pancakes in the winter.

Monday is Wash Day

The porch certainly contained more than its share of grotesque shapes. In addition to the milk separator, airplane plant and cot, there was a cistern pump. Not only did it look misshapen, but it also made eerie squeaks when primed and pumped. Mr. Ed cautioned his children, "Never drink water from the pump. If you take even a sip, you'll be hanging your head over the slop jar all night! This water is to only be used for baths, washing dishes, or watering plants."

Since the cistern water was so foul, Mr. Ed had an extra burden added to his long list of daily chores. Each morning he had to pump drinking water at the distant barnyard well then carry buckets back to the house.

Living on the porch was actually quite pleasant for the cot with the exception of one day each week. Mondays were days of hell! Chaos started before dawn with Mr. Ed's hustling actions. Before heading to the barn to milk the cows, he pumped cistern water into the copper kettle, sat the kettle on a small gas stove, and turned the burners to high. By the time barn chores were completed, the water was boiling. Mr. Ed poured the hot water into a galvanized tub then refilled the copper kettle so the next tubful would be boiling after breakfast.

The Missus scurried through the house gathering up dirty clothes and linens. She dumped them in heaps onto the cot and separated them according to their color. That is, everything except diapers, which received special processing. The cotton diapers were soaked each day in soapy water. In the evening they were rinsed then hung on the spirea bushes to dry. On Mondays, all diapers were sterilized by being dumped into a kettle of boiling soapy water.

In the first years of marriage, the Missus used a washboard to scrub the clothes. The process took time and effort. She had to squeeze the soapy water out of each piece before rinsing it in at least two tubs of cold water.

Mr. Ed was overjoyed at the call he received from his sister, Alicia. After hanging up the phone, he turned to his wife and said, "Well, I guess there are a few generous bones in my sister after all! Instead of taking items from our home she has decided to give something back"

The Missus looked puzzled. Alicia was not in the habit of giving anything but advice. Mr. Ed explained, "A couple of years ago Alicia's home was wired for electricity. She just bought a new electric Maytag washing machine and has decided to bring the old model back to the farm for you to use."

The Missus soon realized that the old washing machine was only a step better than the washboard. She had to manually operate the agitator by turning the handle with one hand. At the same time, with the other hand she carefully guiding pieces through the wringer and into the rinse water. More than once her fingers were pinched between the wringers.

The Missus gave a sighed, "Being poor will not be an excuse for not trying to look our best. If I have anything to do with it, no wrinkles will appear on our clothing or linens." Missus slowly stirred cornstarch into warm water, making sure the texture was smooth with no pasty globs. Items to be ironed were dipped into this solution before being hung out to dry.

On sunny days all the wet clothes were hung on the clothesline that stretched from the garden fence to the walkway. After the clothesline was full, she threw overalls and towels over the garden fence or spirea bushes. Even when it rained the Missus insisted, "I don't care if it's raining cats and dogs. Mondays will be wash days!" When the weather looked threatening the Missus crisscrossed the porch with ropes before starting the washing process. Several of the lines were hung over the cot. Its already damp covers got sopping wet from the dripping clothes.

Monday washing caused the only real argument ever heard between Mister Ed and the Missus. Mr. Ed had changed into a suit to attend a funeral. He tossed the slightly soiled overalls he had been wearing over a bench on the porch. The Missus always washed every cloth in sight so she grabbed the overalls in her arms, then, without looking into the pockets, threw them in the machine. In her haste to complete the washing, she didn't notice that Mr. Ed's new watch was lodging in one pocket. The bath taken by the watch silenced its ticking forever.

As soon as Mr. Ed returned home, he went to the chair expecting to find the overalls. He called, "Honey, what did you do with my overalls?"

She answered, "Silly, I washed them. They're hanging on the clothesline."

Ed groaned and shook his head in dismay. "My overalls didn't need washing!" He thought another second and then growled, "Did you check the pockets before you put the pants in the tub?"

Mr. Ed glared at his wife and reprimanded her actions. "Your too-clean habits are driving me crazy! Do you realize you washed the pocket watch I just bought last week?"

She responded, "Edward, this is not my fault. You are sloppy and don't hang up clothes, and you seem to ignore the amount of dirt you bring into the house from the fields."

The air was so tense that the children tiptoed around the house. The Missus and Mr. Ed did not speak to each other again for a week!

The Missus had to suffer the consequences of wanting everything spic and span. She was allergic to almost all the soaps and cleaners. After washing clothes her hands became an angry red color. They tingled and hurt so much that it was not unusual to see her eyes fill with tears. At night, she rubbed them with a soothing salve before covering hands with soft white gloves. There were times when her fingers were so swollen that her wedding ring would not fit.

Mr. Ed realized that Alicia's gift was not making washday much easier for his wife. Even though money was stretched to its very limit, he used part of the corn crop profits to purchase a washing machine that did not require the Missus to have her hands in water the entire time. Her hands, even though still itching, were now not quite so red and swollen. In addition to a better washing machine, new products introduced to the market came to her aid. Instead of the harsh soap made of lard, lye and ashes she used gentle Ivory Snow.

UNDER THE MAPLE TREE

Kansas is known for hot dry summer months and the mid-thirties are remembered as having some of the worst droughts on record. The temperature was over one hundred degrees most days in August and it was only a few degrees cooler when nights arrived. Even the porch was too hot for resting comfortably, so the cot was placed out in the yard where occasionally a gentle breeze would fan the leaves.

The days spent outside were a trial for the cot's sanity. The constant heat from the sun heated the frame and coils. Even worse, it was placed under the spreading leaves of an old maple tree. The branches of this tree were resting sites for birds, so disaster was inevitable for the cot's covers.

After the sun set in the west on a hot July evening, the Missus suggested, "There's not a bit of wind and the house is stifling. Let's sleep outside tonight." The Missus spread out one of the old cot blankets in the dried grass and Mister Ed claimed the cot as his bed. The little girls started out resting next to their mama, but soon climbed onto the cot and cuddled in their daddy's arms. It wasn't but a minute before little Jane was sound asleep, but her older sister wanted to be entertained.

Mr. Ed gave Mary Lou a hug then said, "Honey, take a good look at the face of the moon. Can you see his big smile? Don't you bet that moon is thinking about the cow that jumped over him last week?" Mary Lou giggled then proudly recited the familiar nursery rhyme for her daddy.

He added another thought. "Mary Lou, do you remember I told you the old moon is made out of cheese?"

Mary Lou gently slapped her daddy's shoulder. "I don't believe it. Last night you said it was really just a big old rock."

Mr. Ed laughed before nodding his head in appreciation, "I guess I can't fool you."

As a shooting star sped across the sky, Mr. Ed directed his oldest, "Hurry up, Mary Lou! Make a wish before the star disappears."

Mary Lou sighed, "It's been too hot. My wish is for a dark storm cloud to appear over our heads and make us all wet."

Mr. Ed steered her to look at a bright alignment of stars, then explained, "We call this formation of stars the Big Dipper. Can you see how they outline a cup and handle?"

Mary Lou thought a minute and replied, "Daddy, I think you are wrong. That's not a dipper. I think the part you say is a handle is a path leading up to a door." Mary Lou realized her father needed more information so asked, "Daddy, do you know why the door is there?"

Mr. Ed was beginning to think this child was developing the habit of telling tall stories. She certainly had good teachers. Both he and his brother Jack were guilty of stretching the truth. He was at a loss to know what his eldest could be thinking, so he shook his head and said, "Honey, I don't have the least idea about that door."

"Daddy, you told us that God lives in heaven and his son Jesus is up there with him. Last year, when grandpa died, don't you think he walked up that path and knocked on that door?"

"Mary Lou, you have been thinking about our Sunday school lessons, and I like the way you think." Mr. Ed pulled the warm body of his sleeping toddler closer and gave his oldest child a hug. He thought, "It doesn't matter that the milk cows are going dry and the crops are burning to a crisp. I am still a lucky man.

EVERYTHING HAPPENS IN THE KITCHEN

Each year when the weather finally cooled a bit, the cot was carted back to its cozy corner inside the house. The room where the cot resided was simply called the kitchen, but it should have been called the Great Room. The reason the cot was so well informed was because everything of importance either took place in the room or was discussed by the family as they sat around the table.

This large farm home had many rooms, but none could compete with the kitchen in the time that the family spent there. The parlor was actually two rooms connected by pocket doors. The Missus kept it clean and neat, ready to receive special company like the local preacher. The girls were the only ones in the family who regularly visited the parlor. They loved the large upright piano that stood in the corner and spent hours banging on the keys. After only a few lessons provided by their Aunt Alicia, Mary Lou progressed from playing "Robin in the Cherry Tree" to the melodies of familiar tunes like "Farmer in the Dell." Younger Jane giggled while using her fists on the black keys to play the tune, "Three Blind Mice." Sessions of practicing the piano were frequent because the girls realized that their mama didn't ask them to do extra work if they were tinkling the piano keys.

There were several bedrooms, but they were upstairs and away from the bustle of kitchen life. These rooms were used for sleeping and storing seasonal clothing or items not used daily. During the coldest months of the winters, two of the bedrooms were completely closed. The others, the sleeping rooms used by children, were never too cold because warm air drifted through the ceiling vents located directly above the kitchen and parlor stoves.

One of the first remodeling tasks was to provide an indoor bathroom. It was built in the space that had once been a pantry. The only entry was near the cot's corner of the kitchen. This meant that the cot was always next to the line of traffic and was the resting site for those waiting their turn to use the facilities.

Before the addition of a bathroom inside the house, the comfort station was located near the garden fence. It was called the Sweet Pea House. Mr. Ed chuckled while naming the small outhouse with only one seat. The name fit because the distinctive vine with its multicolored flowers and sweet aroma entwined itself around the fence then continued to spread its tendrils upward. By the middle of each summer the vines would cover the sides and roof of this privy.

In spite of water and facility limitations, the family members were always clean. Mr. Ed created a shower space in the old smokehouse for use in summers. He draped a rope over a beam. A bucket with holes punched in the bottom was attached to one end of a rope. The other end of the rope was wrapped around a pole and could be tightened to adjust the height of the bucket. Mr. Ed cut a hole in the floor so the water dripping from the homemade shower could drain into a trough and then flow through pipes out to the nearby pasture. Pails of water, placed in the sunshine during the day, were just the right temperature for showers in the evening.

It would have been easy to avoid taking baths in the winters. The cold winter breezes sifted through the cracks in the walls and most of the house was chilly. The only warm room was the kitchen and the warmest spot in it was near the stove. When it was bath time, the Missus placed a laundry tub behind the stove. Water was heated in the copper kettle placed on the gas stove on the porch then brought into the kitchen and poured into the tub. At least once or twice a week each family member was expected to have a turn in the tub.

Mr. Ed had thick brown hair and wasn't too keen about washing it each night. That didn't set well with the Missus. She would say, "Edward, corn could grow in your ears!" She would put a pan of water on the table. Not too gently, she tipped his head over the pan. It was obvious she delighted in scrubbing the Kansas dirt out of his hair.

A small wooden box was purchased to keep foods chilled. Twice a week, starting in late spring and continuing until fall, an ice truck drove up the driveway. The girls eagerly accepted the ice chips offered by the driver. Mr. Ed usually bought a fifty-pound chunk of ice, enough to completely fill the top compartment of the box. As the ice melted, the water slowly drained into a pan stationed at the base of the box. More than once the Missus forgot to drain the pan and water ran over the floor. Mr. Ed teased his wife, "You were just trying to think of an easy way to clean this linoleum."

In the past, the only way to keep foods cool had been to place them in a bucket and have them float in the cool water of the barnyard well. The Missus was overjoyed to have an icebox. She could provide ice tea for lunch and supper in the summer and add all sorts of interesting foods to the daily menu. Until then, leftovers from the main meal had been fed as slop to the pigs or thrown away because there was no safe way to preserve them. The leftover food stored in the icebox could now be served at supper. Salads made with a gelatin base now appeared on the table. Mr. Ed rarely complained about meals. However, he finally confessed, "Honey, I sure appreciate your good cooking and you spread a mighty fine table. But, do we need to have congealed Jell-O with pineapple and cottage cheese served several times each week?"

For many years an old black wood stove purchased by Mr. Ed's grandfather had been used for cooking. Mr. Ed and the Missus had been married several years before they replaced that stove with a smaller range which used natural gas as fuel. A large teakettle always sat on the back burner and was the constant source of warm water. The oven was roomy and the temperature was easily regulated. When the Missus was complimented on her wonderful cakes, she replied, "It's because Ed bought me this new gas stove."

Ed's skill as a handyman was often put to good use. Years ago, one of Mr. Ed's first remodeling projects after he returned home from college was to build kitchen cabinets and counters. He added a sink but it was incomplete because a bucket had to be placed in the cabinet below to catch escaping water. Unfortunately, there was no way to pipe in running water. To wash dishes, hot water from the teakettle and cool water from the cistern was poured into the dishpan sitting in the sink.

The Missus rarely used her better set of dishes. Instead of using the limited kitchen cabinet space, she displayed them in a curio cabinet in the parlor. The mismatched set of plates, saucers and cups were stored in the cabinet above the sink. Most of these dishes were chipped and cracked and had long ago lost their sheen. Stacked under the counter contained an assortment of beaten-up pots and pans plus an iron skillet. These utensils were the few that had not been scrounged by Mr. Ed's siblings. They did not consider them fit for their households. The Missus, with a touch of magic, was able to constantly cook perfect meals using these utensils.

The Missus had a reputation for being a fabulous cook. Fresh bread was made every few days and there were always goodies like pies and cakes ready for snacks and dessert. The Missus prepared food that smelled so delicious the cot sometimes regretted the fact that day beds cannot eat. For the sake of the cot's springs and mattress, it was good that even though Mr. Ed enjoyed eating, he remained trim and slim.

A bulky piece of furniture called a buffet filled most of the space nearest the doors leading to the hallway. The buffet was created from cherry wood, and in its prime, was probably a handsome piece of furniture. After decades of sitting in the kitchen it was in sad need of sanding and a new coat of varnish. The buffet was big and cumbersome and did not seem appropriate for the simple kitchen.

The Missus got almost as mad at the buffet as she did at the cot. The white doilies she crocheted specifically to improve its appearance did not keep their starched clean look. The top surface was also laden with carelessly tossed clutter. The girls, as soon as they started to school, assumed that the buffet was the place to throw all their textbooks and homework. Mr. Ed propped his hat over a vase and was guilty of heaping the surface with newspapers and current issues of magazines. The Missus, who endeavored to have everything looking tidy, would moan, "Someday both this messy buffet and that outrageous cot will be out of here!"

The grandfather clock was on the wall above the cot. The constant ticking and hourly chimes added pleasant, soothing sounds to the kitchen. The clock face displayed a background picture of a ship sailing on the high seas. As Mr. Ed wound the clock each evening, he would sigh and say, "This farm boy would love a tour around the world in a ship like that!"

Chapter 3

NEEDLE, THREAD AND THIMBLE

Acceptance into the Prairie Hill Ladies Aid Quilting Society was akin to entering a sisterhood. The Missus earned the privilege of membership soon after she was hired to be the schoolmarm at a nearby school. For the remainder of her life, she received love and support from the ladies sitting around the quilt. At their weekly quilting sessions these ladies did almost as much gossiping as sewing. They spoke of their past experiences, secret heartaches and aspirations to their sisters of the thimble. Yes, they also whispered about the sins committed by others in the community. Because many of the Wednesdays were spent in the parlor next to my cozy kitchen, I was privileged to listen to them muse about the past, present, and future. Fortunately, I was not asked to adhere to the unspoken understanding that anything said was not to be discussed after the quilting session,

One Who Listens to Gossip Then Tells!

THE TEACHER DISCOVERS A TALENT

T he Missus was delighted with what she had accomplished. At the tender age of twenty, she had successfully completed the preparatory teacher training courses at the State Teachers College located in Pittsburg, Kansas. She was both excited and anxious when carefully filling out applications for teaching positions. She whispered a personal prayer, "Please, please, make it possible for a school to be available in Wilson County." If a position was open in that county, she would live near enough to her family to occasionally check on her siblings. The Missus was only fifteen when her mother died. Since that time, she had tried to fulfill the task of nurturing her feisty younger brother and two sweet sisters. She felt it particularly important that she should be there as often as possible for Marie, her youngest sister, who was not yet a teenager.

Her heart gave a jump in early May when she found a large bulky envelope addressed to her on the table where she lodged. She quickly tore it open and read the news that her application had met the approval of the school board of Shady Grove Elementary School. The Missus whooped in delight. She was familiar with the community, and when still living in her father's home, had once attended a prayer service at the tiny church located only a little over a mile south of the school.

A few weeks later the Missus made a visit to the community. After meeting the members of the school board and signing the contract, she was introduced to the Hatchel family. Mrs. Hatchel shook her hand and said, "Welcome to our little community." After a few minutes of casual conversation Mrs. Hatchel suggested, "Our home is just up the hill from the school. Would you like to room and board with us next year?"

The Missus was pleased. "Thank you for the offer. It would be so much better if I had a place to stay near the school. However, I must share with you that I have absolutely no money and can't pay you rent until I start receiving a salary."

Mrs. Hatchel was well aware of the expenses of attending college and knew that school teachers received a very low salary. She smiled and nodded her head in understanding then offered a suggestion. "What do you think of this idea? Instead of paying cash for a room, you help me care for our children and lend a hand in completing the many chores that are always waiting to be done in the house or garden."

The kindness of Mrs. Hatchel touched the heart of the Missus. This arrangement meant she could start to pay off a student loan and eventually would be able to build a nest egg for her future.

Mrs. Hatchel said, "We are going to be good friends, so from now on please call me Dora."

The toddler Dora was carrying was placed into the arms of the Missus. As the Missus cuddled the tiny child, her proud mother suggested, "Maybe you should see all of our brood before you make up your mind about staying with us. In addition to baby Chad, these two have not yet reached school age." Three-year-old twins with bright eyes and rosy cheeks shyly peeked at the strange lady from behind their mother's apron.

Dora called, "Becky Lynn, Sarah Ann, get over here! I want you to meet your new teacher. They politely shook her hand and confessed, "We can't wait for the new school year."

The Missus was impressed with the two girls who would be in second and fourth years of school."

Dora was hesitant before stating, "Their older brother is not with us. He started weeding the garden early this morning and is still working. Roy will be twelve next month. He's a wonderful boy and such a fine helper." She hesitated then added, "You will soon be aware that school work is difficult for him."

She explained, "When Roy was only three months old, he was stricken with an extremely high fever. His doctor suggested the fever was the cause of his learning problems."

The Missus spent the summer months taking additional college classes, so did not meet Roy until the first day of school the following fall. By the end of the day, he had captured her heart. Without being asked to do so, Roy held the door ajar as his classmates lined up and entered the classroom. Roy had a ready smile, was kind and polite, and willing to assume the responsibility of watching out for the younger children during recess. Each day, a few minutes after dismissal, Roy quietly walked up to her desk and asked, "Miss Chimes, would you like for me to stay after school and help with clean-up?"

Academic achievement was difficult for this child. Roy did not comprehend the relationship between sounds and letters. The only word symbol he consistently recognized was his name. Symbols for math were equally difficult. Roy could count and was capable of simple addition and subtraction using objects but found numerals confusing.

The Missus was determined to be the savior instructor who would identify ways to help this child find success. During a math test she got her first inkling that Roy possessed a unique talent. The other students were using chalk and slates to record sums of addition problems written on the blackboard. Roy was not paying attention to the math assignment. Instead, he was using his piece of chalk on his slate to draw a picture of the wildflowers he had picked for his teacher on the way to school. The Missus quietly peeked over his shoulder to gaze at his creation. He carefully replicated the exact number of petals and distinctive features of each flower.

After the math lessons were completed, the Missus excused the other children for recess but asked Roy to remain with her. When all the other children were outside the room the Missus called, "Roy, please pick up your slate and bring it up to my desk."

Roy's face blushed beet red as he shuffled slowly toward the front of the room, ready to face consequences. He was well aware that drawing was not part of the curriculum.

The Missus picked up the slate, "Roy, your picture is lovely! By looking at your art work it's apparent you are thinking about math." She asked, "Roy, please count how many flowers are in my bouquet and then how many you have in the picture."

Roy slowly but correctly counted the eight flowers in both the bouquet and the picture.

The Missus hugged him, "Roy, you did more than draw the exact number of flowers. You also noticed details like their height and diameter." The

Missus frowned a bit. "The only problem with your picture is that the slate will need to be erased. Will you do me a favor?"

Roy nodded his head. He had expected punishment and instead, received praise. He would gladly say "yes" to anything his teacher might ask him to do.

The Missus handed him a large piece of white paper. She smiled and said, "Now, I want you to make another picture of the flowers for me, but this time, include the colors."

The teacher reached into her desk drawer and pulled out a treasure. "Roy, these are colored pencils I sometimes use for grading papers. You can use them today for this picture and can borrow them any time you wish to draw in the future."

On Tuesday the following week, Roy stayed after school to assist the Missus with chores. After finishing with the tasks of sweeping, cleaning the blackboards, and banging dust out of the erasers, he slipped quietly out the door to sit on the porch and wait for Miss Chimes to finish grading papers and preparing lessons. For several minutes he gazed at the tranquil scenic beauty around him. His eyes sparkled when he recalled that his teacher had offered to share with him the special pencils hidden in her desk.

The Missus looked up from her paperwork and watched as Roy stood before her balancing on one foot then the other. In a hesitant voice he stammered, "Please Ma'am, could I use a piece of paper and borrow your colored pencils?"

"Roy, drawing a picture while you wait for me to finish work is a great idea!" Instead of a little piece of paper she tore off a big piece of the blank newsprint the Herald Tribune had given the school the week before and gave it to him.

The Missus continued grading seventh and eighth grade history essays, a geography report by fifth and sixth graders, third and fourth grade spelling papers and the arithmetic papers of the first and second graders. Almost an hour passed before her school work was completed. She sighed and thought, "Schoolmarms have long days, but it's worth it. Many of the children are showing so much progress."

She had forgotten all about Roy and was surprised to see him still on the porch. He was stretched out on his stomach with the drawing paper in front of him. The Missus smiled. "Thank you for waiting for me, Roy. Before we leave for home, will you show me what you've been drawing?"

Tears came to her eyes as he held up his sketch for her approval. The child had captured the quiet scenes of the Kansas landscape perfectly. The sky was soft blue with billows of white powder puff clouds. A few of the trees were still a mossy green, but most were vibrant shades of orange, gold and mauve. Several cows were grazing in the meadow or resting in the shade of the hedge row, but two were cooling off in the pond. In a distant field Roy's father and neighbor were loading hay onto the wagon pulled by two horses. His two sisters held hands while running on the dusty path leading up to their home. Draped on the right side of the picture were dry withering corn stalks. On the left side three red winged blackbirds sat on a telephone line. The foreground included the school water pump and an old wheelbarrow filled with yellow sunflowers.

The Missus asked, "Roy, last week you gave me a lovely picture you drew of some flowers. May I also keep this one? Both of them are so beautiful."

The Missus and Dora Hatchel thoroughly enjoyed each other's company. As on every other evening, that evening they chattered while Dora washed dishes and the Missus dried then put them back on shelves. While drying the last dish, the Missus asked her friend, "Dora, will the quilting ladies be coming to your house tomorrow?"

Mrs. Hatchel nodded and smiled with pleasure. "Yes indeed. We are almost finished with the quilt for the church bazaar later this month."

The Missus hesitated before making a special request. "Dora, I need to ask a big favor. Could you watch the students after lunch? I need to speak to the quilting ladies."

"I would enjoy seeing the children working on their lessons. As you know, before I was married, I taught in that school." She was curious but did not ask why the Missus wanted to talk to the quilting ladies.

The next afternoon the Missus quietly walked into the parlor. The ladies, belonging to the Prairie Hill Presbyterian Quilting Society, knew she would be stopping by and assumed it was to admire the almost-finished quilt. After praising their lovely work, she said, "I want to talk to you about Roy."

The ladies paused with their needles in the air and waited in anticipation. They thought, "Surely this new schoolmarm is not going to gossip about the child's learning limitations!"

The Missus continued, "I am aware that many of you share a deep affection for this lad. Sunday, after church, I noticed that almost all of you gave him a hug and complimented him about something he had done for your children.

The ladies smiled. This child was very special. Some remembered him as a tiny baby when he was so ill. They had either brought food to the house or taken turns caring for him when their friend, Dora, was in desperate need of rest.

The Missus held up a rolled piece of paper. "I want to share with you Roy's special talent."

The Missus unrolled the picture and attached it to the wall so all could see. The ladies exclaimed, "oh" and "ah," and nodded their heads in agreement when Aunt Be stated, "That's one of the prettiest pictures I've ever seen!" Another said, "This is a reminder of how beautiful our state is in the autumn months."

The Missus smiled and sighed as she gathered up courage to challenge the ladies with a sewing project. "Would it be possible to create a quilt using the Kansas landscape scenes in Roy's picture? It could be a great boost to his confidence."

Aunt Be added, "And wouldn't his mama be proud!"

Fourteen heads nodded agreement.

Annabelle's mother commented, "I have been saving an assortment of cloth scraps with tints that would closely match the autumn shades Roy used in his picture."

Eunice Smith, the mother of several boys, thought a minute and added, "I made the boys tan shirts for school this year. Scraps from those could be used to represent the dry corn fields."

Rose, the mother of four lovely teen-aged girls, was well known for her artistic talent. She could look at a dress in a magazine, duplicate the style and then make adjustments. Each of her girls always had dresses which fit perfectly.

Aunt Be noticed that her artistic friend was gazing at the picture through a rectangular window made using her thumbs and index fingers. "Rose, what are you seeing?"

"I'm taking a closer look at Roy's picture."

The other women nudged for a space to better view the picture and followed her example of using fingers to make telescope triangles, rectangles, and circles.

"Look at the details! It almost looks as if one of the horses pulling the hay wagon is swatting flies with his tail."

"How did Roy ever duplicate the azure color of the sky with those simple colored pencils? He must have smudged the color with his fingers."

Grandmother Shields squinted and moved her ample body to be nearer the picture. "My eyes are so poor that I can't make out the details you are talking about. What I do recognize are the beautiful fall colors.

Rose's mind was racing. "Roy's picture is filled with so many details. To make appliqué sections for a quilt, the scenes need to be enlarged and similar in size."

She continued, "The Herald Tribune is so good about sharing scrap paper." She turned to the Missus. "Could you provide some strips of the newsprint roll the Herald gave to your school? I'll use it to make separate scenes from Roy's picture."

Rose smiled at the Missus and then continued sharing her plans. "I'm going to invite our schoolmarm over for Sunday dinner. She teaches math to eighth graders so her skills in algebra and geometry should be excellent. The two of us will put our heads together to figure the size of the blocks, trims and edging needed to cover a regular sized bed."

The ladies were pleased that Rose seemed more than willing to once more use her artistic talent in creating a quilt. Rose looked around the room. "All of you need to contribute. Collect medium weight cardboard from the backs of your children's tablets or last year's calendars. At our next meeting we'll cut out the figures and transfer them onto cardboard templates."

Rose thoughtfully thanked her friends for their keen observations. "You've already started helping by thinking of cloth scraps that could be useful."

She glanced over at the oldest lady who was feeling a little useless. "Grandmother Shields, thank you for correctly picking out the colored hues needed to accent the quilt."

Annabelle, who rarely said a word suggested, "I love the sunflowers. Maybe we could make pillows embroidered with large sunflowers to go with the quilt."

Aunt Be's eyes twinkled. "Let's not tell Dora the inspiration for the quilt. As far as she is concerned, it can just be one of Rose's creations." The deception worked. Dora Hatchel was enthused when she saw the drawings and never guessed that the real creator of the scenes was her child.

Eunice visited Brad's Dry Goods Store on the weekly trip to Springville. At the next meeting she eagerly displayed her purchase. "I noticed a new bolt of muslin that had a golden hue so went ahead and purchased enough to use for several quilts. If it isn't the perfect background color for this quilt, we can use it sometime in the future."

The following Wednesday, ladies came for the weekly session laden with cardboard to make stencils from patterns drawn by Rose. They also carried boxes filled with colorful cloth scraps. The afternoon was spent swapping pieces until each was satisfied that she had the material she needed to appliqué her chosen section.

Rose assigned the most difficult task to Annabelle. "Honey, based on your suggestion, I sketched a sunflower. Will you lightly outline the flower's pattern into each of the connecting muslin sections so we can quilt it later?"

Annabelle was delighted to be assigned this task. She nodded and beamed as Aunt Be reasoned, "Just think, the reverse side of the quilt will display a field of sunflowers. In the spring and summer, the quilt can be flipped over and make the room seem like it is filled with golden flowers."

The ladies constantly chattered as they worked on their appliqué sections during the Wednesday sessions. It's no surprise that the secret about the creator of the scenes could not be contained. Dora hugged the Missus when she learned the truth. "I wondered why you were so eager to talk to my quilting friends. I never dreamed that you were planning to suggest something so wonderful for my Roy."

A large flat surface was needed to assemble the completed appliqué blocks, connecting blocks with the sunflower design and borders. The only place with enough floor space was the church. The ladies tugged and pushed the pews to the front then covered the wooden floor with sheets. Either barefoot or wearing white stockings, they tiptoed around and over the sheets while arranging and rearranging the blocks and trim.

The quilt was detailed and required many hours of labor. In addition to weekly Wednesday meetings, it was not unusual for one of the ladies to call Dora and say, "I have a few hours available before cooking supper. Could I come and quilt?"

The final quilting stitch was completed the first day of August. It was once again spread out on the church floor for final inspection. The ladies hooted in delight, grabbed each other's shoulders, and danced around the completed product. It was Aunt Be who stopped their silliness by stating, "It's a good thing you didn't stick your toes on the pins that are strewn all around the floor! The quilt looks good, but before it's shown, I've going to take it home and use a cool iron to smooth the seams."

At the county fair in late August the quilt was hung at the entrance of the tent featuring homemaking goods. The quilt caught the instant attention of all entering the tent. Yes, there were other colorful quilts. The Sunset Methodist Church ladies won Best in Show for their efforts and the Favorite of Viewers went to the Valley View Baptists. But the Prairie Hill Presbyterian quilting ladies were thrilled to see the coveted purple First Prize attached to their quilt.

The county commissioners, impressed by the comments made by their wives and neighbors about the quilt, voted to pay expenses for a member of the Prairie Hill Ladies Aid to take the quilt to the Kansa State Fair in

Topeka. There was unanimous agreement that Doris should have the honor. The Missus also granted Roy two days excused absence from school, so he could accompany his mother on the mission.

It was Roy's first visit to the fairgrounds. He was impressed with all the sights and felt immense joy when listening to his mother's comments to strangers. "Yes ma'am, the quilt is indeed unique. I agree with you, the appliqué scenes and all aspects of the quilt capture the feeling of our Kansas farmland in the fall. Did you know the pictures were created by my son Roy?"

All the attention given to the quilt resulted in other children at the school feeling envious of all the attention received by Roy. Most of them begged that their Christmas stockings be filled with paper and colored pencils.

Even though art was never considered a part of the curriculum in country schools, the Missus finally agreed that children who successfully completed their assignments would be allowed to draw. Like Roy's, some designs were duplicated on quilts.

THE NEW DAUGHTER-IN-LAW

In addition to weekly quilting meetings, the members of the Prairie Hill Ladies Aid assumed many other community responsibilities. They served meals at farm sales, funerals, and weddings and organized and ran the ice cream socials and yearly bazaars. They were the pillars of the church and the reason that most of the pews were filled with family groups each Sunday.

The bond of sisterhood was never fully understood by their husbands. The ladies were aware of the faults of quilting sisters, but believed that genuine goodness far outweighed any negative traits. As they stitched, they shared joys and innermost thoughts. They even let off steam and told of personal incidents that made them unhappy or frustrated.

Eunice was the mother of four grown boys. One afternoon she expressed her longing to have a daughter. "My boys love me, but almost from the time they learned to walk, they trailed after their father in the fields or down at the barn. Now that they are older, the boys and my husband go fishing on

Sundays after church and dinner. Meanwhile, I wash the dinner dishes then sit alone in the parlor."

She sighed, "It would have been wonderful to have had a daughter to be with me to help with the housework, garden and chores." She chuckled and added, "The real reason is there would be someone to talk to about something besides crops and how the fish are biting."

A few years later Eunice shared with her quilting sisters her excitement about the upcoming wedding of her youngest son. "You all have watched as three of our boys grew up, fell in love, got married, and now have homes of their own. Henry and I figured it would only be a short time before the nest would be completely empty. Now it is happening. Charlie, our youngest, is smitten with a girl he met from Kansas City.

Aunt Be stopped stitching and looked over her glasses. "Didn't he bring the young lady home a few weeks ago? Did she meet with your approval?"

Eunice sighed. "Yes and no. Danielle is one of the loveliest girls I've ever met. She is tall, has long, curly dark hair, and a radiant smile that must reduce Charlie to jelly. She is also very talented. Did I tell you she plays a harp and sings in her church choir?"

The Missus was curious. "She sounds fine. Why are you concerned?"

Eunice continued her story about the bride-to-be. "Danielle's parents own one of those palace-like houses located in the Plaza District of Kansas City. The girl grew up with maids, cooks and even a gardener. Charlie's a fine lad, but he is just a poor country boy. I am sure he will never be able to provide the standard of luxury she has enjoyed all of her life."

At the next meeting Eunice had more to say. "Charlie told us he got down on his knees and proposed, and Danielle accepted. But, can you imagine this! Charlie wants to stay here and help his dad farm. He and Danielle want to live with us until times get better. Someday in the not-too-distant future, they plan to build a dream house in that wooded area about half a mile east of our home place."

Aunt Be commented, "Eunice, you always wished for a daughter. Sounds like now you will have one."

Eunice returned to the Wednesday quilting session a few weeks after the wedding. A smile was on her face, and she had positive happenings to report. "Danielle shocks me every day with the things she can do. She says she started helping the chef in the kitchen when she was little and had a hankering for lemon squares. I figured she would be getting her beauty sleep with the mornings. Well, I was wrong! She's up at the crack of dawn making biscuits. She helps me with the other meals, and several times, she has insisted she wants to do them by herself."

Eunice continued her praise of the new daughter-in-law. "I had a preconceived idea about a person growing up with wealth. I assumed she would never abide dirt under those long-polished nails. Again, I was wrong. As a child, when Danielle was not pestering the cook, she says she was out in the yard with the gardener. She is no stranger to pulling weeds or digging in the dirt. Only thing that bothers me is she calls my common posies by their scientific names, and I find that confusing."

She shook her head with puzzlement and asked, "Have you ever heard of 'rosemarinus' or 'lavendula?'"

She paused for a breath of air then continued describing the new member of her family. "After church last Sunday, she and Charlie cleared out a section of the garden so she could plant some herbs. This morning her daddy's gardener arrived with a truck full of plants! While we quilt in this cool parlor, that child is out there in the hot sun watering and mulching rosemary, basil, and lavender."

Danielle seemed perfect. Her limitations were not apparent until her first visit to the quilting meeting. Certainly, there was no weakness in her gourmet skills. Danielle walked through the screened porch carrying a triple layered chocolate cake she had baked that morning. As Mr. Ed held the door for her, she hinted, "I heard your wife say you had a weakness for chocolate cake. I'll save a big slice for you."

Mr. Ed grinned. "I'll make sure to come in from the fields a little earlier today."

Danielle was pleasant as she greeted the women she had met previously and graciously shook hands and smiled when introduced to others. She stepped over to admire the half-finished quilt then she sat in the vacant chair next to Aunt Be. As the ladies started stitching, she quietly watched but did nothing. The reason for her idleness soon became apparent. Danielle's long tapered fingers could trail gracefully over harp strings but could not sew a stitch.

The farm wives were astonished. They had sewn all their lives and couldn't imagine that weaving a needle in and out of cloth could be considered difficult.

Aunt Be pulled her glasses further down so they rested on the tip of her nose. She peered over them and asked, "Honey, see that tiny hole at the top of the needle? Pull the thread through that hole."

Danielle squinted her eyes and had hands that shook so much it took several trials before she was successful.

Aunt Be gave encouragement. "Honey, that's fine. You'll want to start about here. Push the needle in and pull gently through all layers of the quilt."

Danielle yanked too hard. Both the needle and long length of thread were suddenly in the air. After several more attempts, Dora Hatchel suggested, "Let me anchor the thread before you practice stitching."

Danielle continued to try but her stitches were irregular and widely spaced. She found the thimble cumbersome so tossed it in her lap. Tiny red stains now dotted the quilt because she pricked one of the fingers on her left hand.

Danielle was relieved when it was almost time for lunch. She quickly jumped up from the chair and volunteered, "I'll be most happy to help set out the food, and I want to prepare a special plate for Mr. Ed. I see he is coming up the walkway right now."

When the young lady disappeared into the kitchen, Aunt Be whispered to the Missus. "Looks like you'll need to pull out those stitches and soak out the blood spots after we leave."

Danielle continued to attend the quilting sessions, but it was obvious quilting would never be one of her talents. She usually spent most of the mornings cooking some grand dish and preparing the table for the luncheon.

On a pleasant spring morning the following year, the casserole she was baking took little preparation, so Danielle had time on her hands. She was reluctant to reenter the parlor and pretend to stitch. Instead, she made her way over to the old cot. She had been feeling tired that morning, so she decided to relax just a minute. The new issue of *National Geographic* on the cabinet caught her eye. One of the articles in it featured the countryside of Scotland, a place she had visited the year before meeting Charlie.

It was Mr. Ed who found her an hour later. He teased, "Hi, young lady. I thought you would be sewing, scrubbing floors, or cooking!"

Danielle rubbed her eyes. "Hello Ed. I apologize for taking a nap. There is something about this old cot. It seems to want to make people comfortable."

Mr. Ed grinned but said nothing. He agreed about the relaxing powers of the cot. He also remembered that the Missus, who never took naps, was sleepy during the first weeks of pregnancy. Instead of questioning Danielle, he commented, "I see you were reading my new issue of *National Geographic*."

"Ed, did you read the article in this issue about Scotland? I visited some of the places it mentions a couple of years ago. The landscape looks even more beautiful than these pictures, and the castles are forbidding and huge."

Mr. Ed ears perked up. As he quizzed her, it became evident that she started traveling to exotic places when still a young girl. He had finally found someone who was fascinated with the world. Much as he loved his neighbors and family, they had little interest in what was happening in places like China, Australia, or the South Pole. Now he and Danielle would enjoy conversations about far-away places.

After lunch, while the other ladies stitched, one of them read stories from the Bible. When Danielle took a turn reading, those listening were entranced. Danielle's voice, as she read with clear melodious intonations, was music to their ears.

The Missus, in her thoughtful quiet manner, gave Danielle the recognition she deserved. "The children taught me so much during the years when I was with them in the classroom. Each child was unique and each seemed to be blessed with a special skill. Adults are no different." She smiled at

Danielle, "Young lady, today we witnessed one of your many talents. Ladies, have you ever heard the Bible read with more eloquence?"

Danielle never learned to quilt. In fact, she never even learned how to mend socks. No one cared. She was a valuable member in many other ways.

THE LADIES OF THE QUILT

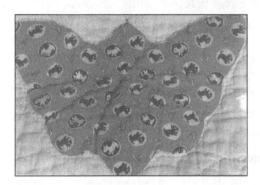

In addition to Aunt Be, Eunice, Dora, Rose and the Missus, there were several other ladies included in the quilting group. Wives of ministers became members of Prairie Hill Ladies Aid. They came in all sizes and behaviors. Some were deeply religious and others wondered how in the world they ever ended up living with a preacher. They came and went so frequently from the community that most never truly became sisters of the quilt.

"Grandmother Shields"

Grandmother Shields was much older than the others. She attended only when her health allowed. She had been a friend of Ed's grandmother and mother. Grandmother Shields was the midwife during the birth of Ed and his siblings. Arthritis had long ago stiffened her fingers and dementia was capturing her mind. She attended the Wednesday quilting sessions because she still enjoyed visiting with the ladies. She tried to add to the quilt. As with Danielle's attempts, the stitches were later removed.

Her quilting friends encouraged her to talk about the "good old days". They smiled and nodded but continued to sew as she recalled when the land was still largely an open prairie; how the Indians frequently camped down by the creek. She described the difficulties faced by settlers when turning their allotted portions of the prairie into productive farms. Grandma Shields remembered Mr. Ed's first toddler steps and went into a chuckling fit when telling the story about the time the family pet, Anamule, had looked like a ghost with big ears when she got caught up in the sheets drying on the clothesline.

Yes, Grandmother Shields fondly remembered facts from the past but she couldn't remember what she ate for breakfast or the names of her grandchildren and great grandchildren.

"Annabelle"

Annabelle was still a teenager. She and her mother arrived later than others for Wednesday quilting sessions, and the reason was evident. A longer time was needed in preparation before leaving their house. Annabelle, at age nine, had suffered from polio. She had recovered, but her left leg, affected by the disease, was at least four inches shorter than the other. She had crutches but was painfully slow when moving from one place to another.

Mr. Ed had always known Annabelle. The childlike nineteen-year-old almost seemed like a daughter to him. One day, while watching her try to maneuver her crutches over the odd shaped slabs serving as the walkway, he thought of a way to help. Ed gave a nod to her mother then hugged and greeted Annabelle. "How are you doing today, Princess?"

Annabelle gave a timid smile. She had always been shy and depressed, but her spirits, even when she was a young child, were lifted when around Mr. Ed.

"Annabelle, I have a great idea. Why don't you put your arms around my neck and I'll carry you into the parlor? It's just too hard to manipulate crutches on the uneven stone slabs of our walkway."

The Missus saw Ed approaching the house with his precious heavy burden. She opened the porch screen door, then scurried ahead of them to prop open the kitchen door. "Annabelle, we are so glad to have you here! We need your fingers for the difficult stitching."

Annabelle couldn't walk and rarely talked, but her quilting stitches were perfect!

"Pauline"

Pauline was the lady who seemed out of place at the quilting frame. The work on farms in Kansas was strictly divided into men or women's work and rarely was there any cross-overs. Pauline was a tall stout woman with firm muscles and hair that looked like straw. Pauline thought the gender division of labor was ridiculous. At the break of dawn each day she accompanied her husband to the barn. She bragged to her quilting sisters, "I can milk a lot faster than Herman."

Dora asked, "Who makes biscuits for breakfast?"

"No one does! In the evenings Herman and I work together baking bread. For breakfast we toast bread and cover the slices with globs of butter and syrup. We don't waste time over the stove when the sun is shining."

Pauline could use a pitchfork as well as any man and delighted in directing the horses as field tasks were performed. When she and Herman purchased a new tractor, more often than not, she was the one holding on to the steering wheel.

This lady's house was a mess, and she was indifferent to personal cleanliness. Her interests and behavior were very different from the others, but they liked her anyway because of her honesty, belief in hard work, and keen sense of humor. Twice a week, on Sundays and for the Wednesday quilting session, Pauline slipped on a dress and tidied up a bit. Unfortunately, she gave no thought to removing the dirt under her fingernails. The ladies hated to hurt her feelings but the quilt often had smudges that were worse on the appearance of a quilt than the drops of blood that flowed from Danielle's pricked fingers. It was the Missus who solved the problem. All the ladies, before working on a quilt, were asked to perform the ritual of rolling up their blouse sleeves and bending over a water basin. Hands needed lots of soap and scrubbing before the quilt was touched.

"Aunt Sarah"

Like most groups, this one had a gossip. Aunt Sarah had a big mouth! She did not believe in secrets, or adhere to the policy of politely sweeping uncomfortable situations under the rug. It was Aunt Sarah who gazed at the preacher's wife and asked, "How can your husband talk to us about the wrath of God when every chance he gets, he takes a nip from a bottle?"

One afternoon she heard Charlene say, "My husband has to attend a Grange meeting every Thursday evening." Aunt Sara looked her in the eye and stated, "Charlene, let me tell you something. The Grange does not meet on Thursday!" She added, "I think your hubby is up to no good, and you'd better find out why he isn't home helping you take care of your young ones."

Aunt Sarah had known Charlene's husband since the time he was a small child. After church the next Sunday, she walked up to him and stated, "I hear you've been lying to your wife about what you do on Thursday nights." She added, "Let me tell you something, young man. When you got married up in front of that altar of our church, you promised to be faithful and loving. It sure would be shameful if your family and friends found out you were not abiding by that promise."

"Flossie"

Flossie, a bubbling twenty-year old, occasionally attended the Wednesday meetings. She was the secretary, receptionist, and accountant at the local grain elevator. Her work hours were long. During the seasons when grains were harvested, the elevator stayed open each day until all the wheat, oats, or soybeans brought in by the farmers were transferred into the elevator bins.

Flossie was around men in overalls throughout the working day. She listened to their constant talk about the weather and crops and was a participant in their jokes and the object of their light-hearted jabs. She confessed to her quilting friends that probably half of the heifers born that spring were named after her.

Flossie missed the company of other women. She yearned for stories displaying feelings and candid appraisals about families living in the community. She particularly enjoyed being around other women as they spoke of nurturing their young. It was her dream that after she married, she would raise, at the minimum, half a dozen children. Her need for female companionship was partially solved by using compensation time from work to attend Wednesday quilting sessions.

The spring day was balmy, so doors and windows were opened to allow the gentle breezes in. The sounds of birds, dogs and Ed's tractor drifted to their ears. Aunt Be chuckled when another sound was heard. "Listen to that old car croak and sputter as it comes into the driveway." When the horn started tooting, she added, "Here's our ray of sunshine."

Flossie rarely settled down long enough to complete serious stitching. She was too busy teasing, questioning ladies, and playing with children and pets.

As the young lady stepped into the kitchen on this particular day, she grinned and teased the Missus. "Are those new curtains? They are sure pretty. Seems like you just redecorated the kitchen a year or two ago."

She ambled over to the old cot and gushed, "My, oh, my! Look at this old cot! It looks mighty nice in this turquoise and tan plaid cover. And look at those fancy pillow shams. Something tells me Ed doesn't rest his dirty head on them."

She continued her thoughts about the cot's appearance. "If that old cot could talk, it would probably thank you for making him look so pretty."

Flossie then danced into the parlor. She squeezed her chubby body around the quilt frame and gave each lady a hug. After spending several minutes greeting her friends, she sat down next to Aunt Sarah. "Ok, Aunt Sarah, let me in on the latest scoops. Who's pregnant? What do folks think about the new preacher? Who's been feeling poorly? Which men have been wasting their money playing poker on Fridays? What do you know about the moonshine operation uncovered over in McDuffie County?"

Aunt Sarah did not have the opportunity to tell all because noises under the quilt distracted Flossie. "Could it be puppies under the quilt?" She peeked under the cloth and exclaimed, "Why, do tell! It's my little darlings, Mary Lou and Little Jane!"

Flossie did not remain in her chair. She instantly scooted under the quilt frame to join her pint-sized friends. She gave Jane a kiss on her rosy cheeks and gently tapped Mary Lou's turned up nose with her finger. "Mary Lou, are you becoming domestic? I thought you would be outside climbing trees."

She cuddled one of Jane's dolls. "Little Jane, is this your new baby? She has golden curls just like you." As she tilted the doll, it made a crying sound.

She gently placed the doll back in Jane's arms. "I think this baby wants her mama."

Mary Lou had important information to impart to her grown-up friend. She took a deep breath and said, "Guess what! Bessie had two new calves in the pen near the barn, Mrs. Broad has twelve new piglets and our cat, White Socks, has four baby kittens.

Mary Lou was wisely knowledgeable for a four-year-old. "I watched when White Socks' kittens were born. They popped out of her behind and were all wet and icky. She cleaned them up, and now they are soft and silky. Guess what! The kittens opened their eyes yesterday."

Young Jane did not use gushing words like her older sister to express her feelings. A look of rapture told of her joy even before she sighed, "I love kittens."

Mary Jane tugged on her friend's arm. "Let's go down to the barn to see the new babies. Flossie, when you hold the kittens, you will love how soft they feel."

Flossie quickly agreed. "A trip to the barnyard sounds fun."

Three heads appeared from under the quilt. Flossie cocked her eyebrows at the Missus and other ladies. "Sorry ladies! Some things are more important than quilting."

Flossie shared the girls' opinion of the barnyard babies. The young animals were beautiful. She lifted Jane up high enough for her to gently pet the soft nose of one of the calves. She helped Mary Lou count the piglets and cautioned, "Be careful not to disturb Mrs. Broad. If she moves quickly, she could smash one of the babies." She shared with the little girls the joy of holding tiny kittens and agreed with girls that nothing was much nicer than petting their soft fur.

Flossie's little buddies pulled her along the yard toward a large maple tree. Mary Lou bragged, "Our daddy put the swing up for us after church last Sunday."

Flossie knew what was expected. "Do you want me to push you while you swing?" For several minutes her little friends took turns reaching their toes toward the sky. During each turn they pleaded, "Higher, push me higher!"

Flossie appeared back in the house just as lunch was served. After finishing a delicious piece of prune cake, she glanced at her watch. "Where has time gone? I've got to get back to work!"

The young lady never contributed much toward the completion of a quilt, but her occasional attendance to a quilting session was like a breath of fresh air for the ladies.

Chapter 4

WEAVING THE THREADS OF LIFE

Each of the quilting ladies touched the life of her sisters. Some, like Dora Hatchel, Aunt Be and the Missus, were close friends. Others were well liked and a few, Aunt Sarah in particular, were tolerated. There were good and bad times, successes and failures. Let me repeat more of their stories

The Cot Who Hears All!

ROSE LAUNCHES A CAREER

The success of Roy's quilt at the county and state fairs spread through Eastern Kansas. Many sought out Rose to show her a drawing made by their child. She heard over and over statements like that of Mrs. Hedgecroft, a visitor from Topeka. "Don't you think my Melissa drew a beautiful tree? Would you make templates so I can piece together quilt appliqué blocks with that design?" Rose always complied and tactfully refrained from expressing an opinion about the amateurishness of a young child's creative efforts.

Even the Missus came to her friend with a special request. "Rose, I've saved that first drawing Roy made years ago of the wild flowers sitting on my desk. It means so much to me. Could you create stencils of the flowers and vase?" She added, "I've saved the material scraps leftover after making my girls dresses for fall. The colors in the fabric are similar to the flowers in the picture. Only last week I bought several yards of cream broadcloth on sale. It will be a perfect background color. I plan to piece the quilt together this winter and ask the Ladies Aid to quilt it sometime next spring. Wouldn't a quilt like that be pretty in our east bedroom?"

Rose knew that one thing led to another when the Missus got in her head a new decorating idea. "Have you picked out the new wallpaper to go with the quilt and asked Ed to help put it up as his next rainy-day project?"

Aunt Be had no children at home. She had no pictures as patterns but she had something in mind as the basis of a special quilt. "Have you seen the morning glories my Jeff planted for me? The blue flowers and vine look beautiful as they trail around the garden wall"

She looked at younger friends around the quilt and gave a shy smile and blushed. "You probably think I'm a silly old woman but, when I look at the flowers, they remind me of the many reasons why I love Jeff."

Aunt Be needed Rose's expertise. "I would love to have a blue quilt on my bed with a quilting design of morning glory flowers. Could you create a pattern for me?"

Rose was talented in many artistic ways but did not feel as proficient when sketching outlines of nature. She was especially reluctant since the floral pattern would have so much meaning to Aunt Be. "Aunt Be, what a wonderful idea. Would you mind if I asked Roy to help me?"

Two long and two short rings made a telephone connection the next morning. "Dora, when will Roy be home? Aunt Be asked me to design a quilt covered with a morning glory applique's. I need Roy to sketch the flower and vine. I can make stencils from his drawings."

Dora quickly responded, "Roy had a friend write a letter to us for him last week. He will be coming home at the end of the month."

The morning glory quilt was forgotten. The remainder of the telephone conversation was reminiscing about the events that had changed the future for this young man.

"How proud you must be of your son!"

"I am. And how blessed I feel that an angel, in the form of a school marm, recognized his talent and started him on the road to success."

"Our Miss Chimes, now Ed's right hand, must represent the aspirations of dedicated teachers everywhere. They seek to find the hidden talent of each student."

"Yes. She was the one who recognized Roy's artistic aptitude, but she needed the help of an angel choir, our Prairie Hill Ladies Aid Society. Isn't it remarkable how his picture was the inspiration for the quilt that won the grand prize at the state fair?"

"We can all be proud that the quilt is now hanging in the gallery of the Kansas Historical Museum."

Dora mused, "Roy had never had more than a few pennies for spending money and was dumbfounded when presented five dollars as his share of the quilt prize money. In the typical Roy manner, his first gesture was to offer to share the money with his family. His dad and I stressed that he should use it to buy something for himself. That is how he obtained the Brownie camera. He still had a little spending money in his pocket and used it to buy film. Roy carried that camera with him constantly. He snapped dozens of pictures of his siblings, school and church friends, and creatures in nature, but his best pictures were of rolling hills, wandering brooks, small waterfalls and fields ripe with golden grains."

"His photos always demonstrated an innate knowledge of composition. You were wise to make an album collection of his pictures."

"I didn't want to get Roy's hopes up, so I didn't tell him I selected several of his landscape pictures for the Heart of America Photography Contest. My heart skips a beat every time I think the judges were so impressed with them that the final result was a scholarship to study photography at an art institute in Chicago."

"Roy went with you to the state fair in Topeka and, if I remember correctly, soon after that he accompanied his dad in the truck when a load of cattle was taken to the Kansas City cattle yards. Those were probably the only two times he has ventured much further away than Springville. Wasn't he frightened at the idea of leaving home and moving to a big city?"

"It worked out fine. Danielle and Charlie made arrangements to accompany him on his first train ride then spent several days familiarizing him with the city. Symbols don't mean a thing to Roy but he has a photographic memory of landmarks. That boy always seems to find his way around. Whenever a little uncertain of directions, he finds someone to help him."

As Rose slowly placed the phone back on the cradle, she smiled, thinking about the twists of fate. Roy, who still had difficulty reading, would probably be hired to work for an important magazine like *National Geographic*. He would eventually visit distant global sites frequently discussed by Danielle and Ed.

It never entered Rose's mind that she should be receiving money for the work she did for others. That all changed because of Danielle.

Danielle, with the encouragement of her mother-in-law, Eunice, asked Rose to create a quilt design with clouds and angels for the precious baby girl who had recently become the newest member of their family. At a baby shower, held at the Plaza mansion owned by Danielle's aunt, the completed quilt was placed on display. The wealthy ladies attending the shower admired the quilt and were impressed by the design created by Rose. They marveled when hearing that she also possessed a special talent of using drawings made by children as the basis for appliqué quilt blocks. Mothers, whether rich or poor, share the same pride in creative work of their children. Ladies of the Plaza Social Club were soon requesting that Rose use one of their child's crayon drawings to create a pattern for a family heirloom.

Danielle listened to their expectations then hinted, "We are living through a depression and these years of drought are particularly difficult for farm families. Rose never asks but could use a financial reward for her creative efforts."

The wealthy ladies instantly opened their purses. Rose couldn't believe her good fortune. She received over twenty-three dollars for exactly the kind of stencils she had previously made from the goodness of her heart.

Rose decided to start a business. She wrote an ad, produced several sketches then sent them to the local paper, *Capper's Weekly* and *Kansas City Star*. Her mail was soon filled with drawings and pictures accompanied with the fee requested for creating stencil patterns for personalized quilts.

Rose was busy with more than a new quilt pattern enterprise. Her four girls inherited her love of clothes and spent hours studying the latest magazines hoping to find just the right style for their next outfit. Unfortunately, they did not have their mother's gift with the needle. She made an agreement with the daughters. She would stitch if they would cook and keep the house clean.

Hand-me-downs were not an option when dressing her daughters. Each outfit had to be customized to fit their particular size. The oldest daughter was petite, and the twins were average in height but insisted they should not dress alike. The youngest girl was all legs and promised to be almost as tall as her father.

Now that the girls were older, they still needed their mom to fulfill fashion requests. The twins were working as private secretaries in prestigious law firms in Kansas City. They convinced their mom that it furthered their careers to look their best with blouses of silk and rayon and suits of herringbone and tweed that only she could make to perfection. Her youngest attended a quilting session carrying the latest edition of a bridal magazine. She thumbed through the magazine then held up a special page for the Missus to see. "This is like the gown I will wear at my wedding next month. Mom duplicated the style, but because I'm so tall, she added a waist panel."

Rose announced upcoming plans. "Helen, my oldest daughter, is coming home for the wedding celebration." She smiled at her quilting sisters, "Please say you plan to attend the quilting session the Wednesday before the wedding. There will be something I want to show you."

The ladies knew exactly what to expect, so of course, were present when Helen arrived. What Helen carried was their immediate focus of attention. The bassinet held a beautiful four-month-old baby who cooed, smiled, and kicked her tiny feet. Thanks to her grandmother's creative talent, she was dressed to perfection in a tiny pink dress with bodice smocking, lace trim and tiny dark pink rosebuds on the collar. The bonnet and panties plus pink booties grandmother crocheted in her spare time completed the ensemble.

After Rose had graciously received compliments about the baby's outfit, she commented, "Roy is coming home to make color photographs with his new camera of the wedding next week. He plans to snap pictures of the bride's gown and going away outfit plus dresses made for my other girls and the baby."

She had a gleam in her eye as she continued. "I plan to use these pictures as a promotion for my new business."

Her friends were puzzled. Rose already had her hands full. What new idea had she though up?

"I helped create personalized quilt blocks for years before realizing I could get paid for it. During the same time, I was creating outfits for my girls. I think there is a need to assist women in personalizing their wardrobes. It's ridiculous that women dress so much alike in shirtwaists covered by aprons."

Good-bye Aunt Be

Mr. Ed answered the telephone with his usual, "Hi-lo." Within seconds his voice was subdued as he asked questions such as, "When did it happen? What are the plans? How can we help?" He slowly hung up the telephone and turned to his wife. "Honey, I have bad news. Our good friend, Jeff, died this morning." His voice choked, "When he didn't respond to the dinner bell, Aunt Be got worried so walked out to the field. She found his body next to the wagon."

A few minutes later the little girls walked into the kitchen and observed their parents holding each other and sobbing. Since Mary Lou was in and out of trouble most of the time, she immediately assumed she was the one who had upset her parents. Did they hear her shouting the cuss words she overheard while listening to the men talking down at the barn? Did they see her tiptoe over the board covering the well? Did they realize that the arm of Jane's doll didn't fall out by accident? She ran over to them, grabbed their legs and said, "I'm sorry. I was a bad girl."

Little Jane had no such concerns. She too ran to them and circled her chubby arms around their legs. Tears were shed because of the tenderness she felt toward her parents.

The Missus finally wiped her eyes and blew her nose. She said, "All the Prairie Hill Ladies Aid members need to be alerted." She rang the central operator and pleaded, "Pricilla, I'm going to need your help." For the next half an hour the Missus placed calls to all the ladies who were close friends of Aunt Be and Jeff. Plans were made to have food available for both the wake and funeral and for someone to always be with Aunt Be until her daughter arrived from out of state.

Providing food seems to be the first response when tragedy strikes a friend. As the Missus talked to her quilting friends, the menu was planned with each deciding to be responsible for taking specific dishes over to Aunt Be's home. That evening the Missus boiled two-dozen eggs. A few were served for supper but most would be used for the deviled eggs and potato salad she planned to make early the next morning. She also baked a chocolate cake and had two berry pies in the oven. The result of so many women toiling in their kitchens would be enough food available to feed an army!

The dairy cows, Lully Mae, Sally Sue, Flossy Ann and Fanny, lifted their heads and stopped chewing lush green grass when seeing their master in the pasture. They were shocked when he hit their flanks with a stick then herded them into the barn for an early afternoon milking. His chores were quickly completed. He explained to the Missus plans for the evening. "I'm heading over to be with Aunt Be. I'll milk Jeff's cows and do whatever else is needed. Honey, I'll probably stay awhile with Aunt Be. She'll need my help in moving the parlor furniture around so the casket can be placed in front of the bay windows. Also, I expect the telephone is ringing off her wall. I'll try to answer most of them for her."

Wakes are described as a watch over a dead person prior to burial and sometimes are accompanied with festivities. It seemed like the entire community planned to participate in the wake for Jeff.

Families arriving at the home were directed to park their cars in the nearby field. The family members held hands as they walked slowly and quietly through the barnyard, stepped under the archway covered with morning glories, then entered the house via the front door. If they noticed friends, they did no more than nod. Eyes were full of tears and noses were sniffing as they approached the parlor. They gazed into the casket in disbelief that their friend was gone. Many stroked his still hands or gently patted his salt and pepper wavy hair.

Even the children were expected to say their goodbyes. Mary Lou looked down at the body of her good friend and said, "Mama says you are going to go to heaven to be with your baby angels. I'll miss you." Young Jane did not understand. She peered into the casket and demanded, "Uncle Jeffie, wake up. I want you to take me for a piggy-back ride."

Aunt Be was in shock and denial that her loved partner had departed. At the wake she was dry eyed and composed while accepting the condolences of friends and neighbors. Her behavior was more like the gracious hostess of a party as she suggested, "Now be sure to pass by the kitchen table. My friends belonging to the Prairie Hill Ladies Aid have plenty of food to share with you."

The dining room table was stacked high with platters of ham, salads, vegetable casseroles and breads and a separate table held pies, cakes, cookies and cobblers. No one drank alcohol or beer but gallons of ice tea were consumed. Folks, with their plates heaped with food, went out into the front lawn and sat in wooden chairs borrowed from both the church and the funeral home.

The atmosphere was almost like a party, but the conversation was mostly about their departed friend. An old timer commented, "Do any of you recall when Jeff courted Beatrice? We teased him because he always brought her posies."

"Yeah, and I once asked him why he always signed his wife's name Be instead of Bea or even Bee like other ladies with the given name of Beatrice.

His answer was he never thought of her as an insect buzzing around a bush. No indeed! She was his be-loved."

Another old-timer sadly smiled, "Jeff was the first one around these parts to be brave enough to purchase a car. I remember the first time he drove it into the churchyard! He scared the shit out of the horses hitched to the fence!"

One visitor remembered an unhappy time for Aunt Be and Uncle Jeff. "He was devoted to both his wife and children. It was a terrible blow when two out of their three young ones died after suffering severe cases of scarlet fever."

Danielle's husband, Charlie, wanted the conversation to be about happier days. "Last spring, several newlywed couples in our church decided to have a romantic outing. It was Jeff who provided the wagon and horses for a hayride. He took us to a special place along Whitman creek where we fished then had a picnic." He looked over at his friend and grinned. "Ed, I bet you know this site. I've heard it was the courting site for young couples a few years ago."

One of the choir members commented, "We're sure going to miss his rich baritone in the choir."

Another nodded his head, grinned then added, "That man sang day in and day out. His cows obediently wandered toward the barn for milking when they heard his voice and when hearing his yodel, the horses would race to the fence for a bite on an apple. When he was younger, his voice could even be heard over the roar of the trashing machine out in the wheat fields."

Flossie listened to the comments and agreed. "Don't you imagine he was singing, "Swing Low Sweet Chariot," when the angels came for him?"

It was autumn before Aunt Be was forced to make hard decisions. Jeff, like so many other farmers during the years filled with depression and drought, borrowed heavily from the bank. Had he lived he would have been able to settle the loans when times got better. As it was, the only recourse was to pay off the debt by selling the land, livestock, farm equipment, and most of the household items.

Mr. Ed helped Aunt Be contact a well-known auctioneer from Ottawa. After establishing the date for the auction early in November, announcements were posted in local papers and store windows. A few days before the auction Mr. Ed and other neighbors cleaned and oiled then carefully set the farm equipment in a line in the pasture near the barn. Caring friends reasoned that equipment in top shape and placed for easy viewing by potential buyers would surely bring in more money for Aunt Be.

The Prairie Hill Ladies Aid did their part. Planks over sawhorses were set up as tables under the maple tree. Hot coffee, sandwiches, vegetable soup and cookies were available for a nominal fee.

Ezekiel Wolfe, the auctioneer, had a booming voice that could be heard from a distance even without the aid of a megaphone. He briefly described the condition of the corn planter before shouting, "Do I hear ten?" When noting that a nod to that amount he would continue, "Now we have ten. Do I hear twenty?" His gavel was tapped when no more responses were forthcoming and shouted, "Sold to Mr. Barnes for twenty-five dollars!"

Aunt Be insisted that she be present during the sale. She held up well while the sales were down by the barn. Losing a cultivator, tractor or rake and even the favorite milk cow, Hanna Lee, did not tug at her soul.

After a half hour break for lunch, the auctioneer moved the crowd indoors. Room by room, he sold personal possessions belonging to Aunt Be. She tolerated losing the sewing machine, stove and tables. Tears came to her eyes and slowly fell down her cheeks as she watched her dishes, vases and a lifetime of handiwork in embroidered dishtowels, crocheted tablecloths and doilies go into the hands of strangers.

Aunt Be tiptoed over to the Missus. "Honey, come upstairs with me before the auctioneer gets to my room." She guided the Missus to the hope chest and pulled out the beautiful morning glory quilt. She hugged the Missus and, with a tearful voice, said, "You are like a daughter to me, and I want you to have this quilt. The flowers always reminded me of the many things I loved about Jeff. When you look at it, I want you to remember the wonderful traits you love about Ed."

The Missus protested, "You should take the quilt with you."

Aunt Be shook her head and sighed, "No. My daughter's small house in Indiana is already filled with young children. The bed I will sleep on is not much bigger than that old cot sitting in your kitchen."

The next day Aunt Be was at the train depot at eight a.m. She carried with her only one trunk and a small suitcase. This once proud, independent, and capable woman would be spending the rest of her days depending on the generosity of another family.

EASTER CLOTHES

The brooder house was thoroughly cleaned, fresh corncob chips were scattered over the floor. The boxes filled with fluffy baby chick were due to arrive in less than two weeks.

The Missus was deep in thought while her fingers busily mended holes in socks. Ed, "Are you planning to buy chicken feed when you go to town?"

Ed responded, "I've been listening to the weather man on WIBW. During his forecast at noon, he predicted a front is coming our way and should dump a couple of inches of rain. Yep. It probably will be impossible to get into the fields tomorrow. It will be a good time to pick up fertilizer and chick feed."

"I'm going to town with you." The Missus paused a minute then asked, "Ed, do you think we have enough cash to buy all the chick feed sacks for the season at one time?"

The Missus was anxious to be with Ed when he picked up the feed for a special reason. The chick feed sacks in the past were rough and scratchy. Now they were made with soft cotton adorned with colorful plaids, stripes and prints. It was possible to cut dress patterns for the small girls out of one sack but the Missus preferred using two. Mary Jane was asking for a full skirt that swirled around her legs, and young Jane would look best in a pinafore.

Flossie was delighted to see one of her lady friends shake the rain drops from the umbrella as she entered the grain elevator. After a quick hug she stated, "You were wise to come so soon after the shipment arrived. You'll have the pick of fabrics."

The Missus was guided to the huge stacks of chicken feed. Flossie expressed her enthusiasm, "Oh my! Just look at the color and pattern varieties they sent this year. You won't always be meeting yourself coming down the street!"

The Missus spied several feed sacks of vivid colors. A bright red background with black Scottie puppies caught her eye. "Mary Lou will love a dress made of this fabric!" Several pastel prints would be perfect for Jane's dress. The Missus finally decided on one that had a soft blue background and tiny yellow, red, and purple wildflowers.

Flossie knew the Missus rarely selected anything for herself. "This should be the year when you treat yourself to a new outfit."

The Missus agreed. "Most of my dresses have been washed so many times they are threadbare. "You're right. I need to make something nice enough to wear to church on Easter Sunday." She didn't like the red checked fabric and was tired of wearing pastels. She smiled in satisfactions when finding an emerald green cloth that was sprinkled with tiny white dots.

Flossie smiled at her friend and said, "How clever you are! This color will look lovely on you."

Ed loaded the chick feed sacks in the truck. He glanced up at the sky then said, "It's a good thing I decided to bring this tarp along to cover our purchases. It is raining cats and dogs!"

As he and the Missus started to back out of the driveway, Flossie ran up to the truck and yelled, "Stop, I have something to share with you. She caught her breath then panted, "I have a new dress pattern you can borrow. It's on my desk so wait just a minute and I'll get it for you."

A few seconds later the jolly wet chunky lady handed the Missus her latest Simplicity pattern. "Just think! Instead of your usual shirtwaist style, this dress will have a dropped waist. Wouldn't it be fancy for you to add a sailor color and cuffed sleeves?"

The Missus wasted no time in creating new dresses she and her girls would wear on Easter Sunday. As she cut the cloth, she was pleased to note that the sacks were in excellent condition with no faded spots or holes. This meant that quite a lot of the cloth remained after dresses were made. The material scraps were carefully folded and added to the growing stash used to piece quilts.

On Easter Sunday Mr. Ed pulled the old Ford out of the garage and parked it near the gate. He stood beside the car for a few minutes patiently waiting for his ladies. Finally, he got restless and blew the horn several times. He muttered, "Why in the world do females need to take so long getting ready? Sunday school will be over and the sermon started before we ever get to church!"

Mary Lou was first to exit the house. She slammed the porch door then twirled like a top on the tiptoes of her new Mary Jane's. The flash of red made her father grin. He had watched his oldest restlessly standing on one foot then the other while her mother sewed the final stitches. He recalled hearing the child delightfully exclaim, "This red puppy dress will always be my favorite." What a happy, lovely little girl! She would have looked perfect coming toward him but her spinning resulted in the new sunbonnet falling to the ground and the strong wind made her hair blow in all directions.

Jane trailed behind her sister. She was the picture of perfection as she slowly walked toward her daddy. She was dressed in a blue pinafore, white blouse with balloon sleeves, and daintily carried a tiny white purse on her wrist. The new white straw hat did not hide her blond curly locks. Jane held her arms up, expecting to be lifted high in the air. "Daddy, do I look like a princess?" Mr. Ed gave both of his girls a kiss and said, "You both look like princesses to me!"

A few minutes later the Missus walked slowly down the path. Mr. Ed grinned with delight at her appearance. Proudly wearing her new green dress, his wife looked as young and beautiful as she did when they were courting. Precious egg money had been used to purchase a new white hat, gloves, and shoes to match the collar and cuffs of the dress! He gently placed the girls in the back car seat, looked fondly at his wife and stated, "All of my girls look like a million dollars!"

He then added, "Just think! All this was accomplished for the cost of chicken feed!"

STASHES OF FABRIC

On a Wednesday morning a few weeks later, the ladies were in the parlor completing yet another quilt. The Missus took a minute off from sewing to put a casserole in the oven and walked out to the mailbox to fetch letters and newspaper. Although she didn't stop to read the headlines, an ad on the back page caught her eye. The bold print stated, "**Sale, Sale, Sale. Gilberts is going out of business. Every thread and piece of fabric is for sale.**"

All quilting stopped while the ladies read the ad. Dora Hatchel was the first to speak. "Prairie Hill Ladies Aid could sure use extra fabrics."

Aunt Sarah agreed, "We need more contrasting colors and a variety in the fabric patterns. Most of the feed sacks are decorated with small flower or plaids.

Annabelle's mother questioned, "Isn't that the store over in Independence, Missouri? That's just too far for any of us to travel."

Danielle was surprised at this statement. "Why, I've driven to Independence several times. It's not far from Kansas City."

Her mother-in-law added, "Charlie and his dad got a new pickup truck last week. Danielle, could you drive it to Independence and collect fabric for us?"

Danielle quickly agreed that this would be no trouble at all. She did plead for help.

Rose, you have such a good eye for color and fabric patterns. Why don't you come with me?"

There was a sudden silence in the room as the ladies thought of a major problem. Even a bargain basement prices, the fabric would cost a lot of money. The Missus pulled down the fruit jar containing precious egg money. She counted a total of two dollars and ten cents. "I need to save at least half of this for buying grocery staples for the next two months but could contribute the rest."

Each of the other ladies calculated how many coins they could spare. The total for all would be less than ten dollars, not nearly enough to make the trip worthwhile. Danielle spoke up. "It's no secret that my parents have given me more money than I can use. I'm not much help making the quilts. Please let me help contribute enough money so we can get the fabric we need."

Danielle and Rose returned late the next afternoon from their shopping spree. In addition to colorful bolts of fabric, they collected batting and a rainbow assortment of thread. The quilts made for church bazaars and for personal use in their homes would be beautiful!

A new problem arose. Where in the world could they store the bolts of fabric? No extra room was available at the small church and most of the homes in the area had no extra space. The Missus spoke up. "Ed's sister, Alicia, took all the furniture from the northeast bedroom so it's almost empty. Maybe Ed could build some shelves for us."

Dora thought a second then suggested, "In Roy's room there's an old table we could use for cutting fabric." Others offered to contribute scissors, pins, needles, and measuring tape.

The Missus knew an easy way to persuade her husband to do her bidding. For supper she prepared one of his favorite meals, baked ham, mashed potatoes and gravy, a fruit salad but, instead of a chocolate cake, made a lemon pie. Her husband anticipated confrontation with the "Honey Do" list because the usual feast for the day was at noon with the evening meal consisting of leftovers. Mr. Ed. patted his stomach contentedly and munched on the last pieces of pie. He chuckled. "Okay honey, what big project do you have planned for me this time?"

Mr. Ed enjoyed carpentry so responded to her request. "You're in luck. Walnut planks cut from the tree that toppled over a couple of years ago are stored in the shed. Maybe I can start building the shelves next Saturday.

The Missus smiled affectionately at her husband then kissed him on the cheek. "You'll be pleased to know that several wives have donated the muscles of their husband's backs and the tools in their hands to assist you."

Ed grinned, "That's great. While we build, Gus, Charlie and Carl can help me plan the lineup for the baseball teams that we'll play in Harley's pasture this summer."

UNDER THE QUILT

Jane decided it was time to change residence of her dollhouse home as soon as the quilting frame was once again set up in the parlor. Her actions resembled those of a mother cat. Her short legs trudged up and down the stairway as she carried each of her dolls from her bedroom then placed them gently in the doll bed stationed under the quilt. She changed the clothes on each baby doll, gave it a quick sip with the tiny baby bottle then sang a soft lullaby while tucking the dolly under the blanket. Satisfied that her dolls were comfortable, she made another trip up the stairs to collect the tiny tea and utensil set. Her final task was to tug and pull a small rocker into the new tent home. She planned to spend hours under the quilt holding and singing to her little family.

On a warm summer day, the Missus noticed sweat was dripping down Jane's neck. She found a long piece of yarn and pulled Jane's golden curls into a high ponytail. Later, when Jane sat in her rocking chair tending to her babies, golden strands of her hair touched the bottom of the quilt. The quilting ladies heard a scream when Jane decided to move from her rocker. Somehow several strands of her hair had been woven into the quilt!

Mary Lou had no interest in joining her sister's motherly care and occasionally even kicked the dolls out of her path. Her time under the quilt was devoted to projects and games. A cardboard box tipped upside down was her table. Treasures under the box included a cigar box filled with broken crayons, stubs of lead and colored pencils, an eraser, blunt scissors and a small ruler. The feathers, bird eggshells, seeds and rocks flecked with mica or interesting in shape stored in a mesh bag were often pulled out then arranged and categorized on the makeshift table.

The Missus noticed her oldest often tore up newspaper pages then reassembled them back into their original place. To satisfy her daughter's interest in assembling pieces, calendar pictures were cut into small shapes and placed into used envelopes. Puzzles became a favorite pastime under the quilt for her eldest.

Pictures of animals found in issues of *Successful Farming* were cut out and pasted to strips of leftover wallpaper. Mary Lou completed several strips to her satisfaction then made a book by attaching the strips together with large safety pins. The book was completed by asking the Missus for help. "Mama, can you write the story I tell you about the animals in my book?"

Mary Lou collected red and yellow yarn and decided to weave it into a potholder by using simple wood and nail frame found in her mother's sewing basket. The yarn was not pulled tight so the result of anyone ever using the potholder would have severely burned fingers. This five-year-old child recognized and was disappointed with the sloppiness of her work. She slowly crawled from under the quilt cave and stood quietly beside her mother. The Missus noticed her daughter's frown and dejected look and observed she was hiding something behind her back. "Mary Lou, is there something you want to show or tell me?"

Mary Lou slowly held up the tangled mess for inspection. The Missus smiled then said, "Learning skills like weaving takes a lot of practice. Come sit on my lap and together we will make a potholder that can be useful when cooking."

Mary Lou then decided to attempt embroidery. "Mama, please put this red thread through the needle eye so I can sew a puppy outline on this dish-towel." The odd rectangle like shape had four long threads that might have been legs and a tangle that only the most imaginative would have called a tail but nevertheless, the Missus was full of praise. "Sweetie, this is lovely. Let's place it on the rack." After a few days the cloth was thrown into rag bag.

A game the girls played under the quilting frame on Wednesdays was titled "Bloomers." The quilting ladies dressed modestly and hemlines of their dresses fell below their knees. When they sat down to quilt, their dresses hiked up and bloomers were in full view. The girls soon were able to identify each of the ladies by her "below the waist" wardrobe.

When Aunt Be was still around she was easily identified because her bloomers were always blue. These were probably made from cloth scraps of the background color of her favorite quilt. Dora, Charlene, Eunice, Annabelle's mother and the Missus made their bloomers out of pastel feed sack material displaying miniature flowers. Since their bloomers were of similar fabrics, the guessers had to pay attention to the length of skirts and thickness of legs. Aunt Sarah actually wore bloomers made out of red polka dot material. Grandmother Shields, who was quite heavy, wore saggy loose bloomers. The fabric, once white, had faded into a dingy yellow. She also always wore thick stockings held up with garters circling her legs just below her knees.

Annabelle had pretty pink bloomers. It was always sad for the girls to look at her legs. One foot was touching the floor and looked similar to those of other women. The other foot dangled several inches above the floor with a shoe not much bigger than the one worn by Mary Lou.

Jane whispered and pointed, "This is Rose." Her bloomers were easy to identify because they were decorated with lace and tiny bows.

Both girls shook their heads with envy and tugged at their rumpled and dingy stockings. Their eyes were gazing on Danielle's trim legs. Danielle did not wear bloomers. What the girls observed when Danielle's skirt hiked up was a beautiful silk petticoat with lace at the hemline.

Pauline didn't bother with bloomers in the winter. Instead, she wore long johns covered with wool stockings.

As the girls played the guessing game, Mary Lou sniffed and wrinkled her nose then took a closer look at Pauline's shoes. She held her nose and giggled as she whispered to her sister, "I think that Pauline was out in the barnyard just before coming here. There's nasty stuff on her shoes. Mama will be washing the floors after she the women have gone home."

Mary Lou had learned to keep a sharp ear on what the adults above the quilt were discussing. Her mother's voice was usually soft and pleasant, but this time it sounded whinny. "I've had the flu for several weeks now. I am so tired and sometimes feel nauseated."

Aunt Sarah laughed, "How quickly you forgot the symptoms. You don't have the flu. You're pregnant. Come about June, I bet you and Ed will have the little boy you've always wanted."

What was this? Mama was going to have a baby boy? Mary Lou was shocked and confused. Would her mother still love her little girls? Would she spend all of her time with the baby and no longer be available to give attention to her girls? Life was going to change in this household, and Mary Lou was not at all pleased.

Chapter 5

THE COT'S BEST FRIEND

It's good to have respect and friendship when two are in close proximity of each other for nearly seventy years. The time could have been longer, but while I was upstairs freezing in the back bedroom while the oak table sat in the middle of the warm kitchen. Our job descriptions were different but both of us were here to serve Mr. Ed and his family. I understood perfectly that my primary responsibility was to provide rest and relaxation. My friend, the table, did not enjoy such a clear job description and was expected to adapt to any task requiring a hard flat surface.

The Fond and Helpful Friend, the Cot

AROUND THE TABLE

An attractive outward appearance can cover up a multitude of imperfections. The table, like the cot, was drab and utilitarian. Yet there were times, when both were gussied up in their finest and made the kitchen look like a banquet hall.

As a young bride, the Missus arrived at her hew home with a hope chest filled with linens decorated with her careful stitches. Loveliest of all was a lace tablecloth crocheted with a cornflower design. It was only used when special company came for dinner.

An entire side buffet drawer was filled with cotton tablecloths of various sizes. Two were made from fabric scraps and matched the cot covers. A favorite was a multicolored granny square cover made with leftover scraps.

Just as the cot had to endure ugly daily covers of feed stack cloth, the table accepted being covered with an oilcloth. The oilcloth was a perfect table covering for daily use. It was wiped clean and never had to be put in the washer and, when old and cracked, was cheap to replace.

The table had a square shape for the daily meals. When company came extra leaves were added. Its shape was then rectangular and took up almost all of the available space of the kitchen. That happened frequently because there were constant reunions with uncles, aunts and cousins. A few times the table was so overcrowded that children sat on the cot and held their plates in their laps. Crumbs and jelly always fell on the cot's fancy company cover!

The counter space was limited so the Missus used the table for food preparation. A large tea towel was spread over the top before the dough for bread or cinnamon rolls were kneaded. When canning vegetables and fruit or making jelly, an oak plank was placed on top of the table. Hot jars, removed from the pressure cooker, were set on the board until they were cool enough to carry down to the cellar. The plank protected the table top from being warped and prevented water ring marks.

Jane pleaded with her mama, "Can we make cookies today? Daddy likes sugar cookies best and I do too."

The Missus answered, "Certainly. We need to get everything ready before starting. After we cover the table with a cloth, we'll shout for Mary Lou to come down from the tree and help us."

Selective hearing is remarkable. Mary Lou, who often pretended she didn't hear most of the time when up in a tree, knew from the tone of her mother's voice, there was something fun to do. She slithered down the tree and started running toward the back door. She did not look where she was going and tripped over a root. Her hands were scratched and grubby, and the scab on her right knee was torn open and bleeding.

The Missus shook her head as she observed her daughter's dirty hands and bleeding knee. "Mary Lou, what am I going to do with you? Are you every going to attempt to be a young lady? Someday you need to accept the fact that girls need to be domestic and not spend their time climbing trees or playing in the barn."

She directed, "Girls, you need to wash your hands and put on aprons. Jane, please bring over two eggs from the icebox, and Mary Lou, help me get the rolling pin, spoons, cutters and bowl."

The girls were soon measuring ingredients, mixing the dough, and cutting out the cookies. They took frequent finger tastes of the dough and succeeded in spilling flour all over the floor. Nevertheless, cookies were served as a delicious after supper treat.

The Missus made sure the children completed their homework each evening before going to bed. She asked, "Mary Lou, don't you have a spelling test tomorrow?"

Jane piped up, "She read the words to me as we walked home, and I know how to spell all of them."

Mary Lou shook her head in irritation. It was not easy having a too smart younger sister.

The Missus asked, "Where is the list of words, Mary Lou?"

The child slowly reached into her pocket and pulled out a crumpled piece of paper. She shook her head and sighed, "I forgot to study them."

"Well, now is the time. You have your slate and chalk. Write each word at least ten times. I'll quiz you to be sure you have them memorized." The Missus noticed the smirk on little sister's face. "Jane, why don't you find ten words in your reader that might be hard to spell, and I'll quiz you on those when I finish helping your sister."

Jane immediately picked several difficult words and spelled them correctly, but Mary Lou failed the test by spelling barrel with only one "r". The Missus tore off two sheets from a tablet and suggested the girls write cursive letters that fit neatly between the lines. She was disappointed because neither of her daughters met her standards of perfection. Script handwriting was not considered as important as it had been when she was a teacher.

Little brother's white highchair was pulled up near the table and both of his sisters scooted as far away from him as possible. The baby, when given the opportunity, found it difficult to resist the temptation of pulling Jane's blond curls. Mary Lou was in even more danger from her little brother because he liked to bang her head with his rattle.

Mr. Ed finished the newspaper's crossword puzzle started earlier in the day by the Missus. When the Misses noticed that Mr. Ed had a pencil in his hand, she stopped whatever she was doing and looked over his shoulder. The couple argued about the choice of words and, when in doubt, opened a tattered book. The Missus nodded her head when Ed said, "Let's check with our old friend Webster." As always, the puzzle was soon completed.

Fingers of the mistress of the household were busy during the evening. After she mended a tear in Ed's work shirt and darned a pair of socks, there was still time to sew for pleasure. The embroidered pillow case was to be a birthday present for her friend Dora.

Mr. Ed was never known to miss an opportunity to talk and, like other evening around the table, explained important information about the world to his children. They only half listened to his words of wisdom. They were much older before they appreciated the knowledge he gained through reading. His favorite sources were the regional newspapers, *The Kansas City Star and Times,* and magazines like *The National Geographic* and *The Reader's Digest.* Ed had long ago accepted his fate of not completing college and achieving a career as an engineer or a scientist. Still, being a Kansas dirt farmer never dampened his interest in learning all he could about almost every subject.

The evening ended on a religious note. Mr. Ed picked up the worn Bible and said, "It's about bed time. I'll read you a story from the Bible then you girls must hurry upstairs."

The children were clever about delaying bedtime. "Daddy, read us another Bible story before we say good-night." Of course, he was most happy to oblige.

THE CUTTING BOARD

Clothes purchased at a store were not an option for this family struggling to make ends meet. The Missus and girls used the table as a cutting board when making new dresses.

The Missus had only a few clothes in her closet but always looked neat when anticipating company. She used the same pattern to make two or three colorful shirtwaist dresses plus a black one to be worn at funerals. When new, the shirtwaist dresses were worn to church, meetings, or shopping in town. When faded and misshapen, they were used as housedresses.

It was not customary for women to wear pants in the 30's but the Missus decided they were necessary for outside work. Ten inches were cut off of the legs of an old pair of Mr. Ed's overalls. They were then short enough so she wouldn't trip head over heels every time she wore them. Her husband's old blue denim shirts protected her sensitive arms from the sun and a large straw hat served as a shield for her face. If a car was sited turning into the driveway, she rushed inside the house and quickly changed into a shirtwaist dress and apron.

Mr. Ed admonished his wife, "Why in the world do you run inside when you see a car turn into the driveway?"

"Ed, there is no way I will let anyone see me looking like a scarecrow!"

During the early 1930's, the Missus constantly denied herself the luxury of extra clothes. In spite of the limited money for the purchase of cloth from the dry goods store, she was determined that her little girls would not be deprived of an adequate wardrobe. They seemed to grow so quickly, and Mary Lou's outdoor activities resulted in dresses that were so ragged and stained they could not be passed on to her younger sister. The Missus enjoyed sewing but was sometimes tired. She sighed, "It seems that I am always sitting at the sewing machine making a new outfit for one of my girls."

Since there were several girl cousins near the same age, the Missus and her sisters frequently exchanged patterns for making dresses. Hems were lengthened or shortened to match the size of children. For the skinny ones, like Mary Jane, the waists were tucked in. For the chubby little sisters, waists were widened and hems turned up. The dresses the Missus created out of inexpensive material or feed sacks looked like designer dresses. Added to the basic dress were cross-stitch designs on the pockets or lovely rosebud embroidery stitches on collars.

The Missus always selected hair bows to match each outfit. She held the squirming girls firmly as she gave their hair a final brush before attaching the bow. She instructed, "Be careful! These bows cost money. Don't be losing them!" The bow stayed in Jane's curly hair at least for a short time, but the one fastened in Mary Lou's straight strands usually fell off while she skipped toward the garden gate.

THE GAME TABLE

Ed, his brother, and cousins enjoyed playing cards in the evenings. The old table was the site of poker, Canasta, Hearts and Pinochle. As much as other games were enjoyed, the favorite game (usually resulting in a lot of yelling and arguments) was called Pitch. Uncle Jack, visiting from far away California, stated, "I'm feeling lucky tonight. Let's play a few rounds of Pitch." While playing, he chewed a nice wad of Pa's Chew. When playing a winning hand, he got so excited that he threw the cards in the spittoon and spit the wad of tobacco in the middle of the table!

Assembling jigsaw puzzles was a popular winter activity. Some of the larger puzzles that took several days to finish were placed on the kitchen table. That meant the family had to find other places to sit when eating their meals. Sometimes it was on the old cot. The cot was relieved when the darned puzzle was completed and the table was once again put to use for meals.

If the table could talk, it would say that its favorite responsibility was to be a site for baths. When little brother was a tiny baby, he was bathed in a large dishpan filled with warm water and placed in the middle of the table. The entire family would sit around admiring the tiny baby as he kicked and splashed. After the baby was clean, he was wrapped in a big towel and carried over to rest on the cot. It was then the cot's pleasure to hold that little one while he was sweetened with powder, diapered, and dressed.

Chapter 6

THE DAILY ROUTINE

Everyone on the farm had special responsibilities. As you know, I considered my job of seeing to Mr. Ed's comfort as extremely important. Mr. Ed claimed me as his special place to be used for a few minutes of repose several times each day. This man was very busy and needed a quiet time on my covers and pillows for relaxation.

Always a Faithful Servant, The Cot

MR. ED'S SCHEDULE

During the depression, keeping the farm productive was a constant struggle. Unlike in the past, when Mr. Ed's father was alive, there were no hired hands to assist him in work. Mr. Ed spent untold hours in the fields or working with the animals. He got up long before sunrise to milk the cows, feed the animals, and prepare the equipment for the field.

After concluding the morning chores, Mr. Ed came into the house and plopped down on the cot for a few minutes of rest. He set the dial of the battery-powered radio to the WIBW station located in Topeka. He wanted to compare the weatherman's predictions with his own expertise of the subject. On a day late in June, the prediction Mr. Ed's made as he gazed at the cloudless sky, was verified by the weatherman. The day would be fair and mild with only a slight chance of a thundershower.

Just as Mr. Ed was getting settled for a little shut-eye, the big old wall telephone, situated right above the cot, jingled three long shrill rings. This was the signal for what, in modern times, would be called a telephone conference. In addition to Ed, there were several clicks as others on the same telephone line picked up their phones to listen and maybe add a word or two.

Ed's side of the conversation was easy to follow. "Hi low, Frank, how are you doin' today? --Good to hear you're over the cold. -- Do you think it will rain? --I don't think so either, so plan to cultivate the South Forty this morning. That cornfield down by the creek is getting mighty weedy, it will be next! --Yes, we should probably be ready to start haying next week. Mine seems to be slower than yours, so maybe we should put yours up first. -- Walt, are you listening? Do you think your son, Bob, will be able to help? -- Alex, what about your fields? --Okay, we'll come to your fields before tackling mine. -- Oh, by the way, I'm going to town for more fertilizer this afternoon. Do any of you need me to pick up anything? --Well, that's all for now. No, wait a minute. The Missus is trying to tell me something. Henry, she wants you to tell Mary that, since the peaches are not ready, she will be making strawberry ice cream and an angel food cake for the social at church next Sunday evening. -- O.K. I'll tell her that if her hens aren't laying that you folks have extra eggs for the ice cream."

Ed left the house as soon as possible after breakfast. In addition to daily morning and evening chores of milking the cows and tending to the livestock, he was busy in the fields for long hours during the spring, summer, and fall. Fields of sorghum, oats, wheat, beans and corn had to be plowed, planted, cultivated and harvested. The alfalfa was mowed, raked, lifted onto the wagon with a pitchfork and hauled to the barn where it was hoisted into the loft.

The garden was never neglected as it provided most of the food necessary for the family meals. When the rainfall amounts were limited, additional effort was necessary. Mr. Ed had to haul buckets of water from the distant well. More than once, he would groan, "It would sure be nice if we still had an Anamule to help with this work."

It took a heap of scheduling, a keen knowledge about the pattern of growth of plants and the ways of animals, a sense of what the weather was going to do, and lots of hard work to complete all that had to be done. Even rainy days were filled with productivity. Mr. Ed. repaired machinery, made needed trips into town, or helped the Missus by paying attention to her "honey do list" always taped to the icebox door.

Ed could look at the position of the sun and correctly identify the time of day. This awareness, plus the rumble in his belly, meant he appeared back at the house just a few minutes before the noon meal. While the Missus completed preparations for dinner (the main meal of the day) he would always rest on the cot. In a few seconds he would completely relax and start snoring. When the meal was ready, the Missus would call, "Edward, the food is getting cold. Wake up now." Sometimes a loud voice did not work. She would have to shake his body and roll him off of the cot's comfortable mat.

Afternoons were a continuation of the hard work in the fields. When Mr. Ed was working a short distance from the house, the Missus would have the children take him a drink and cookies for his afternoon break. Mr. Ed continued working in the fields until twilight then evening chores had to be completed before he even thought of returning to the house. It's no wonder he often fell asleep on the cot soon after supper. (He always claimed that he was merely listening to the ball game with his eyes closed). Later in the evening, the Missus would shake him and state, "Edward, that awful cot is going to break your back. Come on into the bedroom where you can get a decent night's sleep."

THE MISSUS KEEPS BUSY

There's an old saying, "A man's work is from dawn to dark but a woman's work is never done." From what the cot noticed that was certainly the truth.

Mr. Ed worked hard but sensed when his body was tired. Resting on the cot, whether for a few minutes or an hour seemed to provide renewed energy. In contrast, the Missus never realized how she would have felt much better if only she would stop her constant activities and enjoy the cot's soft mattress for a brief time.

Because the cot lived in the kitchen, it was much more aware of the specific tasks that kept the Missus busy every minute of each day. That woman sure was organized! Before marriage, as a school marm, she carefully made daily lesson plans. That habit continued as a homemaker. The Missus had a set time to do certain work and tried to stick with her plan. Even walking out to pick up the mail after the 10:30 a.m. delivery was on her scheduled list.

On Mondays the Missus was so busy with the washings that she always prepared a main dish that took little work, navy beans and ham. The beans that had soaked overnight were placed over a gas flame turned to a low heat while she worked on the porch. A few minutes before noon, she rushed into the kitchen and whipped up a pan of cornbread to accompany the tasty vegetable dish.

Mr. Ed commented, "Honey, I know Mondays are misery for you, but I look forward to them. I know you will be making one of my favorite meals."

On Tuesdays, the Missus rapidly paced back and forth in the kitchen in an effort to complete two major tasks. Soon after breakfast she prepared the clothes and table linens for ironing by dampening them. A soda pop bottle with an attached perforated cap was used for sprinkling starched items. Each dampened cloth was tightly rolled into a ball, placed in a basket then covered with a towel. While waiting for the pieces to evenly absorb the moisture, she hurried over to the counter and pulled out ingredients and utensils needed to complete her second task, making bread. Once the bread dough was mixed, kneaded, covered and placed into a large bowl to rise, she set up the ironing board. Three heavy irons, also used during the summers to keep the doors ajar, were placed on metal plates covering stove burners.

While waiting for the irons to heat she checked to see how the bread was rising. The Missus believed that bread was a better consistency if the rising was controlled so she used her fists to push the dough down at least twice during its rising process.

Satisfied that the bread was doing well, the Missus concentrated once more on ironing. The Missus attached a wooden handle onto one of the iron bases which had been heating on the stove. Before using the iron on a starched piece, she checked the temperature by flicking drops of water onto the iron's bottom surface. A sizzling sound indicated that the heat was at least adequate. The Missus always ironed a piece of scrap fabric similar to the starched piece. Not burning holes into fabric was an art when using the heavy iron. The Missus worked quickly. If all went well, she could iron at least one dress before the iron base cooled and would have to be replaced with another iron from the stove.

By noon, she had pressed several of the girls' dresses, made lunch for Mr. Ed and had the bread and cinnamon rolls in trays. Mr. Ed had hardly finished the last bite of dessert of bread covered with molasses before his wife snatched away his plate. In whirlwind speed the Missus cleared the table, washed the dishes and placed the fat loaves of bread in the heated oven. The Missus sighed with relief a few hours later. The kitchen was filled with the aroma of freshly baked bread and the pressed clothing was folded and returned to proper places in closets and chests.

Mr. Ed thought perfection ironing was almost as ridiculous as washing everything in sight. He once again said, "I can't understand why you make so much work for yourself. The cows don't give a dang whether my overalls are ironed. And why do you need to iron the sheets and pillowcases? No one will see them but us." He also respected the skill in creating fancy needlework but wondered, "Honey, if the furniture wasn't covered with all those fancy doilies you wouldn't have to spend so many hours ironing."

The Missus frowned and shook her head. "Edward, the house always has to be ready to receive visitors. I would hate for your sister, Alicia, to see anything but perfection. I know she would gossip to her town friends that I'm not keeping a neat house!"

Tuesday's work was not over even after ironing and supper chores were completed. When weather was decent, the Missus spent the twilight hours tending to the garden and flowers. She actually considered the flowers her friends and would carry on conversations like, "Well, Miss Lily, you are sure looking perky!" or "Sweet marigolds, you're going to make a beautiful bouquet. Your good looks will spruce up that ugly buffet."

Wednesdays were set aside for The Prairie Hill Ladies Aid meetings. When their pieced quilt was placed on the frame, it needed only a small space in the center of a room. After about ten inches of quilting were completed, the frame was extended outward. By the time the quilt reached completion, it covered almost all the parlor space. As the ladies added the finishing touches of the edging, they sat on chairs tightly wedged between the walls and quilting frame.

It often took months to make the quilt and, for most of the time, it was difficult for traffic to go in and out of parlors. Other husbands grumbled, "The quilting frame takes up too much dammed space." The Missus was the frequent hostess for the Wednesday meetings because having a quilt frame set up in the formal parlor didn't bother Mr. Ed one bit. He preferred to stay out in the kitchen.

The Missus usually planned to churn butter early Thursday morning. Afternoons were spent catching up with the mending and sewing. Fridays she baked again. Saturdays were scheduled as the time to shop and get food and clothes ready for the following day.

SATURDAY SHOPPING TRIPS

The Missus, much to the pleasure of her young daughters, scheduled late Saturday afternoon as the time for shopping. The Missus sternly looked at their dingy clothes and scruffy smudges of dirt on their arms and legs. "I don't want to hear any sass. Each of you will need to take a bath, wash your hair, and put on clean clothes before we venture into town."

The Missus had a lengthy list for the Saturday shopping. As soon as she got out of the car, the toddler was handed over to her husband. She insisted, "You look after this restless child today. If I take him with me, he tries to touch everything on the store counters."

After tossing the kicking boy into Mr. Ed's arms, she quickly hurried off to the dry good store to look at new fabric and thread. She then walked the short distance to the drug store to purchase cold cream, shampoo and a salve to sooth her tender skin. Her last stop was to the grocery store where she bought cinnamon, salt, baking powder, brown sugar, oatmeal, and a few other staples. She noticed cans of vegetables and fruits on the shelves and felt sorry for the town people who had to rely on tasteless foods instead of fresh produce from gardens.

Mr. Ed didn't mind assuming the responsibility of caring for his son. He hugged his youngest and stated, "Son, your mother doesn't know it but I would much rather be sitting out here taking care of you than shopping in the stores. We'll have us a good time." Indeed, they did, or at least Mr. Ed was pleased. Sitting on a bench in front of the hardware store provided him the opportunity to engage in conversations with other men sitting around while their wives also shopped. Conversations were about the weather, crops, and the current political situation. There was considerable skepticism by these stanch Republicans over how well the Democrats were running the show. The possible threat of a war was their biggest concern. The farmers, like people over the entire country, were paying attention to the aggressive German leader called Hitler.

Mr. Ed asked, "Do you think he eventually will try to invade all the countries in Europe?"

Even though many of them had fought in World War I, they nodded their heads in agreement when Uncle Harman stated, "Make no mistake about it, indications are we will be fighting another war with Germany. With the war happening in Europe, you can bet your socks that the United States will eventually be pulled into combat. My teen age son, George, and lots of other young men will probably be called to service." He thought a minute and added, "Since my father came from Germany, George will be fighting against his cousins."

Ed's girls were not concerned about anything but their own pleasure. The Saturday evening shopping trips were considered as the opportunity to see old and new friends. Their strolling pattern was to walk around a block in one direction then spun around and walked the opposite way. They greeted other girls with enthusiasm but, when passing a boy, they looked down at their feet and rarely said more than a whispered, "Hi."

If Mary Lou and Jane were lucky enough to have a few pennies in their pocket, their final destination was the drug store. The soda fountain served several flavors of ice cream and a variety of drinks. The girls carefully read the selections detailed on the blackboard chart then chose their favorite treat, a root beer fizz.

CHICKEN WILL BE SERVED

In modern days people enjoy refrigerators, freezers, and a local supermarket full of food. They can easily go to a restaurant if too busy or too tired to cook. Those who are accustomed to the modern conveniences rarely stop to think how different it was in the depression years. Farm families lived too far from any town to jump in the car and go out to eat at a restaurant. Their only store-bought foods were staples. Everything else served at the table was raised on the farm.

Before electricity, which brought the availability of refrigerators and freezers, sides of ham were cured with salt and hung in the smokehouse until needed. Fish caught in the nearby ponds had to be eaten for supper or, if the weather was cold, fried the next day for breakfast. The cows living on the farm provided milk and butter but beef was rarely served.

Having chicken for dinner for the Sunday meal took advance planning. After dark on Saturday evening the Missus pulled one or two sleepy roosters down from the roosting rafter and placed them into a small pen. Early Sunday morning she or Mr. Ed placed the chicken's necks on the chopping block. The familiar saying, "It's running around like a chicken with its head cut off," is based on the real situation. The headless chickens flapped and flailed around the barnyard until most of the blood had spurted from their necks. The bodies were then hung upside down on the clothesline to drain the remaining blood. The carcass was then dunked into boiling water to make it easier to pluck off the outer feathers. The next step was to hold the carcass over a flame and singe off small pinfeathers. Using a sharp knife, the Missus carefully removed the innards and cut the meaty pieces into serving pieces. As a final step in pre-preparation, she covered the chicken pieces with ice chips, arranged them on a flat pan and placed them in the icebox. After arriving home from church, she hurriedly covered her best dress with a large apron then headed for the kitchen. Lard was heated in an oversized iron skilled. The chicken pieces were dipped in buttermilk and rolled in seasoned flour before being placed in the skillet. Fried chicken served for dinner to family and friends was so crisp and tasty that every piece disappeared.

Mr. Ed read in "*Successful Farming*" about the assets of Angus cattle. He commented to his wife, "Starting a herd of this breed would be a good idea. Maybe those glossy black steers would bring in cash at the market." He sighed, "It would sure be a relief not milking a half-dozen heifers morning and evening."

Having Angus cattle on the farm changed the eating menu. Each year at least one steer, instead of being loaded on a truck destined for the market, was butchered and frozen for family use. Beef became the meat staple instead of pork. Butchered beef was stored in an ice plant in Lila. One or two trips were made into town each week to retrieve meat needed for meals.

THE CANNING ACCIDENT

Vegetables and fruits were deemed ready for canning when they were at their peak in ripeness and flavor. The Missus spent countless hot summer days in the almost unbearably hot kitchen preparing them for the coming winter months.

The cumbersome and dangerous pressure cooker was used for canning. It was early in June when one of the jars of green peas from the hot cooker exploded just as the Missus was removing it from the pressure cooker.

The explosion created a mess all over the kitchen. Peas stuck on the wallpaper and ceiling and pieces of broken glass were scattered about on the table and floor with a few shreds landing on the old cot. The Missus was directly in the pathway of the explosion. Her body was assaulted with bits of glass, boiling liquid and hot peas.

The girls, playing quietly under their quilt tent in the parlor, heard the Missus scream, "Help, I'm hurt." They dashed to the doorway between the parlor and kitchen and were shocked to see their mother with blood streaming down her face and arms and green peas speckled on her hair and skin. The Missus was jumping up and down and running around the kitchen while crying in pain.

Even in her misery, she quickly noticed both girls were starting to rush to her. The Missus shouted, "Get back girls! Don't come any closer. Neither of you have on shoes. Broken glass is all over the floor so you might cut your feet."

She noticed that Jane was started to cry. "Baby girl, please get me several of your doll's blankets. I can wrap them around my bleeding arms."

She then directed Mary Lou into action. "Honey, put on your shoes and find your daddy. He is working in the field south of the barn."

Mr. Ed stopped the tractor when he saw his small daughter running through the rough cultivated field. She was screaming, "Daddy, come to the house quick. Mommy is hurt!" Mr. Ed leaped off the tractor seat, grabbed the panting child up in his arms and ran non-stop to the house.

The Missus was trying to be brave but could not hold back the tears as her husband entered the room. She sighed, "Ed, look what I did to the new kitchen wallpaper." She then looked down at her bleeding arms and sobbed, "The burns and cuts on my arms feel awful!"

Mr. Ed hastened to calm her. He dipped a doll blanket into a pan of water and gently wiped away some of the rivets of blood from her face, arms and hands. He shook his head in concern when viewing the seriousness of her burns. "Try to be calm honey. We'll get help."

He rang one long ring on the telephone to connect with the operator. "Priscilla, get me the doctor as soon as possible. We have an accident down here!"

Mr. Ed sighed with relief when the doctor answered the first ring. It was a miracle that he was not away from the office delivering a baby or attending to a very ill patient. Dr. Gentry listened to the description of the accident and said, "My new Dodge will get me to your house in twenty minutes."

The doctor's car whipped around the barnyard and parked next to the walkway. He jumped out of his car, grabbed his black bag and ran quickly into the kitchen. He quickly examined the Missus to check the extent of her injuries. After cleaning her wounds, Dr. Gentry gently rubbed a soothing salve over her burns. He instructed, "Put this salve on several times a day. Whatever your do, don't break the blisters!"

He patted the Missus, smiled and stated, "You're a lucky lady."

She responded, "What do you mean? I don't look or feel very lucky at this minute."

Dr. Gentry explained, "You are suffering from several burns but only have a few cuts from the glass. The jar that exploded could have easily made severe deep cuts all over your body. You're particularly lucky to have only one bad cut on your face. Say a prayer of thanksgiving because that cut is above your eyebrow and no glass slivers touched your eyes."

WHAT'S FOR LUNCH?

The Missus scheduled several hours of each day for preparation of meals. For breakfast she served oatmeal, biscuits and fruit. Occasionally she treated Mr. Ed to eggs, bacon and slices of toast covered with homemade jelly. There was always a pot of coffee for him and cocoa for the children.

At noon, the main meal of the day was served. It usually consisted of meat, potatoes, bread and vegetables and a rich dessert. Most suppers were leftovers, but occasionally there was a special treat of molasses or syrup poured over pancakes or fried mush.

The Missus accepted cooking as the necessary duty of a farmer's wife. She had a special joy in baking and trying out new recipes. In addition to the loaves of bread baked several times each week, the jolly baker jar sitting on the buffet was always filled with cookies. She satisfied Mr. Ed's sweet tooth by baking triple-layer chocolate cakes or, with almost thoughtless effort, created pies filled with fruit or pudding.

In addition to daily meals, the Missus prepared a large feast every Sunday. There was always fried chicken or ham, in addition to an assortment of vegetables, casseroles, and desserts. She wanted to have enough food to feed her family plus all the invited and uninvited guests who appeared soon after the family returned from church.

It was not unusual for local preachers to drop by homes unexpectedly between Monday and Friday. One particularly hungry parson usually timed his arrival to be just before the noon meal was served. The Missus, by some miracle, was always able to multiply the food so that everyone was satisfied after the meal, and these times were no exception. The minister had a big appetite and ate more than his share.

One time there was only enough pieces of meat for the family so she claimed, "I am just not too hungry today. Reverend, you take this piece of ham. I also made a nice blackberry pie for dessert, so be sure to save room for it."

The busiest and hardest time of providing an adequate meal was when the neighborhood men helped Mr. Ed with the harvesting. On those days the Missus was up by four in the morning. Before preparing breakfast, she had already killed and cleaned the chickens and had them ready to fry, the ham was cooked and the meat loaf ready to go in the oven. To satisfy the hunger of working men, she would peel and cook at least ten pounds of potatoes, pick ripe vegetables from the garden, make gallons of sweet tea and have a large selection of cakes and pies baked for dessert. There was so much to prepare that, on occasion, a neighbor woman came laden with extra food. She stayed to help the Missus serve the meal and clean up the dishes. When the girls were old enough to help, no excuses could get them out of being available to fetch and carry until the last dish was washed.

Hot and sweaty men always arrived from the fields exactly at noon. After a quick wash-up down by the barn well, they strolled through the garden gate, ambled over to the old elm tree and sat down on benches placed beside a makeshift table created with sawhorses and slats of wood. Bowls heaping with food were brought out from the kitchen and passed up and down the table. There was no talking because the men were too busy drinking gallons of sweetened tea and stuffing their mouths with the delicious food.

As the last crumbs of pie disappeared, the men stood up, belched, stretched, rubbed their stomachs and said, "Much obliged for the good meal." Not one of them ever considered how nice it would be to help the Missus. They could have easily scraped their plates and pumped water. This was during the 30's when men never even considered lifting a hand to do anything considered to be woman's work.

TENDING THE GARDEN

The Missus reserved early mornings and the short hours prior to sunset as the times to tend her beloved garden and flowers. (She had painfully learned that working outside during the sunny part of the day resulted in burns and a rash). The Missus believed the magic to gardening was preparing the soil before planting. She layered table scraps and vegetable peelings with leaves and dirt in wooden box. The enrichment of nutrients provided from this compost, plus a load of dirt dug from the old cattle feeding lot, resulted in an ideal garden loam.

It was not easy to provide adequate watering for the plants. Mr. Ed and the Missus filled buckets from the well in the barn lot or house cistern then toted them either by hand or in the wheelbarrow. While the plants were still tiny, the Missus used a tin cup to gently pour water around the base of each seedling.

As the plants grew, she diligently pruned and weeded. Her efforts maximized the possibility that each plant would be the best it could be. She laughed one day as she said to her husband, "Caring for plants is a lot like raising children. They need tender care and attention, but to help them grow to be their best, pruning or spankings are necessary."

Even though the Missus was quite humble about her talents as far as quilting and baking, she was openly proud of her skills in the garden. Flower arrangements were sent to ailing friends and frequently adorned the church altar. The Missus always had several tiny plants rooted in cartons or tins in her porch greenhouse. These were available as gifts and, if a visitor admired a particular plant she would say, "Please take one, I have plenty more."

The Missus had a preference for roses. She believed it a necessary duty to cover the graves of loved ones on Memorial Day with rose bouquets. To be sure of their availability on that date, she planted several varieties so blooms would be continuous from early May until late June. Curling around the fence between the lawn and barnyard was a profusion of yellow roses. She sweetly talked Mr. Ed into building her an arbor in the front yard where her pink and red varieties could be displayed. The aromatic English roses she planted as a border around the garden fence plus other roses planted long ago around the established herb plot, continued to flourish under her care.

The Missus, always the ultimate planner, made sure that, during the entire growing season, the grounds would be covered with displays of color. Snow still lingered on the ground when crocuses began to peek out from under the dead leaves and only a few days later tiny daffodils opened their yellow petals. Later in the spring, the several fragrant lilac bushes and purple iris flowers were in full bloom. During the summer, the two large beds of orange tiger lilies, multicolored hollyhocks, zinnias and marigolds created a patchwork of color.

Sunflowers grow abundantly in Kansas. In the hot, still days of late summer the sunflowers, sometimes reaching ten feet, dominated the garden. Later the rust, gold, and red mums bloomed until the frost arrived in late October or early November. The buffet in the kitchen always held vases filled with blossoms. Even during the winter there was a profusion of color in the kitchen. Mr. Ed would return home from the woods with large twigs adorned with red Bittersweet berries that the Missus used to make a bright and cheerful arrangement for the buffet.

TIME FOR HOUSEKEEPING

Are you wondering which day the Missus scheduled for cleaning? Every day would be a good guess. After breakfast she always took a broom to sweep the latest development of black Kansas dirt off the floor and quickly dusted the furniture. She always fussed over the cot because wads of dust, dirty socks and slippers hid under it and the covers never stayed unwrinkled.

Approximately twice a year, the Missus would go on a cleaning rampage. Her usual plan was to start upstairs and not stop until even the spider webs were missing in the cellar.

The spring after the shelves were built in the north bedroom and filled with bolts of fabrics, she decided to start the cleaning process there. She surveyed the room and frowned. "It doesn't seem right. I provided this space for my friends to store quilting fabrics but they are making no effort to help keep it clean and orderly." Indeed, she was right. The bolts had been put haphazardly on the shelves. Bits and pieces of fabric were scattered over the floor and the old cutting table. The Missus spent the day cleaning and then reorganizing the bolts of fabric on the shelves according to color and labeling boxes for sewing supplies.

Entering the chaotic bedroom claimed by the girls also made her unhappy. She put her hands on her hips, shook her head and sighed as she scanned the mess. "Jane piled all the dolls and doll clothes in the corner and even perched the new porcelain cups and saucers on the bed posts!"

She frowned while she continued to gaze at the clutter around the room. The girls were expected to neatly fold and stack in drawers the clothes she had washed, starched and neatly ironed. Instead of doing as she had instructed, the girls had flung the clothes on a chair. The Missus groaned. "Saints alive, will my girls ever learn to be decent housekeepers?"

The room desperately needed cleaning. She decided to start by dumping every item stored in dresser drawers onto the bed. While working on this task, she complained to her absent daughter, "Oh, Mary Louise, Mary Louise, when are you every going to realize that there's a proper place for everything?" The puzzles made for her eldest by cutting colorful calendar pictures in small pieces were originally stored in labeled envelopes. All of the pieces of puzzles were now mixed together in a shoebox stuffed in the top dresser drawer.

In the second drawer, between slips and panties, she found a library book that had been overdue for months. Mary Lou was always losing hair bows, and at times, it was intentional. The Missus found several of them wadded up and hidden in the bottom drawer. As she replaced clothes to their proper place, she told herself, "There are several dresses that Mary Lou has outgrown and they will even be too small for Jane." The Missus considered throwing them out but, in the tradition of the family, she decided they should be stored just in case someone else might need them.

The mistress of the household continued with the frantic spring cleaning. The feather tick mattresses were pulled off the bed, dragged down the stairs and then taken outside to be aired all day in the sun. All the sheets and pillowcases were laundered and crisply starched before ironing. She had no satisfaction until all the curtains were washed, the furniture was polished and the floors were mopped and waxed.

The cot got a thorough once-over during the cleaning spell! She took its mattress out in the yard and beat it with a broom until no dust remained. Before replacing the mattress, she carefully washed the shiny black metal surfaces.

The Missus also experienced drastic fixin'-up spells. Give praise to the Lord that they only occurred once every three to five years. It was easy to detect when one of the spells was coming on. She frowned every time she looked at the walls and ceiling and she shook her fist and stamped her foot each time her gaze rested on the cot. Sure enough, it wasn't long before she went into town to buy paint and locate a pretty new wallpaper design.

As Mr. Ed shifted furniture to make way for the ladders during one of the cleaning spells, he suggested, "Maybe we should give up farming and take up wallpapering for a living." What a great idea! Had they been so inclined, they could have created a profitable business assisting others.

The wallpapering started early in the morning. The Missus slowly stirred water into flour until she got a pasty substance that looked good enough to eat. Actually, Little Brother found the mixture cooling on the table and thought it was pudding. He stuck his pudgy hand in the bucket and took a good mouthful. This child could eat dirt smothered with worms, but he spit the yucky paste onto his clean shirt.

The paste was strained into a large pail and carried to the buffet, ready to be brushed to the backs of wallpaper strips. Next to them the Missus laid out scissors, yardsticks, blue chalk with a string attached, pencils, and brushes just how a physician prepares his operating table. The ladder, brought in from the shed, was propped in the corner. The kitchen table was covered with faded oilcloth and newspapers.

The Missus methodically matched the wallpaper design, measured exactly and then cut the wallpaper into strips big enough to cover the area from the baseboards to the ceiling. She needed some extra help, so she called her husband. "Ed, come over here and give me a hand." Carefully, the two flipped over the wallpaper strips. The Missus dipped the brush in the bucket and covered the top strip with gooey paste.

Mr. Ed was an expert at attaching the wallpaper to the walls, but he was very cautious. He recalled a lesson he had learned the hard way when he was a teenager. He had been the only son willing to help his mother with wallpapering. Cheerfully and carelessly, he had hurriedly started climbing the ladder but tripped on the second rung. He sprained his ankle and was covered from head to toe with pasty paper.

As an added present-day precaution he pleaded, "Honey, hold this ladder steady while I'm climbing. I don't need another broken ankle."

The strip was attached to the wall next to the ceiling and checked with the chalk plumb line to be sure it hung straight. The final step was to make sweeping motions with a large brush to eliminate all air bubbles under the paper.

Except for a quick sandwich for lunch, Ed and the Missus worked with no break. The entire room had new wallpaper, and there was still time to complete evening chores before sunset.

Mr. Ed. did his share of groaning when assigned to wallpaper duty. But, to tell the truth, he enjoyed the results as much as his wife. The coming Sunday when several friends came to visit, he quickly asked, "How do you like that new floral wallpaper the Missus picked out for the kitchen walls? Doesn't it brighten up this room?"

The redecorating was not over with just new wallpaper and paint. The Missus next turned her attention to the curtains and the cot. She had squirreled pennies for several months and finally counted enough money in the jar to make a trip to the dry goods store.

Decorating always included paying careful attention to the coordination of colors. Once, when the wallpaper had purple flowers, the curtains and the cot wore the same color. This time the wallpaper print was marigold flowers, she decided the curtains and cot cover should be orange. The cot had no complaints. The Missus in her fixin' up spell had made it look almost new.

Chapter 7

I GET NO RESPECT!

Mr. Ed's children were constantly on top of me, but they demonstrated little respect. They abused me and were indifferent to the pain they caused. However, I was thankful they did not share their mother's scorn of my appearance. On winter mornings they jumped out of their beds, abandoning  *the feather tick mattresses and heavy quilts that had kept them snug and warm, rushed barefoot through the cold upstairs hallway, slid down the banister, dashed into the kitchen and made a running jump on me. Each of the three struggled to find a cozy space. My pillows and covers ended up a tangled mess.*

A Cozy Sanctuary, the Cot

KANSAS STORMS

T he cot always welcomed the frightened squirmy company of the youngsters when a storm blew in during the late night. Spring storms in Eastern Kansas are an awesome sight to behold! The cold air from the Rocky Mountains drifts eastward and hits the warm air coming up from the Gulf of Mexico. The clash of air causes angry swirling clouds to gather that frighten even the bravest of souls. These storms, cited by the weather man as boiling up over the plains, usually hit Eastern Kansas somewhere between ten p.m. and midnight. The dark clouds churn and dip and frequent lightning bolts streak from one cloud to another. It is not long before claps of thunder vibrate and flashing of lightening race toward the earth. Hail or tornadoes often accompany the heavy winds and rain.

Mary Lou was less than a year old when an angry storm spread its wrath on the farm. Mr. Ed and his young wife were terrified as they sat huddled in the kitchen listening to the howl of the wind swirling around the house. The bombshell crash told them a huge tree had fallen in the yard and the swishing sound indicated that the roof was ripping apart. The trauma of this experience resulted in the parents' fear of summer storms being passed on to their children.

Mr. Ed had an uncanny awareness of weather conditions. On an early summer afternoon, he returned early from the fields and hustled to complete the evening chores. He made a quick walk around the barnyard to make sure all objects that could fly easily were set inside the shed or barn. He hurried to the house and commented to his wife, "Do you feel the heavy air too? All the critters are aware of the change in atmosphere. The crickets aren't chirping, the birds stopped singing and the cattle have gathered near the barn. Bet this will be a doozy of a storm!

Throughout the evening the Missus and Mr. Ed kept a close watch on the approaching clouds. Meanwhile, three pajama-clad children, too scared to go upstairs for sleeping, considered the cot their sanctuary.

The angry grey clouds rolled in from the west and had swirling cone shaped dips that could easily turn into tornadoes. No chances were taken.

The Missus picked up the baby and Mr. Ed carried little Jane in his arms. Mary Lou started crying and begged to get a ride as well. The Missus sharply reprimanded her. "Mary Lou, you are big enough to walk by yourself to the cellar, so put on your shoes and quit whining."

The family huddled together for nearly an hour in the smelly underground hole inhabited by spiders and other varmints while the winds raged above them. They did not vacate the space until the immediate threat of a tornado had passed. Even though the rain was still coming down in a steady downpour, Mr. Ed said, "It's safe now. Let's head back to the house." The children, still not eager to venture to an upstairs bedroom, curled their sleepy bodies covered with damp clothes in the cot's covers for the remaining hours of the night.

EVERY KID IS DIFFERENT

The oldest girl, the skinny one with bony knees, gave the cot's coils aches and pains. Except for cold mornings and the frequent summer storms she ignored its purpose as a rest haven. Instead, she thought of the cot as a bouncing board and had a thorough workout on it each day. She bounced with the intention of reaching the ceiling. The cot developed squeaking problems and a sagging mattress as a result of her aerobics.

Her mother cautioned, "Mary Lou, be careful. That cot will toss you so high your head really will hit the ceiling, or you'll have a bad fall." She never considered how much the poor cot might be suffering.

It's lucky for the cot that this child had a keen sense of when her mama was going to put her to work. At the first indication that tasks were waiting, she stopped bouncing and disappeared outside. Her goal was to find and climb to the highest possible place. Hopefully, it would be too far away from the house to be able to hear and obey her mama's call. One of her favorite havens was the tall silo located down by the south feeding lot. The carefree child would climb to the top bars and then perform acrobatic stunts. She first let one leg dangle then daringly wave with one arm. It was a thrill to firmly grasp the bars, lean back as far as possible and watch the clouds pass overhead. The experience always made her dizzy and the descent down the bars could have been disastrous.

Another favorite getaway was an old pear tree. If her mother's behavior indicated she would soon be asking for help, Mary Lou would grab her current favorite book and make a dash for its limbs. Mary Lou happily spent several hours reading while clinging to the high branches.

Mr. Ed and the Missus encouraged their children to read, even if it meant shirking some of their duties. They made regular trips to the distant town of Springville just so the girls could borrow books from the library. It is likely the Missus was aware of her daughter's intentions to flee from work but let her escape when she noticed the book under her arm.

One afternoon Mary Lou was not seen for several hours. Auntie Marie questioned, "I haven't seen Mary Lou since I arrived. That's very unusual. She usually hangs around my skirts."

The Missus answered, "She is probably up to some kind of mischief. We'd better go look for her."

As they approached the barnyard, a wailing sound came from the nearby pear tree. "Mama, Auntie Marie, help me!" Just like a kitten, that child had climbed to the top limbs but was frightened when it was time to retreat from the lofty height. Auntie Marie, still young and agile, climbed up to her side and helped her niece carefully descend, limb by limb, to the ground.

That evening after the children had gone to bed, the Missus and Mr. Ed discussed their three growing children. They weren't too worried about busy Little Brother or content Jane. Mary Lou, who always seemed to be tempting fate, was another matter. She tended to daydream, liked to wander and seemed to have a propensity for near disasters. Her knees were always covered with scabs, not because she was clumsy, but simply due to the fact that she always was looking up at the sky instead of where her feet were leading. The cot had more than one reason to dread her jumping. The ugly scabs would often open and blood scattered all over its nice clean cover.

Mary Lou, when only three and a half, became completely bored with inside play. At least a dozen times she pleaded with her mother, who was busy with baking and ironing, if she could venture outside. The Missus finally bundled the child up in a new red cloak but sternly cautioned her daughter, "Stay near the house as you play. It's dangerous for you to go to the barn lot alone."

Mary Lou ignored her mother's directions and within a few minutes was out the gate and headed for the barn. By some hook or crook, she ventured through a fence and into the pen containing a restless angry bull. The red cloak, or perhaps just the presence of a strange small person, scared the bull. Fortunately for the child, instead of charging in Mary Lou's direction, he jumped the fence and raced for the open pasture.

The child seemed indifferent to the perils that could easily harm someone so young. An angry turkey gobbler was the first animal to give her a real scare. The gobbler spread out his wings, gave a gobble, and chased her all around the yard. Mary Lou's climbing skill was put to good use as she found safety by once again climbing to the high branches of the old pear tree.

Soon after his daughter's seventh birthday her daddy stated, "Young lady, you've been playing too long. It's time you started sharing in our workload. From now on it will be your responsibility to locate all the nests in the hen house and barn and gather the eggs each evening."

It was a balmy summer evening and Mary Lou had spent most of the afternoon in a tree. She put off her chores until the shadows grew long and the air cooler. It was so late that her footsteps and banging bucket didn't even disturb the sleepy hens preparing to roost in the henhouse.

Entering the barn a few minutes later was a little scary. It seemed dark as ink and it took a few seconds for her eyes to adjust to seeing with only a tiny streak of sunlight sneaking through the barn door. Mary Lou shuffled slowly until she reached the manger. Her hands slowly groped for any eggs that might be lying in the hay. Instead of identifying the smooth surface of oval eggs, her fingers closed around something that felt a little like her mother's purse. She quickly jerked her hand up and realized she was holding a black snake! He had been coiled around the eggs and the round lumps of his body indicated he had already eaten most of his dinner. The snake wasn't poisonous, but the experience scared the child to death.

Mary Lou screamed so loud and so long that her daddy, who rarely spanked, gave her a swat on the bottom and told her to settle down. "What kind of a farm girl are you if you allow a little old snake to scare you like that?"

The hayloft of the barn, probably because it was so high, was another one of her favorite disappearing places. It was awesome to peer out the cracks to see the distant fields, the church, homes of neighbors, and Fords on the highway. It was also the perfect space for creative play. Mary Lou liked to grab onto the rope that hung over a rafter, take a swinging leap in space then gracefully glide to the other side of the loft before dropping onto another pile of hay. One day she decided that to be a competent acrobat, she should be practicing summersaults and flip flops. She failed to watch where she was going and landed on a pitchfork. This time she was lucky. The only injury was a goose egg bump where the handle hit her head.

The escape areas always contained an element of danger. The sheds, the attic, the woodpile and the barn were often the habitat of less than friendly critters. Black widow spiders resided on the large woodpile where Mary Lou climbed, and brown recluse spiders preferred the dry and dark tool shed which was a perfect place for hiding. It is no surprise that the Missus, more than once, discovered the evil little creatures crawling on Mary Lou.

It took some time for the child to realize that not all animals were good pets. Only after a painful bite on the leg did she realize that some dogs could be dangerous. She also soon became aware that barn cats who hissed might also scratch! When just a toddler, Mary Lou sighted a raccoon that seemed more than willing to let her come near enough for petting and possible arm cuddling Luckily, the Missus arrived in time to pull the child away before she reached for the rabid animal.

Little Jane was a calmer sweeter child and was not in constant trouble like her older sister. The cot was delighted when she took her turn to play on its covers. In the mornings, after Mary Lou had gone to school or outside, little Jane considered the cot a home for her rather large family of dolls. She would quietly dress and feed her little family, then pat their backs gently as she sang, "Rock-a-Bye Baby." It was not unusual for her to curl up and take a nap with her little family.

Jane was usually happy and contented, but there were times when she shed tears of distress while sitting on the cot. She had beautiful curly golden hair that her mama insisted should be brushed into ringlets each day. Indeed, her hair was lovely, but it was always full of tangles. Little Jane often wailed, "Why can't I have straight ugly hair like my sister?"

The girls were four and six when Little Brother arrived on the scene. As a tiny baby, he stopped crying and often fell asleep soon after being placed on the cot. It didn't take long before he appreciated the cot like his father and claimed ownership of its space at every opportunity.

Mr. Ed started taking his son fishing when he was just a toddler, and from that time on, the child had fish on his brain. If Mr. Ed was not available for a fishing expedition to the ponds or creek, the child devised his own fishing plan. Using only a stick, string and safety pin, he would happily spend hours fishing for the tiny minnows in the water trough by the barn.

To accommodate his fishing habit, Little Brother always carried an old tobacco tin inside the back pocket of his overalls. It was filled with dirt and creepy crawly things he needed for bait. As he rested on the cot, those worms often escaped from the tin and crawled onto the covers. The Missus wasn't too happy about the mess they made and was thankful there were extra covers to place on the cot.

To tell the truth, it was almost impossible for the cot to learn the real name of that little boy. Mr. Ed would call him Little Man, Partner or Big Guy. The Missus, who doted on her youngest child, addressed him with titles like Precious, Sweetheart or My Baby. The girls had a consistent name for him. It was Dannydon't. They would yell, "Dannydon't run in the house!" "Dannydon't touch my dolls!" "Dannydon't stick your tongue out at me!" "Dannydon't eat all those cookies!" "Dannydon't pull my hair!"

Four legged creatures were about as welcome in the house as the Kansas dust. The cot only got to meet a few of the pets the children accumulated and only heard about ones never allowed inside. No pets like Anamule were available for this generation of children to have as a companion. Their daddy had filled their head with stories about her. When the children decided to pretend, they had such a wonderful idea. The substitute would be the old arthritic dog, Shep. The dog learned to stop scratching fleas while sitting in his favorite spot by the back door. As quickly as his old legs would let him, he ran to a hole under the barn whenever the children came looking for him.

There were always barnyard animals filling the role as temporary pets for the children. Mary Lou's first pet was a tiny orphaned lamb. Her daddy built a tiny fenced area by the house where it would be easy for the toddler to have access to the pet each day. Mary Lou, who had only recently given up her milk bottle herself, enjoyed feeding milk to the lamb and was guilty of occasionally taking a sip from his bottle. In the succeeding years, baby piglets, a calf, several rabbits and some frolicking puppies took turns living in this pen.

In the spring of each year, large rectangular boxes with tiny holes around the sides arrived at the farm. Strange peeping sounds came from the boxes. Each box was filled with tiny gold chicks. The girls were always delighted to help their mama carefully lift the tiny creatures out of the boxes and then gently place them under a warm lamp in the brooder house.

The girls spent countless hours in the brooder house during the following weeks. They watched with fascination as the yellow chicks chased each other and pecked at food. If the girls sat still long enough, the little chicks crawled over their legs and sometimes into their laps.

Little Jane had a special love for baby kittens. The cot had the opportunity to be well acquainted with them, because when they were tiny, she would temporarily give up the dolls and pretend the tiny kittens were her babies. She was delighted to watch as the kittens played hide and seek under the cot covers. Jane would dress kittens in doll cloths, cover them with her doll blankets and sing and pat their soft fur until all were curled up in balls and quietly sleeping. The Missus probably knew the kittens were on the cot, but she pretended not to see them.

When Dannydon't started roaming through the fields and woods, new critters found their way to the cot. He was very fond of turtles, grasshoppers, ladybugs, fireflies, and little green snakes. Again, the Missus seemed to ignore the fact that these creatures were invading her house. Dannydon't received a puppy for his birthday. The white terrier, Spot, had a single black marking on his back and a ring around one eye. Spot's favorite place to sleep was in the doorway and it was rare he was able to sneak over to the cot.

Tolerance for animals in the house came to an immediate stop because of this animal. The puppy was joyfully playing with the three children on the cot when the children heard the Missus slam the screen door entrance to the porch. They had an inkling of her displeasure, so they hid Spot in the dark cave under the cot's springs. That stupid puppy started barking and quickly came out of hiding just as the Missus entered the kitchen. The Missus put her foot down and demanded, "No animals are to be in this house!" She never bothered to explain that she was extremely allergic to animals with hair and always suffered after contact with them.

No dust bunnies lived under the cot for any length of time, but there were other unwelcome animals who found it a good hiding place. One summer a big black snake somehow got in the house and chose to sleep under the cot. Wouldn't you know, it was the oldest daughter, who by that time was scared to death of snakes, was the one to find the sleeping reptile! She screamed and yelled for hours and kicked the cot's sides because he harbored such a beast. From that time on, she always looked under the springs before starting her jumping antics.

At night, four-legged creatures scuttled across the room and met their final destiny in the mousetraps waiting for them when they ducked under the cot's sides! Someone, who wanted to frighten her sibling, pulled a dead mouse from the mousetrap and placed it in her sister's coat pocket. When Jane's fingers reached for a hankie, she was thrown into a state of complete agitation by pulling out the decomposing mass of flesh. She became even more frightened of mice than her sister was of snakes. Jane fully represented the picture of a lady who jumps up on a chair and screams whenever a mouse scurries by.

Chapter 8

OH, COME, COME, COME

It has been more than eighty-seven years since my journey from Pennsylvania. During these many years the conversation in the kitchen often gravitated to dialogs related to the Prairie Hill Presbyterian Church. The church was located a mile west and half a mile south of the farm via dirt roads. Much preferred by Ed and his brothers was the walking trek traversing across the creek, through the woods and pasture and over the fence into a neighbor's field. Family members made frequent trips back and forth from the house to their place or worship. In addition to Sunday school and sermons, they attended social events on week days.

The Devoted Cot

WHEN THE CHURCH WAS NEW

All the families from miles around piled into their buggies or wagons and came to the church on Sundays when Ed and his siblings were young. The horses were used to pull spring wagons or carriages to the churchyard. The wagons were unhitched and the four-legged animals, tied to the hitching post, waited patiently as their owners participated in Sunday school, church, long periods of gossip and occasional picnics under the old oak tree.

Missing church on Sunday was considered a sinful act. If anyone had to be absent, they made sure that others in the congregation got the word that they were sick in bed or were called to distant places for reasons akin to an aunt's death in another state.

The family had a long-time history with the church. Mr. Ed's father provided an abundant pledge needed for financing, then rolled up his sleeves and provided tools as the building was constructed. His mother taught Sunday school and assumed leadership in endeavors accomplished by the Prairie Hill Ladies Aid Society. Their voices were part of the choir and their duets were requested as special music.

When the weather was decent, Ed and his older brothers did not ride to and from the church in the buggy with their parents. They chose instead to jump across the stream, climb up the steep hillside and stroll through the large pasture they called the South Forty. After only a short walk through a neighbor's corn field they arrived at their destination. It was not unusual for the boys, dusty and sweating, to rush in the door and settle in the pew just as the bell rang the final time.

The parents were very pleased with how well their boys seemed to be behaving during one particular Sunday service, but wondered why their daughter was so fidgety. Jack had proudly collected a large beetle while strolling through the South Forty and concealed it in his pocket. While the parents prayed with eyes squeezed shut, he gingerly slipped the bug down the back of his sister's blouse. His sister, Alicia, couldn't scream in church and could not tell her parents the problem. The parents were unaware of the sibling interchange of stuck out tongues and ugly faces.

In the early 1900's the church was filled with families with young children. After the sermon the adults remained in the sanctuary to gossip. Their children immediately headed for the outdoors where they chased each other around the churchyard and played hide and seek behind the tombstones in the small cemetery adjacent to the church. Young Ed always enjoyed these Sunday outings. It provided one of the few times when he could play with boys his own age instead of tagging after his older brothers.

LOVE AND MARRIAGE

There were several years when Mr. Ed rarely attended the country church. As a teen, he stayed in Springville with his grandmother to attend high school and did not often come home on weekends. Following his high school graduation he moved to Manhattan, Kansas, to attend Kansas State College. After the threatened farm bankruptcy brought him back to the farm, he once again became a regular participant at the church.

It was at an ice cream social held in early autumn that a pretty lady with dark hair and lovely green eyes caught his attention. It didn't take him long to find out that she was the new school marm at one of the nearby primary schools.

Ed did not know the meaning of the word shyness. He immediately strolled over to the side of the pretty young lady. As was his habit in conversation, he immediately referred to the weather. "This has been a beautiful day. Have you ever seen autumn in Kansas so glorious?"

She answered, "Indeed it is beautiful. My students frequently bring me bouquets of flowers they pick along the side of the road to school." She added, "I imagine you know Roy Hatchel. He drew a perfect replica of a bouquet sitting on my desk, then, last Tuesday, after school, he used my colored pencils to draw a lovely picture of the fall landscape."

Ed's smile indicated that he shared the affection others in the community had for the young boy.

The Missus continued, "Roy is a talented artist. Keep your ears alert. You will soon hear of something wonderful that will to happen for the child."

Ed spent the remainder of the evening assuming the duty of seeing that the young lady felt welcome in the community. In his easy conversational style, he introduced her to people around the room. By being her escort, he silently conveyed to the other young men the message, "Stay away, I saw her first."

When it was time to enjoy the ice cream and cake he explained, "I'm an authority on chocolate cake. No one made it better than Grandmother Shields but lately she has been forgetting important ingredients. I think the last time she made the cake she used salt instead of sugar. As to ice cream, Aunt Be takes advantage of the availability of rich cream donated by Maude, the pride of Jeff's dairy herd. She makes the best vanilla ice cream you'll ever taste. I caution you not to eat too much of it, though, if you want to stay slim and trim."

Mr. Ed had never attended choir rehearsals on Wednesday evening, but he decided it provided an opportunity to start a romance. He said, "When my parents attended choir practice, I came with them but played outside. My mother listened to me sing at home, but for some reason she suggested the choir did not need me. Even without her blessing, I am willing to try."

The young lady smiled and said, "If you are willing so am I."

Their first official date, choir practice the following week, was a disaster. Neither of them could sing a note in tune and were extremely embarrassed by the sounds that came from their mouths.

They drove home in silence. Both felt they were failures. Mr. Ed pondered over the situation then started chuckling. "Did you hear when my good friend, Wally, asked if a frog was croaking in the baritone section?"

His date sighed then also laughed at her musical ineptness. "It's a good thing the children at my school were not attending. They've placed me on a pedestal. Hearing me sing might change their minds."

The lifelong sympathy and understanding of each other was established as they accepted their complete lack of any musical talent.

Ed was not about to pick up his Sunday date with his father driving the Dodge, so he resorted to the old-fashioned way of hitching the horses to the buggy. The couple took the long way home by directing the horses to clip-clop along the winding dirt path following Whitman Creek. Mr. Ed pulled on the reins when arriving at a scenic area near the bend of the creek. On their first date the weather was unseasonably warm so Ed suggested, "Let's take off our shoes and socks and wade out to those boulders in the middle of the stream. We can eat that picnic lunch you packed on that big rock."

Taking a long buggy ride to Whitman became a weekly occurrence. The weather quickly turned cooler, so instead of testing the cold waters with their toes, they sat in the buggy and enjoyed jelly sandwiches, hard boiled eggs, apples and sugar cookies.

On these dates, Mr. Ed always talked non-stop. By the time the couple announced their engagement, the pretty lady knew all about Ed's fading hopes of someday completing his college education and becoming an engineer. She chuckled over stories about Anamule but was secretly glad there was no such animal still around. She listened attentively as Ed described the personalities of members of his family. She was concerned over his father's health and was not surprised when he announced that his parents were moving to Springville to be near a doctor. There was no doubt in her mind that she would enjoy his brother, Jack. Before ever meeting her, the Missus decided to be wary of his older sister, Alicia. She even recognized Mr. Ed's special affection for a piece of furniture. It was an old black cot tucked away in an upstairs bedroom.

The Missus announced to friends near the end of her second year of teaching that she and Ed would be getting married in the following fall. Not one of the ladies was the least bit surprised.

When hearing the announcement Aunt Be said, "Ed's been smitten with our school marm since a year ago last September, but he's been very quiet about future plans."

Dora Hatchel commented, "It's my guess that they've had a wedding planned for several months. Since she stays with us, I've observed her every day. There is a glow in her eyes and she spends every evening creating handiwork for her hope chest."

Eunice added, "Ed probably asked her to marry him soon after they were a steady couple at church on Sundays and attended at all the social events in our community together. I think the first year they were a couple, her salary was used to pay off college loans. She probably decided to teach an extra year to build up savings."

Dora gave a nod but added. "Yes, that's true but I think there was another reason she continued to teach this year. She has been totally devoted to her students. As an example, it's been amazing to watch the change in my Roy. Because of her interest and skill in teaching, he has so much more confidence and realizes what he is an accomplished artist and is not as ashamed of his limitations. He will never read books, but he can now recognize words necessary for driving plus other tasks for daily living."

Rose offered a suggestion. "I have a perfect idea of a gift we can get for the bride. When I visited a dry goods store at the Plaza in Kansas City, I saw beautiful bolts of satin, lace, and chiffon on sale. Let's buy some material that she can use to make her wedding gown."

The Missus was speechless when her friends placed yards of ivory satin in her arms. She gently rubbed the material on her cheek then held it up in the sunlight. As each of her friends received a hug she exclaimed, "My dearest friends, I am so thrilled with the exquisite material, but it must have cost a fortune!"

Rose shook her head, "We were lucky. Since materials needed for spring and summer are already on the counters, the heavier fabrics were on sale."

Dora suggested, "Unfold the material. There's even more."

Fingers quickly dug through the material. She soon located a bag containing silk thread, several lengths of Battenberg lace and a beautiful silver belt buckle.

Aunt Be added a small package. "I snipped a little off the length of the material and made a dozen satin buttons for your dress. I can make more if you need them."

Rose was carrying a large packet. "I've been collecting pictures of wedding gowns because my eldest got married last year and it won't be long before the other girls will be asking me to make their gowns. Why don't you look through these patterns and decide on your favorite? I can a sketch a pattern to fit your tiny body."

The Missus spent the summer sewing at the machine by day and finishing the hand stitching in the evening. The finished outfit was a tea-length dropped waist gown. The neckline and sleeve cuffs were adorned with lace and tiny satin buttons. The dress was lovely, and something she could not have afforded without the help of her friends.

As Rose marked the hem of the dress she suggested, "In a trunk at home I have the bridal veil and a pearl necklace that my daughter wore at her wedding last year. We would be pleased if you would wear them when you walk down the aisle toward Ed."

The wedding was in late September. During the 1920's most weddings were held in homes, but Mr. Ed's parents had not returned to the farm from Springville and the Missus had no home of her own. The couple felt that the little church, the place where they fell in love, would be the perfect wedding site.

On the day of the wedding every pew was filled with parishioners, students and parents and others in the area who knew the couple. All gasped as they watched the bride in her beautiful dress step slowly toward the young man they had all known and loved for many years.

After the ceremony the bride threw her bouquet of wild flowers to the giggling cluster of single girls, but her toss was wide. It was Aunt Sarah, a long-time spinster with no prospects in sight, who jumped higher than the others and grabbed the bouquet out of the air.

Tables were set up on the church lawn for the banquet. Each Ladies Aid member tried to outdo the other. A white layered cake with bride and broom figurines at the top was the centerpiece. The Missus, aware of the gourmet favorites of her new husband, had baked a triple layered chocolate cake for the occasion.

Money was very limited, but after announcing their engagement, the couple had saved every penny. Ed, who worked long hours in his father's fields, had made extra money selling the small tables and chairs made out of slats of wood stored in the barn. The Missus, in addition to helping at the Hatchels, had received money by watching other children in the community when parents need to go on a business trip of visit relatives. The couple purchased a black Ford with their savings and still had enough remaining to cover the cost of a short honeymoon. They spent a few glorious days at a scenic Missouri vacation site called, "The Lake of the Ozarks."

Three healthy babies, who arrived to this couple in the following years, were baptized in front of the small wooden alter. The children were expected to attend faithfully but never seemed to share the enthusiasm their parents had for the small church. Perhaps it was because of the small number of other children attending when they were young. It just wasn't much fun to run around the churchyard when only siblings and cousins were available as playmates.

The little cemetery behind the church contained a large family plot. One gravestone had etchings of tiny booties above the name. This marked the site where Mr. Ed and the Missus had buried their first child who lived but a few hours. Mr. Ed and the Missus reserved spaces next to her grave for their final resting sites.

Sunday was identified as the Lord's time. The farmers rarely scheduled any more work than the necessary chores. After attending Sunday school and church for three or four hours, they would return home to enjoy a huge dinner. More often than not, expected or unexpected company appeared at Ed's door and eagerly helped consume the meal prepared by the Missus.

There were only rare occasions when no company came for dinner and the children were unable to convince Mr. Ed that they needed an adventure away from home. Mr. Ed took advantage of this leisure time by enjoying a long nap on the cot. He did not move until time to do the evening chores.

Even the Missus slowed down her steps on Sunday afternoons when no visitors were present. She kept up her constant pace until the dishes were washed, dried and stored neatly in cupboards. The leftovers which did not need refrigeration were placed in the middle of the table and covered with a dishcloth to keep flies away. The Missus told her family, "If you get hungry it's your responsibility to take care of yourselves!" She did not sleep but quietly cross-stitched or completed embroidery on a table runner. Needlework like this was for pleasure rather than a chore.

A SPECIAL CHURCH

Most country churches in the Midwest look similar in appearance, but this one seemed special. The Missus often said, "This church always makes me think of the first line of an old hymn, 'Oh, come, come, come. Come to the church in the wild wood.'" The only difference was this tiny church was located on a small hill instead of in the vale. The land surrounding the church grounds was covered with prairie grasses. Spring provided a blanket of color created by the pink and red roses, purple grass flowers and bits of yellow honeysuckle vines. The abundance of yellow flowers and nearby wheat fields provided an aura of golden glow in June and July. In the late summer the native yellow sunflowers nodded their heads to the sun. Members of the congregation, as their cars turned into the churchyard, often commented on the visual evidence of God's glory.

The building consisted of one large room and a tiny foyer. A raised stage with the pulpit placed in the center sat at the front of the room. When Mr. Ed was a young child the choir sat in seats arranged on each side of the pulpit. By the time his children were attending, there were few singers so the spaces stood empty during sermons. The only time the spaces were used was during Sunday school lessons.

The piano, often out of tune and with keys that stuck, was positioned at the front of the lower left-hand section. The wooden floor had a single red carpet running down the center of the church. On either side of the aisle were long wooden pews. Seating was not assigned, but members tended to choose the same pew week after week. Mr. Ed.'s family always sat on the left side in the third pew from the back.

An old black stove took up a lot of space in the back of the sanctuary. It was ugly and never provided much heat. Mr. Ed took his custodial duties seriously and would always arrive at the church about an hour early. His goal on crisp winter mornings was to get the stove up and going before others arrived.

The congregation sacrificed and saved for stained glass windows. Receipts from donations and bazaars remained minimal, so the decision was made to only add color to the panes having a southern exposure. During the morning services the rainbow rays of light that filtered through the windows were a reminder of God's love for them and their love of each other.

Two familiar religious pictures hung on the walls. One was of Jesus carrying a lamb with other sheep following him. In the other Jesus was holding a small child while engaged in conversation with other small children. Mr. Ed grew up looking at these pictures during the long hours when preachers glorified God's word. He always considered the man in the pictures as his personal heavenly friend. Jesus was there to willingly listen to his needs and be ready to guide him through troubled valleys.

There were times when no rains appeared so crops dried up and grasshoppers devoured the corn and vegetables in the garden. There were other years when too much rain made it impossible to plant the garden and field crops. Mr. Ed was at a loss to ascertain a way to make enough money to provide for the needs of his family during these lean years. It wasn't unusual, in the middle of a week of summer disasters, for him to slowly enter the empty sanctuary, sit down in the family pew, recite the Lord's Prayer and have a heart-to-heart talk with the gentle savior in the pictures. The meditation left him comforted and with renewed confidence that, with God's help, everything would work out for the best.

Mr. Ed and his wife never expressed any doubts about their religious beliefs. They were convinced that God was watching and guiding them throughout life. Their belief extended in confidence that heaven would be glorious. In the land beyond death, they would have constant contact with their savior. They dreamed of reunions with their family and friends who had passed on before them. Heaven was a beautiful place with no drought, insect infestation, pain or suffering.

The denomination of the church was Presbyterian. At the turn of the century the church was so packed that interior doors were opened so the foyer could be used for seating. Attendance was not based on the denomination preference of members. It just happened to be the only church near enough for their horses and buggies to reach by mid-morning and also allow plenty of time to get home before evening chores.

By the time that Mr. Ed was taking his children to church, the congregation was much smaller. Cars now were available for transportation. Many families transferred their membership to larger and more diversified congregations located in nearby towns. The few families that remained at the church felt a strong bond with each other. Their busy lives meant that they rarely had time on any day but Sunday for long conversations. The hour after services was always a special time. Mr. Ed and the Missus gossiped with friends about crops, the condition of the weather, world events and the antics of their children.

Classes were always held during the hour preceding the sermon. It's easy to guess who taught the adult class each Sunday. Mr. Ed was a natural for the task. He liked to talk and knew the Bible from cover to cover. The cot always knew what the Bible lesson would be on Sunday. As the family sat around the kitchen table the previous evening, Mr. Ed presented the context of his planned lessons. Mr. Ed was ready for any doubts and comments expressed by the class the next morning because his children constantly challenged him with questions. They wanted facts, not generalizations.

Mr. Ed never referred to any fire or brimstone bible passages and avoided discussions about hell. He did his best to ignore the evils of the present world and was attentive to the need of kindness and concern for his fellowman. One of Mr. Ed's favorite scriptures was located in Matthew 22. He frequently quoted the commandment, *"You shalt love the Lord thy God with all thy heart, and with all thy soul, and with all thy mind."* He also stressed the second greatest commandment, *"Thou shalt love thy neighbour as thyself."*

Singing several songs from the old hymnal was part of each service. Music was not the best feature of the service. The piano never sounded decent and, since most folks didn't read music, new songs were avoided. The congregation liked to sing old favorites like, "Holy, Holy, Holy," "He comes to the Garden alone," "Amazing Grace," and "The Old Rugged Cross".

Mary Lou and Jane, for one of their dramatic performances, set up a church scene. They lined up kitchen chairs to symbolize pews. Jane's large family of dolls were dressed in their finest and then placed on the chairs to represent the congregation. Jane portrayed the role of the preacher and Mary Lou was the pianist. After Jane's delivery of a fire and brimstone sermon, the girls impersonated the congregation singing. Their performance was an indication that the real flock couldn't carry a tune in a bucket.

THE PREACHERS

Preachers rarely stayed more than one or two years at the country church. The girls might have stretched the truth a bit as they mimicked the unique qualifications of these men of God. Some seemed qualified to stand behind the pulpit but many others demonstrated talents and interests more aptly suited for a different profession. Regardless of any personal feelings of the ability exhibited behind the pulpit, Mr. Ed and the Missus always gave full support for each holy man who found himself called to the rural setting.

Because of the effects of the depression, the congregation simply could not afford to pay more than a small salary supplemented with bonus gifts from their gardens. Perhaps that is why several of the preachers were young bachelors who had no previous experience in delivering sermons or properly guiding the religious life of parishioners.

The young men assumed it was their duty to visit the homes of church members. They made it a practice to arrive at a home just before the noon meal was served. Most of them wore long black coats, severe ties, and felt hats even though it might be one of the hottest days of summer.

When visiting Mr. Ed's home, the young men of the cloth would sit in the rocking chair stationed near the cot in the kitchen and make small talk while the Missus completed dinner preparations. Mr. Ed was very impressed with one young preacher. He made his call early in the morning and was dressed in old overalls. He spent the entire morning helping the men in the fields before heaping his plate during the noon meal.

A few of the preachers had families. Instead of staying in a room provided by one of the local farmers, they rented a small plot of land, raised crops during the week and preached on Sundays. One preacher with a family was a fine man but talked even more than Mr. Ed. When he started preaching there was no stopping. During the context of one sermon, he raised his hands and asked, "Is that all?" And his five-year-old son shouted out, "I surely hope so!"

The preacher who made the best match for the congregation was about the same age as Mr. Ed. He and his wife settled at the farm located just north of the church and became a part of the community. The wife was a special asset. She participated in the Prairie Hill Ladies Aid quilting and welfare duties, taught piano and gave voice lessons to local children. As a gifted musician, she insisted the piano be tuned and guided the congregation in attempting to learn the words of new hymns.

Social events continued to be a focal part of the church. On the fourth Sunday evening of each month members said prayers, heard a brief sermon, and selected a few favorite hymns to sing. The remaining time was spent talking and eating. Mr. Ed's voice was always one to be heard above the hum of chatter. He frequently got so involved in telling stories that his wife and children had to drag him to the car when it was time to head for home.

Each year, in late fall, the church had a bazaar. The feature item up for auction was always a beautiful quilt made by the Prairie Hill Ladies Aid members during their Wednesday meetings. The ladies also contributed colorful aprons, frilly doilies, carefully crocheted, dishtowels decorated with cross-stitch designs and select canned goods like pickles, relishes and peaches. Folks from nearby towns and a few visitors from Kansas City filled the church hall. These visitors knew that a country church bazaar was a great place to buy quality items at basement bargain prices.

A Shivaree

Several years after the Missus and Ed were married, another wedding was celebrated at the church. Mr. Ed's children were delighted to attend the wedding of Flossie and Brett. The couple had spent their entire lives as members of the church and were both thought of fondly by others. Brett was a skilled carpenter who was always ready to lend his hand in helping to build barns and sheds. Flossie had a keen sense of humor and frequently played tricks on others. Mary Lou and Jane, when small, considered Flossie to be their special grown-up friend. Now that they were older, both were pleased that she continued to be fond of them.

Two weeks after their simple wedding the Missus said to her children, "I want you to take a long nap this afternoon. We will be staying up late tonight." "Mama, it's okay for Dannydon't to take a nap, but we're too old!"

The Missus explained, "When I say late, I really mean late. It may be midnight before we get home. Church members and other neighborhood friends are going to have a Shivaree for Brett and Flossie."

The girls realized they had to abide by their mother's decision. "Mama, we will take a rest, but instead of going upstairs, can we sleep on the old cot?"

It was almost dark when friends of the newly married couple drove to a designated spot about a mile away from the couple's home. When all were assembled, they turned off their car lights and slowly drove down the winding dirt road. After they parked the cars in a nearby pasture, folks quietly sneaked into the yard. A few minutes after the bedroom lights were no longer shining the signal was given to start the party. Pots and pans banged, whistles blew, a few firecrackers exploded and people shouted, "Get out of bed!"

Although the exact date was a secret, the newly married couple had anticipated that the Shivaree was bound to happen within a few weeks after their wedding. When they heard the first shout, they quickly jumped into their clothes, rushed down the stairway then opened the door and greeted their evening guests.

As part of the Shivaree ritual the new couple had to perform crazy feats. One was the kissing challenge.

Mr. Ed instructed, "Flossie, you stand on this chair." The young lady quickly jumped on the chair and did a clown dance.

Another chair was pulled up about a foot away. "Brett, you hop up here. Now all you have to do is kiss each other." As the couple started to follow his instructions he added, "Wait just a minute. I forgot one little thing. We need to put this bucket of water between your chairs."

After each kiss, the chairs were moved back a few inches. It wasn't long before the couple lost their balance. Brett landed easily on the floor but his new bride fell into the bucket of water.

Old Joseph took the fiddle out of its case and his brother, Elmer, pulled a harmonica out of his back pocket. Two other neighbors started strumming guitars. The new home soon was filled with lively music. Friends watched and nodded in approval as the bride and groom glided over the floor during the first dance. Many were just a bit shocked as the first couple to join them was the preacher and his wife. Everyone, including the youngest, was soon dancing. Boys did individual Indian stomps around the floor. Girls danced with other girls, their parents or even grandparents. The party lasted until 2 a.m.

Shivarees are now considered an event of the past. Until after the depression years, a couple in Eastern Kansas was not considered truly married until they had experienced a Shivaree.

Ice Cream Suppers

Favorite festivities during summer months were ice cream suppers. Each household provided their favorite ice cream plus a cake or cookies. The

Missus often volunteered to assemble one of her favorite recipes, peach ice cream. This dessert was accompanied by an angel food cake created using expensive cake flour, sugar, and the whites of at least a dozen eggs.

It was delightful to watch how the Missus aspired for perfection as she prepared her dishes for the social. The peaches had to be ripe, the cream thick, and eggs fresh. As the first step in preparation, she carefully washed the angel food cake pans an extra time to make sure all traces of oil were removed. Eggs, taken out of the ice box, were placed on the kitchen counter to warm to room temperature. Each egg shell was carefully cracked on the rim of a cereal bowl. The Missus tipped the cracked half shells back and forth until the white gently separated from the yoke. She worked carefully because even a single drop of yoke could spoil the beaten egg whites. After the ingredients of the cake were beaten and resembled mounds of white clouds, she placed the pan in the oven and cautioned, "Children, don't you start stomping about in the kitchen. Your heavy movements could cause my tall cake to have a dip in the center."

Everyone assumed responsibilities once they arrived at the church lawn. The women covered tables with colorful tablecloths and sprays of flowers then proudly added their assortment of cakes. The men chipped large blocks of ice. The freezer canisters holding the ingredients made earlier in homes were placed in the center of each freezer. Canisters were surrounded with layers of small chips of ice and salt. The children, who had been running around chasing fireflies, were called over to help. "Kids, you need to work too. Come here and sit on top of the freezers and keep them from wobbling." When the freezer paddles would no longer turn, the men carefully removed the top and pulled out the paddles. Children, whose bottoms were by now damp and cold, received the reward of licking soft ice cream off the paddles. Tops were put back on canisters and ice and salt added to the outer section before the freezers were covered with heavy blankets. While waiting for the ice cream to firm, the church members filed into the church for a short prayer service.

It was only proper and polite to take a sampling of each type of ice cream and at least a tiny piece of each cake. It's a wonder that all those people weren't as big as barns!

EASTER CELEBRATIONS

Easter, one of the two religious holidays celebrated in the little church, occurred sometime between the middle of March and late April. In Eastern Kansas it was not a bit unusual for the weather to be gloomy and cold if the holiday occurred in March. Some of the old timers in the congregation even recalled years when snow covered the ground and drifts piled on the roads making it impossible to attend church.

It was one of the early Easters when ingenuity was needed in decorating the church altar. On the Wednesday prior to Easter, six inches of wet sticky snow fell during the evening and night hours. Early Thursday morning Mr. Ed was confronted with two tiny girls stating, "Daddy, will you help us build a giant snowman?" He grinned and assured them that he would help them after finishing chores.

The snowman turned out to be a magnificent specimen. Mr. Ed rolled a huge ball then placed two more of smaller sizes on top of the first. The snowman stood as tall as Mr. Ed but had a much larger girth. Mary Lou decided the snowman should look useful so she placed a snow shovel in the fold of one of the snowman's arms.

Mr. Ed lifted Jane up so she could complete the snowman's attire. She started by placing an old straw hat belonging to her daddy on the snowman's shiny head. Three-year-old Jane started to giggle as she completed the costume by poking a corncob pipe at the side of the snowman's lopsided coal mouth. She proudly announced, "Daddy, the snowman looks like you!"

The Missus had just stepped out onto the porch to shake the dust mop. When she heard her daughter's referral about the snowman's similarity in looks to those of her husband she added, "Ed, that's what you will look like if you keep eating those extra slices of chocolate cake!"

The March sun came out later that day and the warm breezes blew in from Texas and Oklahoma. By Saturday, as Mr. Ed walked to the barn to complete the milking, he noted that all that remained of the snowman was a small hump of dirty snow topped by a wet soggy hat.

It seemed to Mr. Ed that the chores took forever that morning. The melting snow resulted in pools of water standing in every groove and dent of the soil. In the cattle lot, down by the lower barn, the mud was so squishy that tramping through it in his rubber boots was difficult. By the time the cows were satisfied with their meal for the day their owner had pains in his back, a tight chest, and a throat that felt like it was on fire. Mr. Ed walked slowly back to the house and said under his breath, "In five minutes I'm going to be taking a nap on the cot."

The Missus noticed him trudging up the walkway and hurried out to meet him. "Honey, we have a problem about decorating the church for tomorrow's service. There is absolutely nothing blooming that we can use to decorate the church altar. Would you please go down to the west woods and see if any bittersweet berries are still on the vines? If so, Rose and I will use red berries and ivy leaves to add a little color to the church altar."

Mr. Ed slowly sighed. At that moment the winding line of trees by the creek looked miles away. He considered saying "No," but that was never part of his vocabulary when it meant helping the church. He would have preferred to drive the tractor but the fields were simply too muddy for its heavy wheels. Instead, he picked up a basket, kicked some of the mud off his boots then slowly made his journey toward the woods.

An hour later the Missus telephoned her friend. "Rose, I have some bad news. Ed says that there are no bittersweet berries. In addition to that, he looked like a ghost when he returned to the house. He was exhausted and immediately plopped down on the old cot. Ed never complains, but even covered with three of the cot's quilts, he said that he felt as cold as the snowman he and the girls built earlier this week. I stuck the thermometer in his mouth. His temperature registered over 102 degrees."

Rose quickly added assurance about their church assignment. "Don't give decorating another thought. I have a package of rainbow tissue paper and plenty of floral wire. I'll make tissue flowers. Rest assured the church will look beautiful!"

News traveled quickly via the telephone. About an hour after talking to Rose, another friend, Doris Hatchel, was on the line. "Please tell Ed to stay on that cot and not worry about the chores. My husband and Roy will be over early this evening to milk and feed the animals. Roy said that he plans to return and do chores again tomorrow morning. Tell Ed to rest, drink a lot of tea and not worry about the animals."

This was the first and last Easter service missed by Mr. Ed during his life span of almost ninety years!

Most of the Easter Sundays occurred when the weather was much more pleasant. Although the ladies never admitted to competing, each stripped gardens and combed the woods in an effort to provide the biggest and brightest array of flowers for the church.

Easter, the year after Ed's illness, occurred in Mid-April when flowers were abundant. The Missus placed a profusion of daffodils and jonquils from her garden onto the altar space. Rose supplied yellow forsythia and cattails. Doris Hatchel had several fruit trees in her backyard. After she placed stems filled with buds in warm water the result was an abundance of pink and white blossoms. Pauline, who cared little about wasting time tending to a flower garden, combed the woods and found clusters of purple and pale pink Sweet Williams. By the time the members of the Ladies Aid had contributed posies, every inch of the church altar, piano and windows sills were covered. Grandma Shields spoke for all of them when she said, "It's only fitting that we give the Lord back some of the beauty he has provided for us."

There was an additional abundance of color appearing at the church on Easter having nothing to do with horticultural bouquets. Each female, young and old, wore a colorful straw hat or bonnet. Many had on white gloves and wore new shoes. Dresses were created from floral feed sacks or inexpensive fabric purchased at the dry goods store.

Mr. Ed stepped into the foyer and was amused to see all the brilliant outfits. He teased several ladies by stating, "Your efforts to deck the church with flowers are commendable, but do you assume the Lord expects all of you to try to be as colorful as your flowers? After all, he brought you into this world only wearing a birthday suit!"

Rose was indispensable in the weeks before Easter. Dress patterns ordered from the *Capper's Weekly* were shared among the ladies with bodies widely contrasting in shape and size. The differences did not worry them. After all, they had a professional designer in their midst.

Rose was amused when she overheard Flossie, large breasted and wide in the hips, commenting to the Missus. "You and I are the same height. It will be easy for Rose to make adjustments so you can use my pattern."

Rose agreed to alter the pattern for the Missus, but silently she said to herself, "Adjusting a size twelve pattern to fit a size four lady is going to require a lot of tucks and folds."

There simply were no patterns available to fit the misshapen body of Aunt Sarah. The old lady appeared on Rose's doorstep with five yards of cloth featuring a pattern of yellow sunflowers. She peered over her glasses and demanded, "Rose, I need you to make a pattern so I can make myself a new dress for Easter."

As Rose took body measurements of the old lady, she kept silent while listening to a barrage of complaints. "We'll probably suffer another drought this summer. It's already dry and hot." "Have you noticed that Roland has been sleeping during sermons? I can't blame him too much because this preacher's sermons are long and boring." "That Flossie is something else. Have you noticed that she hardly ever adds a stitch to our quilts? All she does is ask questions and tell jokes." "Roy is such a sweet young man but he can only read a few words. His mama should have insisted he study more instead of fooling around with that brownie camera."

Aunt Sarah noticed that the dishes from dinner were still in the sink and the floor around the cutting table was covered with fabric scraps. She sniffed then suggested, "Rose, I hate to mention it, but I've noticed you are somewhat lacking when it comes to housekeeping skills."

Rose bit her lips but said nothing.

As Rose was finishing the last of the measuring, she saw the old lady grimace when asked to raise her arm. Rose also noticed that Aunt Sarah's hands were swollen and her fingers were gnarled. There was no way this lady would be able to sew her own dress.

Aunt Sarah was probably shocked when Rose hugged her and suggested, "Aunt Sarah, leave that pretty sunflower print with me. I'm going to create a beautiful dress for you to wear next Sunday."

Aunt Sarah was all smiles as she carefully climbed the church steps on Easter. She was proud of her matching outfit. The bright yellow dress that fit her perfectly was accentuated with a wide brimmed straw hat Rose had decorated with a yellow satin band and yellow tissue paper sunflowers.

After the service she complimented the preacher on the excellent sermon, gave pleasant greetings to members about the weather and even presented the youth in the congregation with chocolate covered marshmallow bunnies.

Still, total personality transformation due to a pretty new dress was not achieved. Aunt Sarah whispered to the Missus. "My Lord, have you lost control over your eldest daughter? She lost her hair bow before she ever got to church. Now, while the elders are engaged in conversation, she refuses to sit quietly and listen. Look what she did to that pretty red dress you made for her. It tore around the hem when she climbed the fence between the churchyard and cemetery and is all dusty because she sat on the tombstones." She looked even more closely to the wanton child's appearance. "Just look at that! Your thoughtless child even sat in some bird poop!"

CHRISTMAS FESTIVITIES

Each year there was a lot of anticipation as the congregation prepared for the Christmas festivities. Children up to the age of twelve were assured they would be assigned a part in the Nativity pageant. Mr. Ed was always in charge of toting boxes marked "Xmas" from storage in the northeast bedroom to the church.

The children waited eagerly for the boxes to arrive so they could open them and consider which role they might portray. There were old bathrobes with hoods and broomstick staffs for the shepherds. The three wise men would wear the shortened silk and satin robes once worn by their mothers.

Majestic crowns would adorn their heads, and they would carry cigar boxes brightly painted and decorated with old buttons and pieces of jewelry. The younger children hoped to be assigned the roles of manger animals. In addition to wearing masks and tails made by Rose, they anticipated the fun of vocalizing appropriate baas and brays.

No Christmas pageant was flawless, but one year was labeled as a disaster.

At the first rehearsal Mary Lou took a look at the stepladder and selected her part. She informed her mother, "I'll be the angel who stands at the top of the ladder, and tells the shepherds about the birth of Jesus." To demonstrate aptitude for the part, she climbed up the ladder rungs, waved her arms and shouted, "Hey, you shepherds and sheep! Take a look at that big yellow star. It is shining over Bethlehem where Baby Jesus was born. You need to follow its path and go see him right now. He's sleeping in a manger."

Jane stood quietly by her mother's side. She had grown a lot! Maybe she would be assigned a more important part than the lamb she pretended to be the preceding year. Doris Hatchel pulled a pale blue satin gown and shimmering shawl from the box. She hugged the small child and suggested, "Jane, you should play the part of Mary, the mother of baby Jesus."

Danielle's second child, a three-month baby daughter, was selected for the feature role. Danielle smiled and said, "The more noise, the better our tiny baby dozes."

Heads nodded as her proud grandmother, Eunice, sighed, "Won't she look beautiful in the cradle?"

The day of the pageant Danielle called the Missus saying, "Baby Ramona has a cold. I don't dare take her out in this weather. Could baby Dan play the part of the Christ child?"

The performance started well. As the proud parents and grandparents watched, a serene Mary and her husband, Joseph, looked fondly down at the sleeping babe. The Lord's angel, perched on the top rung of the ladder, pronounced the glad tidings to the shepherds that a miracle had happened. Children sang "Away in a Manger" as they slowly marched from the foyer to the stable. When the song ended, the youngest children, dressed as animals, happily started making appropriate sounds. The mooing and braying startled the sleeping seven-month-old baby.

This pageant occurred long before the child had acquired the nickname of Dannydon't but his two older sisters were already assuming the responsibility of altering his behavior. The Madonna smile on Jane's face turned to a scowl as she whispered to her baby brother, "Hush that crying!"

Baby Dan continued wailing so Jane tried to cover his mouth with her hand. This made Baby Dan angry. Now, in addition to crying he kicked his arms and feet and tried to pull himself out of the cradle.

Mary Lou, still standing high on the ladder, realized she needed to help her sister discipline baby brother. In the haste of climbing down the ladder her foot got caught in the hem of the white gown. She fell several feet and, while doing so, twisted her ankle. Her cries were almost as loud as baby brother's.

The preacher called intermission so Mr. Ed could carry his eldest off the stage and the Missus could replace the screaming baby with a doll.

This was also the holiday season when the Missus was caught telling lies. The previous Christmas her eldest was disappointed with the meager gifts left under the tree. As the current Christmas drew near, Mary Lou reflected on the unfairness of toy distribution and finally asked, "Mama, why doesn't Santa like poor children?"

The Missus quickly responded, "That's not true, Mary Lou. The jolly elf who lives at the North Pole loves all children."

Mary Lou frowned then stated, "Last Christmas Jane only got one doll and all I got was a scarf and hat. I wrote to Santa and told him I wanted a real puzzle." She added, "Do you remember when we went over to Danielle's house to see their tree? There were boxes and boxes under the tree for her little girl, and I bet this year there are just as many toys for baby Ramona!"

The Missus cleared her throat then suggested, "Danielle's daughters have rich grandparents living in Kansas City. Maybe they were pretending to be Santa's helpers."

Mary Lou accepted this answer but added, "You must be a Santa helper too. I peeked in your sewing box and noticed you are making new mittens for us. Will we pretend they are presents from Santa?"

Nothing more was said until Christmas Eve. Soon after dusk a man wearing a red stocking cap peeked in the window. The Missus called, "Mary Lou and Jane, come and look. I think Santa is coming to see you."

Mary Lou took a quick look then angrily shouted to her mother. "Mama, that's only Uncle Dave pretending to be Santa." Her eyes filled with tears as she challenged her mother's truthfulness. "You've lied to us. Santa Claus is not real!" Mary Lou rushed to the cot and covered her head with its pillows.

The Missus felt almost as sad as her daughter. What her daughter said was true. She, like so many other parents, projected the myth about the jolly fat man who lived at the North Pole. She had never once considered the consequences of telling this story and wondered what to do.

The Missus gently removed the pillows from her daughter's head. As she pulled the child to her arms, both of them were crying. The Missus choked as she said, "Mary Lou, you are such a smart girl. You are right. Parents pretend there is a Santa. I guess we do it because it is so much fun. Little children are always so excited when they wake up Christmas morning and find gifts under the tree."

She continued to hold her daughter tightly. Finally, she said, "Mary Lou, why do we celebrate Christmas?"

Mary Lou immediately responded, "God's son was born on Christmas. Jesus is God's gift to us."

The Missus was pleased with her answer. "You're right. That is the reason we celebrate. The other part is just a game. Now that you know the truth do you still want to help daddy cut down a tree and help me decorate it with berries and popcorn? Do you think it would still be fun for us to make presents for each other and put them under the tree?"

Mary Lou was not quite as angry. She answered, "Yes, mama. It is fun walking with daddy in the woods to find the best tree and we always have fun decorating the tree." She thought a minute then asked, "Even though I don't believe in Santa can I still get some presents on Christmas morning? Can I ask for a puzzle of United States?"

WHAT WILL YOU BE?

Mr. Ed continued the practice of nightly lectures to his children and some of them were about religious beliefs. During one such lesson he discussed predestination and reincarnation. Mary Lou surmised, "It sounds to me like predestination could be the words of a song, "Whatever will be, will be." She thought a minute then added, "I don't like this idea that everything is pre-planned for the future. I think each of us should be responsible for deciding what we want to do and should work to obtain that goal."

The concept of reincarnation sounded ridiculous but the children later decided it had some merit.

Mary Lou flapped her arms and danced around the room. I must have been an eagle because I would love to be able to soar to high places."

Jane retorted, "I bet you were a butterfly because you always are flitting from one thing to another."

Dannydon't stated, "I know what you were, Sis. My guess is you were an ugly turkey buzzard. You would have swooped around in the air then zoomed in for the attack like you do to me."

Jane couldn't decide, "Was I a beautiful medieval princess or a sweet Persian cat?"

Dannydon't had no doubts about his previous life. "I was the biggest bass to ever live in the pasture pond."

Chapter 9

SPARE THE ROD

I truly loved and had the uppermost respect for Mr. Ed. He was a fine man and did just about everything right. If any complains were to be made, it would be that he tended to be soft hearted when it came to disciplining his kids.

The Critical Cot

DISCIPLINE GUIDE

Mr. Ed recalled the strict discipline he faced as a young child. His daddy had insisted that a firm hand was necessary if the future result was to be worthy young men. When only one of his boys misbehaved, it was deemed necessary that all of them receive a spanking.

Mr. Ed's three older brothers, especially Jack, were mischievous and did tend to ask for trouble. But their pranks were not the real cause of so many spankings. The boys were punished because their sister felt it her duty to report to their father any misdemeanors her brothers made and some they never even thought of trying. After hearing of a misdeed, the father ordered the brothers to stand in a line, pull down their overalls, turn their backs to him and bend over. As Alicia smirked, each boy got one or two bottom swats. Mr. Ed, even though small and innocent, got more than his share of spankings. He made up his mind as a child that when he was grown up and a dad, he would never mistreat his children.

Mr. Ed's children were usually well-behaved, but they did push limits. When the children sassed their mama or teased each other more than necessary, the Missus would say, "Edward, you talk to those kids and make them behave." He knew exactly how to handle the situation. He placed the temporary enemies on his lap and explained that Jesus wanted them to love each other and always show kindness. Mr. Ed listened patiently and allowed each of the adversaries to describe his take on the situation. Step by step, he guided them into negotiating a truce.

Since Mr. Ed did not spank, the Missus felt it was her responsibility to see that the children were adequately punished. If the misbehavior was slight, she made them sit five minutes on the cot. (She considered that to be punishment and the children were smart enough to not tell her anything different.) If the misdemeanor was more serious, the Missus drew a circle on the wall and instructed, "Peek at the old clock ever so often. You are to stand with your nose in that circle for ten minutes." When the crimes were severe, like saying naughty words or hitting, she administered a much more effective punishment. The offender was marched out to the yard and instructed. "Look for a fresh twig from a bush or a tree that can be used as a switch." More than one swat on the bottom of the legs was rarely needed before the criminal was pleading, "Mama, I promise to never do it again!"

Mary Lou got more spankings than her brother and sister. She complained that it was because she was the oldest, but the truth was she invited trouble. One of her first hard spankings was due to her budding gourmet skills. Her daddy built her a special outdoor kitchen. On one tipped wooden crate he painted circles to represent burners. The other crate housed an assortment of small cans, jar lids, dishes and stick utensils.

Mud pies became her specialty. The ingredients consisted of good garden dirt and just a tad of water. The pies seemed to lack the right sticking consistency so she had the bright idea of collecting eggs from the hen house and adding them to the dough. The completed dessert looked yummy! She decided to feed several pieces to her baby brother. The baby didn't mind a bit, but the Missus had a fit when she found him with mud covering his cheeks, nose, and tongue.

Little Jane enjoyed playing with paper dolls almost as much as the seven sweet faced porcelain dolls. Her tiny hands carefully cut pretty models from outdated Sears or Montgomery Ward catalogs. She stored her cutouts in an old shoebox and carried the box from room to room under her arm. She often took the models out of the box and lined them up on the cot or the table. Jane saw to it that her paper ladies attended pretend dances and ice cream parties.

Mary Lou was frustrated. "Jane, why do you spend so much time playing with dumb pieces of paper? Please come out and have an adventure with me. We could climb that cottonwood tree that fell during the last storm or pretend to be pirates guarding the treasure chest hidden in the cliffs by the creek." When her sister refused to join her in the great outdoors, she tore the heads off of the paper models in frustration. The end result was that Mary Lou got a sore bottom, and the next time the family went into town, Jane got to purchase a real paper doll kit.

IN TROUBLE

The girls walked to and from elementary school with Oliver. This young fellow had excellent memory skills and could flawlessly repeat stories he overheard. He was the same age as Jane, but was much more knowledgeable about the ways of the world than the girls were. Whenever possible, he thought it great fun to shock his innocent friends.

One evening Oliver heard his father comment to his mother that several friends were coming over to play poker. Instead of retiring to his bedroom as instructed, Oliver hid in the hall closet. He could not see any card action from this hiding place but could hear every spoken word. He was delighted to have this opportunity to learn a whole new assortment of jokes, stories, and songs.

The next morning Oliver greeted his friends with the statement. "You will never believe all the things I will tell you when we walk home after school." The girls knew he was planning to share something delightfully naughty. At recess they pondered how they should respond to the stories Oliver would tell. Jane suggested that they not let Oliver see them wide-eyed and shocked. Later, when he started to relate his naughty stories and songs, Mary Lou pulled out her tablet and commented, "We can't remember all the things you are telling us. We'll jot them down on a piece of paper." Mary Lou soon tired of taking dictation so Jane completed the task by writing each word of the song, "Nelly, lay your belly close to mine!"

The girls were aware that their mama would be very disapproving of their newfound knowledge. Once home they quickly hid the pieces of paper between the cot's mattress and springs. They soon completely forgot their intention to destroy the hidden manuscript. On a spring day, a few months later, the girls walked into the kitchen and were confronted by a very angry mother. "Girls, it's beyond me to know how you two were even aware of such shameful things. We're going outside to pick out the longest sprig on the spirea bush." The Missus jerked off the green leaves then swished the sprig in the air to create maximum effect. It was punishment enough to endure more than a few swats, but the girls also went to bed without supper and did not get to attend the next school party.

Chapter 10

VISITORS

*Mr. Ed, the Missus, and children were always in and out of
the kitchen and neighbors and family stopped in frequently.
I've also been entertained by meeting or hearing about quite
a few characters. Would you like to hear about some of them?*

The Welcoming Cot

THE MAN WALKING DOWN THE ROAD

The wooden doors on the big farmhouse never had safety locks. The
simple latches attached high on the screens provided no security
from intruders. Their purpose was to confine smaller members of
the family to inside the house. Three-year-old Jane stood in the kitchen
doorway yearning for her mama to unlock a latch and give her permission
to play on the new swing. Her alert eyes spotted a man walking up the path.
"Mama, a man is coming to visit us."

A few seconds later the young man tapped on the screen door. He was
a strange sight with a freckled red face and a shaggy rust colored beard. The

ends of the matted hair were dripping wet from sweat. The plaid shirt and overalls had long ago turned ragged and were covered with dust from the roads. He pulled out a handkerchief from the overall pocket and wiped his forehead before he pleaded, "Ma'am, could you spare a few scraps of food? I'm very hungry."

The Missus took one look at the young man and immediately poured water from the pitcher into a large glass. She instructed, "Looks like you covered many miles today in this heat. Take a rest on the porch swing and I'll fix you something to eat. There are plenty of fresh leftovers from dinner."

It wasn't long before the Missus presented the visitor with a pie tin filled with two pieces of fried chicken, green beans, mashed potatoes, pickled beets and two slices of bread. She even had dessert for him: a thick slice of cherry cobbler.

The hungry man probably had had very little to eat for several days, because tears filled his eyes when the Missus handed the tin to him. As he quickly devoured his feast, the Missus decided he needed more than one meal. She filled a lard pail with several pieces of the bread, a slab of cheese, some carrots and two apples.

The Missus frowned and jabbed both hands into her apron pockets. She gazed at the kitchen cabinets for several minutes before slowly reaching up to the highest shelf to grab the cracked jar filled with pennies and nickels. She sighed, "I was counting on saving up enough egg money this year to buy pretty new cotton prints from the dry goods store. The girls have grown so much that they need new dresses for church." She shook her head and decided, "The Lord will provide what is necessary. This young man needs help more than my girls need new dresses. Besides that, the chicken feed sacks are mighty pretty this year." She pulled the jar from the shelf, shook out most of the coins and dropped them into the pail.

The visitor wiped his mouth with a scrap napkin then sincerely stated, "That was the best meal I've had since I left my mama's home in Illinois. I thank you kindly for your generosity."

The Missus smiled and responded, "I wish you well on your journey."

The young man nodded in appreciation and slowly started down the steps. He paused on the bottom step as the Missus called, "Wait just a minute young man! You'll be hungry in a few hours so I packed some of our leftovers for your supper."

As the young man retreated toward the gate she called out once more. "Sir, please come back to the porch. We have a couple of items that will be helpful on your journey. I know the hot August sun shows no mercy. My husband, Ed, bought a new straw hat just last week. I know he would be pleased for me to give this old one to you."

He nodded in gratitude then placed the hat on his head and started to leave once again. He was detained because the Missus thought of another gift. "I expect you take a rest every so often by the side of the road. I just washed this cot cover from earlier this summer. It's covered with berry stains but it will do fine as a rest mat."

During the next several years it was a common sight to see men walking on roadsides or riding freight trains. They had the undignified titles of hobos and tramps. Most were like the young man who shyly strolled up to the screen door on a hot August day. They were making journeys across the country in search of work.

GREAT GRANDMOTHER NICHOLS VISITS

The Missus answered the three long rings coming from the wooden telephone hanging on the wall above the cot. She responded to the voice on the line. "Yes, Uncle Fred, we would love to have Grandma Nichols visit for a few days. Certainly, she can stay as long as she wishes, but it will probably only be for two or three days. She always says that guests that stay any longer start to smell like dead fish."

Grandma Nichols arrived a few days later with two small fabric travel bags. One was filled with clothes and the other with dried herbs, lotions, and a tonic that looked and smelled like whiskey. Grandma Nichols was a tiny dried-up thing and had walked this earth for nearly eighty years. Her movements were swift and direct and it was evident she still had many miles to go.

Her ancient black dress was adorned with at least forty tiny buttons lined up from the high collar to her ankles. She wore black high-topped pointed toe shoes and a funny square hat perched atop her gray hair. The few necessities she needed frequently were contained in the small black mesh bag she carried over her left arm.

Grandma Nichols had raised thirteen children. She was solely responsible for their upbringing after her husband, when still a relatively young man, was killed in a freak hunting accident. Two of her sons had died on the battlefield during the First World War. Two other sons had contracted tuberculosis during their service in France. Her middle daughter had assumed the role of a nurse and helped to take care of sick brothers after they returned home from the war. It was not long before the daughter also suffered and eventually died from the dreaded disease. The remaining children and grandchildren lived in Canada and in all corners of United States. Two daughters even lived in the distant state of California.

A travel bug bit Grandma Nichols when she reached the senior age of sixty-five. In order to see her many children and grandchildren she frequently rode the Atchison, Topeka, and Santa Fe Train to California and visited other relatives by boarding a Greyhound Bus.

On journeys to distant places, she always carried a long hat pin in her mesh handbag. It came in handy when the man sitting next to her on the coach was snoring or leaning against her. One day, as she was sitting on a bench waiting for the arrival of a bus, a robber sat down beside her. He glanced around to see that no one else was near then poked a gun into her ribs. He growled, "Old lady, give me all the money you have in that funny black bag!" The robber assumed she was grasping for dollars but, with her gnarled fingers, she managed to pull out the hatpin as well as several dollar bills. As the man lowered the gun then extended his other hand to grab the money, she quickly jabbed his hand with the pin. He immediately yelled, dropped his gun and ran.

Mary Lou and Jane enjoyed Grandmother Nichol's infrequent visits. Soon after her arrival they begged, "Grandma, tell us the story about when you were a young girl." She responded, "Girls, I'll be glad to oblige in a few minutes. First, I need to take a few nips of my tonic and remove these old shoes. My corns are hurting like the devil."

Grandma Nichols limped toward the old cot. She plumped down on the cushions and gave a satisfied sigh when she heard the familiar squeak of its coils. She patted then rearranged the pillows and pulled a cover over her thin body before starting the story.

"My family trekked from Illinois to the Kansas Flint Hills in a covered wagon. They were planning to go as far as Oregon but I guess my folks must have been too tired to go any further. They built the sod hut right smack in the middle of a prairie with endless miles of tall grass around it. Thank goodness, there was a spring nearby the hut that never ran dry.

"One day, my brother, Jerome, looked out the doorway and saw three Indians stalking toward the hut. Maw was frightened out of her wits. Would they all be scalped? Would her children be kidnapped? Would she and the oldest girls be raped? She took a deep breath and said, "Lucy, take the baby. Jerome, I want you to help the little ones hide in the tall grasses. I'll stay here to find out what them Injins are up to."

"Only a few minutes after we were hidden the Indians silently entered our hut. They took no scalps that day but indicated their hunger by pointing to the pan of stew Maw had brewing in the fireplace. The natives sat silently on the floor eating the stew, sour dough biscuits, and other bits of food that Maw placed before them. After consuming every scrap available they expressed their appreciation to Maw through use of nonverbal gestures of rubbing their stomachs and chomping their gums.

"Prior to coming to our hut, the red-skinned men had obviously scouted out our home and had taken note of the number, sex and ages of the children in our family. On their next visit they brought moccasins for the girls, a cradle swing for the baby and hunting tools for the boys."

Grandma Nichols continued to visit the farm for several more years and always had interesting stories to tell about her travels around the country. Each time she visited, it seemed she relied more and more on her liquid "medicine."

It wasn't unusual for her to stop in the middle of a sentence and start snoring while on the old cot. On one of her last visits the Missus realized her grandmother was again sleeping. She pressed her index finger to her lips to indicate silence and made another signal telling the children to tiptoe out of the kitchen. She gently took the tonic bottle from the old lady's hands, unbuttoned the dress and pulled off the old black shoes. A favorite soft blanket belonging to the cot was gently placed over her frail body. The Missus patted the wrinkled cheek and whispered in the old lady's ear, "I love you, Grams."

VISITORS FROM THE CITY

"Mama, can we have a picnic after church?" It had been a long, hot, dreary summer with days consumed by farm tasks of raising and harvesting crops, then preserving fruits and vegetables for the long winter ahead. Seven-year-old Mary Lou pleaded with both voice and eyes that it was time to have some fun.

The Missus quickly responded, "Why Mary Lou, that's a wonderful idea! All of us need a day to relax. We can have a picnic by Whitman Creek. That's where daddy and I went for picnics before we were married."

Mary Lou remembered the complications which frequently occurred on Sundays. "Mama, can you pack our food for the picnic before we go to church? We can leave the church as soon as Daddy quits gabbing. That way we won't be home if someone comes by."

"Sorry, Honey, but that won't work! In this hot August air, the food would spoil while we attend church. We'll rush home and have the lunch packed in no time." Then she added, "Mary Lou, can you suggest what each of us would like to eat?"

Mary Lou was delighted to have the responsibility of selecting the menu. "Danny is easy. He'll want milk, crackers, and applesauce." She looked at her little sister and asked, "Jane, do you want a gooseberry jelly sandwich?"

Jane nodded her blond head enthusiastically at the idea of her favorite snack. Mary Lou made her personal selection. "I want two slices of bread covered with cat soup." In the past year the child had developed a love for the tomato sauce her mother made. She spread it on bread, crackers, mashed potatoes and sometimes even cookies. She enjoyed the taste so much she actually dipped ice chips in her mother's rich cat soup.

"Me and Jane."

The Missus, a former teacher, was not about to let her daughter start bad grammar habits. "Mary Lou, think what you are saying. Which name should come first?"

Mary Lou shook her head and twisted the toe of her shoe in a circle before continuing with menu suggestions. "Jane and I like the sugar cookies you made yesterday. Put lots of those in the picnic basket."

The Missus felt her daughters should feast on more than breads and sweets. "Even on picnics you need to eat fruits and vegetables before dessert. What do you suggest?"

Mary Lou cared little for veggies so the choice was difficult. "Please don't put in any pickled okra or beets. Potato salad and onions are just about as bad. Can we just have carrot strips?"

"Honey, think about what your daddy would like. He got up before dawn to do the chores. He'll be very hungry again by lunch."

"Daddy is easy because he is always hungry and eats everything. He would like a hard-boiled egg and you can fry some ham for his sandwich. He doesn't like much mayonnaise or mustard. Maybe he would like some cat soup on his bread." She thought a moment before corrected herself. "No, that wouldn't do. Daddy would choose sliced tomatoes instead of cat soup."

Mary Lou sat by her daddy at each meal and was well aware of his sweet tooth. "Daddy loves your chocolate cake. You can pack that for his dessert."

The Missus shook her head. "Daddy won't get any cake at the picnic because it is gone. He ate two pieces for supper then had another piece after his nap on the old cot."

The Missus had one more suggestion, "Mary Lou, do you remember how you helped me yesterday by climbing the tree to pick fruit? We can add ripe peaches to our lunch basket."

Just at that moment Mr. Ed entered the kitchen. The little girls rushed to their daddy and joyfully danced around his legs. "Daddy, Mama says we can have a picnic after church. We will go to that place near Whitman Creek where you took her before you had us. I bet that's where you asked her to marry you."

Mr. Ed winked at his wife then quickly responded to the gleeful anticipation of his little girls. "That sounds like a grand plan. After the picnic your brother will probably take a nap so your mama can relax. You girls can go wading, and I'll take along a fishing pole. I've heard the bass in Whitman Creek are a foot long. If I catch a batch, we can have a fine supper."

Elaborate planning does not guarantee success, and, on the lovely Sunday, they were completely destroyed. Immediately after the minister's last words, the girls grabbed their daddy's arms and pulled him out the church door. (It was one of the few Sundays when he didn't spend nearly an hour talking to the minister and parishioners.)

Once home, the Missus quickly changed the baby's diapers and suggested the girls carefuly hang up their Sunday garments and change into old clothes.

She directed, "Mary Lou and Jane, please pack some towels and extra clothes. You two will probably get wet and will need to change into something dry. Oh, yes, put a couple of the old cot covers in the basket. We'll need to sit on them because the grass is dry and itchy."

As the girls eagerly rushed to do their mama's bidding, a cloud of dust indicated that a car was turning into the driveway. Seconds later, Uncle Hugh and Aunt Opal stepped out of their new Buick.

Uncle Hugh and Aunt Opal lived far away in Kansas City. Instead of going to a fancy restaurant they could well afford, they chose to drive over fifty miles to partake in a Sunday meal created by the Missus.

Jane sighed and nodded her head in agreement as her sister groaned. "Daddy, Mama, please tell them we are leaving for our picnic." In the eyes of the girls and probably their parents, these drop-in visitors were their least favorite people.

The Missus shook her head. "Girls, we'll have a picnic another day. Remember, we always welcome visitors to our home even if they interfere with our plans."

Jane stuck out her lower lip and buried her teary face in a doll blanket. Mary Lou was so mad she kicked the legs of the old cot before pouncing on it. She hid her furious face in the pillows and moaned softly so her mama could not hear, "I wish those ugly old bats would disappear forever."

Both Uncle Hugh and Aunt Opal seemed completely unaware of good manners and consideration of others. They also looked and acted strangely. Uncle Hugh was short and fat. His thick spectacles constantly slipped down to the edge of his nose, so he looked over the rims rather than through the glass. He had only a few remaining wisps of hair around his ears. A few long strands were plastered over the top of his head in an effort to hide his baldness.

Uncle Hugh always dressed in a brown suit. The coat could not button so the brown plaid vest and a bit of his fat belly underneath were visible. He walked with a shuffle step in his highly polished brown shoes.

Mary Lou watched Uncle Hugh as he entered the kitchen. She whispered to her sister, "We should call him Mister Brown Penguin."

Uncle Hugh, actually a distant cousin of Mr. Ed, had little to say. After nodding a greeting to his hosts, he borrowed a straight kitchen chair and retreated to the shade of the maple tree. The old man moved from this chosen site for only three reasons. As the brilliant sun made its progress across the sky, he moved his chair a few feet into the shaded area so his bald head would not get sunburned. At regular intervals he walked to his car and took a nip from the bottle he kept hidden under the seat. Before returning to his chair, he always visited the sweet pea house. His only other motivation for moving was when the Missus rang the dinner bell.

Mr. Ed, always the courteous host, tried to encourage his guest to join him in casual conversation. "What do you think of this hot weather?" Uncle Hugh just blinked and shook his head.

Mr. Ed continued on the subject of weather. "There are rings around the sun. Maybe that means we'll have a good rain soon. The crops sure need a drink."

Noticing that the weather was of no interest to Uncle Hugh, he switched to the topic of baseball. "Are you keeping up with the Royals? That team is having a great season." Still there was no response from the brown form sitting nearby.

When all else failed Mr. Ed turned to politics. "I'm a good Republican, but I must admit that the Democrat now in office seems to be doing his best for poor folk. What do you think of Roosevelt's New Deal Recovery Program?"

Uncle Hugh didn't answer. His eyes were closed and he was softly snoring.

Mr. Ed heard his wife call from the kitchen. "Ed, come and get the baby. He's had his lunch and wants to play before taking his nap."

Mr. Ed was more than willing to carry the baby, an old cot cover for a mat, the Sunday papers and a few toys out to the shade of the maple tree.

Mr. Ed looked at the smiling baby on his lap and said, "Son, Uncle Hugh was not in the mood for conversation, but you seem interested. I'd like to ask your opinion about a few things."

He started with a question about the weather. "Do you think it will rain soon?"

The baby's cross-eyed glaze indicated that, while it might not rain outside, his diapers were getting wet.

Mr. Ed continued, "Explain your opinion of these hot dog days of August to me."

The baby's response was to pass a bit of gas.

Mr. Ed cautioned, "Hold on son, you don't have to demonstrate your opinion. Your mama is busy cooking, and I'd have to be the one to change your diapers!"

"Son, what did you think about Rev. Roth's sermon today?"

The baby clapped his hands and broadly displayed four tiny new teeth.

His daddy laughed, "I'm surprised you enjoyed the sermon so much. It seemed to me that you were asleep the whole hour. Anyway, can't say I agree with you. Mr. Roth is a fine man but he always preaches about sinners going to Hell. Instead of always telling us God's anger, the minister should remind us of God's great love and of the gifts on earth he has willingly shared with us."

Mr. Ed changed the conversation. "Now, let's talk about baseball."

The baby recognized the word ball. He quickly picked up his red ball, and after a few quick chews, gave it a mighty overhand toss.

"That's a good idea, son. Looks like you might someday be a great pitcher for the Royals."

Mr. Ed was finding this chat with his son quite enlightening. "Uncle Hugh wasn't interested in politics, but you seem to have some mighty good ideas for one only a year old. Do you think, with this New Deal firmly in place, folks will not be so hungry?"

The baby often heard his mama ask him about hunger so he responded to his daddy's question by rubbing his fat tummy.

Mr. Ed laughed then asked, "I have one last question that's been worrying me. There's a lot of unrest over in Europe and war might break out. Do you think this president can keep us out of a war?"

The baby had no idea what his daddy was talking about so he answered with one of his new words, "No!"

Mr. Ed hugged the baby and said, "Thanks for the conversation, son. Now, why don't you sit down on the cot cover and play with your toys while I read the Sunday paper?" Mr. Ed quickly became engrossed in both the front page and sports sections. When he looked up the baby was out the garden gate and toddling toward the water trough by the barn. A lifelong interest in water holes started early for this child.

Aunt Opal was the opposite of her husband who had almost nothing to say. She gossiped nonstop about her neighbors and relatives. The couple had no children of their own and had a general dislike for anyone under twenty. She had firm opinions of how children should be raised and felt it necessary to point out to the Missus mistakes she and Ed were making as parents.

Aunt Opal frowned and questioned the Missus, "I'm surprised that baby is clothed only in diapers and you let your girls dress up in those old clothes on Sunday. Shouldn't they be wearing their best on this Lord's day?"

She listened to Mary Lou banging on the piano while Jane sang nursery rhymes in a loud screechy voice. She sighed, "I always believed that children should be seen and not heard. You and Ed are too lenient with your children. You must let that oldest child stay outside half the time. Her skin is so dark! She looks like an Indian. And the little one's hair is a mess. I thought you said it was bushed every day! All three of your children are spoiled!"

The Missus bit her lip and thought, "Aunt Opal is almost as difficult to be around as Ed's sister!"

Aunt Opal was short in stature like her husband. In her youth, before she became addicted to sweets, she had been petite. Now, her short arms were flabby and her jeweled fingers stubby. Attached to her sticklike legs were tiny feet enclosed in green high-heeled shoes with pointed toes and gold bows as decoration.

Her pinched facial features were even more striking because her graying hair was pulled back in a severe bun. The black band attached to her thick eyeglasses hung loosely around her neck. The eyeglasses were irritating so she frequently jerked them off. She puffed her hot moist breath onto the glasses, shined them with a hankie which had been hiding in her sleeve, then carefully placed the glasses back on her thin nose.

Time and age had left their damaging marks on her torso. She wore a corset, but it failed to keep the added hip poundage in check. A very noticeable disfigurement was the huge double balloons which billowed out just below her chin and draped down over her lost waistline.

Aunt Opal never helped the Missus by assisting in food preparation or even in setting the table. Instead, she sat in the rocker placed near the cot and continued having incessant chattering and making judgments. She was so short that, as she rocked back and forth, the tips of her shoes barely touched the floor.

Five-year-old Jane stopped singing in the parlor and wandered into the kitchen. She was fascinated by the uneven back-and-forth movements of the chair. Jane thought, "Perhaps Aunt Opal needs help with rocking." Jane climbed on to the back of the rockers and proceeded to add her assistance. Indeed, her pushes helped the rocker move better. In addition to forward and backward movements the rocker gradually shifted into a position facing the cot. Jane eventually tired of the activity and jumped off the rockers. Her dismounting caused the chair to jerk forward and catapult Aunt Opal into space. Luckily, there was no injury because the old cot was there to catch the leaping woman.

Aunt Opal slowly got up off the cot, replaced her glasses on her nose then tugged her dress down so her bloomers would no longer show. Her only comment was, "Well, I never!"

The couple made a hasty retreat soon after the meal. It was several months before they revisited the farm.

THE MISSUS KICKS UP HER HEELS

Frequent visitors to the farm were brothers and sisters and nieces of the Missus. There was at least one family get-together each month plus almost daily telephone conversations.

The fondness and clinging to each other of this family was a result of a troubled, unhappy childhood. They were so poor that adequate food was scarce. The children wore tattered clothes and rarely had shoes to fit their growing feet. Their father struggled, sometimes unsuccessfully, to make ends meet. When problems were too stressful, he tipped the whiskey bottle for comfort. As an alcoholic, he was irritated by children and often spanked them. Their mother, a kind and caring lady, was simply too weak from tuberculosis to assume full parenting responsibilities. During the last months of struggling with the disease, she was placed in a shed a distance away from the house so the children would not be exposed to her illness.

While still a teenager, the Missus assumed the role of mother to her siblings. She was always very protective of her brothers and sisters and continued to look after their welfare even after they were grown with families of their own.

The Missus, her brother, and one of her sisters all married within the space of two years and their children arrived in waves of two or three. All were girls except for Dannydon't. As the offspring grew, interesting trends in personalities emerged. The oldest three tended to be mischievous and were constantly in trouble. (One year they got in big trouble because they nearly destroyed Uncle Elbert's watermelon patch. In their search for the ripest melon to eat, all the watermelons of any size were methodically smashed against a huge rock.) In contrast to their mischief, the younger sisters and Dannydon't were well-behaved and sweet.

When the families had family gatherings there was a consistent theme of play between the children. The three oldest girls hid from the little sisters and were delighted when the younger ones started to cry.

Dannydon't received adoration from all the adults in the family. The uncles would pat Mr. Ed on the back and congratulate him for having a boy who would grow up to be a fine helper with the farm work. The aunts raved on and on about his precious round nose, pretty eyes and perfect little body. It's no surprise that the girls had little appreciation for this child. When the adults raved about his attributes, they would look at each other and gesture as if they were about ready to vomit.

Dannydon't wanted no part of their game, "Chase the older girls." If the girls were to have any fun, they had to change the game to, "Chase the little guy." As soon as he was old enough to escape, Dannydon't got away from the girls by grabbing his fishing gear and disappearing to one of the nearby ponds.

The similar aged cousins begged for more time together. The Missus, suggested, "Let's draw straws to determine which group of youngsters would be under their care for the following day or two. The losers get the oldest girls, the seconds will gladly take Jane's age group, and the winners will go home with only their baby."

Auntie Marie was amused at the discussion and confided to her married siblings, "When I am older and have a home of my own, all of them can come and stay with me." Little did she guess that, years later, when she lived in town, the teen aged girls, who resided on farms a distance away from school, would stay with her so they could attend ball games, skating and dances parties.

One cold and rainy Sunday the adults finished their meal and were lingering at the table sharing gossip over a final cup of coffee. Nearby, on the cot, the youngest toddlers were napping. The older children were not engaged in their typical banging of doors as they ran in and out of the house. Jane's buddies were playing with her growing family of paper dolls. Mary Lou and her companion explorers had climbed up to the attic and started rummaging through old picture albums.

The older girls soon rushed downstairs with their discovery. Mary Lou held out a large colored print and said, "Mama, is this you?" The picture was of a beautiful young woman dressed in a royal blue flapper dress. The young lady in the photo had a long string of pearl beads around her neck and a blue velvet headband decorated with a blue feather encircling her bobbed hair.

The children looked at the Missus in awe. They just didn't see the Missus, their mother and aunt, in the same way as the cot and Mr. Ed did. To them she was a mom who wore old shoes, a simple shirtwaist print dress, and an old blue shirt to protect her sore arms from the sun. Her hair was a glossy black, but the heated rollers of her latest permanent made it fuzzy. As the girls compared the picture with the Missus standing in front of them, they realized for the first time that this lady, a relative so constant in their lives that her physical features were ignored, was quite pretty.

Uncle Dave laughed at the children's question and confirmed that indeed this was a picture of his sister. He told them a story they had not heard before. "When I thought I was old enough to attend the local dances, I asked for permission to use the family coupe. My father agreed but insisted my older sister could tag along. I was furious with the arrangement. Each time, as soon as we entered the dance hall, I escorted her to a vacant chair and then disappeared."

He grinned then added, "I'm telling you, a pretty young girl sitting alone is something young men do not resist easily. Before long all the boys, that is all of them except me, were inviting her to dance. My sister was the belle of the ball at this and all the other parties we attended."

As Uncle Dave told the story, Mr. Ed snapped his fingers and grinned. He quickly browsed through the chest containing the old collection of wax cylinder records. After finding the one he wanted he wound up the old Edison phonograph. A lively song, "Charleston," floated through the room from the phonograph's large morning glory amplifier.

The children stood with their mouths gaping open as the Missus with expertise, energy and rhythm kicked up her heels to the music.

A Witch Lives in the Attic

The day was gray and rainy, so Mr. Ed's children remained indoors. Four-year-old Dannydon't collected his toy farm equipment and animals. The moss green fabric covering the pillows represented pastures for his cows, and the cot's new brown and green striped quilt became a cultivating site for his red tractor. The child was most happy to be by himself without his sisters pestering him.

Jane suggested, "Let's play dress-up." After her sister quickly agreed, they bounded up the stairs two at a time. They raced into the bedroom where the cot had once spent many lonely and neglected years. The girls did not share the disgust the cot had for the room. For them it was the stage for their impromptu theatrical productions.

The room was large with only a few pieces of furniture. In the center of the room was an antique iron bed adorned with the beautiful morning glory quilt Aunt Be had given the Missus. The matching pillow shams were blue with the outline of a large morning glory embroidered in the center of each. The two straight-backed wooden chairs sitting next to the bed looked fancy because the Missus had made blue cushions and top backings to match the pillow shams and tied blue bows on the back of each chair.

The room provided ample evidence that the family never threw anything away. The closet and wardrobe held topcoats, suits, vests and shirts for the men and dresses and cloaks for the women. The wardrobe had drawers at its base where assortments of shoes worn in past years were stashed.

The tall walnut chest positioned near the wardrobe was filled with ties, gloves, blouses, scarves and items normally hidden from public view like bloomers, pantaloons and long johns. The girls found several long white petticoats and wondered which ancestor wore them. It was not until much later, when listening to one of Uncle Jack's stories, that they identified them as once belonging to a great grandmother.

The girls were granted permission to use a large antique trunk as their special storage space. In the bottom section they stored a wide assortment of hats. The top compartments was filled with feathers, rings, belts and a collection of necklaces and other pieces of jewelry.

An antique hall tree was the most interesting piece of furniture in the room. It stood at least five feet tall. The base had a bench where men had once sat to remove their dirty boots before entering the parlor. Near the top was a shelf for hats and pegs for coats were directly below the shelf. Mary Lou and Jane were always attracted to the large vertical mirror adorning the front of the hall tree. It was yellowed and had small cracks where the glass had pulled away from the backing. Still, it sent back a reflection to the young actresses as they appraised their attire during dress up sessions.

The girls had developed an uncanny ability to guess what the other was thinking. This skill meant they had no problems creating short skits. For the first act of the day, they would mimic a scene they had watched many times downstairs.

Jane rummaged through the closet and found a couple of her daddy's old work shirts. Mary Lou watched her for only a minute before creating an accompanying costume of an old housedress belonging to her mother.

Mary Lou, using her mother's voice demanded, "Edward, take off that old shirt and put on the clean one I placed on the old cot."

Jane frowned and shook her head. "Ah, Honey, I've only worn this shirt for two days. It is just now beginning to feel good."

Her sister shook her head and stated, "Nonsense, it looks dirty and your sweat has made it smell. I even see oats sticking to the back of your shirt. You will soon be itching." She gazed closely at her sister before continuing. "Edward, your lovely thick hair is the color of Kansas dust. As soon as you have taken off that shirt, come over here to the table. I'll put some water in the wash pan then wash your hair for you."

Jane shuffled over to the trunk while her sister rummaged through their toys and found a tin pan. Jane wore a frown on her face but dutifully bent her blond head over the basin.

Mary Lou proceeded to scrub her sister's curls for a minute then burst into laughter. She made a popping sound then pretended she was pulling something out of Jane's ear. As she held up the imaginary object she commented, "Well, I'll be! You really do have corn growing out of your ears!"

Mary Lou took off her mother's old dress and looked through the wardrobe for another interesting costume. She pulled out a brown coat and vest then looked for a man's pair of brown shoes by digging through the bottom drawer. Jane frowned and shook her head to indicate she was a little confused. Mary Lou gave hints by yawning and pretending to tip a bottle. Jane smiled and immediately put on a fancy dress and stuffed the bodice with a large pillow.

Mary Lou commenced the play by stating, "Opal, I'm feeling mighty hungry."

Jane stuck out her chin and responded, "Well, don't look at me. I don't cook and the maid is gone because it is Sunday."

Mary Lou, pretending to be Uncle Hugh, gazed up at the ceiling in thought before suggesting, "We could go and visit Ed and his family at the farm. His wife always spreads a good meal. It's about time we take our new Buick for a drive out in the country."

"We can go, but let me tell you I'm not happy about this trip! You always go out and sit under a tree, but I have to stay in the kitchen and listen to those three brats yell and sing!" She hesitated a second then added, "It has been quite a while since we visited the farm. By now Ed and his wife might be making those kids behave!"

The girls broke out in gales of laughter. When younger they were unaware of how they tested the sanity for these unwelcome visitors. Now, older and wiser, they knew just what behaviors would make the visit less enjoyable for the old couple.

Jane put on a striped shirt and a bow tie then searched through the wardrobe until she found a formal black jacket. This time Mary Lou had no idea of the character her sister was planning to portray. Jane was pleased she had fooled her sister, but she knew the character would be identified as soon as she added one more prop. She rolled up a piece of paper then gave a big toothy smile while holding the paper roll at the corner of her mouth.

Mary Lou gave a nod and said, "I get it." Her sister was pretending to be an important dignitary who often appeared on the front page of Mr. Ed's daily newspaper. To compliment her sister's costume with one of her own, she pulled a fancy long sleeved gray dress once worn by her grandmother over her head. Accessories included high heels, a felt hat with a feather and several strands of long beads.

The girls listened each day as their mother and father discussed the world situation, so they had fairly accurate ideas about what the conversation might be like between these two important people they were impersonating.

Jane started the play by frowning and taking a big puff from her play cigarette. "Eleanor, this is one tough job. It seemed that the country was just getting on its feet and the New Deal program was successful. Folks had jobs and there was plenty to eat. Now we are getting into war with both Germany and Japan. I have to ask young men to leave their families. Who will be available to build the needed ships and tanks? How will the wives and children they leave behind survive?"

Mary Lou stomped her foot and sniffed. "Franklin, no one ever told you that living in this White House and directing the country would be easy! It's your responsibility to see that our country helps fight that terrible man Hitler and those evil Japs with slanted eyes!"

Mary Lou remembered hearing a description of the personality of the First Lady. She continued, "Look at me. When you were ill and now that you are in a wheelchair, I proved I was perfectly capable of taking care of the family. Let me tell you that the women in this country will rise to the occasion. They will take over the important jobs of building war machines and ammunition, and at the same time, they will find ways to successfully raise their children."

Mary Lou added a comment based on what her own mother would dictate. "I have just one more reminder. If you are determined to smoke, go out to the Rose Garden!"

The afternoon continued with the girls creating several short plays. They adorned themselves in the Gibson dresses smelling of lavender that their grandmother once wore. When fully attired in the long dresses, high-heeled white shoes and large hats with feathers they strolled around the room singing, "We were strolling through the park one day in the merry, merry month of May." Later, when they put on cowboy hats and plaid shirts, the room became a western range. They galloped on stick horses, yodeled at the top of their voices and tied up their horses to the chair back so they could go into the local saloon and enjoy a glass of sarsaparilla. Before tiring of dramatics, they pretended to be outlaws, ballet dancers, clowns and gypsies.

Jane decided it was time to do something different. "Let's go up to the attic to check if any ghosts or witches have come to visit." The girls opened the attic door located in the corner of the room. They slowly started climbing the creaky stairs. The rain made the attic seem more eerie than usual. There was only a dim light sifting through the cracks in the wall. The soft rain made pattering sounds and the wind caused the shingles to rattle.

As the girls approached the last step a mouse scampered across the room seeking a hiding place in the cracks between the boards of the floor. Jane shrieked but her older sister insisted, "Oh, don't be silly. That tiny mouse won't cause any harm!"

The attic was filled with reminders of the past. There were old trunks, broken chairs and tables, stained chandeliers and bent picture frames. Mary Lou speculated, "This attic would make a perfect home for a witch."

The girls tiptoed back down the stairs and into the bedroom with an idea of how to make the dreary afternoon much more interesting. The old hall tree sitting in one corner was a perfect form to use when creating a witch. The sisters jerked and pulled until the furniture was positioned in the middle of the room facing the hallway door. A large army blanket draped around the base represented a skirt for the witch. They found and added a long trench coat then pinned gloves to the sleeves. A round pillow with a glossy purple cover was placed on the top shelf of the hall tree. It had no features but that made no difference since a large floppy hat shaded the face.

They practiced moans and shrieks were practiced. It was decided the Mary Lou, accustomed to making wailing noises in the course of her daily antics of bouncing on the cot, made the most frightening sounds. She hid behind the hall tree, ready to make the proper auditory sounds while flapping the sleeves of the coat.

An audience was needed to appreciate this latest drama. The girls quickly decided that they could provide a show for the only creature available, one small brother quietly playing downstairs.

Jane ran into the kitchen searching for Dannydon't. There he was, quietly playing on the old cot, happily minding his own business. Jane exclaimed, "Guess what, Danny! There really is a witch living in our attic. She came down to the bedroom to visit us!"

"That's silly. Mama told me not to believe you girls when you try to scare me." Dannydon't, even at a young age, was learning to not trust the things either of his older sisters told him.

Jane put her hands on her hips and challenged, "If you don't believe me, come and see with your own eyes!"

Dannydon't crept slowly up the stairs behind his sister Jane. She opened the door into the dim bedroom. Peeking inside he saw a huge witch waving her arms and making moaning cries. He quaked in fear when the witch said in a raspy whisper, "Little girls are my friends but I eat little boys."

Dannydon't flew down the stairs and ran to fetch his mama who was busily organizing tools in the garden shed. Dannydon't screamed, "Mama, a witch lives in our house and might eat me!"

"Child, that's nonsense! Sweetie, your sisters are just playing a trick on you. Let's go see what they are up to this time."

Dannydon't didn't feel it was safe to go upstairs. However, with his mama's arms to protect him, he reluctantly decided to be brave and climb up the stairs one more time.

During the short period while Dannydon't rushed to find his mother, the girls stashed the clothes in the closet and pulled the hall tree back to its rightful place in the corner.

As the Missus reached the top steps she called, "Girls, what's this I hear about a witch living in our home? Mary Lou and Jane, you two nearly scared your little brother to death!"

The girls shook their heads and looked innocent. "Mama, we have no idea what Dannydon't is talking about. We are here on the bed quietly reading books we checked out from the library."

For years Dannydon't refused to explore the attic and was not happy about sleeping upstairs. Many nights, after the other family members had retired to their beds, he would tiptoe downstairs and into the kitchen. He felt safe spending the night between the cot's covers.

RELATIVES VISIT

Aunt Alicia, Mr. Ed's older sister, exhibited the same personality as an adult as she had as a young girl having to contend with several brothers. She constantly scolded and told others what to do. In the Missus' opinion, her only one truly redeeming feature was she was quite fond of her young nieces. She enjoyed buying outfits for them and, on a recent trip to Chinatown in San Francisco, returned with lovely silk pajamas and slippers that were perfect fits for the two little girls. She was also most willing to be their piano instructor even though there was rarely egg money available to pay for lessons.

When visiting the farm home, Aunt Alicia would explore each and every room. She would gaze at a bowl or picture and say, "I just know that my mama would want her only daughter to have this!" The Missus would grit her teeth, but because her sister-in-law was so kind to the girls, would say nothing.

On one visit Aunt Alicia noticed a lovely blue vase holding a cluster of spring flowers. Aunt Alicia tossed the flowers over the fence and started to place the vase in her large handbag. The Missus grabbed the vase out of her sister-in-laws hand and snarled, "I'm sorry, but this is one of the few pieces I have which belonged to my mother! I know she would want her daughter to keep it!"

Uncle Jack, Mr. Ed.'s older brother, lived in faraway California and only was able to return to the farm for a short visit every two or three years. He was everyone's favorite person. Even the Missus didn't fuss when he chewed tobacco and took frequent nips from the bottle. Uncle Jack always brought gourmet surprises from the land of sunshine. In addition to sweet oranges, he introduced his brother's family to unusual foods. The children thought eating artichokes by pulling off the leaves and dipping them in butter was a real treat. However, they did not willingly accept the taste of black mushrooms and other strange looking Chinese food when he tried to convince them that these were special delicacies.

The children cherished the visits from this uncle. He took the time to listen as the girls played their newest songs on the piano. He was attentive during their dramatic scenarios and added interest to their plays by creating roles for himself. On his visits, he took daily trips to one of the ponds with Dannydon't. He explained to Dannydon't that Old Fighter was lurking somewhere and it was Danny's responsibility to try and catch him.

Uncle Jack talked even more than his younger brother, Mr. Ed. He constantly told stories about when he was a little kid at the farm. Of course, Anamule, his favorite pet, was always included in the conversation.

During his visits Uncle Jack and Mr. Ed talked to the wee hours of the morning. Although the Missus had a bed turned down for him upstairs, he always said, "Now, don't go to any bother. I'll just rest my bones on that old cot." Within seconds after crawling under its covers, he was sound asleep and snoring so loudly that the house shook.

UNEXPECTED GUESTS

Mr. Ed and the Missus were not always well acquainted with guests who came to the farm. Wild John had grown up in a desolate area of Western Kansas. He remembered hearing stories about cousins back in Eastern

Kansas, so decided it was time to make a trip back East and make their acquaintance. This uninvited and unknown guest tested the hospitality of even gracious people like Mr. Ed and the Missus.

Wild John brought along a companion, his girlfriend, Ely. This lady, who weighed at least 300 pounds, had probably never experienced a bath except in a river or a downpour of rain. When asked a question, she responded by mumbling. She did not make eye contact with the Missus and was very indifferent when introduced to the children. She did, however, appreciate the cherry pie the Missus had made just that morning and proceeded to eat every bite of it!

Wild John was six-foot-four inches tall. His long unwashed steel gray hair was so stiff it stood straight up. The overalls he wore had more than ten years of wear but had rarely seen the inside of any washing machine. He liked to tell jokes and, as he finished the punch line, gave a near toothless smile and slapped his knees. That caused a swirl of dust to float up into the air.

Wild John always carried candy in his back pocket. He smiled broadly when he met Mr. Ed's sweet children, reached into the back pocket, pulled out several pieces of squashed candy, and offered it to the children. As the children extended their hands to receive the gift, the Missus intervened. She said, "Now children, you know you can't have candy before the meal. I'll keep it for you." The candy Wild John offered was tossed into the trash when no one was looking and she substituted candy she kept hidden for special occasions.

Sleeping arrangements for Wild John and Ely were a problem. It was pretty obvious Ely was too big to climb the stairs to the bedrooms and, if she did, the bed she selected would probably break. Ely mumbled something and went out to their old jalopy. She had brought along her own roll and planned to sleep under the stars.

The cot sure had a lot of admirers! Wild John sat on the cot and bounced up and down a few times. The springs shrieked and dust rolled from his clothes onto the clean cover. He stated, "This is one fine cot! Right here will be a fine place for me to take my rest!" As you might expect, the Missus approved of his choice.

After the couple departed the next morning, the keen eyes of the Missus quickly spotted tiny white lice on the cot's pillows. All of the pillows and covers were burned. As an extra precaution, she also washed the mattress with lye soap and aired it out in the sun for several days.

A VISITOR WITH FOUR LEGS

Some of the visitors who came to the farm had more than two legs. One spring day a fat, young, pink pig arrived at the kitchen door. Mr. Ed and the Missus understood none of the nearby neighbors were raising pigs, so they decided that he must have fallen off one of the large trucks carrying animals to the stock market in Kansas City.

The young pig was adorable. Like Anamule, the pet of the past, he ignored the barnyard and preferred to stay in the large yard surrounding the house. Mr. Ed fed him appropriate animal food, and the Missus added to his diet with scraps from the table. As he grew older and fatter, he was named Mr. USA because the pattern of United States was clearly outlined on his back.

Farmers enjoy raising their animals and get a kick out of their antics. Nevertheless, folks who work on a farm understand that the purpose of animals like cows, pigs and sheep is to provide food for the table. Mr. USA was eventually old enough and fat enough to be called to duty. During a Sunday dinner Mr. Ed took a bite of a pork chop and said, "Right now, I'm eating a part of North Dakota."

Chapter 11

TELL US A STORY

Uncle Jack was the historian of the family. Each evening, during his visits from California, he told stories of the past. Uncle Jack sat in the rocker holding Dannydon't on his lap, and the two pajama-clad girls took their places on top of my covers. Uncle Jack's stories were vivid and detailed. He knew many true facts about the family history, and using his acute imagination, was able to fabricate what he didn't know.

Another Historian, the Cot

COMING TO THE NEW LAND

"Uncle Jack, tell us about our great, great grandfather William." Uncle Jack had hardly had time to greet everyone before his two nieces were begging for stories. Fortunately, he was happy to oblige.

"Kids, I don't know how many greats you need in front of this grandfather's name, but I can tell you a little about William. He was a bright young gentleman living in England a long time ago. He was lucky to have wealthy parents in a time when many people were poor and starving. They were able to pay for him to have an excellent education. After he graduated from Oxford, William's parents purchased a private school for him to operate.

"Schools in that era were called colleges, and only young men were allowed to attend. I expect he taught teen-aged boys Latin, math, and other subjects the boys would need to know before they went on to a university. William taught for a couple of years but found the job tedious and boring.

"William, like so many other young lads, had heard many tales about the new land across the ocean. The land was full of opportunities and vast areas were still unexplored. William decided he should have the excitement of settling in the new land. He sold his school and put his money and everything else he owned of value in a large trunk. He then booked passage on the first ship available heading for America.

"The journey to America took over two weeks. Just as the ship was nearing the new land, there was a terrible storm. The waves eventually tossed the boat up against the rocks so hard that it broke in half. Many of the sailors and passengers died."

Jane frowned and shook her head. "Did William die?"

"Sweetheart, of course he didn't! He was your ancestor, and if he had died, none of us would be here. Nope, William was a strong swimmer. Since he was a smart young man, don't you think he might have grabbed a wooden plank and held on to it as he paddled to shore? He was soon safe from the raging water but everything he owned was in the trunk that had sunk with the ship to the bottom of the ocean. All he had were the clothes on his back and a few coins in his pocket.

William could easily have chosen to become a teacher in the new country but that career was not exciting enough for him. Instead, he was accepted as part of a surveying crew. A few months after he learned this trade, his crew was sent to survey an area way out West at a place which would eventually be called Chicago."

Uncle Jack paused to see if the children understood what he was talking about. "Mary Lou, what do you know about Chicago?"

Mary Lou, then only nine-years-old, had gained an interest in geography by listening as her daddy constantly described interesting sites around the world. She quickly responded to her uncle, "I know all about Chicago, Uncle Jack. It's the second largest city in the United States. It's located on the southwest side of Lake Michigan. It's in the state of Illinois."

"Mary Lou, you must be listening to your teacher and my brother! Let me explain. When William went out West, there was no state named Illinois and the area to be surveyed was a marshland by the lake. William worked all summer surveying the area later to be nicknamed the Loop. It now sits right smack in downtown Chicago. He stood all day in the murky water and battled mosquitoes and black flies. He was just plain miserable about the whole adventure.

"The company owners who hired the surveying team found themselves short of cash. They decided to offer the workers an alternative to wages. The crew could have money or one out of every seven lots surveyed that summer. Your great-grandpa William stated, 'This place is nothing but a dammed swamp! I will take the money and leave!' William thought he was smart, but he sure made a bad decision. If he had chosen to take the lots you probably would be worth millions, and the family would be living in a fancy Chicago penthouse."

Mary Lou thought for a minute and commented, "Maybe he was smart after all. You and daddy have always told us we are living in a piece of paradise. I think a farm is a lot more fun than a stuffy old penthouse in Chicago."

BROTHERS IN THE CIVIL WAR

The next night Uncle Jack said, "Do you want to hear a story about two brothers who fought in the Civil War?" After seeing nods of interest, he continued. "When the war broke out, the older brother already had a wife and two small children. The other young man, your great grandfather, had just purchased some land in Kansas where he wanted to build a fine new home. Both young men dropped the plow, so to speak, and put on the Union's blue uniform.

It wasn't long before the brothers were separated. Alas, the older brother ran into trouble and was captured by the Rebels. He spent several years in a terrible place, a prison in Andersonville, Georgia. He was sick and almost starved to death, but he didn't die. Instead, he got a little crazy in the head. When the war was over and prisoners were released, he returned to Eastern Kansas. In no time at all he gathered up his wife and children and moved to a remote area far beyond Dodge City. He wanted to be in a place far away from civilization where his family would not be affected by the world. I heard that his wife died the following year. His children grew up with no education and no one to tell them how to behave."

Mary Lou thought a minute and commented, "I'll bet Wild John was the grandson of this uncle. He came back to see us last summer!"

Uncle Jack continued. "Now, your great grandfather was luckier than his brother. He was with a troop that fought in areas of Murfreesboro, Tennessee, and Marietta, Georgia. He was assigned sentry duty. While the other men in his regiment were sleeping, he was to keep a watch out for the enemy troops and wild animals. Your great grandfather got mighty sleepy while on this watch so he started brewing coffee. Sipping the strong caffeine drink would help him stay awake until dawn.

The delicious aroma of the coffee filled the air. It reached the nostrils of a young man from Kentucky, Mr. Childs, a soldier for the South. He was sitting only a short distance downwind from your great grandfather and assigned to a similar lookout watch for the Rebels. One of the things he loved most was a good cup of strong coffee, but it was almost impossible for soldiers fighting for the South to obtain because of blockades. Finally, he could stand the smell no more. He yelled over to your great grandfather, "*Hey, Yank, "I'll gladly swap some tobacco for a cup of your coffee.*" The young men, who were supposed to be enemies who shot at each other, spent many a night drinking coffee and smoking mellow tobacco. When the war ended your great grandfather walked home to Kentucky with Mr. Childs before returning to Kansas."

Uncle Jack noticed the look of disbelief on the faces of his nieces. "You kids look like you don't believe that these men who were enemies became friends! There is proof of their friendship. Every year, as long as he lived, Mr. Childs sent a sack of tobacco to the farm. Don't you remember the story I told you about how tobacco was used by most of the folks living on the farm and Anamule became addicted to tobacco?"

GREAT GRANDMOTHER'S PETTICOATS

Each night of Uncle Jack's visit had the same ritual. After supper, the children brushed their teeth and quickly put on their pajamas. Mary Lou did not give the cot her usual bouncing workout. Instead, she and her little sister puffed up the pillows and quickly curled into balls on the cot's covers. Little Dannydon't enjoyed the privilege of being the youngest and therefore very special. He held up his arms and said, "Put me high, Uncle Jack!" Uncle Jack swung him high up in the air before settling on the rocker with the young child in his lap. Mr. Ed and the Missus sat nearby at the kitchen table and worked a crossword puzzle. They too were anxious to hear the next family story. The couple was aware of the real facts, so they were amused by the exaggerations of their favorite family member.

This particular evening, Mr. Ed sat at the table, finishing a crossword puzzle. The Missus cleared up the table and, before doing the dishes, offered coffee and a piece of rhubarb pie to Mr. Ed and Uncle Jack.

Uncle Jack thanked her then chuckled. "This family is mighty lucky. Ed, you married a woman who is an excellent cook, homemaker, and gardener. On top of that she is always organized." He then added, "I remember our mother was the same way, and my wife certainly keeps the world straight for me."

Uncle Jack asked his nephew, "When you ask your dad permission to do something, how does he answer?"

Dannydon't had an immediate response. "He says, 'Go ask your mother.'"

Uncle Jack wondered aloud, "In the Bible, in our history lessons and even with the stories I've been telling you about your ancestors, a man is usually the hero. Something is wrong with this picture. It just doesn't jive with what I observe in the families I know. In all of them the woman holds the family together. If truth be told, women are the ones who make most of the important decisions. Perhaps women get their satisfaction out of knowing that, through their guidance, husbands and sons can achieve great things."

He took a gulp of the coffee then turned again to the children. "Listen closely. I want you to understand that, in our family history, there are womenfolk who are just as important and interesting as their husbands. Tonight, I want to tell you about the one who was known as a healer."

He asked, "Have you ever heard of Great Grandmother Ruth?"

The girls nodded their heads. Jane commented, "I think there is a picture of her in an old album upstairs."

Mary Lou added, "I remember what she looked like because I asked daddy about the picture. She was smiling. In most of the old photos the people look like they are mad or ate something that tasted like rotten eggs."

Uncle Jack chuckled. "I think you will admire Ruth. She had determination and the ability to do what she thought was right."

He recalled, "Ruth was the only child of a family doctor in a little town located in the state of Connecticut. The doctor and his small daughter had mutual admiration for each other. When very small, probably about Jane's age, she would sit on his lap and tell her daddy that, when she grew up, she wanted to be a doctor just like him.

The good doctor would give his little girl a hug and say, *"We'll see."* He was not about to tell her that there was no chance that a young lady would be allowed into a medical school."

Uncle Jack took a large bite of rhubarb pie then continued his tale. "The front room of the family home served as the doctor's office. After the school day was over, young Ruth rushed home with the intention of acting as his receptionist. She invited those waiting to see the doctor to have a chair in the foyer then would serve them warm tea. She was overjoyed when he asked for her assistance in the office. She watched and listened and soon became proficient in mending broken arms and bandaging wounds.

The doctor always had his horse and buggy nearby because he was expected to make house calls to patients too ill to come to the office. Whenever possible, his young daughter jumped into the buggy seat beside him. Sometimes she remained quietly in the buggy while he tended the sick. There were other occasions when she followed him into the house and assumed responsibility as his nurse.

The years passed by. Ruth finally realized that because she was a woman, she would not have the opportunity to attend medical school. Nevertheless, she continued to help her father care for the sick and injured. By sixteen, the young lady had read all of his medical books and memorized most of the facts in them.

When Ruth was only eighteen-years-old, she married your great grandfather. He was a fine young man but was restless. He agreed with a popular saying at that time, *'Go west, young man, go west.'* Soon after their marriage, he convinced his new wife they should head in that direction.

Their first home was a small frame house near a town called Peculiar, Missouri. Your great grandfather was a hard worker. He toiled long hours at a mill and saved every cent of his salary. His goal was to save enough money to purchase land and have a farm of his own.

In early May, William and Ruth toured the countryside in search of a site for their permanent home. After riding their horses for nearly two days over the prairie, they stopped to rest by a small creek. Ruth was delighted with the beauty surrounding them. The water in the creek was crystal clear. She and William looked down into the deep pools and saw fish swimming and, in shallow areas, the mica on rocks was shining like diamonds. Ruth noticed that featherlike ferns covered the ground where she was standing. *"I love this place. Let's call our future home Ferndale."*

Ruth slowly turned in a circle and, as she did so, took note of the pristine countryside ablaze with the colors of spring flowers. Clumps of violets, wild Sweet Williams and Jack-in-the-Pulpits were in the shady areas by the creek and wild roses and daisy like flowers blossomed in the nearby sunny areas. Clusters of trees were an unusual occurrence in this prairie area. Ruth and her husband were more than pleased with the canopy of trees surrounding both sides of the creek.

William knew that Ruth was smitten with the wooded area but made a thoughtful suggestion that building a home so near the creek would not be a wise decision. In years when the spring rains are abundant, it could become a flood plain."

All the listeners, including Mr. Ed and the Missus, were nodding their heads in agreement with Uncle Jack. "William reached down and grabbed a handful of black dirt. He surmised they had been traveling for two days and this is the best land seen. It would be wise to get a deed for this section as soon as possible. The couple looked around and decided a site several hundred yards north of the creek looked like a fine place for their future home. William kissed his wife and made a promise. *"I'll build you a white framed house. It will have bay windows facing toward the wooded creek area you like so much."*

The girls grinned at each other. Jane said, "I bet we're sitting in that house right now."

Uncle Jack acknowledged that their guess was correct before continued his story about Ruth. "In those days doctors were few and far apart. I expect the nearest doctor lived in Kansas City or Independence. Of course, people got hurt and few medicines were available to treat serious diseases. It didn't take long for folks to recognize that Ruth was capable of helping them get better when they were sick or injured.

Her doctoring started in Missouri, long before they lived at Ferndale Farm. A boy about eight, who lived nearby, ran to her house crying, *"I think my mamma might die. She is bending backward and forward and holds her stomach. When the pains come, she screams and moans. Daddy is away and I don't know what to do.!"*

Ruth gave the boy a hug and responded to his fears. *"Maybe you came to the right place. I'll see if there is something I can help your mama to feel better."*

A few hours later the mother had a smile on her face and two new babies in her arms. The happy mother wasted no time in telling all the neighbors how Ruth was there to help in her time of need. The wish Ruth made when a small child was coming true. Her days were filled with helping people regain their health."

Uncle Jack took a bite of pie and a sip of coffee then continued, "I've already told you that Ruth was very intelligent and independent. When her husband and his brother signed up to fight in the Civil War, she reassured him that she was perfectly able to take care of herself!"

Young Jane's eyes lit up. "I know who her husband was! When he was in the war, he drank coffee and smoked tobacco with a man who was an enemy."

Uncle Jack complimented his niece on her quickness at making connections. Then he continued. "Would you like to know about some of the ways which indicated that Great Grandmother Ruth filled the role of a fantastic person and doctor?"

After nods from the children, he continued. "Ruth seemed to understand a lot more than most people did at that time about diseases and germs. She believed that close contact and improper cleanliness habits encouraged the spread of germs. Girls, you know how your mother constantly is cleaning the house? Well, Ruth was like that. Also, like your mother, she always insisted that her husband and children wash their hands after a trip to the outhouse or before eating. Your mama sees to it that you children and your daddy have frequent baths. My father, Ruth's son, used to shutter as he recalled how she demanded he take baths even when the water was icy cold.

In those days, if one family member succumbed to an infectious disease like scarlet fever, it wasn't long before the entire family would be ill. The first thing Ruth did when entering a home having a member with a contagious disease was to see that the healthy inhabitants did not get near the sick ones. She proceeded to wash all touchable surfaces like knobs on doors, dressers and counter tops with water and a strong soap made with lye, grease, and ashes. She then stayed by the bedside of the ill person until they got well or died.

Ruth believed in being prepared. She took to always wearing an extra white slip. Then, if someone was injured, she had cloth available to use for bandages."

Mary Lou looked startled. She turned to her sister, "Jane! That's why so many petticoats are in the dresser in the bedroom. Do you remember? We found them when we were playing dress-up."

Uncle Jack continued, "Ruth loved the woods down by the creek. On her long walks in that area, she would look for small fallen limbs. She gathered these and kept a few stored on her buggy. The limbs were needed as splints when setting a broken arm or leg."

Uncle Jack paused, "Girls, have you noticed all the herbs that grow at the side of the garden? Your great-grandmother, Ruth, knew about the medical benefits of herbs. She had lavender for insect bites, peppermint for pain, witch hazel for swelling, as well as herbs like garlic, thyme, cloves and all sorts of other plants needed to sooth and speed up the healing process. Her herbs were dried in the smokehouse then placed in her medical bag. She also always kept a bottle of whiskey available."

Uncle Jack took a quick look at the Missus before continuing. He was aware of her complete disapproval of all alcohol. He decided to explain why it was of importance to Ruth. "The whiskey helped deaden a patient's pain when she performed surgeries."

He completed his description by adding, "There is one more thing I want to tell you about your great grandmother Ruth. She cared so much about others that she could feel their anguish even when she was not near them. My father recalled that their family could be happily eating a meal, and even though there were no telephones, his mother would stop eating and seemed to be listening to someone talking. She would jump up from the table and announce that one of the neighboring families needed her. In no time she grabbed her medicine bag, hitched her horse to the buggy and raced down the road."

Uncle Jack concluded by stating, "Yes, indeed, she was a wonderful woman. There were a lot of folks who remained alive because of her."

Jane looked at her uncle and made a promise. "Uncle Jack, I want to be like my great grandmother. When I grow up, I will help people who are ill."

Uncle Jack smiled his approval. "Honey, you have all the makings of a nurse or doctor. I've noticed how you take special care of your pets so they stay healthy, and you often pretend that your dolls are sick and need your nursing, don't you?"

Mary Lou was not to be excluded. "What about me, Uncle Jack? Do you think I could be a doctor?"

Uncle Jack shook his head and said, "I don't think so, Mary Jane. You can't even stand the sight of blood. I've noticed that when you scrape your knee, your little sister cleans the wound and puts a bandage on it."

Mary Lou was not pleased. "Well, if I can't be a doctor when I grow up, what can I be?"

Uncle Jack grinned and pinched her cheek. "Mary Lou, there are many things you could do. You like to make collections and often trade these with your friends. Maybe you could run a store. Also, you like younger children and seem to know how to explain things to them. If you ever learn to spell correctly, you might make a fine teacher."

Mary Lou was not a bit pleased with these suggestions. They didn't sound like exciting professions.

Uncle Jack noticed her disappointment. "Or your calling might be in the circus. You like climbing to high places. Maybe you could walk on the wires strung at the top of tents."

Uncle Jack chuckled as he thought of another possibility. "Mary Lou, do you recognize the name Houdini?"

Mary Lou thought a second and asked, "Didn't he do some kind of magic?"

Uncle Jack nodded his head. "That's right, honey. He was known as the best escape artist in the world. You have an uncanny ability to disappear about the time your mama needs your help. Houdini is no longer alive, but I bet you could be the disappearing lady for another magician."

A Famous Ancestor

Uncle Jack's vacation was nearing an end, but there were many more stories to tell. The next night he had another almost true story to tell about a past member of their family. "Did you know that your mama also had some fine ancestors? Jane, have you ever heard of Abraham Lincoln?"

Jane nodded her curly blond head. "He's that tall man with a black beard who wears a black hat. His picture is on the wall at school."

Big sister reminded her, "He was very important! He was the president of the United States during the Civil War. After the war, a bad man shot him while he was watching a play at the Ford Theater."

Uncle Jack continued with his story. "You are right about old Abe. He was very important for the United States. He was successful and had a fine career before he ever went to Washington. One of his important jobs was to be a lawyer in Springfield, Illinois. Abe became well known and was very busy. He hired a bright young man to be his secretary and help him with many legal matters. That young man was your mother's great uncle. He was in Abe's law office for several years.

"This uncle was also known to be successful in business and a strong leader in his community. He held several important offices both in the state of Illinois and for the United States. At one time he was even appointed to be an ambassador to France for our country.

"This famous man had a brother who wanted to homestead in the Flint Hills area of Kansas. He willingly gave his brother money so he could buy the oxen, wagon and other materials needed to move a large family to the Flint area in Kansas Territory."

Mary Lou made another connection. "I'll bet that he was the brother of Grandmother Nichol's father. She told us that her father died in a hunting accident soon after moving his family to Kansas."

"Uncle Jack, what is the most ancient ancestor you know about?" It seemed to the children that their uncle had all the answers about their history. They never stopped to consider how he could possibly know all the information and if there was complete truth in what he was saying.

Mr. Ed looked up from the crossword puzzle and gave his wife a grin. They were curious about the response Uncle Jack would concoct for this question.

Uncle Jack found this question a challenge to his imagination. He though a minute then grinned. He was not going to resist the opportunity to make up a new story. "Children, this is just oral history from the distant past. Nothing is written but I have a pretty good idea about one of our ancient ancestors. Do you know about King Arthur's court? King Arthur had many brave knights that sat with him around the Round Table. There was one handsome young man named Richard. They say he slew dragons with ease and was a favorite of many of the ladies. He just might have been one of your great grandfathers!"

MORE ANAMULE STORIES

The children always wanted to hear stories about when Uncle Jack and Mr. Ed were young boys on the farm. It was their uncle who added to the many stories they already knew about Anamule.

Uncle Jack started this story by reminding the children about Anamule's mother. "Black Jenny was already twenty when Anamule was born. That's mighty old for a mare to give birth. Old Jenny gave up the ghost within a few days after this baby arrived. Perhaps she died solely due to old age, but more than likely, it was the shock of seeing her offspring standing beside her with skinny legs, big ears, and a forlorn look.

The owner, our Aunt Mildred, didn't want to bother with the young mule, so she gave it to us boys to be our playmate. Until Anamule was grown, she was a delight for all the kids in the family and a headache for the women folk. She refused to stay in the barnyard. Near the kitchen door was her favorite grazing area.

With the womenfolk fussing so much about her presence, we had to find a way to make her useful. I take pride in being the one who saw the opportunity to make Anamule more respected. Each day the womenfolk asked us to bring up buckets of water from the barnyard well. That was back breaking work and took quite a lot of time away from our play. I suggested we hitch Anamule to a cart. That silly mule thought this was a new game so she willingly pulled the cart filled with water buckets from the well to the kitchen door. Even my mother decided that that mule might be worth something after all."

"Uncle Jack, tell us about Anamule and the 4th of July parade." The children had heard this particular story several times. It was their favorite.

It was a delight for Uncle Jack to elaborate about this familiar tale. "The 4th of July was considered a special day in this community. One year we decided it would be fun for all of us to be a part of the parade. We decorated that cart we made for carrying water with red, white, and blue ribbons. The same colors were woven into Anamule's mane and tail. We painted a sign reading, 'Pike's Peak or Bust.' All of us kids dressed ourselves up to represent pioneers heading west. Your Aunt Alicia pretended to be the mama and your daddy was the little boy. They were assigned to ride in the wagon while the rest of us would guide Anamule in the right direction down Main Street.

On the day of the parade everything: the cart, our parents, us kids, and even the small mule were loaded onto a large spring wagon. It was slow going, but we arrived in town just in time to get in line for the parade.

When we gave the command, 'Giddy Up' Anamule only twitched her ears. Her legs were like stone pillars.

The parade started moving down the street. We were holding up the line and we were afraid they would require us to go to the sidelines. Something had to be done because Anamule wasn't about to do her part. My older brother had a great idea. He suggested that we put Anamule in the cart. After we had hoisted her into the cart, all of us boys grabbed the reins and started pulling. Everyone watching thought the situation of the mule taking a ride was mighty funny. We won a prize for the most interesting entry in the parade."

Chapter 12

THE GOOD YEARS

The 1930's, years filled with of depression, drought, and floods in the Midwest retreated to the past. Unfortunately, disasters seem to follow each other. Just when it seemed conditions were getting better, Pearl Harbor was bombed. The Second World War was not quite as unsettling for this family as it was for others living in the United States. Since they lived on a farm, there was always plenty to eat. They were fortunate that no man in the immediate family had to be called into service. Mr. Ed was considered too old to be drafted, and Dannydon't was

still a little kid. Ironically, these years, in spite of the war, were some of the best for Ed and his family.

The Wise One, the Cot

OUT OF DEBT

M r. Ed and the Missus planned carefully and were always frugal. These habits, plus their hard work, had positive results. Mother Nature also played a part in making their situation much rosier. The change of the weather pattern brought several years with ample rain. Even better, rain seemed to come whenever it was needed the most. After several years of bumper crops, Mr. Ed was able to pay off the loans on the farm incurred by his father years before and still enjoy a margin of profit. He hugged his wife and gleefully said, "Put away your red pen! By golly! Now we will see our bank statements in black!"

Ever since the time he was asked to give up attending college and come home to helped keep the farm from bankruptcy, Mr. Ed had made do with hand-me-downs and leftovers. The extra money now sitting in their bank account provided the opportunity for Mr. Ed to make his first big purchase for his own personal use, a red Farmall tractor. His new tractor made him feel like a kid who found the toy he wished for under the Christmas tree. The day it was delivered, he telephoned all of his neighbors and offered to come over to their place and use his new vehicle to help with their planting.

Ed called to his wife and children, "Everybody, come out here to the barnyard right now! I want you to see my new wheels." Ed gleefully lifted each child onto the tractor seat then instructed, "See if you can make a powerful right turn with the steering wheel." Long after his children grew bored and went back to their play, he continued to examine every part of his new machine. Mr. Ed joyfully kicked all four wheels and probably would have peed on them if the Missus had not been watching. Ed smiled a silly grin and said to the Missus, "Now I can do twice as much work in half the time."

A new tractor was not the only large purchase for that year. However, the next one was unexpected. On an early Saturday morning in July, the Missus filled five buckets of water and set them where the sunshine would beam on them the entire day. Her family no longer questioned her demand for cleanliness. They knew they would each have a turn using the warmed water in the makeshift shower setup in the shed before going into town that evening.

Each family member dutifully showered and decked out in clean clothes before jumping into the ancient black Ford. When Mr. Ed tried to crank up the motor, the only sounds heard were click and clack. Mr. Ed spent nearly fifteen frustrating minutes tinkering with almost every part of the engine. Finally, he shook his head and said, "Seems like this old car has gone its final miles! We will need to buy another car."

Dannydon't was secretly glad they would not be going to town that evening. He knew his friend, Marvin, was away visiting his grandmother. With no friend to play with, he would have to stand around while his dad talked nonstop to other old men about problems in a distant place called Europe. Since they were home for the evening, maybe his dad would take him fishing.

The others were not pleased. The girls were disappointed that they would not be seeing their friends while walking in circles around the city block and were unhappy because they were missing the opportunity to enjoy ice cream or a root beer float at the drug store. Mary Lou groaned, "There's nothing interesting to do at home this evening. We've read all of the books we checked out of the library." Jane added, "Fiddlesticks, we can't even listen to the radio because it needs new batteries. We'll miss listening to our favorite Big Bands."

The Missus looked at her long grocery list and shook her head. "My containers holding staples are nearly empty and the dry goods store had an advertisement in the paper saying floral patterned material was on sale. I was planning to buy several yards to make summer outfits for the girls."

Mr. Ed voiced his personal concern. "I just paid off the loan on our property at the bank and used the extra cash from the sale of last year's corn crop to buy the tractor. Hell, I'm going to have to ask for another loan so we can get a car. Honey, I hope you didn't throw away your red pen. You'll need it after we borrow money from the bank to buy the car."

The Missus, who usually worried about money more than her spouse, thought a minute then offered words of reassurance. "Ed, you told me the crops are looking good this year. Don't worry too much. We'll do fine."

The Missus thought about events happening the next morning and realized a means of transportation was necessary. She sighed, "Tomorrow is a special day at church. We could walk but it's going to be difficult because I was assigned several dishes to bring for the annual church picnic. What are we going to do?"

Mr. Ed smiled, "At least that problem can be solved. I'll hitch the hay wagon to the new tractor. You all can hop on board the wagon and have a great ride."

At the picnic after church, Mr. Ed moaned to other men about the demise of his old car. Charlie, Danielle's husband, had an immediate suggestion, "Ed, I need to make several trips to local towns in my truck next week. Ride along with me, there will be plenty of time for you to bargain with car dealers." By Wednesday afternoon, Mr. Ed drove home from Olathe in a bright green second-hand Chevrolet.

The Missus loved the new car. In the past, she usually waited for Mr. Ed to come in from the fields before making trips into town. She reasoned that since the new tractor had lights, he would probably stay out in the fields until it was dark. After returning to the barnyard, he would need to complete chores like milking the cows so would not be eager to drive into town.

She suggested, "Honey, don't you worry about taking me to town to run errands after you've had a full day of working in the fields. Driving the new Chevrolet is a delightful experience, and I am more than willing to assume that responsibility."

Dannydon't liked to ride in the car but had no interest in going to town with his mom when he could be fishing or playing around the fields where his dad was working. His older siblings had a different attitude. One afternoon they noticed the Missus getting into the car so begged, "Mama, we want to go with you."

The Missus looked at her scruffy daughters and directed, "You may go to town with me only if you clean up and put on decent dresses." She thought a minute then added, "Don't forget to change your underpants. I want you to be clean all over just in case we are in a wreck."

Mary Lou quickly responded, "Mama, that's silly. No one is going to see our panties. And, if we are in a wreck, they will cut off our clothes and our panties will be all covered with blood."

The Missus grew irritated whenever her children gave her any back talk. She sniffed, put her hands on her hips and stated in a firm voice, "If you want to ride with me in this car you will clean up, comb your messy hair, and change all of your clothes."

ELECTRICITY ARRIVES

The evening ritual of sitting around the kitchen table after supper was no longer as pleasant as it once was. Mary Lou was the first to complain. She snatched her glasses off her nose, blew on each glass then rubbed them vigorously with a tea cloth. After putting them on again she whined, "Mama, the words in my book are still blurry. Am I going blind?"

Electricity had finally arrived to rural areas of Eastern Kansas. Almost all of their neighbors were pleased, but the Missus was correct in expressing her doubts about its value for their family. Prior to the event of electricity, natural gas was piped in from a well located west of the house. Illumination on winter nights was provided by the gas chandelier plus kerosene lamps on the table and buffet. Another source of light was the soft glow of the stove casting dancing lights and shadows throughout the room. The Missus stopped stitching and agreed. "No, Mary Lou, it is not your eyes. Like you, I am having trouble seeing tonight."

She looked up at the dangling light bulb of only forty watts dangling over the table. "Sometimes modernization is a mixed blessing!"

On the other hand, the Missus was most appreciative of the new electric refrigerator. It kept foods cooler than the old icebox, and she no longer had to worry about ice water spilling out from the holding pan onto her kitchen floor. Mr. Ed assured her that part of the profits from next year's corn crop would be used to purchase an electric washing machine. Hopefully, that would eliminate some of the agony she suffered because of her hands being in wash water each Monday.

Mr. Ed changed some farming practices as a result of electricity. As soon as he had the pastures surrounded with electric wires, his dairy herd was minimized to only a few heifers to provide milk and butter for family needs. Now he owned nearly fifty black and glossy Angus beef cattle that liked to graze in the pastures south and west of the barn. It took only a short time for the cows to fully respect and shy away from the wires designating their areas of confinement.

Mr. Ed warned the children not to touch the wires. They heeded his warning and, like the cattle, kept their distance. The electric fence, surrounding the south pasture, separated the farm buildings from the creek, silo and cliffs waiting to be climbed. The three children had to find a way to overcome the new obstacle. To reach these play destinations, they learned to avoid a jolt of electricity by carefully rolling on the ground or scooting on their tummies under the wire.

Unfortunately, the children did not fully understand electric currents. One afternoon Dannydon't received a dare, "Hey, little man, I bet you can't piss on the electric wire from three feet away." He was successful with his aim but retained a lifelong memory of the resulting pain.

PEEKING THROUGH CRACKS

Nine-year old Mary Lou's ears perked up as she listened to her dad's early morning telephone conversation with Murray, the local veterinarian. Mr. Ed finished his call then said to the Missus, "Raising feed cattle sure is different than having a dairy herd. The time I once spent milking is now taken up mending fences. I have to walk around the pastures each day to

177

check the electric wires. It's not unusual for a snake or stick to get tangled in the wire and cause a short in the circuit. The cows seem to know when the wire isn't hot. They get out of the field and wander all over creation. Two wandered into the neighbor's pasture across the road last week!"

Mr. Ed continued, "Today we are required to do another kind of work which comes from having stock cattle instead of a dairy herd. Murray said that he would bring the equipment needed to castrate the male calves."

Mr. Ed thought about his children and requested, "Will you see that the girls stay in the house this morning?" Mr. Ed had the belief that his girls should not be exposed to some of the grim facts of life around the farm.

The last the Missus saw of Mary Lou she was heading upstairs with a book recently borrowed from the library. The Missus assumed that the child would stay in her bedroom the entire morning in hopes of avoiding work.

The Missus continued her kitchen duties and failed to notice when Mary Lou tiptoed down the stairs and rushed out the side door.

Mary Lou hurried to the barn and climbed up into the hayloft before her daddy herded fifteen male calves up from a pasture near the creek. Murray was driving his truck into the barnyard by the time Mr. Ed had the calves in the holding corral. Through the cracks in the hayloft walls Mary Lou watched as Mr. Ed and Murray lifted a wood contraption that looked a little like a huge crate off the truck bed. Mr. Ed and Murray, with a lot of yelling and pulling of ropes, finally enticed one of the young bulls to enter the crate.

Mary Lou, always a curious farm girl, was knowledgeable about the husbandry associated with raising animals. She helped the Missus chop the heads off of chickens and had seen pigs slaughtered at butchering time. Mary Lou was very aware of many aspects of animal behavior. She had watched the birth of a batch of kittens and had actually been swinging on the barn door when Bessie delivered Lily, the sweet new calf. She also understood the function of bulls. After all, she had kept a sharp eye out for the males of the bovine species since the time when, as a small child, she had wandered into the angry bull's pen.

Her previous exposure to animal husbandry did not prepare her for what transpired on this day. One by one, each calf was herded into the crate.

As the vet performed a quick operation, each calf gave a blood-curdling scream. After being released from the crate the poor animal would race through the barnyard and seek sanctuary in the nearby pasture.

Mary Lou closed her eyes and held her hands over her ears. The child thought she could not bear another minute of listening to the torture of the animals but did not dare leave her hiding place.

Finally, all the calves but one had endured the operation. This last male was a beautiful animal quite a lot larger than his brothers. Whenever Murray and Mr. Ed approached the animal he would paw the ground before shaking his stately head back and forth in an arrogant manner. Mr. Ed finally said, "Murray, this young bull doesn't want to become a steer. I guess he feels that he is destined for something better in life then ending up as steak at the table."

Mary Lou was able to sneak back into the house without either her mother or father knowing her whereabouts. She was quite subdued when she entered the kitchen. Instead of running over to the cot and jumping to test its springs she quietly crawled onto the cot, pulled up the covers and hid her head under a pillow.

The Missus came over and gently removed the pillow. She looked at her daughter with concern. "Mary Lou, you look pale." She felt her daughter's head then declared, "You must just be tired because you don't have a fever."

Mary Lou felt better as the day progressed. She thought she was fine until supper was served. When she saw the meat dish, she turned green, jumped up so quickly her chair was turned over then gagged as she rushed out the screen door. The special delicacy served was braised rocky mountain oysters!

SHADOWS OF WAR

The Missus went shopping on a Saturday fall evening in 1941. As usual, Mr. Ed sat in front of the hardware store visiting with several farmers and local merchants. As it had been for several years, the conversation quickly turned to Germany's invasion of European countries.

One of the men stated, "We should just stay on our continent and mind our own business."

Mr. Ed reasoned, "War is inevitable. For years Hitler has been aggressively destroying his neighboring countries. The question is not if we will go to war, but when. Uncle Sam will soon decide he can no longer sit on the sidelines and watch the devastation of countries like England, France and Poland."

Another man argued, "We stuck our heads in the last war and look what happened! Too many soldiers died and others had to live with injuries."

Mr. Ed was firm. "We are not living on an isolated island. As part of the world community, citizens in the USA need to quit ducking their heads. Let's stand up and accept our responsibilities to help the allies!"

Mr. Ed knew that all was not well on the Pacific side of the world. Nevertheless, like the rest of the citizens in United States, it was a complete surprise when, on December 7, 1941, Japan destroyed most of the navy ships based in Pearl Harbor.

Drastic changes happened almost overnight. Young men either enlisted or were drafted into the service. Uncle Dave decided to enlist in the army, and Danielle's husband quickly signed up for the Air Force. Mr. Ed was too old for the draft and, had he tried to enlist, probably would have received a 4F rating because of a bum knee. He reasoned to his wife, "The best war effort I can contribute is to put my tractor to good use and increase crop production."

Mr. Ed felt that, for once, fate was on his side. Demands of the war would determine that factories should now be producing airplanes, ships, tanks and jeeps. Had the war started a year earlier, it would have been impossible for him to purchase the needed new tractor. He smiled as he thought about the additional luck of having the old Ford stop dead in its tracks. The Chevrolet purchased that summer was in good condition and sporting four fine new tires.

He was surprised that the Missus continued to have frequent errands into town and always needed to go somewhere in the Chevrolet. He cautioned, "Honey, be careful about the amount of gas you siphon from the holding tank. That gas is supposed to be limited for tractor use." He thought a minute and made another suggestion to his wife, "We are lucky to have new tires on that car. Remember, they will have to last the duration of the war. Both of us should drive slowly and take it easy on the curves."

One of the first food items to become scarce on the grocery shelves was white sugar. The Missus thought about the amount allotted by rationing and warned her husband, "Ed, you can forget about chocolate cakes." She then turned to the girls. "The two you won't be finding anything in the cookie jar. I will need all of our sugar allotment for preserving fruit."

Luckily their neighbors, the Hatchels, had placed several bee hives near their orchard. The bees were producing more than enough honey for their family's personal use. Dora Hatchel was allergic to chicken feathers and always had sneezing fits when going into the henhouse. Only the year before, she had decided the poultry had to go. The flock slowly dwindled as Doris served delicious chicken meals to her family.

When the Missus mentioned the lack of sugar for sweetening, Dora said, "Since we don't have chickens any more, I'll be most happy to swap honey for eggs."

The children were not too disappointed that cakes and cookies were no longer part of their daily menu. They were perfectly content eating biscuits smothered in butter and dripping with honey.

The Missus noticed that a barrel in the grocery store was filled with cheap unrefined brown sugar that required no rationing stamps so quickly purchased several pounds. Mr. Ed rubbed his stomach after eating several slices of fresh baked whole wheat bread covered with melted butter and brown sugar. He said, "We should feel guilty eating delicious food like this when many people around the world are starving!"

When butter became scarce in towns and cities, the substitute was a new product called margarine. Margarine came as a colorless substance the consistency of lard. Enclosed within each package of margarine was a small bubble filled with orange liquid. Even though there was ample butter on the farm, the girls begged their mother to purchase margarine. It was great fun to squeeze the liquid from the bubble into the white mixture then stir until the substance turned golden.

The Missus carefully checked the rationing books. She started to chuckle when noticing that the allotment for shoes for each person was limited to two new pairs per year. Neither she nor Mr. Ed had purchased a new pair of shoes in years! Mr. Ed owned only his rubber boots for rainy days, heavy work boots, brown shoes for church and slippers that the Missus insisted he wear when inside the house.

His work boots were getting old, and the local cobbler had replaced the soles several times. Even though the leather was holding up, the shoestrings were so rotten they finally crumbled into unusable short pieces. No shoestrings were available in stores. Mr. Ed was forced to use lengths of bailing twine. The substitute was not very successful. It was difficult to lace the twine through the eyelets and untying knots was almost impossible.

Mr. Ed spent a rainy day cleaning up the tool shed. He just happened to notice an old set of reins dangling from a hook on the wall. These had once been used to guide Anamule as she worked in the fields. Using a sharp knife, he carefully cut narrow leather strips from the reins then laced them through the eyelets of his boots.

The Missus also had a limited supply of foot wear. After heavy rains, she slipped her feet into knee high rubber boots before venturing into the muddy vegetable garden. When the soil was dry, as an accompaniment to her scarecrow uniform, she wore an ugly pair of work boots. Day in and day out, whether in her house, at Ladies Aid, shopping or going to church, she wore a sturdy pair of black slippers. Oh yes, tucked in a box at the back of the closet and rarely worn, was the pair of white high heeled shoes she purchased years ago as an accessory to a special Easter dress. She rarely wore these even in the summer because they hurt her toes. The only other covering for her feet were crocheted footies. These she wore in the evenings before going to bed.

She frowned when thinking of the rapidly growing feet of her children. Jane, who was already taller and bigger than her sister, complained that shoes purchased only a couple of months ago were pinching her toes. It made sense to purchase new shoes for Jane and have Mary Lou put her small feet into Jane's old shoes. The Missus looked over at the cot and chuckled, "You better be ready for a beating. Mary Lou is going to be furious when we tell her she has to wear her younger sister's old shoes. She'll probably take her anger out by kicking your sides."

When planning for one of the regular monthly family Sunday get-togethers, the Missus and her siblings discussed the problem caused by the rapidly growing feet of their children. They decided to pool all of the shoes sitting in closets or presently worn by children. If children wore hand-me-downs, the only necessary shoe purchases would be for those having the biggest feet.

The following Sunday all the children removed the shoes they were wearing and tried to find another pair which provided a comfortable fit. Dannydon't was mortified to realize that the only pair of shoes fitting his feet was a pair of black Mary Jane slippers belonging to a cousin. He complained even more than his older sister had when she was told to wear her younger sister's shoes. He shouted, "I won't wear girl shoes! I would rather go barefoot all year!" He sighed with relief when he realized the family was just teasing him. He would get new shoes if necessary, or could wear hand-me-downs supplied by one of the older boys in the neighborhood.

ASSISTANCE ON THE HOME FRONT

The fall, following the Japanese attack on Pearl Harbor, the girls arrived home from school with exciting news. A soldier visiting their school had explained how children could help in the war effort.

Jane, in her careful third grade handwriting, had listed ways he suggested children could contribute to the war effort. She took a deep breath and started reading the list to her parents. "Number 1: Save paper." She explained, "Instead of wadding paper in a ball and throwing it in the wastebasket, kids should carefully place it in a box. The recycled paper can be used to stuff boxes packed with guns and other weapons as they are shipped from factories to war zones."

Mary Lou looked at her dad. "You get a newspaper every day. I know you use lots of the old newspapers in the garden to keep down the weeds, but could we have the others to put in the school paper box?"

Jane continued to read her list. "Number 2: Buy war stamps."

Again, her sister had additional ideas of how to contribute. "Mama, you give us only a weekly allowance of a nickel. If you gave us more money, we could buy war stamps."

The Missus looked at her daughters and had an alternate suggestion. "No, I will not increase your allowance. What I will do is list jobs and the earnings to be received by completing each task. For example, churning butter would be worth two cents. Dusting the parlor furniture to my satisfaction would be worth a penny. Are you girls willing to work to earn money for war stamps?"

The girls looked at their mother and nodded their heads. They realized she always was one step ahead of them and there was no use arguing.

Jane smiled as she read the next item on her list: "Number 3: Collect milkweed pods."

Mary Lou shook her head in wonder. "After the milkweeds open I love to blow on the plant and watch the feathered seeds float in the wind. I won't do that again. Did you know they are used to stuff the lining of jackets? I guess they help keep pilots warm."

Jane had a frown on her face as she read. "I don't understand Number 4 on the list. It says we should help supply white cloth."

She looked at her mother and questioned, "I know the quilting ladies have used all the extra sheets for bandages. What can we kids do?"

As always, the Missus had an answer. "Girls, for years you have been playing pretend upstairs in the west bedroom. Do you remember that there are petticoats belonging to your great-grandmother stored in the dresser? Tell me, why did she have so many petticoats?"

Jane remembered the story Uncle Jack told. "She always wore an extra petticoat and would cut strips from it to use as bandages if someone was hurt."

The Missus nodded her head and asked, "Don't you think your great-grandmother would be pleased if her descendants continued to use her petticoats to help someone in need?"

Jane read the final recommendation on her list. "Number 5: Collect scrap metal." She thoughtfully added, "Mary Lou and I found several pieces of an old car on our way home from school. That can be the start of our scrap metal stockpile."

Mary Lou, even though she had not bothered to take notes while the soldier was talking, continued to add her two cents worth of information. "Guess what, each elementary school in the county will compete in a scrap metal drive. The school that collects the most junk metal will be rewarded with a trip to the zoo in Kansas City."

The Missus smiled at her children then spoke with determination to her husband. "Ed, this is your great opportunity to help your children contribute to the war effort. This family has never thrown a thing away. Our old Ford is still sitting in the barnyard and those pieces of farm equipment used years ago when Anamule and horses were the power sources are rusting out in the west pasture. We must have enough scrap metal around here to build a tank!"

It was almost time for the Missus to enter another one of her leaning up spells of the entire house. She looked around the room and said, "Speaking of scrap metal, I see a piece of furniture made out of cast iron which would be a worthy contribution to the scrap pile."

Mr. Ed saw her eyes glancing to the corner of the kitchen. He replied sharply, "Don't you even think of getting rid of that old cot! He's part of our family!"

On the surface it seemed that many daily events remained the same during the war years. The Ladies Aid still held regular Wednesday quilting sessions in the parlor. Children still played under the quilt, but now, instead of Mary Lou and Jane, it was Danielle's two little girls playing with dolls.

Lunch had been served and dishes washed, dried and put into cabinets. The ladies quilted as Danielle read from the Bible. As she read the familiar story of Ruth's devotion to the land of her husband, her voice, usually clear and melodic, choked. Finally, she stopped reading and sat quietly with tears streaming down her face.

Eunice quickly moved from her chair in the quilting circle to go to the side of her precious daughter-in-law. She put her arms around Danielle's shaking shoulders and said, "Dearest, please don't worry. You'll hear from him soon."

Eunice quietly explained the problem to their quilting friends. "Do you all remember when Charlie, as a teenager, learned the art of barnstorming? When the war started, he was the first in this area to enlist." Her voice shook as she continued. "Charlie kissed Danielle and the two little girls good-by and explained, *"Honey, pilots are desperately needed in this war. I have to fight for my country."* He then looked over at us and said, *"Mom and Dad, take good care of my precious girls while I am away."* The mother-in-law's grip on Danielle's shoulders tightened as tears also streamed from her eyes.

She continued in a choked voice, "Charlie wrote to Danielle almost every day. Even though he couldn't tell her exactly where he was stationed, we all knew it was somewhere in England. It has been obvious that he is constantly going on bombing missions over Germany. Danielle hasn't heard from him for over six weeks. We hold our breath when the mail arrives each day and will be so relieved to get a letter and know he is not missing in action or something worse."

Each of the ladies stopped quilting and seemed lost in their own thoughts. The war had affected all of them more than expected. Almost all had a family member fighting the war. The Missus whispered to herself, "That old goat, my brother Dave. Why did he have to enlist when he is already in his mid-thirties?" Her thoughts brightened a little with the thought that, since he was older than most soldiers, he had been assigned office work instead of being placed in the midst of battle.

Dora thought of her son Roy. He had physical and mental limitations, so was not qualified to enter the armed serves. Nevertheless, he was on the front lines, first in Africa then in Italy, for the duration of the war. He had been hired as the photographer to work with a famous war correspondent. Dora frequently recognized his pictures in the paper and knew he was in constant danger. She whispered, "My son has faced so many problems with a positive attitude. He wouldn't want me to worry now."

Flossie was sitting next to the Missus. Her new husband, like Charlie, had been one of the first young men in the area to enlist. Thus far, he was stateside, but he would probably be sent to Europe soon. For once, Flossie was not talking or joking but sat quietly with tears running down her cheeks.

At the start of the war, Rose was thankful that her children were girls so they would not have to serve. She was wrong. Her oldest daughter and her husband, both with medical backgrounds, were now stationed at a military hospital in San Diego. The twins, who were crackerjack secretaries, were snatched from the insurance companies and hired as girl Fridays for generals. Thanks to her friend, Pauline, her youngest daughter was talked into joining her in working in an ammunition plant near Ottawa.

Flossie was the first to speak. "Instead of crying we should be doing something to help in the war effort."

Dora Hatchel agreed. "Tearing up old sheets and making bandages isn't enough. Does anyone have any other ideas?"

The Missus thought about the messy pile of fabric stashed in the upstairs bedrooms. "For years we've been collecting fabric for quilts. The shelves Ed built for us have long ago been filled and stacks of fabric are piled up around the room. We've quit using feed sack material, but we still have a lot of it on hand. Several pieces of drab fabric we ignored when making quilts for the church bazaar have not been tossed away. Could we use these unused and unwanted pieces to make quilts for soldiers?"

Rose chuckled, "If other men are colorblind and unconscious of patterns like my husband, we won't need to worry about matching fabrics as we make quilts."

Eunice added her two cents. "I'm almost certain soldiers are allotted heavy olive-green covers. If soldiers can't use our quilts, they could be supplied to people in Europe who have lost their homes and belongings. The newspaper says many people are freezing as well as starving."

Rose immediately started organizing. "Let's go upstairs and look at the material on the shelves. Each one of you should select several pieces of fabric to take home. Cut out six-inch squares and sew the pieces together. Remember, a double layer of batting is needed because these quilts may be the only source of warmth for users. At our meeting next Wednesday, we'll finish the quilts by tying yarn in the center of each square.

Annabelle thought a second and questioned. "We've always made standard or queen-sized quilts using the frame as a guide. How will we know the quilt size needed to fit a twin bed?"

Flossie grinned, "No problem! We can take the measurements of the old cot sitting in the kitchen." She added, "You know that cot has an ego because it gets so much positive attention. In addition to taking note of its proportions, we can use it as the form when inspecting completed quilts. Showing off will provide the poor structure an immense pleasure."

A Second Garden

Farmers always planned ahead when selecting the crops to be planted in the spring. As Mr. Ed rested on the cot in late February, he had an inspiration about an improvement he wanted to make. He stated to his wife, "Honey, we could use more garden space."

The Missus looked at her husband like he had lost his mind. "Why do we need a bigger garden? Half of what we grow is given away!"

"Honey, listen to my idea. Now that we have an electric fence that keeps the cows from wandering, I could section off a part of the south pasture and use it to grow vegetables. An ideal space would be down by the creek." He added a further comment in an effort to change her mind. "If we used that area for the veggies requiring a lot of space, then you could plant more of your posies in the garden by the house."

The Missus was looking through the new seed catalog as Mr. Ed was talking. She had already picked out several flower seed packets and a few vegetables not readily available at the local hardware store. She just happened to notice an advertisement describing, "Aunt Sadie's Miracle Plants." Perhaps this would be an ideal year to experiment with new produce.

Mr. Ed made a wise decision. The soil in the new garden was particularly rich in organic matter because, in former years, it had served as the loitering ground where the cows waited patiently for winter feedings of hay.

The garden was located only a short distance from the stream. Mr. Ed easily rigged up an irrigation system to use during the dry season.

The perfect setting for the garden, plus the added ingredients of sun and moisture, encouraged more than vegetable seedlings to grow. Weeds sprang up and threatened to take over the garden. Mr. Ed needed the assistance of his family to fight the weeds. The Missus tried to do her part but could only occasionally help at the end of the day when sunlight had dimmed. The girls had not inherited the work ethic of their parents and found every excuse possible to avoid the garden. Jane remembered that she needed to practice a lesson on her new violin, and Mary Lou wouldn't go near the area after a tiny green snake slithered over her toe.

On a clear July evening, only young Dannydon't seemed more than willing to help his dad. While yanking at the stubborn weeds, he caught several critters and placed them in the tobacco tin can kept in the back pocket of his overalls. The bugs would make great bait! He reached the last row needing weeding and was pleased that the task was finished so quickly. He took note of the long shadows and joyfully realized there would be few treasured minutes available for what he liked to do best. He said, "Daddy, we are almost finished weeding the garden. I think we need to spend a few minutes trying to catch Old Fighter."

Taking a few minutes to relax by the pond was a special time for father and son. Dannydon't was happy that the fish immediately nibbled on his bait. As for Mr. Ed, at this moment he was feeling mighty pleased because of many reasons. He commented, "Son, stop staring at the bobber and look at our beautiful world! The corn in yonder field will get as high as an elephant's eye, the wheat fields are ready for harvesting and should reap abundantly, the pastures are lush, and those steers are getting fat."

He looked up to the sky and savored the scene of the setting sun's rays touching the clouds and creating a sky filled with gold, red and purple hues. As he gazed upward, he prayed, "Thank you, Lord, for this beautiful world you have provided. We give thanks that this horrible war will soon be over and appreciate how you looked after our friends like Roy and Charlie."

He thought of the richness of his life and added, "I want to thank you especially for this young son standing by me and his mama and sisters who are preparing supper for us up at the house."

The summer progressed from a mild June into the long hot days of July and August. As time rolled on, the family was amazed at the produce available from the lower garden. The regular vegetables performed far beyond expectations. The sweet corn was over six feet tall and had perfect ears. Okra plants were always full of blossoms and produced pods needing to be picked daily. The tomato vines were so sprawling that Mr. Ed had to erect a fence to hold their weight. Mr. Ed bought new scales. Dannydon't thought it was to weigh his fish, but Mr. Ed's reason was to verify the total ounces of his large red tomatoes. Ones weighing a pound became the rule rather than the exception.

Aunt Sadie's Miracle Plants fulfilled their promise and produced abundant plants. More than a bushel of zucchini and summer squash were picked each day. The family was even more astonished by the growing results of the cantaloupe seeds. The healthy vines gradually invaded over half of the garden space. As the abundant fruits turned from green to orange, they grew to be as large as watermelons.

The Missus was also quite pleased with the odd variety of shapes of Aunt Sadie's gourds. After being picked, the gourds were stacked by the shed until completely dried. The Missus instructed Mr. Ed to drill an opening approximately the size of a silver dollar in the side of each gourd. The Missus, with more than willing help from her girls, painted a lovely floral design on each gourd. The Missus decided to offer most of the bird houses as contributions for the church bazaar. People would hang them from tree limbs or garden fences. The wren or sparrow parents would consider them perfect homes to raise their young.

The bountiful harvest had drawbacks. The Missus finally declared, "I simply will not spend another day in this hot kitchen pickling okra or canning the squash and tomatoes!" She added, "Besides that, the few remaining canning jars will be needed for applesauce. At least our children will eat the applesauce! That isn't true of the food picked from the lower garden. Mary

Lou turns up her nose at the okra, Jane refuses to eat the squash, and our son thinks that tomatoes are poison."

Mr. Ed had always been more than willing to share the harvest from his gardens. In addition to pleasure, he derived from helping others, he treasured the minutes of conversation with receivers of his garden crop. It was soon noticeable that the cousins were rarely visiting the farm. They simply did not want more zucchini tossed in the back seat of their Fords! Mr. Ed took some of the extra produce into town and waited patiently for someone to walk past the truck. However, Ed.'s friends waved at him from across the street then hurried away. Mr. Ed sighed, "It's almost like I have a contagious disease!"

Chapter 13

THE COUNTY FAIR

The summer responsibilities of caring for livestock and raising crops seemed unrelenting and totally time consuming. The farm families looked forward to late August when most of the harvesting was completed. To celebrate the end of the season, Ed's family would attend the county fair held in Springdale.

The Observant Cot

LEARNING TO SEW

"Mary Lou, please pay attention to what you are doing! Just look at your stitches! Unless that finished apron is better than this, it will not qualify for your 4-H sewing project. You most certainly should not display it at the county fair!"

The Missus looked closely at her daughter. "Where in the world are your glasses? You should know by now that those glasses are to be worn constantly! No wonder you are sewing poorly. It's obvious you can't see what you are doing!" The Missus, always a perfectionist in her work, sometimes became frustrated with her older daughter's lack of interest in domestic activities.

"Mama, I don't like sewing tiny stitches on this ugly apron! It just doesn't seem fair. Girls have to stay in the house doing cleaning, sewing and cooking while the boys are outside having lots of fun."

Mary Lou was perceptive about how gender influenced the roles of children living on farms. Young boys, even while still toddlers, tagged after their dads. They played at the side of the field while Dad cultivated and harvested crops and were present when men sat on the fence by the barn and swapped colorful stories. Boys, by the time they were Mary Lou's age, were helping with the milking, feeding animals and sometimes, if their legs were long enough, driving the tractor while dads and hired hands tossed the hay onto a wagon.

Mary Lou speculated how her restricting situation could be improved. "If only Dad would give me the responsibility of raising a calf! I would see that the beast had the best of care. Maybe he would even win a purple ribbon as the best specimen submitted as a 4-H project."

Mary Lou stopped daydreaming and turned her mind back to the sewing project. She reasoned, the apron shouldn't be difficult to complete, and it would please her mother if she at least tried making decent stitches. Alas, the apron was not the least attractive. The pocket was basted at a crooked angle on the right side and the hemline was jagged. At least the side seams sewn with the sewing machine were acceptable.

Mary Lou and her sister were both competent when using the machine. They had learned to sew using the ancient treadle machine when they were only seven and nine years old. Mary Lou was amused to think of how they had to improvise manipulating the machine because their legs had been simply too short to reach the treadle. When one of them was sewing, the other girl had sat on the floor and pushed the treadle back and forth. The girls had been successful practicing sewing skills using fabric scraps not set aside for quilts. In no time at all, they had been creating shabby dresses for Jane's doll family.

Soon after the house was wired for electricity, Mr. Ed presented the women of his family with a special Christmas gift, an electric White Sewing Machine. It was the fancy kind with attachments for flocking and sewing zippers. Mary Lou and her sister loved the machine and thought it would not be long before they would be creating gowns fit for queens. They did progress from making simple doll clothes to creating broomstick and wrap-around skirts.

The novelty of the electric sewing machine soon wore off for Mary Jane. Why should she be fiddling with material when the outdoors was waiting? In contrast, Jane continued to have a great appreciation of her daddy's gift and was intent on becoming a skilled seamstress. She made shirts for her dad and brother and a blouse with long sleeves for her mother. Jane didn't forget the old cot. She took his measurements and made him a new denim cover.

4-H Club Meeting

Mary Lou had dawdled away most of the afternoon by reading, playing the piano, and taking a nap. When it was time to start chores, she hid the apron in the bottom drawer of the oak chest. She immediately forgot about the apron, and since it wasn't visible, her busy mother failed to nag her about working on the sewing task. The apron would miss the deadline of being completed for the next meeting of the Bentley 4-H Club.

The following Thursday Oliver and Jimmy were bouncing a ball by the gate as the Missus drove the girls into the Mitchell farmyard. Jane nodded to her friends, while willingly helping her mother carry cooking supplies into the house. Mary Lou was not eager to go inside the house to face the bitter music about the unfinished apron. She stalled off the inevitable by joining in the ball game with two boys.

The boys were well aware of Mary Lou's distaste for housework and her desire to be outside. Jimmy taunted, "Mary Lou, it's too bad you have to go inside to learn how to cook and sew. At the last meeting we boys learned all about machinery. Some of us even got to drive the tractor."

He added, "Yeah, Mary Lou. You could have helped us as we greased the wheels on the cultivator and wagon. You must be pretty good with the grease can. I've noticed that in school last year several of your skirts were covered with grease blotches."

Oliver snickered, "Mary Lou, we heard that you want to raise a calf. I shouldn't tell you this, but today we boys are going to have animal husbandry lessons. The extension agent thinks we're old enough to learn the bull and heifer version of the bird's and bee's story. He says we have to know all about the characteristics of mama and papa cows before we pick out a calf to rear as our 4-H project for next year. If we are to be successful farmers in the future, we need to understand all about livestock breeding."

Mary Lou stuck out her tongue at her adversaries and ran inside. She was embarrassed and angry. She would have to learn to not disclose so many thoughts to her sister. Jane and Oliver were in the same grade at school and had been close friends since first grade. It was obvious Jane had told Oliver about her oh so-secret desire to raise a calf.

Miss McGraw, the home demonstration agent, stood at the door greeting each girl. Most of the girls had brought one of their sewing projects and held it up to hear her praise. Miss McGraw noticed that Mary Lou entered the room empty handed. She hugged Mary Lou then asked, "Honey, I bet you're still working on your apron and dishtowels. Are they almost finished?" For once the child had no answer.

Miss McGraw was young and pretty. She was just a little quirky and knew how to make the meeting fun. She directed, "Girls, you know the procedure. Put a book on your head and walk around the room until I say to take a seat. Try to keep the book on your head for the remainder of the meeting. Each time a book falls, a mark will be put by your name on this chart. At the end of this session the girl with the least points will receive a prize."

When the girls had taken a seat, the home demonstration agent continued, "Girls, look how you are sitting in your chairs! Some of you are slumping. It's ladylike to sit with your backbone next to the back of the chairs and your head held high. Jackie and Helen, your legs are crossed. Remember what we talked about last week? When you cross your legs there is a tendency for the hemlines of your skirts to pull up over your knees. That is unacceptable!"

The leader felt that these young girls needed to learn about manners as well as cooking and sewing. She smiled at her charges and said, "Now, before we start our other lessons, let's review what we learned about greeting others." For the next few minutes, the girls practiced how to make eye contact, the proper ways to shake hands and how to introduce adults to adults, children to children, and adults to children. They also engaged in small talk about the weather or a function happening at church.

Mary Lou performed much better on social lessons than when trying to improve her homemaking arts. She was often at her father's side at church or community socials. Now, at this session, she mimicked his behavior of never meeting a stranger and seeking to make all feel welcome. This friendly manner was an exception to the behavior of most children living on isolated farms. It was not unusual for younger children to hide behind their mother's skirt and older ones to disappear when someone came to the door.

"Okay, girls," said Miss McGraw, "it's time to share what you've learned while completing your 4-H sewing projects. Ginger, tell us where you feel you have made improvements."

It was apparent that the book on her head was going nowhere because Ginger sat straight and tall in her chair. Ginger, who had just turned thirteen, was an excellent seamstress. She quickly responded, "It has been so much fun to use the attachments on our new sewing machine." She held up a skirt and continued, "Look, I learned how to use the zipper foot. See how smoothly the material folds over the zipper?"

Miss McGraw turned to a quiet child sitting next to Ginger. "Nancy, what have you accomplished? Have you learned some sewing techniques that have been helpful?"

Nancy was from a poor family and had several brothers. She responded, "The boys are always ripping their pants. I can now help mom patch them. It is also good that I've learned to darn socks over an apple. My little brother, Alex, has holes in the toes of all his socks."

"Jane, I know you like to sew. Is there any sewing where you feel improvement has been made?" Miss McGraw thought to herself, "If all the girls were talented like Jane my job would be easy."

Jane beamed, "My mom makes beautiful quilts. Someday I want to make quilts for my home like she does. This year I learned how to cut out and attach fabric squares. I don't play with dolls anymore, but I am making a quilt for the small bed holding antique dolls."

Miss McGraw gaze fell on the child sitting next to Jane. She noticed that Mary Lou did not eagerly raise her hand indicating she wanted to share information about her projects. When she ducked her head in an effort to avoid Miss McGraw's eyes, the book perched there tumbled to the floor. The instructor ignored the reluctance of response and stated, "Mary Lou, I know that sewing isn't your favorite pastime, but surely there is something that you enjoyed making."

Mary Lou thought a minute and responded, "Well, I've been embroidering designs on dishtowels. Mom says the handiwork isn't too bad, and she might put them on the dish rack rather than using them for rags."

When the sewing review was completed, Miss McGraw led the girls into the kitchen and asked them to stand around the large table. "Girls, most of you have been helping your mothers for several years and know how to cook. In our 4-H lessons I've tried to teach you the vocabulary found in cookbooks. The recipes don't say two or three handfuls of flour, a tad of butter, and a pinch of salt like your mothers tend to do. You will need to use measurements like one cup, a quart of milk or a tablespoon of sugar."

Miss McGraw continued, "I've also been teaching you about special cooking tricks. At the last meeting you learned how to whip cream to the right consistency and you now understand that, if liquids are slowly added to a mixture of dry ingredients, lumps will not form. We are ready to learn a new trick. I want each of you to scoop into the flour bin and fill your cup with flour."

There was a little too much enthusiasm. The girls giggled as puffs of flour scattered on their faces, arms and aprons. Miss McGraw let them have fun but then instructed, "Do you see how most of your cups are overflowing?

Please take the side of a knife and carefully level the flour to the rim of your cup. Remember, adding too much flour will destroy the consistency of your cakes."

The time came for the final cooking lesson of the day. She asked, "Ginger, please read the cake recipe for us. How much shortening is to be added?"

Ginger responded, "It says to add one-half cup."

"Girls, like the flour, your cake should have exactly the amount of shortening called for in the recipe. Don't use more or less. Here's how you can be certain of the amount." She proceeded to show them how to fill a measuring cup half full with water then add the shortening until it reached the one cup mark.

When the lessons were completed, Miss McGraw called to the boys and men standing outside, "It's time to wash up and come in for a treat. Hurry boys! Today we are eating the cookies your mothers brought instead of cooking creations made by the girls."

After snacks everyone went out to the large open porch. The fathers had left their fields early to join their wives and children. The musicians pulled out an accordion, guitar, and fiddle and Fred started blowing into his harmonica. As the musicians picked up their instruments Big Jim directed, "Boys, don't be shy. Choose a girl to be your partner." When one or two children stalled, he suggested, "Everybody needs to be dancing, so you might need to select your mom or dad as your partner."

Big Jim continued, "We are starting out with a simple folk dance. Boys, you stand on the inside of our circle. Girls, take the hand of your partner." He watched with amusement as the pushing, shoving and unkind faces made it clear that a brother and sister were not happy as partners.

He intervened by saying, "Junior, that's no way to treat a lady. Your sister won't even be your partner after the first verse of our song. Now, ladies and gentlemen, sing along and follow the directions." As soon as the dancers heard the first notes of, "Jolly is the Miller Boy," they started skipping in a circle.

The fiddler picked up his bow and strummed the introduction to "Turkey in the Straw." Big Jim directed, "Boys, find a new partner. Form a long line facing your partner. We're going to have a great time dancing the Virginia reel." It wasn't long before Big Jim was suggesting they make up squares of four couples each. For the remainder of the evening dancers would do-see-doe, bow to their neighbors, and promenade with their partners around the dance floor.

ATTENDING THE FAIR

Each girl belonging to a 4-H club was assigned several sewing projects. The item considered her best work would be judged for excellence at the fair.

It was only two days before the fair and Mary Lou had nothing ready to exhibit. She had completed a nice neat broomstick skirt but had worn it several times. To her dismay, as she was sliding down a tree the hem caught on a branch! The skirt was ripped halfway up the front and couldn't even be worn to school in the fall. Only the embroidered scenes of Sunday and Tuesday had been finished on the "Days of the Week" dishtowels. The potholders were completed but the weave was too loose. Her mother shook her head when inspecting them. She scolded, "Mary Lou, anyone using those potholders will get severe burns on their hands!" Then there was that hideous apron. It had remained hidden in the bottom of the chest.

Mary Lou curled up in the corner of the cot and pondered a way to solve the problem of having no sewing projects for display at the fair. She had almost decided the best solution was to accept the disappointment of her mother and Miss McGraw when Jane entered the kitchen carrying her completed apron. Jane held the apron up for her mother's inspection and beamed when she heard, "Honey, your apron is beautiful! I am so proud of your work. Your hand stitches are almost perfect!"

Mary Lou's eyes lit up and she grinned from ear to ear. She now knew an ideal way to solve her apron problem.

After the Missus went into the parlor, Mary Lou hurried over to her sister to share special information. "Guess what! I know where Mistress Matilda hid her new kittens."

Jane felt her heart warm. There was nothing nicer than to watch and hold the tiny creatures. "Oh, that's wonderful. Let's go see them right now!"

Mary Lou scratched her cheek and pretended she had just thought of an idea. "Jane, I will show you the kittens but you have to promise to do something for me."

Jane was overjoyed to see that Mistress Matilda had four new babies hiding in the old tire stored in the tool shed. Two were beige with black markings. One was totally black and one was a soft bluish gray. Jane tenderly made a new home for the tiny animals by lining a discarded cardboard box with scraps of cloth. Since Mistress Matilda was very fond of Jane, she didn't seem to mind as the child tenderly held each new baby close to her cheek before gently placing it in the box.

Mary Lou grew impatient with the loving absorption her sister had with the kittens. "Okay. You've seen the babies. Now let's go back to the house so you can fulfill your part of the bargain."

The next day Mary Lou's apron was completed with pockets perfectly balanced with each other, and an even hemline decorated with red rickrack. The Missus was pleased to note the perfection now obvious in her oldest daughter's sewing. Neither sister ever shared how Mary Lou's stitching seemed to improve overnight.

On the morning of the fair, Mr. Ed had the cows fed and milked by the early hour of six. He came into the house and kissed his wife goodbye, saying to the girls, "I've loaded the truck with one of the largest of the piglets and have two of our best Angus calves. I also collected samples of my wheat, oats and corn and will place them in the grain exhibit hall. You can come later in the car with your mother, but your brother will be going with me in the truck."

Mr. Ed and Dannydon't spent several hours getting the animals into the pens provided on the fair grounds. They also saw to it that the pig and two calves were properly fed and groomed. When work was finally done Mr. Ed hoisted Dannydon't onto his shoulders and said, "Son, let's have a good look around the fairgrounds." They admired the handsome animals and were impressed with the variety of grains on display. Mr. Ed appreciated even more the opportunity to say "howdy" when meeting friends. What a wonderful opportunity to enjoy a few minutes talking with others about the weather and yield of this year's crops.

The Missus and girls entered the homemaking exhibit tent at mid-morning. The Missus proudly lined up some of her prettiest canning jars on a long table that other farm wives had already laden with preserved fruits and vegetables. She was more than pleased with the praise she received over her jars of spiced peaches and sweet pickles.

The girls carried a large bundle as they trailed behind their mother over to the area where quilts were displayed. They set down the bundle and retrieved from it a beautiful quilt, which they placed over a rack. It took more than a year to complete the quilt. During the long evenings in winter, the Missus had cut out and pieced butterfly shapes using scraps of fabric left over from dresses made for the girls. The butterfly shapes were attached to white squares then all sewn to a bright yellow background.

Mary Lou gazed at the butterflies and exclaimed, "Mom, looking at this quilt is so much fun! I can remember the dress made out of this material." She pointed to the square displaying a bright red butterfly. "This red doggie dress you made for me when I was only five was always my favorite!" She sighed when glancing at the butterfly square created with a green plaid scrap. "Do you remember that I ruined this jumper the first day I wore it by sitting in a pool of black oil? You made me wear it to school all year even though the other kids teased me."

Jane hugged her mom as she commented, "It's so easy to identify how you selected fabrics for our dresses. Mine are made with pastel blue, pink and lavender and often the fabric has a floral pattern. You always dress Mary Lou in bright colors like red, green or orange and the design on the material is plaids, stripes or animals."

The Missus' quilting friends had also been impressed with the butterfly quilt. They agreed with Dora Hatchel when she suggested, "Before we start working on our quilt for the church bazaar, let's finish this one. It should be exhibited at the county fair in August." Not one of the ladies was the least bit surprised to notice how every person visiting the homemaking tent stopped to admire the beautiful creation made by the Missus. They also shared in their friend's pleasure as the judges presented her with the coveted purple ribbon.

In the 4-H tent girls were taking turns demonstrating their expertise in cooking in front of a panel of judges. Mary Lou and her cousin Ginger had decided to share how to mix their family's favorite chocolate cake recipe. The judges were impressed with the baked sample of the cake brought from home. The Missus had assisted the girls in making it so it was both attractive and tasty. Ginger and Mary Lou might have won more than a white ribbon if Mary Lou had been a bit more careful. The judges were not impressed when she cracked an egg on the rim of a bowl and eggshells landed in the mix. Several points were also lost when she licked the mixing spoon!

Mary Lou was not too disappointed. She had more important things on her mind than unimpressive showing about housework. Now that her duties were completed, she could hurry to the Midway. She ignored the stands and easy rides for little kids and rushed over to the side of the Ferris wheel. She stood by the massive piece of equipment and pondered how she could get a ride. She just had to have the thrill of getting strapped into a seat then slowly moving up into the sky. From the top, she would be able to observe all the main events occurring at the fairgrounds and would have an excellent view of the town. It might even be possible to get a glimpse of the ribbon of the gravel road leading toward her home.

Mary Lou had a problem. The few pennies she had saved for the fair had been spent on hot dogs and ice cream. While she tried to figure out how to get a ride, she recalled a story Uncle Dave shared about when he took his sister to dances. Mary Lou decided that what worked for mama might work for mama's daughter.

Ginger walked by with two other girls she questioned, "Mary Lou, do you want to join us as we stroll down the Midway?" Mary Lou waved them on their way and continued to remain standing where she was.

At the end of the day, she announced to her mother. "I remembered the story Uncle Dave's story about you being the belle of the ballroom. I decided the plan might work for me. I stood all afternoon by myself next to the Ferris wheel."

The Missus looked confused so Mary Lou explained further. "I was alone a few minutes before Harvey Pembroke ambled by. Even though he has a pimple on his nose and ears that stick out like wings, I liked the sound of money jingling in his pocket. Harvey asked me to ride with him two times. A little while later Oliver and Jimmy noticed I was standing there alone gazing up at the top seats. When I admitted to having no money, they offered to pay for my ticket."

Mary Lou knew her mother was not happy, "Mama, I know how you feel about me talking to strangers. Don't worry. The only boys who invited me to ride belong to our 4-H Club. It was so much fun! I got to touch the sky eight times!"

Chapter 14

THE COT'S NEW FRIEND

In an earlier chapter I described the cozy kitchen where I spent so many years. I explained how the table, buffet, cabinets, icebox, sink and stove performed specific duties. The room gradually changed as electric appliances and gadgets were added. One new addition was a replacement for a cumbersome battery-operated radio which offered more static than voices and music. He became my constant companion in the kitchen. I am proud to now introduce you to my buddy, Mr. Jabberbox.

A Friend, the Cot

CONSTANT NOISE

few weeks after the house was wired for electricity a new radio was placed on the side table near the cot's pillows. This gadget was boxlike with a knob on the front which controlled both on and off and volume. It was not attractive but fulfilled its duty of providing constant entertainment.

Each time one of the family members entered the silent kitchen, the radio knob was turned on. When they went about their duties outside the kitchen, they neglected to turn the knob off. The only time the radio was quiet was late at night or when all the family was gone for the day. Because the cot did not have the option of leaving the room, it heard every sound the radio emitted. No wonder he, an inanimate object, was nearly as knowledgeable about world affairs as Mr. Ed.

Mr. Jabberbox was the supplier of information not immediately available from the weekly newspaper or gossip with neighbors. The sounds coming from the box amused its listeners, informed them about the weather and world events and alerted the Missus about new products appearing on the market.

Mr. Ed always turned on the radio when he returned to the house after the morning milking. As the Missus prepared his breakfast, Mr. Ed listened to a singsong voice telling him about the weather throughout Kansas and Missouri. The weather report was followed by another twanging voice informing listeners about the price of cattle and hogs at the stock market in Kansas City. The same voice also supplied details about the expected yield of grains and predicted the rise or fall of their market prices. Mr. Ed claimed he needed this information to become a better farmer. The cot questioned how much it helped his master improve his farming expertise, because Mr. Ed was always snoring when the reports were given.

Mr. Ed was concerned about the war. He listened closely to Mr. Jabberbox when Edward R. Morrow and other commentators described the battles fought in Europe and Asia. Mr. Ed placed a world atlas on the side table. As he listened to descriptions of the battles fought, he located and marked their sites on the map.

Mr. Ed, always kind and gentle, grieved over the soldiers killed in battle. He was angered by the horrors faced by Jews and prayed for all the innocent people who just happened to be in the way of battling troops. Mr. Ed would sigh, "This war makes no dammed sense. Both the Germans and Japanese could gain much more by negotiation."

Mr. Ed, even though he hated the war, was knowledgeable about war tactics. He learned the names and functions of tanks and other artillery and easily identified the aircraft used by both the allies and enemies. After listening to Mr. Jabberbox's news commentary, he would state, "You can have the best weapons in the world but they don't win battles. Success is dependent on well trained troops and outstanding leadership." He had great confidence in General Patton and General MacArthur but in his mind, General Eisenhower, a native of Abilene, a little town in Kansas, was the outstanding military leader. Mr. Ed confided, "If anyone can put an end to this terrible situation, it will be General Ike."

After peace was restored, Mr. Ed turned on the radio for more pleasant listening. Mr. Jabberbox provided him the opportunity to closely follow play-by-play of his favorite ball teams, the Kansas City Royals and the St. Louis Cardinals. Mr. Ed faithfully recorded statistics of each player's hits, runs and errors and became a walking encyclopedia of knowledge about the physical history of each player.

The Missus claimed she grew tired of all the noise in her kitchen caused by Mr. Jabberbox. However, it was quite obvious that she treated the radio with much more respect than she did the cot.

The Missus had favorite programs of absolutely no interest to anyone else. Even the cot considered her choices totally boring. Early on Sunday mornings she listened to gospel singers from St. Louis as they joyously sang, "Shall We Gather at the River," "Swing Low, Sweet Chariot," and "Joshua and the Battle of Jericho."

The Missus had many talents, but singing was not one of them. When no one was listening but the cot, she loudly and joyfully sang along with the choir. The cot was always thankful that his pillows helped blot out part of her Sunday morning singing.

Little attention was paid to the weekday programs called soaps or the half-hour home extension programs discussing food preparation. However, when the programs broke for commercials, she stopped working and listened closely. After hearing the commercial for Rinso soap, she hurried to the store to purchase a box. Perhaps "Rinso Blue" might solve her washday agony.

The Missus actually sat down with pen and paper when listening to home advice specials suggesting new and better ways to clean the house. What a ridiculous waste of her time! She should have been the one telling others how to clean.

Dannydon't listened less than his sisters or parents to Mr. Jabberbox but did have favorite programs. He thoroughly enjoyed stories about the Lone Ranger, his Indian sidekick, Tonto, and the loyal horse, Silver. After listening to the weekly episode, he would get on a stick horse and gallop through the house and yard shouting, "Hi ho Silver and away we go!"

Listening to radio programs helped him build up a defensive response to his sisters' frequent accusations. When asked if he was responsible for a crime, he would respond in a deep and slow voice, "Only the Shadow Knows."

Dannydon't developed preference for a specific type of music. He overheard his sisters stating that they thought hillbilly music sounded ridiculous. He delighted in turning Mr. Jabberbox up to the loudest possible volume whenever that type of music was on the air. He knew that within seconds, one or both sisters would be pitching a fit.

WELCOME SCARLETT

The good years, with abundant yields from farm products, made it possible to provide the girls and Dannydon't with spending money. Each Saturday, before the trip into town, the Missus took the jar holding egg money down from the shelf. If the children had completed their assigned duties and demonstrated good manners, they received an allowance.

Money was used as leverage. If the children were too lazy and did not complete their chores properly or became too sassy, the money was withheld. In order to get her fair share, Mary Lou spent a lot less time hiding in the highest branches of the pear tree. She needed to have the cash to buy clothes, earrings and smelly lotions. Mary Lou earned a few dollars by teaching beginning piano lessons to neighborhood children, but those funds were insufficient in providing the needs for one who was almost a teenager. The funds from the Missus were necessary if she was ever going to successfully change her image from a pixie tomboy to a potential glamorous movie star.

The entertainment world mushroomed in the 30's and 40's. In addition to most households having electric radios, movie theaters were opening throughout the country. Mr. Ed and the Missus did not care to go to movies but would drive into town and visit with Auntie Marie or other friends so their daughters could gaze at screen heroes.

Mary Lou and Jane joined the national frenzy over Margaret Mitchell's saga "Gone with the Wind." They went to the library in hopes of checking out the book but were discouraged to find sixty or seventy names ahead of theirs on the waiting list. Even though they had not read the book, they were very familiar with the characters and plot of the story. Clippings from newspapers and movie magazines were saved in a scrapbook and reread on a regular basis.

Mary Lou dreamed of love scenes related to the movie. She signed, "I would drop in a faint if Rhett Butler held me in his arms and kissed me like he kissed Scarlett in this photo!"

Jane had outgrown playing with paper dolls and had packed the dozens of boxes holding them on the highest shelf in the closet. On a visit to Springville, she noticed a paper doll set featuring Scarlett and Melanie dolls and couldn't resist returning to her youthful play. The new set provided long gowns, gloves, and hats similar to the costumes worn by Southern Ladies during the antebellum years. Jane created even more outfits for the dolls by tearing pages from wallpaper sample books then using her new set of colored pencils to draw curves, pleats, and accessories.

Mary Lou was quite small in stature. Girlfriends her age towered above her and even her younger sister was two inches taller. Mr. Ed frequently called her "Little Bit," and, when Uncle Jack came for a visit, he held out his arms and called, "My little half-pint sweetheart, come and give your old uncle a hug." Dannydon't face lit up with a wide grin and his eyes gleamed when he realized that being short was his sister's newest worry. He taunted her by suggesting, "Mary Lou, you are so short and weird looking. We should call you Dopey the dwarf."

It was amusing to read about the difficulty Scarlett had lacing up her corset. Mary Lou wondered, "How does Scarlett's waist compare to mine?" She searched in her mother's sewing basket for the tape measure then draped it around her waist. She said to herself, "Well, fiddle-de-de, can you image that! The beautiful lady from the South had a waist measuring at least two inches less than mine!"

Both girls imagined that Tara resembled their beloved farm home. It was easy to envision ladies in lovely gowns stepping out onto the front porch to greet gentlemen who were waiting on the expansive green lawn. Jane wondered, "Did Tara have roses circling the fences and was there a big vegetable garden in the back?" She giggled then added, "Do you suppose they had a sweet pea house with only one hole like we do?

Daily the Missus listened to the plea, "Mama, we just have to see that movie." Finally, she agreed. "Girls, get all your chores completed early this week. Next Saturday we'll go to Kansas City. Gone with the Wind is showing at Lowe's Theater."

The three sat spellbound during more than three hours of the beautiful Technicolor movie. Colors on the screen were fascinating because the previous movies the girls had seen in local theaters had been in black and white. Rhett charmed them, Melanie was loved and, although Scarlett was an irritating bitch, they admired her spirit. By the end of the movie, the Missus and her daughters had red eyes and runny noses.

THE BIG BAND ERA

On trips to Springville, the first stop was to get an ice cream soda at the local drug store. Before leaving the premises, Mary Lou and Jane always bought the newest issue of a fan club movie magazine. During the following weeks they read it from cover to cover.

The girls knew all about the sordid love affairs in Hollywood and often chatted about the distinctive features of their favorite stars. They dreamed of growing up to be beautiful like the ladies they saw on screen.

Jane decided, "If I let my hair grow longer, a strand can be draped over my eye. I'll look like Veronica Lake."

Mary Lou admired the bluish-purple sheen of Hedy Lamar's long dark hair. In an effort to create the same effect, she rinsed her hair in bluing. The experiment failed and her hair turned a dull mousy color. It looked so bad that the Missus made an appointment for her daughter at the local beauty salon. After the dull strands were removed the only possible styling was a cut ending the hairline just below her ears with bangs hanging over her forehead.

In no time at all, Dannydon't realized Mary Lou hated the new hair style. He gleefully teased, "I was wrong. You're not Dopey the dwarf. Now you are Helga the sheep dog.

A store frequently visited on trips to Springville was Frank's Music Store. The salesman, a long-time friend of their Aunt Alicia, was always delighted to see the sisters enter the door. He knew they would ask him lots of questions and would spend at least half an hour scanning the stand holding the sheets of popular music. Mary Lou would ask permission to play pieces on the grand piano. As she struggled to sight read the notes, Jane hummed the tunes. The girls always left the store with new sheet music. Once home, they practiced until both the notes and lyrics were memorized.

The girls pleaded with their mother to let them stay up late to hear Mr. Jabberbox relaying music from dance halls across the country. They easily recognized the music of bands directed by Harry James, Guy Lombardo, Benny Goodman, Glenn Miller and others. No one was around to be their dance partners as they listened but that didn't stop them from twirling through the kitchen and down the hall.

The Missus was amused when she spotted her young daughters sway and twirl to the music. She just had to intervene when they tried to kick like Ginger Rogers and instead, plunged to the floor. "Girls, if you are going to perform dance routines like that, spread your arms forward then lean back to keep your balance."

The Missus proceeded to demonstrate how to do some of the more intricate dance steps. Mr. Ed and Dannydon't returned from the barn to find the females kicking up their heels to the lively music of Harry James. Supper preparations had been completely forgotten.

Male crooners who were lead singers of bands were easily recognized. The girls were fascinated with the humor as well as the delightful voice of Bing Crosby. They learned many of his songs by going to the Bing and Bob's Roadshow movies and listening to his hit vocals on the radio. As they washed and dried dishes, folded clothes, or dusted, their soprano and alto voices harmonized while singing songs like, "I'll Be Seeing You," "In the Cool, Cool, Cool of the Evening," "Swinging on a Star," and "High Hopes." At the yearly Christmas program, Jane brought tears to eyes of the listeners as she sang a song made popular by Bing called, "White Christmas."

It wasn't too long before another young skinny singer was their idol. Young Jane would fall on the cot in a swoon when listening to Frank Sinatra croon love songs like "Night and Day." She continued to worship this star until she attended college. Her adoration then turned to a young man from Memphis, Tennessee, who completely captured her heart when he sang, "Love Me Tender."

The cot listened to the Big Bands and lead singers with the girls. It agreed with their tastes in band music and appreciated different lead singers. It preferred to listen to female singers like Gisele MacKensie, Dinah Shore, Peggy Lee and Doris Day. The cot's favorite singer was Jo Stafford. When she sang "You Belong to Me," the coils would tingle.

The girls considered the best way to keep up with popular new songs was to listen each Saturday night to a program called, "Your Hit Parade." They sat quietly on the old cot and listened intently from the first announcement of, "Lucky Strike means fine tobacco," to the final phrases of the chorus singing, "So long for a while. That's all the songs for a while."

Each week, as they listened spellbound to the top ten songs, the sisters memorized specific parts of the newest songs. Jane quickly learned the words while Mary Lou paid attention to the tune and harmony. After the show was over, they hurried to the piano sitting in the parlor. Mary Lou easily picked out the melody on the piano, and her sister sang the lyrics with emotional spirit.

After songs were perfected, Mr. Ed, the Missus and Dannydon't were invited to be their audience. Mr. Ed and the Missus always whistled and clapped as they expressed their appreciation of the musical mini-shows. They felt the talents displayed by their girls made up for their own inability to play musical instruments or sing.

Dannydon't did not share the pleasure his parents felt as he listened to the musical performances by his sisters. He thought they looked and acted like idiots! He expressed his opinion with disgust, "You two sound like two cats fighting in our garden!"

Jane decided to mimic Kate Smith in an impromptu performance for her family. She applied pink lipstick and added rouge to make her normally rosy cheeks even brighter. Her older sister helped by arranging her hair in big curls. High-heeled shoes and a shirtwaist dress were found in the upstairs closet. Jane stuffed the front of the dress with two of the cot's pillows. It was quite charming to hear Jane belt out the words to "God Bless America" and "When the Moon comes over the Mountain."

Favorite Radio Shows

The radio provided situation comedies throughout the week. Mr. Ed swiftly completed the chores so he could get inside in time for favorite shows and the children hurriedly finished homework assignments. The Missus made sure that treats like popcorn, apples and cookies were available. The family gathered around Mr. Jabberbox, ready for laughs and entertainment. Mr. Ed kicked his shoes off and stretched out on the cot. The Missus sat in the rocker and held her son while the two girls claimed a couple of the cot's pillows then sat on the floor with heads resting on the cot's side.

Sunday evening had a series of interesting features. One of the earliest half-hour programs was Dannydon't favorite. He stated. "Can I go visit Uncle Jack in California? Maybe he could take me to see Gene Autry at Melody Ranch."

Mr. Ed was highly amused by all the problems King Fish caused his friends on the Amos and Andy show. It was not unusual for him to mimic the actors by saying, "Ain't that right, Andy?"

Jack Benny was a favorite comedian of all the family members. They liked his wacky attempts to play the violin and appreciated the appearances of his friends, Dennis Day, Mary Livingston, Phil Harris, and Rochester. After so many years of having little money, the Missus fully understood why Jack kept a tight-fisted hold onto each penny. The Missus laughed and said, "It makes a lot more sense for Jack Benny to store his money in a vault in the basement than it does for me to bury a tin filled with coins under that big rock at the side of the house."

Whenever possible, they listened to shows occurring on weekday evenings. They rarely missed a radio visit with their friends living at 79 Wistful Vista. It was a forgone conclusion that sometime during the show set in a little house on that street Fibber McGee would forget about the impending disaster that would occur if he opened the cluttered hall closet.

They also were amused each week as George Burns tried to understand the wacky logic of his wife, Gracie. Mr. Ed speculated, "I can almost anticipate the future. Mary Lou will probably cause her husband the same kind of frustrations! She is always putting things in strange places so it wouldn't be a surprise if the thermometer ends up in the refrigerator. When she is in one of her daydreaming spells, she pays little attention to the tasks at hand. Her husband will complain because she's likely to wash his underwear with her red blouses."

Mr. Ed appreciated many advances in the technical world and kept up to date by reading scientific magazines. He commented to his children, "When you grow up and have families of your own, you won't be sitting around listening to the radio."

Mary Lou questioned, "Daddy, why not? Listening to the radio is a lot of fun and isn't expensive. People would be crazy to give up this kind of entertainment."

He continued, "The popularity of the radio will be replaced by television. You will still gather around the entertainment center in your home but will be watching, as well as listening, to the characters appearing on its screen."

Both girls shook their heads in disbelief. Mary Lou said, "Daddy, you are putting us on! I bet you will even tell us that people will instantly communicate with people all over the world just by punching a few keys on a keyboard. You might even try to tell us that a man will soon be going in a spaceship to the moon!"

Chapter 15

TURN, RISE AND PASS

Obtaining a good education in the 30's in rural areas of the United States was not easy. Children often had to walk at least a mile to and from school regardless of weather conditions. Textbooks were passed on as students moved on to the next grade and, since there were only a few copies available, were shared between students. Sometimes it was difficult to find good teachers. During the depression, it was too expensive for young people to attend college and obtain a teaching certificate. In spite of obstacles, providing a good education for children was considered very important to families living in Eastern Kansas. This attitude was particularly true of Mr. Ed, the ex-collegiate, and the Missus, the retired school marm. Mr. Ed and the Missus made sure that their children missed very few days of school and insisted the children always completed their lessons. Since I was confined to the kitchen, I never saw the inside of the elementary school and only met the teacher once. Nevertheless, I listened and learned!

The Knowledgeable Cot

ARE YOU READY FOR SCHOOL?

"Eat your oatmeal! You need to finish your breakfast and get ready for school."

"But I don't like oatmeal! You make it early in the morning for daddy's breakfast. What he doesn't eat sits on the back of the stove and gets thick and sticky."

"Eat it anyway!" replied the firm mom.

A few minutes later Jane wailed, "Ouch! Mama, it hurts when you brush my curls. You don't brush Mary Lou's ugly hair. Why do you bother with mine?"

"Sweet one, I do it because you have beautiful long blond curls that tangle easily. Your sister has straight hair that won't even hold a hair ribbon."

The voice disliking breakfast now wailed, "Mama, I can't find my shoes! Maybe I should stay home today!" As usual, Mary Lou wasn't too organized.

"Nonsense, Mary Lou, your shoes are under the cot. That's where you kicked them last night before you started cot jumping."

This was a typical dialogue in the early morning. The girls loved school, but it sure didn't sound like it in the mornings. A few years later, Dannydon't had even more delaying tactics and excuses than his sisters. He would play with his animals in the yard instead of getting ready and he would often made comments like, "I think dad needs me to stay home and help him in the fields today." Or, "I should go fishing so we'll have perch to eat for supper."

Finally, the girls would be ready. Faces were clean, hair was combed, the wrinkles of cotton stockings were straightened and dresses were properly buttoned. The Missus stuffed their books and homework in two of the cot's old pillows so they would be easier to carry during their mile walk to and from school.

Jane and Mary Lou, who didn't eat much, always wanted their lunch pails heaping with food. They planned to swap the delicious sandwiches, cookies, and cakes made by the Missus with the store-bought food Oliver and Jimmy carried in their paper sacks.

LEARNING TO READ

Mary Lou had been six years of age for only three months when she started first grade. The Missus and Mr. Ed assumed their daughter would do well in school. The child could easily assemble puzzles which had at least one hundred pieces and had been playing piano pieces with two hands for more than a year. Also, they had no reason to question her intelligence since she constantly outwitted other members of the family.

It was somewhat a shock when, after the first week in school, the teacher commented to her parents that Mary Lou barely recognized the letters of the alphabet. The Missus realized she was at fault. Even though she had spent several years as an elementary teacher before getting married, she had been negligent about helping her own daughter prepare for school. She had simply been so busy with her many gardening and housekeeping chores plus the responsibility of raising two lively girls and a new baby.

The Missus decided it was absolutely necessary to set aside time each evening to help Mary Lou with reading lessons. As her daughter struggled to read the words in the primer, the Missus noticed that she held the book close to her nose and traced letters with her index finger.

Aunt Alicia came to the farm to give Mary Lou a piano lesson a few days after the Missus noticed the problem. The Missus questioned, "Alicia, you have always raved about Mary Lou's ability to play the piano. I also noticed that, only a few weeks ago, you asked her to practice several songs in Thompson's Third Grade Music Book."

Aunt Alicia thought about the situation for a moment. "Mary Lou was playing songs like, 'Mary Had A Little Lamb' and 'Robin in the Cherry Tree' when she was barely four. Last week I gave her a new piece, 'Pirates March.' It's quite complicated in both fingering and rhythm but she already has most of it memorized."

Aunt Alicia paused before continuing to describe her observations. "Mary Lou refuses to sight read. She always insists that I play every new tune two or three times. As she listens, she closes her eyes and moves her little fingers like she is playing the keys. Now that I think about it, she does recognize the notes but always takes the music off the piano rack when looking at the pages. I've also noticed that she traces the notes with her index finger."

The Missus promptly made an appointment with Dr. Gentry. During the examination Mary Lou could see the large "E" easily. As she tried to read the letters on other lines, she squinted and tilted her head right, left, up and down. The efforts were to no avail. The letters were a blur.

After Dr. Gentry completed the examination, he put Mary Lou on his lap and gave her a piece of peppermint candy. "Young lady, we'll fix you up with new glasses so that school work will be easier. You will even be able to read what Miss Simons writes on the blackboard." He continued, "Your mother says you like to climb trees. You'll need to wear your glasses even when climbing. The only time to take them off is when you take a bath or go to bed."

Dr. Gentry knew well the personalities of the babies he had helped to deliver. "Now, Mary Lou, don't lose your new glasses. It will cost your mommy and daddy a lot of money to replace them."

The new glasses made an immediate difference. Mary Lou skipped into the house when returning from school each day. Her bounces on the cot were wild and joyful and made springs on the old cot squeal. First the Missus, then Mr. Ed when he returned from the fields, were required to sit down and listen as their child joyously gushed detailed descriptions about all she had read. School was going to be a fine place after all!

Tiny Jane sat quietly at the table listening to her sibling's tutoring lessons. To keep her occupied, the Missus supplied her with an alphabet chart and a pencil. The Missus and Mr. Ed were in for a shock. The younger daughter, only four-and-a half years old, soon recognized the letters of the alphabet and their sounds, could count to one hundred and easily solved simple addition and subtraction problems. She even could read the books brought home by her older sister. The parents reluctantly decided that young Jane should start first grade the following fall.

The first year Jane was so little that Mr. Ed or the Missus drove the sisters to school in the car or hitched the wagon to the tractor. During the fall months, Missus would often pick Jane up at school soon after lunch and take her home because she needed an afternoon nap.

THE ONE-ROOM SCHOOL HOUSE

Mary Lou and Jane attended all eight elementary grades in a one-room schoolhouse. Each morning and evening they walked a half-mile east to reach the highway then turned south for another half-mile.

The educational system in Kansas was rapidly changing. These would be the final years for the one-roomed schools in Kansas. Dannydon't spent most of his elementary school years riding a bus and attending a consolidated four-room school several miles away from the farm.

The girls attended a small white rectangular building sitting on a hillside. Two acres of surrounding land served as the playground. The tiny building was simply furnished. The space in the front of the room held the teacher's desk, a large coal stove, and an old upright piano. A blackboard covered the entire front wall. Attached above the blackboard were roll-down maps, one was of the world and the other of the United States. Hooked to the right side of the blackboard was the national flag. There was no space for storage of school supplies. A globe, a music book, and the manuals Miss Simons needed for lessons were stacked on top of the piano. Stationed directly in front of the teacher's desk was a pew borrowed from the church. It was designated as the reciting bench.

The bulk of the room was filled with five rows of desks. The last row had desks large enough to comfortably seat several almost-grown young men. Mr. Ed commented, "These boys have to drop out of school early each spring and help with farm work. It will take some of them as long as ten or eleven years to complete their elementary education. A few will not even consider attending high school."

At the opposite side of the room were desks tiny enough to seat six-year-olds attending school for the first time. The three other rows of desks were graduated in size to fit growing children. At the start of each year, children tried out each seat until they found the one where their feet comfortably touched the floor. Children were delighted when they were big enough to have a desk with an inkwell hole in the upper left-hand corner. Inside their desks, children stored tablets, books, rulers, pens and one or two pencils. There were no individual crayons or scissors. Art was not considered part of the curriculum.

At the rear of the room two more blackboards were at the sides of the door. Cloak closets located on adjacent side walls housed coats and lunch pails. Two small library shelves were built at the sides of the closets. The miniature library got a lot of use because Miss Simons and the children's parents had instilled into the students a love of reading. Some of the books belonged to the school and had been there many years. Once Jane giggled and rushed over to her sister with a tattered book in her hands. She directed, "Take a look at this book. It is really, really old. There's Daddy's name on the inside page."

The county had wisely set up a lending library between the rural schools. The books were very popular because if they were not read during the month they were loaned to a school, it might be a couple of years before the same set of books would once again be available.

The door in the middle of the back wall opened to a small porch. This area was often cluttered with muddy boots and rain gear. (Children walked to school, rain or shine). There was a scraping rod at the side of the porch to remove mud between the heels and soles and a large mat for the final cleaning of shoes. A standing rule was strictly obeyed. Shoes always had to be cleaned before the child entered the classroom.

MISS SIMONS

Miss Simons was only twenty years old when starting her long professional teaching career. This was the same year that Mary Lou entered first grade. The tiny lady was in charge of approximately twenty-five children who ranged in age from five to sixteen.

This young school marm always had the classroom under her complete control. Perhaps other children heard what the Missus told her children, "If you get into any trouble at school, you may be sure that we will see you get punished at home."

Mary Lou learned this painful lesson in second grade. She had not studied her spelling words and was having difficulty during the weekly test. Mary Lou cautiously pulled the spelling book out of her desk and searched for the correct spelling of a word when she thought that Miss Simons was looking in the other direction.

Miss Simons, like most teachers, seemed to have eyes in the back of her head. Mary Lou was caught in the act of cheating. Miss Simons strongly reprimanded this behavior. She said, "Mary Lou, you know better than to cheat! Come up to the front. Sit on the stool and face the corner. When the other students go out for recess, you will return to your desk and study spelling words." A note was sent home explaining the transgression. Mary Lou got a lecture from her father about honesty and a whipping with a fresh green switch from the Missus.

Miss Simons managed the classroom so well and with such precision that it worked like a well-oiled machine. After the flag salute and opening announcements in the morning, she immediately started lessons. She would call, "First grade students, collect your readers from inside your desk then turn, rise, and pass. Please take your places at the reciting bench." When that lesson was concluded children marched like little soldiers back to their desks and another group was called forward.

The children quietly and diligently completed assignments at their desks. As they worked ears were tuned to lessons taught to other groups seated at the reciting bench. Jane, an excellent student, always knew everything she was going to learn in the upper grades.

Teachers in modern day schools tend to teach only one grade and, if they work with older students, only one subject. They must be in awe that, in times past, a single teacher would teach reading, writing, spelling, social studies, science, geography and math to multiple levels of students.

Miss Simons emphasized memorization. No errors were accepted when students recited poetry as they stood in front of the classroom. They were also expected to show proficiency in chanting multiplication tables through twelve, spelling words correctly, recalling names of presidents and knowing the capital of each state.

Strategies used by this instructor were successful, and her students made rapid progress. Her biggest challenge was time management. There was simply no way she could give the smaller children the constant attention they needed. To address this problem, she assigned older students as tutors. It worked well in most situations, but in Jane's situation, roles were reversed. It was not unusual for Jane to be the one helping an older child solve a difficult problem.

Competition was encouraged. In the interest of time, Miss Simons ignored grade and age differences. The spelling bee format was used to quiz students in several areas of the curriculum. Children were divided into teams and stood in lines in front of opposite walls. Each child had a turn to answer a question. Instead of sitting down when someone made an error, a member of the opposite team had the opportunity to give the proper response. Points were given for correct answers. The team with the most points often enjoyed a special treat such as cookies baked by a parent.

Writing tablets were available but no one wasted paper. Both the front and back of each sheet was used. If the report was short, the child was instructed to use only half a sheet of paper. Several children had small slates. The slates were used for practice of math problems and, when the teacher was not paying attention, drawing pictures.

The blackboards, both in the front and back of the room, were in constant use. The blackboard was often divided in half horizontally. The older children wrote their answers on the top half while, at the same time, the smaller children utilized the lower portion of the space.

The constant use of blackboards resulted in them requiring a good cleaning at the end of each day. After every inch of the board was erased, a wet cloth was used to bring back the shine. Children enjoyed the task of cleaning erasers by pounding them together or beating them on the sidewalk. When Mary Lou or Jane assumed that duty, the Missus would greet them when they returned home after school saying, "The boards at school must have been used a lot today. I can tell you girls cleaned the erasers because you are covered with white chalk dust."

PARENT INVOLVEMENT

Mr. Ed and the Missus never heard the term parental involvement. They just assumed it was their responsibility to be aware and a part of everything that happened at the school.

Each fall, a few days before the start of school, parents prepared the facility for the following year. Inside the building blackboards were painted, the wooden desks were polished and floors were cleaned and waxed. Outside, the men mowed the grass, added gravel to the driveway, put a fresh supply of coal in the shed, and mended the swings and seesaws.

Two outhouses, with crescent moon windows on their doors, were located at the edge of the schoolyard. Fall duties included throwing fresh lime in the toilet holes and killing the critters that had used the small buildings as their summer homes. Slick pages of the Montgomery Ward or Sears catalogs were ready for instant use. Pages were looped over a bent coat hanger which was hooked over a nail in the wall.

The Missus made sure that her little family always looked good for the first day of school. She saved her egg money so new shoes could be purchased to cover growing feet that had been barefoot for most of the summer. She made the girls new dresses and purchased large hair bows to match each outfit. When Dannydon't was old enough to be in school, the Missus always stitched a new plaid shirt for him.

Mr. Ed did more than his share to make the school comfortable. On cold winter days he would take his children to school then stay until the coal stove made the room feel warm as toast. If there was a snowstorm, he shoveled the driveways and paths leading to the outhouses. The Missus also was a frequent visitor at the school. Miss Simons was rarely ill, but when she did have to stay in bed, the Missus was only too happy to be the school marm for the day.

RECESS

Since the children did not socialize during class time, recess and playtime after lunch were considered the highlights of the day. It was their opportunity to compare notes, tease each other, participate in organized games like baseball or simply enjoy free playtime.

Mr. Ed and the other fathers built several pieces of playground equipment. There were three swings. Two had seats close to the ground and were used by the younger children. The other was constructed to satisfy daring older children. One afternoon, Bob and Howard, two sixth grade boys, enjoyed pumping with vigor as they stood face to face on the swing. They made the swing go extremely high and those watching thought they might make a complete loop around the bar.

Two seesaws were provided. Jane and her small friend, Sue, always headed straight to the seesaws at recess and, once they were on them, were reluctant to share turns with others. Mary Lou was impatient about having her turn and decided to best way to get it was to help the younger girls with their math concepts. She said, "I bet if the two of you got on one side of the board it would be balanced if I got on the opposite side."

If Jane and her friend were not quick enough to reserve a place on the seesaw, they wandered around the playground looking for another place to play. One of their favorite spots was under a massive maple tree. In the crevices between its knees, they created a palace. Leaves, rocks, flowers and sticks were utilized to set up the throne room. The rocks were giant chairs, the leaves represented beautiful rugs, and sticks covered with flowers were the ladies and knights of the castle.

Mary Lou continued her habit of scouting for trees good for climbing. The large apple tree near the ball field was her favorite. When high in the branches, she could see most of her world. She thought to herself, "I feel like I am in the center of a saucer and the horizons are the rim." As she looked to the west, she could clearly see the white church and its steeple. By turning her head slightly to the right, she could identify the roof of the barn and very tip of the large maple tree near to her house. She turned her head south to north and saw the highway sneaking toward the town and knew it would eventually take travelers into Kansas City.

Mary Lou felt like the full leaves on the branches made her invisible. While standing on her perch on a warm fall day she could see all that was going on without being seen. On the grass near the building, the older girls were practicing cheerleading movements. Near them several boys were playing with marbles. There was no official baseball game that day and the older boys, who seemed to have mitts glued to their hands, were playing catch. She watched as Jane and her friend jumped off the swings and ran to the base of the tree where she was hiding. Within a few minutes, they had assembled yet another palace ballroom out of sticks, leaves and flowers. Oliver and his buddies were huddled behind the school. Oliver had his hand cupped over his mouth and was whispering so that only his buddies heard him. The boys responded by hooting with laughter, slapping each other's backs, and jumping around like monkeys. Mary Lou thought, "Oh, no. Oliver is telling another of his naughty stories!"

The leaf cloak provided invisibility so Mary Lou was the witness to secrets not known to others. One day she watched with curiosity as Ralph and Jennifer, two eighth graders, kissed behind the school. It wasn't long before, hand in hand, they strolled away from the playground. The two, who thought they were hidden by the tall grasses of the nearby field, intensified hugs and kisses. Mary Lou knew what might happen next and was tempted to climb down the tree, race into the classroom and alert Miss Simons. Fortunately, the clang of the bell brought the older students to their senses so they came quickly back to the schoolyard.

Mary Lou also knew why Miss Simons sometimes looked sad. She had silently watched as a young man stepped out of his car and greeted her teacher. As the couple walked around the playground, they were unaware of a child's presence in a tree. Mary Lou heard Miss Simons ask, "Do you really have to enlist?" The young man nodded sadly and said, "You know I do." He promised, "As soon as this war is over and I return home, we'll think about plans for the future."

Climbing days were over at the school playground when Miss Simons happened to notice Mary Lou twenty feet up. The angry teacher ordered, "You will break your neck if you fall from that tree. Come on down. I don't have time to worry about you." Mary Lou had to stay in the next recess and write one hundred times on the blackboard, "I will not climb trees on the playground."

During recess some games were organized with detailed rules. Students played dodge ball and a game, resembling soccer, called, kick the can." A favorite game was called, "handy over." The students divided into two groups. One group threw the ball over the school roof. The other team, after catching the ball, sneaked around the building and chased the other team. Anyone caught had to join the opposing team.

It's no wonder that most of the young men were excellent baseball players. In the spring and fall of each year, most recess periods were spent playing baseball. Sometimes there were not enough good players available so girls and younger children were drafted. That wasn't a great idea because younger children did not have gloves, couldn't even try to catch the ball. They were easily distracted and, instead of watching the action of the game, became much more interested in finding four leafed clovers, picking tiny flowers and chasing butterflies. There were often bumps and bruises because of their indifference to the game.

When snow covered the school ground, children brought their sleds to school. They would spend recess time first sliding down the steep slope east of the building then trudging back to the top to be ready for another turn. There was a barbed wire fence near the end of the slope. A child, riding the sled on his tummy, could easily glide under the fence. When children rode double, the one on top had to roll off just before the sled went under the fence. No one ever considered the danger of this activity, and Miss Simons didn't notice because she was inside preparing lessons.

Five minutes before the end of recess, Miss Simons would come to the door and ring a bell. Children immediately stopped their play and raced to the outhouses. By the time Miss Simons rang the next bell, children were waiting to enter the building. The line was formed according to seating assignments with the youngest going in first. Talking was over. Each child stepped quickly to his seat and went to work.

FESTIVITIES AT THE SCHOOL

The tiny school building was the center for neighborhood social activities. The first event of the year was Halloween. On the last day of October, the children only worked on lessons during the morning hours. The afternoon was spent decorating the room. Their first task was to create and hang colorful scary paper creatures on hooks and from lights. Later students hiked through the countryside searching for beautiful red, yellow, and brown leaves that would complete the autumn setting for the festivities to be held that evening.

Everyone attending was expected to dress in costumes for the party. Mr. Ed and the Missus went to great length to disguise their identity by wearing masks and dressing up in ridiculous outfits. Costumes were judged in two categories. One was for originality and the other on how well the costume concealed the identity of the ones hidden behind the masks. Mr. Ed and the Missus frequently won in both categories.

The entire evenings were filled with fun like apple bobbing, relay races, and spooky versions of familiar games like, "Pin the Tail on the Donkey." The final event of each Halloween Party was to build a giant bonfire. Friends talked and joked about the enjoyment of the evening events as they drank apple cider and roasted hot dogs and marshmallows.

Mr. Ed and other fathers constructed a stage in back of the tiny room to accommodate the yearly Christmas programs. All the children, young and old, participated in the one-act plays and sang in the chorus. Mary Lou could play the piano well enough to accompany most of the singing by the time she was in third grade. Little Jane, blessed with a sweet voice, sang her first solo, "Away in a Manger," when only five. At each program in later years, she was expected to entertain the audience.

Valentine's Day was celebrated by having a box supper. All of the women and girls carefully made beautiful baskets or boxes and filled them with delicious food. The unnamed boxes were placed for display on a large table. The boys and men took a lot of time inspecting the colorful boxes. They appreciated the creativity and beauty of the boxes but were much more interested in who made it and what tasty goodies it contained.

Mary Lou and Jane were busy creating their Valentine Boxes at the old kitchen table on the thirteenth of February. Mary Lou was slapping paste on the backs of red hearts then randomly sticking them on the sides of a white rectangular box. Jane was carefully decorating a blue basket with pictures of kittens.

The oldest suggested, "If you want Andy to bid on your box and be your picnic partner, you'll need to give him some incentive. You could hint that your box is filled with fried chicken and mama's snicker doodle cookies."

Jane questioned, "How will Andy be able to identify my box?"

Mary Lou quickly replied, "That will be easy. You talk about kittens and constantly draw pictures of them. Besides that, our daddy always makes the first bid of five cents on our boxes."

The final day of each year was celebrated with a picnic. Children spent the first part of the day straightening their desks, cleaning the blackboards and putting the library books back on the shelves. Miss Simons gave a cheering talk about what fine students they were and how she was looking forward to seeing them back in school next fall after Labor Day. She then passed out the dreaded report cards. Most of the students had smiles on their faces but a few blushed as they read comments like, "I know you will try harder next year."

By midmorning parents and grandparents and everyone else living in the school district had arrived at the school. Picnic tables, set up under the large oak tree, were laden with fried chicken, vegetable casseroles, slaw, potato salads, bread, and an assortment of cookies, pies and cakes.

A ball game, initiated after the picnic, lasted until it was time to leave for home to perform evening chores. On their team Mr. Ed pitched, Jane substituted for the third base player, and Mary Lou assumed pigtail duty. (The pigtail person stood behind the catcher and chased the balls escaping into the outer field. The position was assigned to uncoordinated kids who had difficulty catching and throwing the ball.)

The girls always remembered the year when the last day of the school year was not pleasant. Miss Simons was very quiet all morning. She said, "Children, will you please do all the cleaning? I don't feel well." Her pains became worse. By the time the parents arrived she was vomiting and holding her stomach.

The Missus recognized the symptoms and hurried home to telephone the doctor. Dr. Gentry must have flown out the door because he was at the school within twenty minutes. He gave a diagnosis after a quick examination. "Young lady you have a bad case of appendicitis. It's almost ready to burst."

Miss Simons was rushed off to have an operation in the nearest hospital the center of Kansas City, at least a two-hour journey.

The illness occurred long before antibiotics were available and there was a real fear that this special lady might not survive the ordeal. Due to the alertness of the Missus, the teacher recovered and continued to be a special member of the community.

GRADUATION

The eight years of attending a rural elementary school were drawing to a close for Mr. Ed's oldest daughter. Mary Lou and the other teens planning to attend high school had to take a series of academic tests. Even though she did not achieve the status of valedictorian or salutatorian, she was one of the four young people in the county selected to sit on the stage during the commencement program.

Mary Lou earned this prestigious place on the stage. This child, who spent her young life finding ways to get out of work, diligently practiced piano lessons. She was actually talented and had frequently been asked to perform for local events. Mary Lou was both pleased and frightened when Miss Simons stated, "Mary Lou, I've submitted your name to be one of the performers for the graduation ceremony in May."

The Missus was very proud to hear that her daughter was selected to display her talent and wanted her to look her best for the occasion. She decided it would be best to take Mary Lou on a shopping trip to Kansas City. A beautiful white blouse with red buttons and ruffled sleeves and a flowing red plaid taffeta skirt were selected to wear on the stage. The Missus did not consider the attire completed until she found a matching red ribbon. Mary Lou responded to her mother, "I absolutely will not wear that ribbon!"

In addition to the lovely skirt and blouse, on the day of graduation Mary Lou was wearing new black slippers with two-inch heels and, for the first time in her life, nylon stockings. They were held in place just above the knees with loose garters. Mary Lou confessed to the smiling girl sitting next to her who was waiting to play an accordion solo, "I feel like my stockings are sliding down my legs."

The girl planning to play an accordion giggled and whispered, "You aren't the only one. Mine are just as bad. Even worse, I need to go to the bathroom."

Most of the audience was attentive as the dignified superintendent talked about lofty opportunities in the future for young people. He was almost ignored by the two girls on stage concerned about the present. They giggled about how silly they would look when they got up to perform and their stockings slipped down to their ankles.

Mary Lou heard her name called by the superintendent. She looked out at the audience and felt her knees tremble. She wondered, "Will I make a complete fool of myself?" Slowly she stood then walked over to the huge grand piano. As she looked at the white and black keys, she felt the impulse to run and hide behind the side curtains. How could she possibly remember notes of the difficult piece? She took a deep breath, straightened up her back, placed her new black slippers on the pedals and faultlessly skimmed her fingers through the arpeggios of the composition, "Valse Chromatique."

Chapter 16

ON TO HIGH SCHOOL

*Ed's children were growing up. Their sprouting caused anguish
for the elder members of the household. The Missus wanted her
little boy to stay a baby. I was disappointed that Jane never
played with dolls on my covers and Mr. Ed shook his head in
disbelief at the thought that his oldest was ready for high school.*

The Ignored Cot

THE FIRST DAY OF HIGH SCHOOL

The day following Labor Day was rainy with a preseason chill in the
air. Mr. Ed was sipping his second cup of coffee after breakfast when
his eldest daughter emerged from the bathroom. She was dressed in a
green plaid jumper and a starched long sleeved white blouse. White anklets
and new brown and white oxford shoes completed her attire.

Mr. Ed admired her appearance, "You certainly look neat and pretty in
your new clothes." He grinned as his daughter glanced at the mirror over
the buffet and shook her head in disapproval of her image. He added, "This

first morning of school the bus will not come down our road. Why don't I drive you up to the corner so you won't get wet while walking? You'll want to look good for your first day of high school."

A few minutes later their Chevy was parked at the corner near the busy highway. Both occupants of the car, for once, were silent. Thinking about high school was both scary and exciting for Mary Lou. Meanwhile, her daddy was wondering, "How in the world did the years fly by so quickly?" His babies were growing up too soon.

Mary Lou broke the silence, "Daddy, I feel like I need to go to the bathroom."

Mr. Ed replied, "Nonsense, child, you must have been in and out of the bathroom at least five times before you left the house, and I even saw you run out to the Sweet Pea House when Jane was using the inside facilities."

Mr. Ed hugged his daughter. "Honey, you're scared because your world is changing. You'll be fine in high school." He added, "Your mama and I are so proud of you and your brother and sister. You all have done so well in elementary school and high school will be no different."

He thought a minute then added, "Mary Lou, you are always climbing trees and keep trying to get to the highest branches. Think of going to high school in this light. You are simply moving up to a higher branch of your life."

The rains continued throughout the morning and early afternoon. A little before four in the afternoon, Mr. Ed decided it would be wise to pick up his younger children from their school. They returned home and, after telling their mama about two new students who had entered the school plus a few other events of the day, they sat down at the table and worked on math assignments.

Mr. Ed followed his usual routine of glancing at pictures in the *National Geographic* before picking up the daily paper. He grinned when noting that his wife and failed to complete the crossword puzzle. His vocabulary was more extensive than hers but his spelling was phonetic and often not correct.

The Missus sat quietly mending socks, but frequently got up to glance out of the window. There was an air of quietness in the room comparable to the stillness before a thunder storm.

At half past four the screech of the bus brakes gave a signal that the tranquility of the room was soon to be over. A few seconds later those sitting around the table heard first the squeak of the garden gate then the slam of the porch door. It seemed like a tornado entered the kitchen, and the creature causing the storm looked like she had been through one herself. Her starched white blouse was rumpled and ketchup stains were on the collar. A button was gone from the green jumper and both the white anklets and new oxford shoes were splashed with mud.

The creature instantly headed for the old cot. She lunged for the center, ignoring creaks and groans and even failed to notice she was getting mud all over the newly cleaned cover. "Wow, high school is awesome!" To the rhythm of bounces she proclaimed, "I–loved–every–minute!"

The Missus poured lemonade and placed a batch of oatmeal cookies on the table. "Mary Lou, please stop bouncing. Come over here to the table. We all want you to tell us about high school." The Missus and Mr. Ed knew their talkative child would describe every minute of the eventful day.

"Daddy, remember how scared I was this morning? Well, everyone on the bus must have been as scared. There wasn't a peep out of anyone. Ginger and I sat on the same seat and held hands. Both of us were trembling."

When the bus finally arrived at the school there were big burly football players waiting in the rain to gallantly assist us as we stepped off of the bus. One of the biggest and most handsome boys took my hand! I was so excited that I tripped. Thank goodness, he was there to steady me before I fell! Anyway, we were sent inside to the registration desk then later upstairs to the study hall."

Mary Lou giggled, "The study hall is a little like our elementary school. There are six long rows. Seniors sit on the far side by the windows, and the freshmen are on the opposite side by the doors. We had to play musical chairs until each grade was lined up alphabetically. I am seated near the back since my last name starts with an R."

She had another thought, "Guess what! There are forty-one freshmen. That's the largest class in the school."

Mary Lou took a bite of cookie and a sip of lemonade before continuing. "I was surprised to realize that I knew several other students. In addition to our cousin Ginger there were several friends Jane and I met at 4-H district meetings."

Without pausing she continued, "Do you remember Allison? She played the accordion at the county graduation ceremony last spring. Allison will be my best friend. We are taking the same classes and agreed to sit together."

Mary Lou described Allison's personality. "She is lots of fun and giggles all the time. Even the teachers start to smile when they look at her."

MEET THE TEACHERS

Mr. Ed asked, "Did you like the principal and teachers? It's my guess you will be giving us a description of each. Also, what classes are you taking this year?"

"Well, Mr. Swartz, the principal, wore a black suit and vest. He tried to look mean but that probably was just an act. I saw him put his arms around a pimply freshman boy. Allison said he was Mr. Swartz's son. Anyway, in the study hall before the final bell rang Mr. Swartz paced back and forth and kept pulling out his pocket watch. After the bell, he led us in the Pledge of Allegiance and said some serious sounding welcoming words about the fine quality of students and teachers in the school."

Jane perked up her ears as she listened to her sister's descriptions. It would not be long before she too would be going to high school. She was just a bit jealous that her sister got a head start but decided it was wise to learn from her sister's challenges. "Did you like your classes?"

Mary Lou shrugged. "Some of them were okay. Others were dumb."

Jane prodded, "Go ahead, Sis. We know you would tell us every detail even if we weren't interested and we are!"

Mary Lou started with the first class of the day. "Mrs. Tyler teaches algebra. Mama, I think you know her. She and her husband always come to the church bazaar. She probably has lung problems like you. She hacked and spit several times during the class." Mary Lou giggled, "Maybe she should teach English instead of math. She had a's, b's, x's, y's and z's written all over the blackboard. Algebra is going to be hard for me to understand. Ginger, who is smart in math, said she could help me."

Mary Lou took another sip of lemonade and gulped for air. "The next class was American History. Even though Mr. Swartz is busy running the school, he has to teach that plus two other classes. His first assignment was for us to read a chapter in the textbook about our state of Kansas."

Mary Lou rolled her eyes. "I think it's neat to have the principal as a teacher. The secretary came to the door every few minutes with important messages, and he even had to leave the classroom a couple of times. Whenever he left, we all whispered and giggled but were smart enough to stop when the door opened. If we get into trouble, would he send us to his office or deal with us in front of students in the class?"

Without pausing the young lady continued, "Did you know that Home Economics is a required course for freshmen girls and Industrial Arts is required for all the freshmen boys? That's such a silly arrangement. Our class is made up of girls who learned to cook and sew by helping their mothers when they were little and through lessons taught by home demonstration agents during 4-H meetings. We should be learning about tools, electricity, and machines and the boys should learn how to cook!"

Mary Lou gave a look of disgust and added, "The Home Economics teacher's name is Miss Please Her."

The Missus looked down at the paper with Mary Lou's class schedule and corrected her daughter. "No, Honey, her name is Miss Plesher."

"No, Mama. She distinctly told us to remember Miss Please Her. She expects us to always make her happy and told us points would be taken off our grades if we failed to do so."

The Missus snapped at her child. "Mary Lou, this is just the first day of school. You shouldn't rush to judgment."

"Mama, she treats us like we are only six years old. I'll pretend to be Miss Please Her and show you how it sounded."

Mary Lou pulled her glasses down further on her nose. She looked over them and talked in a shrill squeaky voice. "Girls, see if you can name the cookware and utensils I am displaying. What is this? Yes, this is a two-quart saucepan. Yes, this is a tablespoon. Yes, this is a teaspoon. La, la, de-dah, la, la, de-dah."

Mary Lou speculated, "Miss Please Her didn't listen to our answers. Allison loudly gave the wrong name every time and was never corrected."

Mary Lou completed a negative review of Home Economics by explaining the assignment for the following day. "Tomorrow we are going to learn how to boil water so we can make plain Cherry Jell-O! When we really become experts at this cooking business, we will make sugar cookies to share with the boys taking Industrial Arts."

Dannydon't was a little bored with the description of classes. "Did you have recess?"

"No we didn't, silly boy! Grown up kids don't have recess. We have P.E. classes. Today we only had a walk through. I saw the bathroom and lockers assigned to girls. Did you know we have to change clothes and take showers in front of the other girls in the class? I'll die when they notice that my boobs are so small."

Dannydon't questioned more. "Why didn't you have P.E.?"

"We didn't have class because no teacher was available! Coach Williams was assigned to teach us but he refused. He told the principal that he was hired to teach Industrial Arts and coach football, basketball, baseball, and track. He did not have time for silly freshmen girls. Someone said that the lady who teaches shorthand and typing has been asked to supervise our physical education classes. She is tall and skinny and looks like she might blow away in the wind. How can someone who has problems moving possibly be a physical education teacher?"

Jane questioned further. "We've talked about how great music classes will be. Did you play the clarinet in orchestra? What about glee club?"

Mary Lou shrugged her shoulders. "There were no music classes today for anyone. We had to sit in study hall and pretend to study during the periods assigned for music. It's a good thing to have a new friend with antennae for ears. Allison told me that the teacher hired last spring sent a letter in August stating he was breaking his contract. She also heard the secretary tell the principal that a new man accepted the position and would be at school tomorrow."

The Missus continued looking at the class schedule. "I see you have two other classes. What about English and Geography?"

"The English class will be fun. When we entered the room there were sentences written all over blackboards. It was a sure bet we were going to have to search for nouns, adverbs and stupid stuff like that, but we didn't get around to it today. The teacher is Miss Livingston. She greeted us with a big smile and suggested that today we should get to know each other by telling our names and where we attended elementary school. I think she likes all of us.

Everything was going fine in the class until she noticed Allison. It was so funny! Miss Livingston is pudgy. Allison is pudgy. Miss Livingston has frizzy blond hair. Allison has frizzy blond hair. Miss Livingston smiles all the time and Allison does too. When Miss Livingston looked at Allison, they both started to giggle. They continued to giggle so much that Miss Livingston suggested that Allison go out to the hall and get a drink of water. In a few seconds she followed. Allison shared with me earlier that, when she has one of her giggling spells, she wets her pants. I bet both of them had damp panties after that."

Mr. Ed was looking at the geography textbook. "This book sure looks interesting. Tell us about this class."

"Daddy, I'm going to ace that sucker and never even have to crack the textbook."

The Missus did not appreciate this kind of attitude. "Mary Lou, how can you make a statement like that?"

"Mama, take a look at what Daddy is doing. He is already reading the first chapter of my textbook. By midnight he will have read the whole book. All I have to do is tell him the reading assignments. He'll gladly reread the pages and tell me what the book says plus other interesting information he knows about the country or area. Thanks to Daddy's interest in geography and facts of yesteryears, I will impress the teacher with all I know."

Chapter 17

MUSIC FILLS THE AIR

I've explained that Mr. Ed and the Missus had no musical ability. They could not sing on key and had never developed the skill of playing any musical instruments. In contrast to their parents, both Mary Lou and Jane loved to sing, dance, and each had learned to play several instruments. It's a good thing that the small high school hired a music teacher who

could take the talents of these girls and other students to new levels.

A Music Lover, the Cot

STUDENT ROAD SHOW

High School had been in session almost two weeks. As was her ritual, when Mary Lou returned home, she ran from the bus and dashed into the kitchen like a whirlwind tornado. The cot braced his coils for another session of bouncing. These episodes were getting difficult. It was harder for the cot's coils to cope with the present ninety-five pounds than with the wimpy sixty pounds she had weighed only a few years earlier.

"Mama, guess what!" stated the child in aerial motion.

"Mary Lou, please watch what you are doing! I've told you before. You aren't too big for that cot to toss you off onto the floor!" The Missus still never considered the abuse the cot was receiving.

"Mama, remember I told you we have a new music teacher named Mr. James? He's really groovy. All the other teachers are at least thirty years old! I think Mr. James is only twenty-five."

Mary Lou stopped bouncing and sighed, "Today he came up to my desk in study hall and asked if I could accompany him to the music room."

The Missus perked up her ears. Teachers did not often pull the students out of study hall.

"Mama, the whole music room was filled with boys! Mr. James has formed a men's glee club. He asked if I would help by playing the piano accompaniment."

Mary Lou went back to her bouncing. A twang indicated a spring of one of the cot's coils. "After the class was over Mr. James said I did very well. He asked if I would consider helping out on a regular basis."

The Missus was skeptical. "Mary Lou, you have already given up one study hall to sing in the girl's glee club and another to play clarinet in the orchestra. Young lady, just when do you plan to study?"

"Mom, that's no problem! I'll bring the textbooks home and study each evening. You know that all of us do our best work here at this old kitchen table. It will be a perfect place to spread out the books and papers. I can easily complete written English assignments and math. I inherited my daddy's poor spelling skills. While I'm doing homework at the table, I can ask either you or Jane how to spell words"

"Young Lady, we won't help you! Here's the old dictionary to use for that."

Mary Lou had an additional thought. "There will be a lot of reading required for English. Whenever I need to read a chapter or two, I'll climb up the pear tree and sit on one of its branches."

"We'll see," the Missus responded. "If your grades start to slip in any subject, you'll have to give up music classes." The Missus knew how much Mary Lou loved music. The threat of canceling any one of them would keep her on task in other subjects.

"Thank you, Mama. I sure don't want to disappoint Mr. James." Pleasing the teacher was only one of the minor reasons for Mary Lou's eagerness. Not many girls had the opportunity to be in a room alone with so many boys.

That afternoon a conference transpired after school between the principal and Mr. James. The principal was curious as to why the music teacher had asked for a few minutes of private time. He asked, "Is there a problem, Mr. James? I've heard no complaints about any of your classes."

"No sir. All of the music classes are doing fine. I just want to talk to you about my observations of the students in this school. Two things are very apparent. First, they are shy and seem to have very little confidence when talking to adults. Several of the other teachers have told me it is difficult to get them to answer questions in class. There is another trend I've observed. Many of the students have musical skills. This is particularly true of the freshmen class. Several girls and boys have beautiful voices and there is actually music coming from the orchestra room."

Mr. Swartz agreed. "Music seems to bring out the best in them. I know my own son looks forward to each of his music classes. Your enthusiasm is catching."

Mr. James stated his purpose for asking for a conference. "I've lived in this community for only a short time, but it's obvious that there is not much in the way of entertainment. Folks seem to be limited to going to church, attending dull civic meetings, and coming to high school games. What I have in mind is to assemble a traveling music show which will be available for enjoyment to community members."

The principal's eyes lit up. "You may solve a big problem for me. A committee was here yesterday from the Lions Club. They are having a district meeting in October and asked to use our facilities. They also asked if the school could provide some sort of entertainment. Having a program for their meeting could serve as a way to introduce your musical show to the community."

Mr. James wasted no time in putting together several acts. When teaching the boy's glee club class that afternoon, he divided the boys in groups of four. He soon identified four talented young men to sing in a barbershop quartet. A senior with a deep voice was selected to sing bass, two sophomores could sing the lead parts of baritone and second tenor and a freshman was a natural for tenor. This young man had a high-pitched voice that sounded like Dennis Day, the singer who regularly appeared on the Jack Benny's radio show. In addition to singing with enthusiasm, it was soon obvious that these four boys were clowns who would not be afraid to show off during performances.

There were so many girls interested in singing that selection was difficult. Mr. James ended up choosing enough for two sextets. He told the girls they would rotate appearances in the show. The girls of this era idolized the women who were lead singers with Big Bands. The music leader had no difficulty in selecting girls to feature in duets and solos.

Students too shy to talk to adults seemed to ignore this feeling when on stage. Mr. James discovered that Phillip, the young man who sang baritone in the barbershop quartet, could throw his voice like a ventriloquist.

He even owned a dummy doll named Homer. Another comedy act was the principal's son. He could change his voice to sound like Donald Duck and the skits he created always had the audiences laughing.

Several students played the piano or other instruments. Mr. James once again had so many available that he promised them they could make guest appearances on a rotating basis.

THE SUNFLOWER SWEETIES

Mr. James had heard that Allison played the accordion. He asked her to bring it into the band room after school and play a few tunes for his enjoyment. After only listening for a few minutes, he realized she could play a song after hearing it only once and had the fantastic ability to remember the words of songs. He thought it would be a great idea to form a special musical group to be a part of the road show and appointed Allison as the leader.

Allison was delighted and suggested, "The name of our group could be, The Sunflower Sweeties."

Mr. James, with Allison's help, chose girls to be a part of this band. Betty, who played the violin eloquently in the orchestra, easily made her instrument sound like an old-time fiddle. Helen, a master at percussion instruments, gladly agreed to play the washboard and any other object which would supply a basic rhythmic beat. Helen was a perfect selection for this group. In addition to the skill of playing percussion instruments, she could yodel at the top of her voice. Iris, a quiet sweet girl with an abundance of talent was asked to play the piano or bass fiddle.

Allison asked that her friend Mary Lou be included. "Mr. James, you have Mary Lou playing piano for the boy's glee club, and she plays first chair clarinet in the orchestra. Did you know that she also plays guitar?"

Mary Lou had indeed learned fingerings for chords of the instrument and played well considering she had no formal lessons. The child had improved her skill when about ten years of age by practicing each evening as a way to get out of work. Mr. Ed had assigned her the duty of going out to the pasture and bringing the milk cows to the barn each evening. She hated the chore. Since she rarely wore shoes in the summer, her feet were abused by stepping on stickers in the field. Even worse, the soft squishy stuff contributed by the cows often got between her toes.

Mary Lou noticed that milking cows seemed attracted to music. One evening she picked up a guitar and started strumming while singing loud enough to get the attention of the Flossie, Jasmine, Maribell, Hannah and Lizzy who were happily munching on grass in the nearby pasture. The strategy worked. The cows ambled toward her while listening to the songs "Get Along, Little Doggies," and "Red River Valley". From then on, Mary Lou usually resorted to this easy strategy of sitting on a fence post and providing entertainment that would entice the cows toward the barn.

Mary Lou was pleased to be asked to join the Sunflower Sweeties but realized she had a problem. She jumped off the bus and rushed into the kitchen screaming, "Mama, I'm one of the chosen five to be in a group called the Sunflower Sweeties! They might not accept me because I don't have a western costume to wear!"

The Missus immediately backed out the Chevy, and the two headed for town. They rushed into the small department store where Mary Lou, with her mother's approval, selected a red cowboy hat, a denim skirt, and black cowboy boots. They then went into the dry goods store where the Missus spied an attractive red plaid fabric. "Mary Lou, I can make you a cowboy shirt out of this material." She examined the bolt another second and decided, "Since the material is on sale, I'll buy extra yardage and make a new cover for the old cot."

The musical road show rehearsed several times a week. By Mid-October the acts were perfected enough to perform for the Lions Club. The musical repertoire impressed the audience. The word was soon out. In no time, the community became aware of the availability of the students for musical entertainment. There were constant requests for the students to perform. Because of this demand, Mr. James was pleased that he had selected rotating acts to perform at shows.

The five Sunflower Sweeties became close friends who spent many hours together after school. They enjoyed frequent practice sessions and canceled other events, including dates, if they had a chance to perform. There were many times when the girls, toting the bass fiddle and other instruments, were delivered to the farm gate by Bus #8.

The evenings the girls spent at the farm were always so boisterous that no one even pretended to sleep. On one such evening the girls realized they were very hungry after playing their instruments and singing at the top of their voices for several hours. While nibbling on snacks provided by the Missus, they shared stories about school life. Each experience related would send the others into giggling fits.

Helen moaned, "Can you believe all the horrid experiences we have in Home Economics?"

Alicia agreed, "Miss Please Her certainly is not happy with our culinary skills. She was furious last week when we were not paying attention to the cooking time and let the entire batch of cookies burn on the bottom." She giggled then added, "Instead of throwing them in the wastebasket she should have given them to the boys in Industrial Arts. They'll eat anything."

Iris rolled her eyes, "Miss Please Her wonders why we don't seem interested in making aprons and skirts. She has never once considered that we might have made these things at home or as 4-H clothing projects."

Mary Lou informed her friends, "Miss Please Her was happy with my crocheting project. Ha! Little does she know, Mama agreed to complete the doily with a border of colorful pansies so I could spend extra time studying for the algebra test."

Mary Lou thought of another situation that would cause hoots of laugher. "Did you know Mr. James was so furious with me last week that he broke his baton by whacking it on the music rack?"

Allison looked surprised. "Mary Lou, Mr. James always acts like he appreciates you playing the accompaniment for the boy's glee club. Whatever did you do?"

"It's what I didn't do. I was so busy flirting with Jason, the cute senior baritone, that I didn't see the downbeat of the baton."

Mary Lou chuckled, "Mr. James apologized for getting mad, and I promised to pay better attention. Actually, it was amusing to watch him direct singing with only about four inches of the broken baton in his hand."

It was Betty's turn to turn on the laughter. She jumped off the cot, put several books on her head and slowly glided around the tables and chairs. She asked, "Girls, who am I?"

In unison they shouted, "You're Miss Herbert walking around the desks in the typing room."

Helen was sympathetic. "Girls, don't be too hard on her. I think she walks with her head tilted back so her thick glasses won't fall off her nose."

Iris giggled and instructed, "Young ladies, it is time for Physical Education. Let's start with stretching exercises." She proceeded to pretend that it was impossible to bend further than her knees.

Helen again took the teacher's side. "You girls don't understand her problem. None of you are taller than five foot six. She's at least six feet tall. She has to reach down a long way to go in order to touch the ground."

The girls had a real affection for the math teacher but that did not stop them from imitating her snorting, hacking and spitting. The girls agreed when Allison said, "Miss Tyler is very patient with all of us and really is great about explaining all of those equations she puts on the blackboard."

Mary Lou nodded her head in agreement. "It's amazing! I am actually beginning to understand algebra."

Iris asked, "Who's your favorite teacher?" Her friends quickly responded, "Miss Livingston."

Betty described their English teacher. "She continues to act like she is really interested in all of us and is excited about what we are learning. Have you noticed that even the lazy boys are enthusiastic about completing assignments?"

Helen reflected, "Miss Livingston doesn't just assign books to read. She stimulates interest by telling a little about the author and reading a short synopsis of one of her favorite books at the beginning of each class."

Allison had shared earlier with her friends the problem she had when giggling too much. It wasn't long before the word got around that Mrs. Livingston also had difficulty controlling her bladder.

Betty laughed and said to her friend, "Now that all the students are aware of the problem you two share, they are determined to find ways to make you laugh. It was so funny last week when both you and Miss Livingston rushed out the classroom door."

The girls did not forgive the coach for not wanting to teach them in Physical Education. Iris commented in her quiet sweet voice, "We get in trouble for chewing gum, but Coach Williams is always chewing his cud."

Betty added, "That's nothing! I bet you have all seen him doing this." She proceeded to mimic how he adjusted the crotch of his pants and scratched his behind.

Allison had one of the funniest stories to tell. "I was asked to play my accordion last Saturday evening to entertain the inmates at our local mental institution. A warden assumed I was an inmate leaving the premises and stopped me as I carried my big heavy accordion case across the institution's grounds. He roughly guided me into a building and placed me in restraints. It was a long time before I could convince him this was a case of mistaken identity."

Boyfriends were not free from scrutiny. If one girl professed to be in love the others felt it their duty to point out his shortcomings. Funny ears, inability to sing harmony or doing poorly on a test were quickly detected. Mary Lou was always informed that her special guy tended to flirt with other girls when she was not around.

On one of the overnight visits to the farm, the girls decided to find out for themselves if Mary Lou had made a correct assessment of the cot. She had professed several times that its squeals and squawks would make it an eligible instrument for their band. Each girl took a turn jumping up and down on the old structure and challenged his tired springs. Just as Betty started to jump, she took a good look at the cot's covers. She exclaimed, "Why Mary Lou, that old cot really is planning to join our group. He is dressed up in material just like your cowboy shirt." There were crescendos of laughter as all five girls leaped on the cot. The glee continued as the cot made proper squeaks and groans. Allison's giggles expanded into a fit of hysterical laughter. (It's a good thing she brought along an extra set of underclothes.)

The musical road show's popularity grew. As Mr. James predicted, it filled a void for the community. The show gained such recognition that they occasionally played in nearby towns. The musical road show also accomplished the goal of helping the students gain self-confidence and self-esteem.

Each year, as seniors graduated, new students were added to the show. When Jane entered high school, her talent and interest quickly made her an important member. She sang in sextets and duets and even occasionally sang a solo of one of the popular songs she learned by listening on Saturday night to "Your Hit Parade."

The Sunflower Sweeties performed all four years of high school. In addition to being an important number in the musical road show, they accepted additional invitations to provide entertainment for civic organizations in Eastern Kansas and Western Missouri. The girls were elated when they were asked to perform at the American Royal Cattle Show in Kansas City. A few months later, their spirits were only a little dampened by the fact that they did not make the cut when auditioning for Ted Mack's Talent Show. If four out of the five girls had not made the decision to marry immediately after completing high school, the group might have decided to do more than play for events like school reunions and community affairs.

Chapter 18

LIFE GETS BUSY

"The years with a quiet ebb and simple flow were gone. A few things remained the same. Mr. Ed and the Missus still enjoyed visiting with friends after church on Sundays and the Missus rarely missed attending the Prairie Hill Ladies Aid quilting sessions. The problem was, in addition to predictable activities, were multitudes of events associated with having two active teen-aged girls plus providing adequate attention to an adolescent brother.

Mr. Ed and I continued to be friends. However, during the years when his girls were in high school, I felt neglected. About the time Mr. Ed would get comfortable and relax his graying head on my pillow, Mary Lou or Jane would rush into the kitchen and plead, "Daddy, we need to go to the basketball game," or "Daddy, I have a play rehearsal tonight so need to go back into town." They were likely to suggest, "You might want to bring along a book to read, Daddy. It may be a long wait."

When the girls weren't asking Mr. Ed to take them somewhere it was Dannydont's turn for attention. "Dad, we need to go fishing. Old Fighter is hungry and might try to take our bait."

The Lonely Cot

RESEARCHING THE PAST

The high school, although small, was fortunate to have an excellent faculty. Miss Livingston, still a favorite among the students, had also established a friendly teasing relationship with her fellow teachers. They, like the teenagers, usually found themselves smiling when in her presence.

Mr. James was not at all surprised when Miss Livingston tapped him on the shoulder as she passed by him in the hallway. "My goodness, fancy me meeting you here in the hallway, Mr. Music Man! Guess you aren't in that orchestra room every minute of the day!"

She put her hands on hips and stated, "I have something important to say to you!"

"Oh, oh," he responded. "Are you upset because members of the choir have been coming to your class several minutes late? I promise it will stop after the concert on Friday."

"No, that doesn't bother me at all. I'm proud of the way you've turned those little hens into singing canaries. You can also be commended for inspiring students who play horns like Benny Goodman or Tommy Dorsey."

Her eyes twinkled, "You are getting a lot of credit for the inspiration you provide students. It's time you have some competition. Move over, sir. I'm challenging you for the title 'The Teacher of the Year'!"

He laughed, "Just what are you doing?"

"You found the talent hidden in their voices. I have uncovered the talent in their fingers." Miss Livingston added, "Can you spare a few minutes? Come into the English classroom and see for yourself."

The two teachers walked quickly up to the desk cluttered with papers. Miss Livingston pulled out several files filled with essays in various stages of development. "Just take a look at these."

Mr. James glanced through the first file. "This writing looks like chicken scratches. I thought English teachers expected good handwriting from their students."

She chuckled, "Most of the students have not had shorthand. These are the notes they took during initial interviews with people in the community. They scribbled because the interviewees had so much to say. I suggested that we keep the papers just in case they are needed for reference as essays are completed."

She then held up another file. "Here are the drafts students are still touching up before final submission. When these are finished would you like to read them? You'll learn a lot both about the students and the local history."

Mr. James was curious. "Just how did all this unfold?"

Miss Livingston continued her story, "Each student was assigned the task of interviewing a parent, grandparent or someone of the older generation. They returned from this assignment with amazing stories. Students were shocked to learn that the community had not always been populated with folks who read their Bibles daily, never missed church on Sunday, and frowned on anyone who dared to let liquor touch his lips."

She took a sip of water, caught her breath then continued. "Names of local sites, Olathe, Paola, Osawatomie, Shawnee, Wea, and Pottawatomie roll off their tongues, but they failed to consider these were names of Indians who once inhabited this area. I asked them why their state was once called "Bleeding Kansas." Their research revealed that some of the early settlers were gun toting whiskey drinkers who liked nothing better than a good fight. Just before the Civil War, many acts of violence ignited in this area. The anger was spurred over a difference in political beliefs. Most of the people who settled in this neck of the woods came from states in the Northeast and felt a strong alliance with the Union. The settlers in our Kansas Territory rarely set eyes on anyone with skin darker than their own. Even so, they were abolitionists who championed the concept that Negroes deserved the right of freedom. These attitudes did not set well with radicals having the opposite viewpoint who lived just a few miles across the border in Missouri."

Miss Livingston again smiled mischievously. "This research even has the attention of Mr. Swartz. He is most impressed that students are searching in history books for more facts. They are particularly curious about why John Brown, known for the Harper's Ferry incident in Virginia, is somehow connected to Osawatomie. They also wonder why the name of William Quantrill, who led ruffians in the massacre in Lawrence, Kansas, keeps popping up in local stories."

Mr. James continued leafing through student folders. He laughed as he saw the short poem, "Ode to a Toad." "Who did this?"

"You probably know Oliver. The poem is ridiculous. But at least the language is clean. That young man knows too much for his own good. I refused several of his essays. He had to spend several extra hours redoing assignments before I would give him a passing grade." Miss Livingston sighed, "I hope he learned a lesson. No filth will be allowed in this school."

JANE'S ESSAYS

Mr. James eyes were directed to one of the folders "This student's folder is thicker than the others. Is someone working for extra credit?"

"All of these essays were written by Jane. You know her. She is Mary Lou's young sister. She's probably active in your music program just like her sister. Anyway, Jane keeps a note pad with her at all times. The ideas popping into her head often turn into poems.

"This young lady has an excellent knowledge of local history. I think there are members of her family who like to share stories of the past."

How right the English teacher was. Jane did not have to go out of the home to do research. Reviewing stories she had already heard was particularly easy when Uncle Jack visited the farm. As always, the evening started out by Mr. Ed and Uncle Jack yakking several minutes about the weather, fishing, and crops. Jane interjected a question, "Uncle Jack, could you elaborate on the story you told us many years ago about Grandfather Richard?"

That was the only motivation needed. For the next hour or so she took notes as her dad and uncle talked about the experiences and personalities of family characters. She also. researched old newspapers for interesting stories related to early history in the Kansas territory. Occasionally, she was shocked over past events like the Marais des Cygnes Massacre when five men were shot to death by John Brown and his followers. Old John might even have trekked over Mr. Ed's farm land when he went over to Missouri to rustle cattle.

Each afternoon, when the bus stopped in front of the house, it was typical for Mary Lou to be the first to jump out of the bus and run quickly through the garden gate. In contrast, Jane waved good-by to friends, and the driver then slowly stepped off the bus. While strolling the lawn she took time to notice the color of trees, smell the flowers and watch squirrels or birds flitting from tree to tree. One day was different. Jane jumped off the bus and rushed to the tool shed where her dad was overhauling the tractor.

The anxious child wanted confirmation of stories researched that day. "Dad, guess what I heard! At the turn of the century, there was a saloon where the hardware store now sits. Is that true?"

Mr. Ed grinned, "When I was a young boy, I would hear comments from the men working in the fields about a trip they were planning to take on Saturday evening to the Sundown Midwest Saloon." He scratched his head before concluding, "So, I guess it's a fact."

Jane was a little too shy to ask her father about the truth of additional information whispered. Her gossip source stated that dancing girls working in the saloon lived in the house next door and were very free with their favors.

Jane had enough confidence to ask him about an additional story about ancestors of two students in her class. "Dad, we read about a famous murder mystery that was never solved. Based on the names written in the newspaper, the lady was identified as Julia's grandmother, a married woman with two children. She fell in love with a man who was the grandfather of John Charles. The paper states that a few months after rumors about their affair started someone shot the husband. The articles indicated that her lover was under suspicion but was never convicted. Can this story be true?"

Mr. Ed gave his youngest daughter a look of disapproval. "Jane, don't be looking too deep in closets of other families. Just about every one of them will have a skeleton. Even ours has a few. Think about it. Would you be happy to hear about a crazy act committed by one of your ancestors?"

"Dad, you always think of how others might feel. I just hope I grow up to be so caring. You are right. I imagine both Julia and John Charles feel embarrassed."

She shook her head and added, "However, the cat is out of the bag. Most of the kids in the class read the article, and Frank stated he plans to do more research and someday write a book about this unsolved murder."

THE ORPHAN TRAIN

Early in the spring quarter, Miss Livingston gave the students in the creative writing class a new challenge. "Review the historical essays you wrote during the year. Select one of these and develop it into a play." She added, "Mr. Swartz has agreed that the best play will be presented during a school assembly."

Jane was pleased with this assignment and knew it would be easy. After all, she and her sister had been setting up scenarios and acting in them since they were toddlers. She carefully leafed through her file of essays and decided the story about the Orphan Train would be perfect.

Miss Livingston was always fair when reviewing work of students. She read through all the plays they created. There was no question in her mind about the winner. Jane's play touched her heart and would have the same effect on the audience. When the play was read to classmates, they too were impressed and quickly volunteered to act in her production.

The stage background setting for the first act contained large cardboard boxes painted to represent shops and houses in New York. A large rectangular box was positioned in the foreground. The lead actors played the parts of a brother and sister, Pauline and Jerome. The young girl, playing the part of Pauline, sat cross-legged next to the box she was using as a temporary home. She blew her nose and wiped tears away with the tail of her tattered coat. She looked up as her brother neared the box. She sobbed, "I can't believe that Ma got pneumonia and died last week." Her brother, Jerome, paced in front of the box while shaking his head to indicate he too was confused by all that had happened. He added, "Yeah, and Pa was killed only a year ago when the scaffolding collapsed, and he fell fifty feet."

Pauline sighed, "I'm hungry and this packing box doesn't provide much shelter from the cold winds."

Jerome placed his hands on his hips and said with determination, "Sis, crying isn't going to help. If we want to eat and have a place to stay, we'll have to find work."

The children hugged good-by and went separate ways. Jerome knocked on the shop doors. When the proprietors opened the doors, he would plead, "Sir, can I help you sweep and clean up?" Each time the proprietor slammed the door in his face.

Pauline approached a large house. As a housewife opened the door she pleaded, "For only a few pennies I will be most happy to help in your kitchen or watch your children." The lady shook her head and said "No" then quickly shut their door. At other homes she received the same response. One woman even chased her away with a broom.

Pauline was the first to return and crawl into their temporary home made from cardboard. She brushed the tears from her eyes, shivered with cold and clutched her stomach. Thoroughly dejected she speculated, "People in New York have very little sympathy for orphans."

A few minutes later her brother joined her. He shared a few precious pieces of bread then imparted important news. "Guess what, Sis. I overheard other street children talking about an organization called the Children's Aid Society."

His sister responded, "What does that have to do with us? No one seems to care if we have anything to eat or a place to sleep."

Her brother continued, "This organization does. It provides food and clothing for abandoned children in the city then arranges for a train to take them out to the Midwest states. There, in some far away community, a farm or small-town family might decide to adopt a child needing a home."

Pauline nodded her head in agreement when her brother suggested, "Let's try to get a seat on the Orphan Train."

The second act stage was set up with one section representing the inside of a train and the other half a platform next to a depot. Several students, including the boy and girl assigned the roles of Pauline and Jerome, pretended to be orphans riding on the train. When the conductor announced a stop in a town in the states of Illinois, Iowa, and Missouri, children left their seats and filed out of the train. They quietly stood in a straight line on the platform, willingly accepting the inspection of waiting crowds of people. Each child whispered the same prayer, "Please God, have one of the families pick me." Children chosen waved good-bye to the other children, quickly stepped down from the platform, and walked off the stage.

The conductor announced, "The next stop will be in Springville, Kansas."

Pauline and Jerome looked at each other and shook their heads in disappointment. Kansas was near the end of the journey, and they were among the few children still remaining on the Orphan Train. Pauline moaned, "I guess no one wants us because, at ten and eleven, we're not cute or cuddly."

Jerome took the hand his sister's hand. "That's not the main reason. It's because we insist on staying together. Some families just can't see taking care of two children."

Richard, a local landowner, just happened to be picking up supplies when the Orphan Train stopped at the local train depot. His heart went out to the brother and sister holding hands as they stood on the depot platform. Even though Richard's home was already full with his growing family, he went up to the brother and sister and asked, "How would you like living on a big farm?"

By the end of the final scene of the play there was not a dry eye in the audience. Miss Livingston asked that Jane, the author of the play, take a bow. She accepted the applause then explained, "This is a special story of our family. Pauline and Jerome were real children and the man who adopted them was my grandfather."

TOSS THE ARSENIC AND OLD LACE

In addition to monthly assemblies displaying talents of students, the school presented both junior and senior plays for the enjoyment of the community. Mary Lou and Allison, thanks to frequent appearances in the musical road show, were not afraid of the stage. In the junior play, Allison played the part of a crazy senile aunt while Mary Lou was a skinny niece who was always trying to build up muscles in her arms.

At the beginning of their senior year, Miss Livingston gave the girls the script to the play, "*Arsenic and Old Lace.*" She instructed, "Girls, the two of you would be perfect for lead roles of the two old women in the play. Since there are so many lines to learn, perhaps you might start to memorize the parts this fall."

The girls loved the script and enjoyed debating which of their innocent classmates they would get to poison on stage. The girls were in for a disappointment. After the Christmas holidays, Miss Livingston announced to them, "The committee voted against presenting this play."

"But why?" questioned Allison. "We've already memorized our parts."

Miss Livingston sympathized with the unhappiness felt by the two girls. "It has nothing to do with the two of you. The decision was made because that play has very few characters in the cast. The committee felt the senior play should include most of the senior students." The two girls did have parts in the substituted play, but they did not display the enthusiasm generated for the roles of little old ladies who killed visitors entering their home.

THE WEEKLY NEWSPAPER

The small community had an excellent newspaper. Even those who did not bother to read daily papers like the *Kansas City Times* and *Star* subscribed to *Winston Weekly News.* Mr. Banks, the editor, dutifully wrote articles about high school events such as games and plays. So much was happening at the high school that reporting about them was taking up entirely too much of his time. He came to see Mr. Swartz asking for a solution for his problem.

He stated, "I'll gladly donate the entire fourth page of the weekly to your school if someone here will write the articles."

Mr. Swartz, smart principal that he was, handed the problem over to Miss Livingston. She immediately accepted the challenge. "My advanced students are required to hand in frequent written assignments. One of their weekly assignments could be to submit an article for the paper.

The editor, principal, and teachers were amazed at the response the students made to this request. They were enthusiastic about learning how to set up the dummy sheets and willingly met the deadline for submitting appropriate articles each week. Features included the usual calendar of events and spotlighting of teachers, football jocks and winners of beauty contests.

Students quickly thought of other clever ideas about what would be interesting reading.

Betty, with Mary Lou as her assistant, initiated a gripe and solution column. Their classmates submitted their gripes, and the girls came up with solutions. The following are some typical comments found in the column.

Gripe: There are too few typewriters for those assigned to class. This is a serious situation. How can one possibly learn to type if their fingers don't touch a machine?

Response: The school needs to buy more typewriters! If no funds are available then we suggest the class be split in half with students dividing their time between study hall and the typing room. You are correct. You can't learn to type by watching someone else tap the keys. That's like learning to drive a car when someone else is at the wheel.

Gripe: What can be done about the cafeteria ladies insisting on serving bean sandwiches?

Response: Ask them to switch to egg salad or peanut butter sandwiches. If that doesn't work, go on a hunger strike or bring food from home.

Gripe: Why is there plenty of equipment available for guys to use for sports but almost none available for the girls to use during physical education classes?

Response: This situation has to change. Girls have as much right as boys to enjoy sports and develop physical skills. Share the equipment Coach Williams!

Gripe: Why are boys always assigned to Industrial Arts while girls have to take Home Economics?

Response: We are constantly told education is to prepare us for the future. It is only reasonable that the boys need to learn how to boil water and heat soup, and the ladies need to know how to change a light bulb and tap a nail into wood with a hammer. We suggest that each Friday be a flip-flop day for the two classes. Perhaps the boys will put more effort than the girls do into trying to please their cooking instructor!

Gripe: Why are girls not allowed to wear jeans or slacks to school?

Response: Girls, you are liberated. Your mothers earned the right to vote and for you to think for yourself. The fashion magazines demonstrate that pants can be both comfortable and attractive. Stand up for your right to wear pants!

Gripe: My girlfriend has a mood ring. Why does it always turn blue when I am around her?

Response: We bet friends are telling you that this indicates she just doesn't like you. That may not be the case at all. Have you ever heard the expression, "Cold hands - warm heart?"

Allison initiated a gossip column for the newspaper. She was perfect as its reporter because no secret in the school escaped her attention. It was a sure bet, when Allison's giggle was heard as another student whispered in her ear, some interesting tidbit would soon appear in her column. She knew about love attractions of those still reluctant to openly express their interest, heard about lover's spats, and always knew when someone was two timing their special friend of the opposite sex. Even teachers were included in Allison's comments. Mr. James was seen sitting by the pretty school secretary at a basketball game. Allison speculated that romance was in the air. Sure enough, the next time the two were seen together, the secretary was wearing a diamond.

Friends were not exempt from teasing. Mary Lou was mortified to read in Allison's column, "Henry says if a certain junior is getting tired of grapefruit halves for size enhancement, she can borrow a pair of his socks."

Mary Lou, scrawny and skinny as a young child, had not changed all that much. Her boobs had increased only to the size 32A and, indeed, she was guilty of trying to improve the contour of her body by stuffing her bra.

Chapter 19

AFTER SCHOOL HOURS

Since I am just an old cot, it doesn't seem logical that I knew all about dating and parties. As always, my source came from paying attention to those who constantly talked in the kitchen area. I rarely interfered with the goings on of the family, but one time, I knew it was necessary. The silly oldest daughter needed my protection.

The Helping Cot

GROWING PAINS

Mr. Ed's eldest daughter made a slow and painful transformation from a scrawny and skinny brown pixie to a reasonably attractive young lady. The first indication that she was aware of growing up was when she spent her limited savings on a bra. Even though the size was only 30AAA she proudly wore it each day.

One summer day her wanderings took her to the creek. The water looked so welcoming that she quickly stripped down to her panties. The new bra, shoes, socks, and shirt were placed carefully on a rock located a short distance from the swimming hole. Mary Lou ignored time and what was going on around her while she splashed and floated. After enjoying the refreshing swim, she walked to the rock to retrieve her clothes. Everything was just as she left it except for the bra. She looked everywhere for it to no avail. After returning home, Mary Lou went to the cot, her favorite spot for weeping and moaning. She knew good and well her mama was not about to let her buy another bra until the garment was really needed. That might be weeks or years!

Dannydon't enjoyed listening to the pathetic agony his sister expressed about the loss of her newest garment. Finally, he suggested, "Don't feel so bad Sis. As I was fishing in that stream this afternoon, I noticed a big old bullfrog hopping near the rocks. He was wearing your bra. I grabbed the frog before he jumped away and tugged the bra away from his slimy body. See, I brought it back home for you." The devilish grin on his face gave a clue that this was payback time for all the times his sister had teased him.

Soon after Mary Lou's twelfth birthday, she and others in the congregation quietly sat and listened to the preacher's long Sunday sermon. When the final prayer was completed, the congregation slowly stood up and stretched their cramped legs. The Missus and Mary Lou immediately noticed that Bonnie, sitting in the pew directly in front of them, had a large red stain on the back of her dress. The Missus quietly whispered to the young girl's mother about the problem. The two ladies stood behind Bonnie, quickly guided her past the preacher who was shaking hands with parishioners in the vestibule, then shuffled her down the steps and out to the car.

During the ride home after church, the Missus mentioned the incident to her husband. "I keep thinking of Mary Lou as a young child, but she's a couple of months older than Bonnie. I guess it's time I talk to her about some facts of life."

After lunch, before Mary Lou disappeared to the great outdoors, her mother directed, "Mary Lou, I want you to come back in the kitchen and sit down on the cot. Please don't start bouncing. We need to talk seriously about you growing up."

Mary Lou listened as her mother explained what she called the monthly visitor. She tried to act indifferent and stated, "Oh mom, I know all about menstrual periods." Actually, her ideas were vague but she did admit concern by saying, "Mama, I am afraid. I'd die of embarrassment if what happened today to Bonnie would happen to me in a public place."

Her mama suggested, "Let's make an emergency kit for you."

After the mother-daughter talk, Mary Lou always carried her mother's old purse. When her friends would ask her about the purse she would reply, "I seem to always have a runny nose caused by a cold or hay fever. I keep hankies in the purse." Indeed, a few were stuffed on top but the items of importance contained in the purse were several strips torn from a white sheet, two large safety pins and a sanitary belt.

It was almost three years before she had any need to use the items hidden in her purse, and Mary Lou grew worried. One day, after listening to her friends talk in the locker room about painful periods, she came home from school, flopped down on the cot and did her usual moaning. "Mama, all the girls call it a curse. I haven't been cursed like other girls. I'm certainly not a boy, and since I'm not becoming a woman, maybe I'm just an It."

Mary Lou had always been an expressive, emotional child. It's no surprise that during her transition years when hormones raged, she constantly wavered from highs to the depth of depression. She would giggle and laugh while attending a 4-H event which included square dancing and singing. Later, she would cry herself to sleep because no compliments were made about her sewing or cooking projects. She was in ecstasy when chosen to play the piano piece for the county eighth grade commencement but cried for hours at the thought she might be compared with two students who were on stage for their academic achievements.

Dannydon't was delighted to see his older sister in distress and quickly learned the buttons to push to make her scream or cry. He frequently asked her embarrassing questions. "Mary Lou, is that a pimple I see on your nose?" Another time he would ask, "How come your knees are so knobby?" When the newest young puppy ran to Jane, he commented, "Mary Lou, what did you do wrong? Even this dumb dog acts like he doesn't like you." When he heard the name mentioned of someone Mary Lou admired, he suggested, "That person doesn't even know you exist."

In response to his teasing, Mary Lou would scream an ugly comment back at him then start to cry. Her younger brother would walk around with a smile on his face. He was more than pleased with her reactions whenever he teased.

Mary Lou became fascinated with mirrors. She used her daddy's mirror with magnification to note if any blackheads or pimples were appearing to mar her reflection. When her mother's hand mirror was held at an angle to catch the bright light coming in the bathroom window, she noticed that her skin seemed shiny. She decided to remedy the situation by generously using the puff to spread her mama's powder over her face. The powder looked like snow on her dark skin.

The vanity in the guest bedroom had three sections of mirrors. The one in the middle was stationery but the two side parts were movable. By adjusting the angles, Mary Lou, when standing in front of the vanity, could see dozens of self-images. Not one of them was pleasing to her sight. She also turned the side mirrors to check how her hair looked as it fell over her shoulders. She frowned and almost sobbed because it looked dull and straight.

Dannydon't, sprawling on the cot, was delighted to be present as she peered into the mirror over the buffet and wailed, "Mirror, mirror, on the wall. Why am I the ugliest of all?"

Dannydon't, in a squeaky witch voice, moaned, "You were made that way, Dearie. You have ugly straight brown hair you never comb, so it hangs down over your face. Your weird glasses give you frog-looking eyes. You have space between your front teeth. Your skin is so brown that there is no pinkish color in your cheeks. You have a pimple on your chin." He finished his description by stating, "And you have a hook nose!"

Mary Lou turned to him and shouted, "I do not have a hook nose!"

Mr. Ed was sitting in the rocker beside the cot. He had been so absorbed in his newest Zane Grey novel that no attention was paid to the conflict between his children. After Mary Lou's verbal outburst, she ran into the kitchen and plopped into her father's lap and, while doing so, knocked his book to the floor.

She cried, "Daddy, what am I going to do? I am so ugly!"

Mr. Ed could see she was serious and felt sorry to know she was in agony. He hugged his oldest daughter and looked at her fondly. "Mary Lou, where did you ever get that opinion of yourself?" As he patted her soft dark hair he added, "Did you know that you are beginning to look like your mama did when we were courting? I can tell you that I thought your mama was about the prettiest woman I ever saw and I still do. I think you are perfect just like you are, but if you are concerned and want a makeover, why don't you talk to your mama and Auntie Marie?"

Mary Lou found it much easier to approach her aunt. "Auntie Marie, what can I do about my hair? It is so straight and won't stay in place. Half the time it is over my face? Can you help me?"

Auntie Marie smiled. By the request she heard she knew that her dear niece was finally growing up. "You came to the right person. I am an expert on giving home permanents. Why don't you stay overnight with me on Friday? We'll get up early Saturday morning and I'll give you some curls." As a result of her aunt's efforts, Mary Lou's black hair fell to her shoulders in a soft wave.

It was not easy to approach her mama because the Missus believed, "Pretty is as pretty does." Color on the face would not make one bit of difference in her book. It took some pleading before she reluctantly agreed that the next visit into town Mary Lou could use her spending money to purchase lipstick and a little rouge.

Mary Lou had worn glasses since first grade. She was so near sighted that, in the past, she actually appreciated the way they helped her vision. Now they were a hindrance in her campaign of becoming more attractive. There were many mornings when she ran out to meet the school bus but the glasses remained on the old buffet.

The mirrors over the vanity assured her that her looks were improving. With that goal accomplished, she focused on her wardrobe. She wailed, "Mama. I wear blouses and homemade broomstick skirts every day. Lots of the other girls have circular skirts and some even have a poodle patch for decoration."

She reflected a minute then added. "I have my Sunflower Sweetie skirt and shirt, but I can only wear them when we perform. I don't have a decent sweater and the only good outfit is the one I wore at the eight-grade commencement."

"Mary Lou, you have the sweet green jumper you wore the first day of school and you made a couple of skirts before starting high school. What happened to them?"

"I love the green jumper but when I was writing a book report with that new fountain pen, I got black ink all over the front. You washed it but the ink stains are still there. As for the skirts, they should be thrown away. Mama, you know that my sewing skills are limited. I have a hard time with zippers, and the ones in those skirts have already pulled out at the seams. When they are worn, I have to fasten the gap with safety pins."

The Missus counted the egg money and added that amount to a check Mr. Ed had recently received after selling corn at the grain elevator. She declared. "Mary Lou, you've convinced me the world might fall apart if you don't have some new clothes from the store. Next Saturday I'll take you and your sister to Kansas City. We'll look for clothes at the Jones Store plus other department stores located near First and Main."

"Why are we taking Jane? She is still in elementary school and doesn't need new clothes! Besides, she is good with the sewing machine and can make nice skirts and dresses."

The Missus was angry, "Mary Lou, I'm ashamed of you. Your sister deserves new clothes as well as you. She is already two inches taller than you, so she can't wear your hand-me-downs. Just yesterday, she complained that the shoes I bought just two months ago were pinching her toes."

The trip was a joyous one for the mother and two sisters. Each girl returned home with a new coat for winter, two sweaters, several blouses, two skirts, and new shoes. The Missus did insist that the girls get dark skirts instead of pastel pink ones. "Girls, that type of skirt would be soiled in no time, and the material doesn't wash well."

The girls were happy with the clothes purchased by their mother. Mary Lou used some of her allowance to complete her wardrobe by purchasing a pair of gaudy dangling earrings. They were a source of pride even though they pinched and turned her ear lobes green.

DATING

Mary Lou's quest to improve her physical image was successful. It wasn't long before the telephone was constantly jingling. Each time three long rings were heard, the neighbors sharing the same line picked up the phone to listen to conversations between a silly girl and a timid boy.

More often than not it was young Jane, still too young to date, who answered the phone. The sisters did not look a bit alike, but their voices sounded identical over the phone. Jane enjoyed pretending to be her sister and often had long conversations with boys. She thought it was great fun to accept dates on behalf of her sister. She hung up the phone after one of the calls and yelled, "Mary Lou, you have a date with Taylor next Saturday night. The two of you will double date with Ginger and her boyfriend. After the game you'll go to Ginger's house. Her mom said she would serve cookies and cocoa."

The girls were allowed to date once they started high school, but Mr. Ed and the Missus set up restrictions. The girls had to be in the company of parents or another couple and needed to be home at the designated early hour. Mr. Ed and the Missus insisted on always knowing all the boys the girls dated.

A few weeks after school started in Jane's sophomore year, the Missus heard her accept a date with someone named Mark Stevens. She was quite skeptical. "Jane, we don't know anything about this boy. How old is he and where does he live?"

Jane commented, "He is sixteen, just one year older than me and he lives about six miles west of town. Mama, you would like him. He's a nice boy."

Mr. Ed listened as Jane described the potential date. After thinking for a minute, he commented, "If his home is on Winding Osage Road, then he must be the son of Andy Stevens. Andy dated and married one of the

Andrew sisters who went to high school with me in Springville. Andy's parents are upstanding citizens." Mr. Ed looked over to his wife and assured her by stating, "With parents like that the son must be a fine young man."

Mr. Ed then looked at his daughter and demanded, "When this young man comes to get you, I expect you to bring him into the house to talk with us. We want to meet him, and I'd like to hear how his mama is doing."

Setting up dates was complicated because of the limited availability of cars. Even families who enjoyed some wealth were limited to only one car. It was not unusual for the dating couple to be accompanied in the car with the boy's mom, dad, brothers and sisters. Jane commented after one date night, "I like the sister and parents better than my boyfriend."

There was a great deal of organization by boys in arranging transportation for the evening. If one boy was fortunate enough to have the use of the family car, he suggested to his friends, "Why don't you get a date and come along with me?" The cars were often filled with as many as six young people.

There were times when the boys were not able to borrow the family car. Mr. Ed heard more than once a plea like the one Jane made to her dad. "Keith says the brakes in his dad's car are out, and they had to take the car to the shop. We have no way to attend the game Saturday night."

Jane thought a minute then suggested, "Dad, you like to go to the ballgames. Why don't you and I pick up Keith and his dad in our Chevrolet?"

The Swing Era became a way of life across America. Like Mary Lou and Jane, many young people diligently listened when the weekly radio show announced the top ten songs of the week. Thanks to access of radios, record disks for phonographs, and gala movies featuring popular music, both young and old were well acquainted with popular bands.

It was almost impossible to listen to the rhythmic swing music and not start moving. Songs like Artie Shaw's "Dancing in the Dark," and the orchestra of Harry James playing "I Cried for You," created the need to sway. "Chicago" played by Tommy Dorsey's band, and Glen Miller's fast paced "Chattanooga Choo Choo" and "Pennsylvania 6-5000" had everyone twisting and leaping.

The students in high school in this rural area had a problem. They needed a place to jitterbug. There were dance halls in faraway places like Kansas City, but the students were too young to travel long distances and return home at a time acceptable to parents.

Allison, as president of the student council, chaired the group designated to discuss the problem with Mr. Swartz. "Sir," Allison pleaded, "you know how we all love music. We enjoy singing and playing instruments in the orchestra but most of us want to dance. Is there any way we can get a phonograph for the school, so we can have dances in the gym after games?"

His response was agreeable. "You have my approval for organizing dances here at the school. I am sure that if you politely asked them, some parents and teachers would act as sponsors. You young people could share your own records. The problem you are facing is one we face every day at this small school. There simply are no funds available to purchase any equipment."

The principal tugged at his chin and thought a minute. "I am constantly amazed at how all of you have learned to solve problems. Can you think of a way to collect the money you need to buy the phonograph?"

The fact that Mr. Swartz gave his approval for dances gave Allison and her committee all the encouragement they needed. The following week, instead of poking fun at someone in her gossip column, Allison asked students to help raise the money to buy a phonograph. The response was immediate. Students formed car washes and went around town offering to do odd jobs like weeding the cemetery, painting sides of buildings, and decorating store windows. Parents set up tasks at home beyond the usual duties of their teenagers and paid them for their efforts. The Missus and other mothers made sandwiches and drinks to be sold at school events. It took only three weeks for all the needed money to be collected and a phonograph purchased. As a result of combined efforts, after basketball games students used the gym to dance to songs like Glen Miller's orchestra playing "In the Mood," or Doris Day singing, "Sentimental Journey."

On a lovely October day, Mary Lou and Jane again rushed home with news they considered very important.

Jane announced, "Mom, Dad, the road show troop is planning to have a hayride and party next Saturday."

Her sister added, "Billy's dad is providing his tractor and large wagon for the ride, but someone needs to offer their home as the site for the party."

The girls were quiet but turned their heads and gazed wistfully into their large double living room. Both parents knew instantly what their daughters had in mind. The Missus said, "Yes, girls, our home is about the right distance from school for your ride and we would love to host your party."

Mr. Ed whispered something into his wife's ear. After her nod he directed, "Girls, since the party will be here you might enjoy receiving your Christmas present early."

The Missus instructed, "Go up to the guest room. In the closet you will find a big box. Please bring it downstairs."

Mary Lou smiled. "I've looked at that box several times and wondered what was in it. If it hadn't been sealed with tape and twine, I probably would have peeked to see what was in it."

The girls lugged the rather big box down the stairs to the kitchen and placed it on the table. Mr. Ed pulled his trusty knife out of his back pocket and used it to cut the twine and tape. While doing so he asked, "Girls, do you have any idea what this might be?"

Jane made a wise guess. "It is something we can use for the party? Maybe it's a new set of dishes."

Her father chuckled and said, "Child, you are way off the mark. This is something you and your sister will love."

Mary Lou was finding it difficult to wait. "Daddy, don't make us guess any more. Please open the box."

Mr. Ed pulled back the flaps and invited the girls to peek inside. The eyes of both girls grew large when they saw it contained a new record player. They screamed and hugged their parents. "This is a perfect gift for us. Now we can listen to our favorite records any time we wish."

At school the next morning the girls quickly told their friends about the early Christmas present. Mary Lou commented, "Now we have a phonograph to use at the party!" She bit her lip and added, "There's another problem. Jane and I only have four records. We'll have to dance to the same songs over and over."

Betty quickly replied, "Heavens, that isn't so. Many of us own several records. We can bring them to the party."

The girls helped their mother prepare refreshments the day of the party, and Mr. Ed was responsible for setting up the parlors for dancing. He looked around and found assistance. "Son, it's a good thing you have grown so much this year. You will be a lot of help in moving this furniture and rolling up the rugs." Dannydon't had no interest in preparing for the festivity, but could not resist helping because his father had noticed he was growing bigger and stronger.

The party was boisterous and noisy. The phonograph was turned to its highest volume. Probably even the cows were listening as they rested in the small lot by the barn. Those attending were dancing most of the time and only stopped for refreshments during slow songs.

At some time during the party, guests sat briefly on the cot while waiting for a turn to use the bathroom. The Missus had dressed the cot up in the plaid material, the same fabric as she had used for Mary Lou's Sunflower Sweetie cowboy shirt. More than one student frowned in thought then commented, "I think I've seen this material before."

Mr. Ed was more than pleased as he watched the young people dancing to the Big Band sounds. He commented to the Missus, "This old house is lively like it was years ago when my brothers and sister returned home from high school for their summer vacations."

Young people always felt welcomed to visit the farm. Mary Lou and Jane's girlfriends considered it their second home. Even though there were extra bedrooms available for sleeping upstairs, the young visitors would often say, "I don't want to be any trouble. Why don't you let me sleep here on this old cot?"

Boys also regularly stopped by the farm. Mary Lou and Jane were amused by their visits. Jane agreed with her sister, "These boys say they are coming to see us, but we are ignored. Instead, they eat our mom's cooking and have long conversations with our dad."

THE SWEETHEART DANCE

On one of the first days in February of her sophomore year, Mary Lou made a mad dash into the house. Even though she was older now and had more self-control, the cot was destined to suffer from this workout. She jumped on it and bounced a few times while shrieking with delight. "Mama, guess what. I have a new boyfriend. His name is Tony. He asked me to be his date for the sweetheart dance."

She bounced so hard that another coil popped. "Mama, he is so g-o-r-e-. No, he is so g-o-r-g-o-u-s. Well anyway, he sure is cute!"

"Mary Lou, if you don't know how to spell words you had best look them up. The correct spelling is in the old dictionary. It's sitting on top of the buffet. Your daddy was using it when working the crossword puzzle this morning."

The Missus frowned at the statement made by her daughter. "Let's discuss your potential date. Your father and I don't know this boy Tony. Don't you remember the rule is we must be acquainted with the boys you date?"

"Mama, of course I remember the rule and I told it to Tony. He is coming down to meet our family this Sunday. I told him that you often had fried chicken for dinner, and he thought that sounded delicious."

Tony arrived soon after the family returned from church on the following Sunday. He did his best to charm each family member. He was new to the community so was interested as Jane told him stories about the shady history of the past. As a natural athlete, he suggested pointers of how Dannydon't could improve his skills of throwing a ball. The Missus was complimented about her cooking and he seemed to enjoy the lively conversation with Mr. Ed about politics as well as fishing. By the end of the day, both parents felt it acceptable for Mary Lou to attend the dance with this new boy provided it was a double date with another couple.

Mary Lou then realized she had a fashion problem. "Mama, I absolutely must have a pretty new dress to wear to the party."

Her eyes were pleading and her voice wistful as she sighed, "What I would really like to wear would be a black velveteen dress with rainbow sequins on the collar."

The Missus sighed at the request. She always had a difficult time saying no to her children. "Mary Lou, you haven't had any nice new outfits since we went to Kansas City last year." She peered at her daughter before continuing. "You seem to have grown at least two inches since the start of school. Most of the hems of your dresses are now above your knees, and we can't have that. You will get your dress. Tomorrow we'll go into town to pick out a pattern and fabric."

She added, "Mary Lou, you know that velveteen material is expensive. You'll have to help with the purchase by using some of the money you've earned teaching piano to the neighborhood children. Money in my jar is limited because the hens are not laying many eggs this time of the year."

The Missus used the old kitchen table as the cutting board. After she had pinned the pattern onto the fabric and started snipping the fine fuzzy lint made her sneeze. As she finished sewing the first seams her fingers were tingling. By the next day her fingers were so stiff she could not sew.

Auntie Marie, visiting that afternoon, noticed her sister's discomfort. "Let me finish the dress for my demanding niece."

Auntie Marie cornered Mary Lou as soon as she arrived home from school. "Mary Lou, put on your dress. I want to see how it looks."

Mary Lou whirled and twirled in the lovely dress. Even though it wasn't finished, it fitted perfectly on her petite body. Auntie Marie said, "Your mom is having trouble with her allergies so I'll work on it too. Stand on a chair while I mark the hemline. After I finish stitching the hem I'll attach the sequins to the collar, and your dress will be ready."

The task was not easy. Auntie Marie fussed, "Honey, will you please stand still and not pretend to be dancing? If you keep moving, the hemline will look like ocean waves."

Auntie Marie looked at the clock above the cot and sighed to her sister, "I can't finish the dress today because I told my neighbor I would pick my girls up by five."

She looked at the Missus and cautioned, "Now don't you touch that dress. I'll be back here to finish it tomorrow."

Later that evening Auntie Marie called her sister to say, "My youngest came home with a high fever. She will need to stay in bed. Sorry, but I can't come down and complete Mary Lou's dress tomorrow."

The Missus sighed. Even though her hands were sore, she made the final stitches so the dress would be ready in time for the Friday night dance.

Her daughter went to the dance decked out in a lovely new dress. The Missus, because of the terrible reaction to the fabric, was home suffering with swollen red hands, a puffy red face, and eyes that were almost swollen shut.

AN IMPERFECT WORLD

"Whew, that was close!" Mary Lou entered the kitchen just as the grandfather clock struck 10:00 p.m., the hour of her curfew.

The only reason the Missus and Mr. Ed had allowed her to be out this late on a school night was because the basketball team was playing in the district play-off. Winning this game qualified them to participate in the state tournament in Hutchinson, Kansas. Mary Lou had convinced her parents by pleading, "I just have to attend this game for Tony. He says that seeing me in the cheering section will give him confidence to do his best."

The almost sixteen-year-old stopped in her parent's room to assure them she was home on time. She shared the highlights of the game with her dad and proudly stated, "Tony scored twenty-two points, probably because he heard me screaming."

Mary Lou kissed her mom and dad goodnight, dashed up the stairs and entered the cold bedroom. In the soft glow of moonlight, she took note that her sister's body was curled in a ball between the feather tick mattress and several of their mom's quilts.

Mary Lou tiptoed over to the bed and whispered, "Move over, Sis." Jane, still in a deep sleep, flopped to the other side of the bed. Everything would have been fine if Mary Lou hadn't stuck her cold feet on Jane's legs.

Instantly Jane was alert. She snarled, "You cad, I've been wondering for months how I ended up on your side of the bed."

Since the girls were now awake, they turned on their tummies and gazed out of the south window. The moon was so bright that the barn, sheds and fences cast long shadows. The tranquility of the evening was only broken by the distant howl of coyotes and the barking response of the dogs.

Mary Lou's eyes were growing heavy when she became aware that her sister was silently sobbing. She gave her sister a nudge, "You've never awakened before when I asked you to move to the cold side of the bed. I figured what you didn't know wouldn't hurt." She added, "I won't do it again."

"Bet your life you won't! If it happens again, I'll kick you out of bed, and you'll land on your butt." She choked back a sob, "Besides, that's not why I'm crying."

Mary Lou was baffled. She asked, "Whatever makes you so sad at this time of night?"

Jane decided it was time to alert her older sister about the imperfect world. "Mary Lou, you are so smitten with Tony and busy with the road show that you don't pay attention to things that are happening around school."

"I'm not that dense. Mr. Swartz looks at his watch every five minutes and paces back and forth. Mrs. Tyler is snorting more than ever. Coach Williams looks angry and Miss Livingston seems to have lost her giggles. All the teachers are walking around with long faces. Come to think of it, I've seen several boys shake their heads like they are trying to get rid of bad thoughts and some sit around with their hands covering their faces. Explain to me what is going on."

Jane stated, "Let's go back to the beginning. This fall Mr. Swartz realized that our high school had enrolled many more students than expected. He convinced the school board that another teacher was needed. They hired Mr. Whipple to teach American History, a new class in World Geography, and relieve Coach Williams of teaching Industrial Arts."

"None of my classes are with Mr. Whipple, but he's handsome and seems friendly. He hasn't been around the school for several days. Where is he?"

"Mr. Kellerman, Ralph's dad, pointed a shotgun at his head and chased him out of town!"

"That doesn't make sense. Why would he do that?"

"Oliver told me the whole story. Mary Lou, do you know the definition of pedophile?"

"Well, I know the definition of the word pedicure. Pedophile sounds a little like it, so it must have something to do with feet."

"How can you be so stupid? A pedophile is someone who takes sexual advantage of a minor! Mr. Whipple is a pedophile, and he took advantage of several freshmen boys!" Jane blew her nose and wiped the tears from her eyes.

Mary Lou gasped. "How could this have happened? Most of the freshmen boys live on farms and go home on one of the school busses. They aren't around anytime except during school hours."

"That's where you are wrong. Mr. Whipple suggested that the boys in Industrial Arts select a special project. Ralph was making a bird apartment for Martins. Jason was designing a greenhouse for his mom and Carl was doing final touches on a gun rack for his dad. The boys were having trouble finishing their project on time, so Mr. Whipple suggested they take turns staying after school. He offered to take them home in his Chevy."

"If this really happened, why didn't the boys resist or say something?"

"I think Mr. Whipple made them think it was completely their fault. He must have had them scared silly."

"How did Ralph's dad find out?"

"You know how Ralph is, talkative and energetic. His parents grew worried when he had nothing to say, ate little, and immediately went to his room after supper. When his dad drilled him about problems at school, he broke down and told what had happened."

"This is weird. Does everybody in school except me know about Mr. Whipple and what has been happening?"

"Like you, a lot of the students know something is not quite right but don't know the story. Oliver was taking the Industrial Arts class, but he had his project completed. I think Ralph or one of the other boys must have confessed to him. You know that Oliver and I have been best friends since first grade. Even though he likes dirty jokes and acts worldly, this was a shock to him. I guess he needed to talk about it with someone, and that someone was me."

Jane hesitated then continued, "Even though I sometimes hate your guts and think you are dense, you are my best buddy so I had to tell you. Now, I know that Allison is your best friend but you must promise not to tell her. It would be terrible if she hinted about this in the school newspaper. Remember, the boys promised not to mention this problem at school. They were told to pretend that it never happened."

Sharing the terrible secret seemed to relieve Jane's mind. Within a few minutes she was sound asleep. Meanwhile Mary Lou tossed and turned most of the night. Her worried thoughts were about the boys. "Will these boys have nightmares for months? Will it change their personalities? Will this assault disturb them for the remainder of their lives?"

GOING STEADY

Until the middle of her sophomore year, Mary Lou enjoyed dating but had no special boyfriend. Now, she was smitten and frankly acted a little giddy. Dannydon't liked the new boyfriend but thought his sister was going crazy. He danced around the kitchen table teasing her. "Tony does this and Tony does that. I think my sister is in l-o-v-e."

Tony, a junior, asked Mary Lou if she would be his date at the junior-senior prom. By this time the Missus had learned her lesson. Instead of trying to make a formal, she and Mary Lou made another trip to Kansas City. Mary Lou came home with a beautiful gown. The flowing skirt was white with tiny red embroidered flowers embedded in the material, and the bodice was made from a red satin fabric.

The night of the prom Mary Lou once again stood in front of the three-sided vanity mirror. She was pleased at how the gown's long swirling skirt and the fitted waist accentuating her slimness. The v-shaped neckline and padding in the bodice gave a suggestion of curves, and the red color enhanced the shine of her dark hair. She applied a deep red lipstick, rouge, and a tiny bit of eye shadow to her face. She thought a minute about the makeup she had just dabbed on and decided it best to wear her glasses while still in the sight of her mama. Hopefully, the makeup around her eyes would not be noticed.

Mary Lou finished preparing for the date by tucking an artificial gardenia over her left ear. She had purchased it when she realized it had chemical properties that made it glow in the dark. As she looked at her image she chuckled, "The flower will act as a beacon for Tony as he kisses me goodnight under that sweet smelling honeysuckle vine." Mary Lou took one last look at her reflection and sighed in satisfaction. "It took forever but I made it. I finally am a woman."

The day after school was dismissed for the summer, Tony went to Western Kansas. He needed money and his uncle suggested that joining his wheat harvesting crew would be a good way to earn the needed funds. The crew would be working in wheat fields in Kansas, Nebraska, South and North Dakota, and Minnesota. Tony would not return home until two weeks after the start of school the following fall. He did not seem sorry to leave Mary Lou and even had the nerve to suggest she might enjoy dating other boys.

The cot's pillows were soggy because, for the next two days, Mary Lou did nothing but cry. When her tears were gone, she sighed, took a long bath, washed her hair and said to her sister, "Two weeks ago it seemed like I was grown up. Now, I've been acting like a baby. It's time to get on with my life and forget about Tony."

During the long summer Mary Lou thoroughly enjoyed her friends and family. In addition to having fun, she made money giving music lessons and assisting at a church camp for young girls.

The Missus and Mr. Ed were pleased that their daughter said nothing about Tony. The Missus stated, "He's a nice boy, but I hate for Mary Lou to be tied to one boy when so young."

Mr. Ed asked his wife. "Did you ever have a serious conversation with her about birds and bees? Too many young people around here have to get married because of an unplanned pregnancy." Mr. Ed knew his wife was quite shy about talking about sex. He added, "If you don't say something to her about this, then I will."

The parents wrote off the romance between Tony and their oldest daughter too soon. When Tony returned home the second week after school started, the couple decided to go steady. Mary Lou was more than pleased that she was the special girlfriend of a senior who played left end in football and was the basketball center who chalked up a minimum of twenty points each game.

The tokens representing going steady put her in a state of rapture. On a date after a football game, Tony gave her his purple athletic letter and suggested she sew it onto the jacket she wore when sitting in the cheering section at games. A couple of months later, after a basketball game in January, he placed his senior class ring on her finger. It was made to fit by adding several layers of masking tape.

Tony brought Mary Lou home after yet another basketball game and dance. Tony was hungry. Instead of kissing Mary Lou good night at the door, he suggested, "Let's go into your kitchen. Your mom is sure to have some tasty tidbits somewhere." Once inside, he immediately headed for the refrigerator and cookie jar.

Mary Lou sat quietly on the cot watching the love of her life devour the leftover meat loaf, a glass of milk, and all the snickerdoodle cookies. After Tony had finished gorging himself, he plopped on the cot beside Mary Lou. For a short while they simply held hands and talked about the game and class assignments. Tony's arm went around Mary Lou's shoulders. Within a few minutes they were enjoying innocent hugs and kisses. As hormones kicked in, the kisses and caresses became intense.

The old cot had to do something to protect this foolish girl. It thought only a moment before formulating an appropriate action plan. It could protect this almost grown child and, at the same time, enjoy the opportunity of paying her back for long years of abuse. The child had jumped up and down on it so many years that his springs were weakened. Now, as the couple wiggled and squirmed, the cot responded by making squeaks and creaks so loud they awakened the Missus. She yelled from the bedroom, "Mary Lou, is that you?"

The Missus was no dummy. As soon as Tony made his hasty goodnight retreat, she came into the kitchen and gave the lecture she previously had avoided. It was properly titled, "If you know what's good for you." The Missus pointed out loudly and clearly what happened to girls who did not realize it was their responsibility to firmly say, "No."

Chapter 20

MOM, WE MISS YOU

A dark cloud had gathered which would topple the joyous spirit the family had enjoyed for several years. The Missus never whined about how she was feeling. Perhaps I was the first to recognize just how much she was suffering. Some nights, especially after doing the washing on Monday, she paced the floor because her hands and arms were stinging. During the fall months she often sat in the rocker all night and struggled to get her breath. Her health continued to deteriorate and eventually resulted in a crisis for the family. They needed faith and love to survive the following year.

The Caring Cot

ILLNESS TAKES OVER

The Missus had been bothered for many years with allergies. Her reactions seemed to be getting worse. She couldn't be around any animals without her eyes starting to water, the feather pillows made her sneeze and the soap used for washing clothes on Mondays caused her skin to become red and swollen. She had to eliminate the work of tending to her beloved flowers and garden vegetables because of sun poisoning. The only time she dared to tread outside was in early morning or at twilight.

The Missus developed an additional ailment. She now was having difficulty breathing. Instead of getting a decent night's sleep in a bed, she spent the entire night sitting in the old rocker placed next to the cot in the kitchen. Night after night the cot heard her gasping for air.

Mr. Ed was worried and tried to help in every way possible. He took over the Monday morning clothes washing and insisted he did not need her help with the garden work. He pleaded to his daughters, "Girls, can you please spare some of your telephone and primping time and help your mother?" He also expected Dannydon't to do his part. "Son, keep your pets a good distance from the house and help by doing errands for your mama." The efforts made by her family did nothing to improve her health. The lady seemed to get weaker and thinner every day.

Mr. Ed. expressed his concern, "Honey, I'm really worried about you."

She sighed and responded, "Now, you know there is nothing that can be done, I just have a lot of allergies."

The Missus got thin as a rail and started running a fever. Mr. Ed insisted she make an appointment to see Dr. Gentry as soon as possible.

Dr. Gentry shook his head as he watched the Missus enter his office. The feverish eyes and blush in her cheeks foretold the news he would soon have to share with her. After only a short examination he delivered the bad news. The Missus, in addition to all of her other problems, now had tuberculosis.

In those days anyone diagnosed with this disease was immediately sent away to a sanitorium for treatment. The children watched with heavy hearts as their mother packed the bare necessities: a toothbrush, a comb and a few nightgowns. The Missus dared not kiss her children good-by because of the infection. Her voice choked, "Children, take good care of your daddy. He'll need a lot of help."

The doctors at the sanitorium discouraged visits from young people. Mr. Ed's children rarely saw their mama for several months because the rules were so strict. When they see her, it was from across the room. They were never allowed to get near enough for pats and hugs.

The Missus had been Mr. Ed's constant companion for more than twenty years, so he was determined to see her as often as possible. Each Sunday, immediately after church, Mr. Ed jumped in the car and drove to Kansas City. He would stay through the afternoon but always had to return in the evening to the farm to complete the milking and other chores.

On his weekly visits Mr. Ed did his best to lift the spirits of his ailing wife by providing a monologue about the previous week. "Tony came home from college last weekend. Evidently, he and Mary Lou had a big fight because he had accepted a sorority girl's invitation to attend a dance. I hoped maybe the romance was over, but before he left on Sunday, they were lovey-dovey again."

The Missus nodded but said nothing.

He continued. "Jane is writing poems about our farm. She had to hand them in for the teacher to review. I can probably bring them for you to enjoy next Sunday."

The Missus blew her nose as tears filled her eyes.

Mr. Ed knew she desperately wanted to hear about the activities of her children. "Danny seems to be very proud of his calf, Billy. I've raised a lot of cattle but this is the first time I've seen one that acts like a puppy. He follows Danny all over the farm. Danny is taking excellent care of his animal. In addition to brushing Billy each day, he is learning techniques of how to lead and display his pet. It will be interesting to see Danny show his calf at the county fair this fall."

Her heart was breaking. The Missus cried and moaned, "Ed, I am so homesick for my babies, my flowers, and my kitchen. I even miss the old cot! Will I ever be released from this bed and these four drab walls?"

Mr. Ed tried to be consoling and hide his own doubt. Both he and his wife were aware that tuberculosis could be fatal. Nevertheless, he responded, "Sure you will, Honey. The doctor says you are doing all the right things. Your fever hasn't been as high this week."

MOM, WE NEED YOU

Mr. Ed had always been a busy man. Now he was doing double duty and almost never had time to rest on the cot. He and the children had not realized how many daily tasks the Missus had always done for them without comment. It was a struggle for the family to survive without the guidance and helping hand of the Missus. They missed her precise schedules and sense of order. Even though the girls had assisted her for years, somehow, they had not learned how to properly complete household tasks.

It's fortunate that Mr. Ed had learned how to handle the washing. He continued to do it on Mondays unless a crop absolutely needed attention that day. He had different standards than his wife. He didn't think it was necessary to wash his work clothes so often and he suggested to his children, "It won't hurt you to wear an outfit more than one time before it is washed." After taking the clean clothes off the clothesline, Mr. Ed. always heaped them on the old table or the cot. The girls, when they returned from school, could not ignore what was to be their afternoon job.

Most of the clothes were made of simple cotton. In order to have clothes looking neat, shirts, skirts, and blouses needed to be starched and dampened just before they were ironed. The girls and even their young brother, Dannydon't, used the new electric iron whenever they had a few extra minutes. The ironing board was permanently set up in the living room next to the piano. This was a furniture arrangement the Missus never would have allowed.

A final rehearsal for the junior play was called, so Jane returned home late in the afternoon. She walked into the parlor to find her dad ironing the dress she was to wear that night. While doing so tears were rolling down his cheeks. Missing his wife, trying to fulfill so many responsibilities on the farm and caring for his children were stretching his optimism and patience.

There were other changes happening. The Kansas dirt, which the Missus fought so vigorously, was finally winning a battle in the old house. Each piece of furniture located in the upstairs bedrooms was covered with a fine layer of dust. The kitchen floor was given a once over with the broom each week but was only washed when it was so sticky that walking was difficult. The dark space under the cot was now the permanent home of dust bunnies.

Dannydon't had to spend many hours alone and needed company. Mr. Ed found a perfect pet for his son, a wiggly German shepherd puppy. The puppy was not satisfied with the bed made for him on the porch using one of the cot's old covers. It took only a few scratches at the back door and a sad look to help Mr. Ed decide that it would be acceptable to allow the puppy inside the house. The pup helped by cleaning up all the crumbs falling on the floor, but his destructive behaviors caused problems. A throw rug, Mr. Ed's slippers, and several of the cot's pillows were torn to shreds. The puppy, just like Mr. Ed and the children, liked to rest on the cot. It wasn't long before the cot's covers smelled like a wet dog.

Mr. Ed could fix just about anything, and did so willingly. He never complained about most household tasks and would even sew on buttons or stitch a torn seam using the sewing machine. Unfortunately, he never mastered the art of cooking. This intelligent man, who could read directions of how to assemble complicated pieces of farm equipment, was at a loss when reading simple cooking recipes. He never baked even when the girls prepared a casserole, put it in the refrigerator then wrote simple instructions like, "Take the meat loaf out of the refrigerator. Turn the oven to three hundred and fifty degrees and bake the meat for one hour." In hungry desperation, Mr. Ed finally learned how to use the skillet to fry eggs and bacon for breakfast.

The girls had learned how to cook when they were young by helping their mother and had received additional training through 4-H Clubs and Home Economics in high school. However, both were deficient in taking an inventory of pantry needs and planning menus in advance. They would tell their daddy he was going to get a gooseberry pie for dessert only to learn that there was no sugar in the canister and that pie certainly took a lot of sugar. They decided to bake cookies or bread then discovered that the flour was so old it had bugs. The first winter the Missus was away from the farm the cellar was filled with canned vegetables and fruits that could be opened and served easily. During the next summer there was an abundance of fruits and vegetables but no one canned. It was fall before the girls realized that canned goods, no longer available from the cellar, needed to be added to the grocery list.

The girls, because of busy school schedules, had difficulty including time for domestic tasks. They thought it much more important to be present to cheer for sporting events, perform in plays and all musical productions, and attend each time they were invited to a party or asked to go on a date. Boiled hot dogs became their specialty. They were served so often that Dannydon't, when an adult, hated the sight of them. Mr. Ed had an abundant supply of potatoes stored in the cellar. Each evening one of the girls quickly cleaned and boiled a few for the meal. The wonderful breads, baked so many years by the Missus, were replaced with brands from the store like tasteless Wonder Bread. Within a few days the loaves became soggy and developed a green mold around the edges.

During weekdays Mr. Ed worked in the field until noon. Since the children were in school, he had to make his own lunch. He often dined on bread and molasses or made himself a cheese sandwich. After the snack he continued to always take a few minutes to rest on the cot and, while doing so, dozed during the market and weather reports.

The Missus missed many important events in the lives of her children. She only could write letters to Jane congratulating her on high grades and honors. She missed hearing her sing "Blueberry Hill" when the road show performed for the county fair. She regretted that she could not enjoy watching her daughter deliver faultless lines for one of the plays created by the writing class.

She was not around when Mary Lou broke up with her boyfriend. Perhaps it's just as well. Had she heard Mary Lou sobbing over her lost love and listened to her concerns about being an old maid, she would have sniffed and commented, "Good riddance."

The Missus only heard about the Sunflower Sweeties being invited to audition for a national radio talent show and missed hearing the group practice long hours in preparation for this audition. She also missed Mary Lou's high school graduation and was not present that summer to help her make final preparations for college.

LITTLE BROTHER

Dannydon't felt the absence of his mother far more than Jane and Mary Lou. His siblings had been correct in their observation when they said, "He's the apple in mother's eye." He was aware that his mama's eyes had always lit up when he entered the room. When he was younger, he had received far more hugs and kisses than he wanted. His mother had always had time to listen to his tales about his latest fishing expeditions. After school she would drop what she was doing to help him complete homework. Before bed she enjoyed reading animal or adventure stories to him.

Six years earlier, Dannydon't oldest sister had begged to be given a calf to rear for her 4-H project. She thought it sounded a lot more fun than making aprons and cooking biscuits. Her dad had responded, "Honey, you need to learn to be a good wife. Raising a calf is a project for boys."

The spring before the Missus went to the sanitorium, Dannydon't was presented with a calf. As a 4-H project, it would be his responsibility to see that the calf was groomed and well fed. If he turned out to be an outstanding specimen, Dannydon't would show him at the county fair. As soon as the calf was weaned, he was guided by his master to the greenest pastures, and more than once, allowed to graze on the lush Kentucky Blue Grass surrounding the house. Billy followed his master everywhere, even to the creek or pond. More than once, Dannydon't was irritated because the calf stepped into the water just as a fish started nibbling on the baited hook.

After his mother went to the sanitorium, Dannydon't continued to fish but he stopped bringing his catch back to the house. He groomed Billy and cuddled the new puppy but did so in a listless manner. Mr. Ed was not surprised to read on his son's report card that Dannydon't needed to be better prepared for lessons.

Dannydon't sisters finally realized the depth of his sadness when he stopped tormenting them. As soon as they arrived home from high school, he disappeared to the pond or barn and delivered not one teasing word. At the supper table he made no sassy comments about their cooking and ate almost nothing. During the evening hours he listened to the radio and went to his bedroom long before asked to do so.

Jane asked her sister, "What can we do for the poor kid? He looks so sad all the time."

Mary Lou thought a minute then answered. "We've been pretty mean to him. I guess it is time we change the way we treat our little brother."

The following afternoon Jane rushed from the bus and quickly changed into a pair of overalls. She called, "Come on, Dannydon't. I want to go fishing with you."

Dannydon't looked up in surprise, grinned and immediately collected the fishing gear. "Jane, you hate to bait the hooks with worms. I'll do that for you."

Mary Lou did not accompany them because she had an assignment to complete before starting the meal. She called to her siblings, "Bring home some fish and we'll fry them for supper."

She noticed that Billy was preparing to follow Dannydon't and his sister to the pond. She got a firm grip of his halter and said, "I'll keep Billy with me. If he gets in the water, he'll scare the fish. I'll even give him a good brushing while you are gone."

The evening meal featured a large platter of fried perch caught by Dannydon't. As he ate everything on his plate, he babbled about the fun he had had with Jane. He even teased, "Mary Lou, it's a good thing you didn't come along because we saw two snakes."

The gentler, kinder sisters continued to give their brother the attention and affection he desperately needed. They made hot chocolate and baked his favorite cookies. Mary Lou borrowed the car and took him to see Lone Ranger or Gene Autry movies shown on Saturday afternoons. Jane always took the time to check his homework and quiz him before tests. The biggest change of all was the sisters started calling him Dan instead of Dannydon't.

THE MISSUS RETURNS

At the sanitorium, the Missus was receiving special treatment designed for patients with tuberculosis. In the forties, medicines like antibiotics were not available. Instead, the patients stayed in bed most of the time and ate vast quantities of fatty foods. Breakfast included oatmeal, biscuits, eggs, bacon and fruits. Dinner and supper were both full meals including breads, gravy, creamed vegetables and rich sauces. Desserts such as puddings and pie were always on the tray. Each evening, just before bedtime, a nurse would bring the Missus a large bowl of chocolate, strawberry, or vanilla ice cream. The Missus slowly got better and, while doing so, got fat. She went to the sanitorium weighing less than a hundred pounds and came back home weighing over one hundred and seventy pounds.

The Missus followed the doctor's orders and spent many hours sleeping. When awake she sat in the easy chair by her bed reading or doing needlework. Her busy fingers created two beautiful lace tablecloths for the old kitchen table. The cot was proud to be remembered with a new crocheted pillow cover. Mr. Ed thought all were too elegant to use, so he stored them in the cedar chest.

The Missus finally was well enough to be released from the sanitorium. Upon returning home she was surprised by so many changes. Mary Lou attended a distant college and returned to the farm only on rare weekends or holidays. Jane was no longer the quiet younger sister. She was now totally absorbed with high school activities and spent many hours with her friends. Dan, her sweet baby, was an adolescent with a squeaky voice. He was happy to have his mother home but thought that he was far too big for her hugs.

Mr. Ed reassured her that things were just as they should be. "Honey, it's only natural that our children grow up and make their own way. You can rest assured, they know we much love them, and they love us. Think of it this way. If the circle of life goes as expected, it won't be many more years before grandchildren will be here taking their turn to jump on the old cot!"

Making their own way did take the children away from the farm for several years. Mary Lou, who thought she would be an old maid at seventeen, was happy that her life turned out as it did. She studied to be a teacher and, while doing so, had a wonderful time dating and going to parties. When Mary Lou was having difficulty with an advanced biology course, a graduate assistant offered tutoring lessons. The two quickly fell in love and were married the following June. Mary Lou, her husband and two sons lived in the nearby state of Nebraska for several years. On holidays or during the summers, while her husband was absorbed in fieldwork related to his professional entomology position at the university, Mary Lou and the boys always loaded up the car and headed for Mr. Ed's farm.

Jane often listened as her dad dreamed about traveling around the world. He frequently asked her to sing one of his favorite songs, "Far Away Places with Strange Sounding Names." Jane completed a nursing degree, worked in a New Orleans hospital, and later married a career army officer. For the next twenty plus years, she moved from coast to coast and spent several years in Europe. She, her husband, and children considered the farm their only constant home.

Dan, who by now, had forever dropped the "don't" part of his name served several years in the navy and was assigned to a ship called Yorktown. Soon after returning home, he married a charming girl from Independence, Missouri. Dan's family settled in a town only about thirty miles away from the farm. Dan was available on weekends to help his dad with the garden and field work. He often brought his boat along when he came to the farm. If the work was completed, he and his dad would try out the excellent fishing lakes located not too far from the farm.

Mr. Ed treated the Missus like a queen. In respect to her frailties, he did the heavy work and lifting. He was ever thoughtful and offered a helping hand for canning and the heavy housework. He pushed the vacuum cleaner even though he swore no dust was visible. Ed hung the wet clothes to dry on wash day so the Missus would not be exposed to the sun. When a man does a woman's work, it is sometimes referred to as "hen pecked," The term did not apply for Mr. Ed. because the Missus never asked him to do a thing.

The Missus slowly regained her strength and tiny figure. She missed her children, but realized how precious and fleeting these years were for her and her husband. They now had time to thoroughly enjoy each other's company. One anniversary in September was celebrated by enjoying a second honeymoon at the Lake of the Ozarks. They also made regular weekly visits to Dan's home and enjoyed extended trips to visit daughters each year.

Most of their time was spent quietly on the farm they both loved. Summer evenings were special. They sat under the big maple tree, watched the fireflies and stars, and listened to the singing of the evening critters. As the sky grew dark, they tuned in the battery-operated radio to hear the sports announcer describing baseball games played by the Kansas City Royals.

Chapter 21

GRANDPA! THERE GOES OLD FIGHTER!

In the eyes of the grandchildren, visiting the farm was a perfect vacation. They were greeted by adoring grandparents, always had fabulous meals containing food they liked to eat and found the farmland offered endless sources of adventure. Mr. Ed stocked the three ponds with fish. On summer nights after supper Grandfather and the children collected poles and dug for long red worms behind the bar, then tried their luck. Yes, they caught fish. The children were frustrated that one, Old Fighter, always got away.

The Aging Cot

GREETING GRANDCHILDREN

The long shadows of the maple trees indicated it was getting late in the afternoon. For the last two hours the Missus and Mr. Ed had been sitting in lawn chairs placed near the edge of their front lawn. Sitting a distance from the barnyard, they could hear when cars turned from the highway onto their dusty road and could identify the color and make of the cars when they drove over the hill.

The Missus started to worry. "Do you think Mary Lou had an accident? She should have been here by now."

"Now, Honey, you know that girl is always late. There's not a thing to worry about. I'm not watching for that orange Studebaker any longer. I'm going inside because in a few minutes Mr. Jabberbox will start to relay the battle between the Kansas City Royals and the Boston Red Socks. Besides that, I can hear my old cot calling me."

Before starting to rest Mr. Ed turned the window air conditioner up a notch and tuned the radio to the station broadcasting the game. He patted the pillows and crawled on top of its covers. After all these years the cot's old mattress perfectly fit the form of his long body. It made him feel quite cozy and comfortable, and within a few minutes, he was snoring softly.

Only a short time later, Mary Lou tiptoed into the kitchen holding a tiny bundle. She placed the bundle in her father's arms before gently nudging him. "Wake up, Daddy! You need to meet your first grandson."

The baby's blue eyes looked up at the older blue eyes, and his little legs started kicking at the sound of grandpa's voice. "Now aren't you something special! You are mighty little so you need to get big really quick because I hear Old Fighter calling us from the pond." Grandpa's mellow voice continued to tell this tiny child all the things he planned for them to do together. The baby seemed to comprehend instantly that this big person was to be a very special person in his life.

Mr. Ed was special for this child and for the seven others who came to the farm within the next few years. Each of the six boys and two girls were placed in grandpa's arms and rested contentedly with him on the cot's old mattress. Mr. Ed had conversations with each baby, and the tiny ones seemed to understand perfectly the wisdom of his words. Roger gave his old grandpa his first real smile when he was only a month old, and Hank took his first wobbly steps toward his grandpa.

The grandchildren always seemed to cherish the cot and didn't seem to mind at all that it was getting mighty old and squeaky. Even when they grew a little older, they hurried down from the bedrooms each morning and cuddled with their grandpa on its pillows. The cot was often pretty crowded. Jimmy, the oldest when five, had enjoyed the time spent alone on the cot with grandpa when he was the only grandchild. He was not happy when three cousins and his baby brother also demanded space. The cot tried but simply could not hold them all. Poor Jimmy rolled off onto the floor. If looks could accomplish miracles, all of the interlopers would have disappeared to outer space.

The old table once again enjoyed holding babies while they had their baths. The bright oilcloth protected him from spills, but some things were different. A plastic baby tub replaced the old blue galvanized washtub, and the mothers used all sorts of smelly things to rub into the soft bodies of their babies. Also, there were differences in the bath routine. Mary Lou and Jane represented modern mamas who did not adhere to the complete modesty that the Missus had when her babies where in the company of others. After the baths, naked babies were placed on the cot to kick and squirm. The cot was thankful that the Missus saw to it that a plastic sheet was placed over its cover as protection from bare bottomed babies.

SUMMER VISITS

The close bond developed in their childhood continued between Dan, Mary Lou and Jane. Each time Jane and her family visited the farm after distant travels, Mary Lou and her boys would make their appearance. Dan, his wife and two boys also found Jane's visit a magnet. The old house, permanently inhabited by only two senior citizens, was filled to the brim with twelve to sixteen bodies.

In the mornings of these family reunions the cot felt like a bench in Grand Central Station. Jane's oldest girl, Casey, was the first to rush into the bathroom. She was always sure to stay inside several minutes. The Missus regarded her grandsons looking mighty uncomfortable waiting their turn to use the bathroom. "Boys you don't need to be sitting on that old cot squirming around and crossing your legs. You need to quit moaning and looking so miserable. There's the old sweet pea house outside, or you can always pee behind the bushes!"

Mealtimes brought back memories of the many times when the neighbors came to help Mr. Ed. with the harvesting. Preparation of the food was not so complicated or time consuming with all the new appliances. Instead of working in a frenzy preparing the noon meal like she did for the workers long ago, the Missus, with the help of Dan's wife, spent the summer prior to family reunions filling the new freezer with casseroles, vegetables and desserts which could be thawed quickly then put on the table.

The Missus was most happy to oblige when her daughters suggested they take over the final minutes of meal preparation. They shooed her out of the kitchen saying, "Mom, why don't you play with the babies? We'll call you when the meal is ready."

The girls cherished these moments when they were together with no children demanding attention. It gave them the opportunity to catch up on what had happened in each of their lives since their last visit. Jane suggested they make a pact, "When our children are grown and our husbands gone, we will come back and live on the farm."

Jane wrote the following poem about the life she and her sister would lead as senior citizens:

We'll sit on our rockers, you and me
Remembering Grandmama, poetry and tea
Dad: long summer evenings, watching the cars,
listening to ball games
and checking the stars.
Mom: quilts so beautiful, "Edward, comb your hair,"

fresh baked bread and pies and someone to care.
sunsets in Kansas
bathing suits in the snow
a pesky little brother who finally did grow
a lamb, Spot, Butch and kittens we had
cayotes howling and winds blowing bad
rain on the tin roof
and an attic with a ghost,
a barn with a hayloft and summers that would roast.
You got stuck in a pear tree and lost your first bra
We picked gooseberries and wild plums and flowers we saw
long walks on a country road
the cows chasing me, a little white church and
grandfather's knee.
I talked to your boyfriends-pretending to be you
We fought over clothes, money and cigarettes too.
Two beautiful daughters and four handsome sons,
Six little grandsons and two granddaughters dear
Two husbands thriving on gin and on beer.
You'll think of your tennis, your schools and your brats
I'll think of my travels, my dogs and my cats.
My joints won't bend and my eyes barely see
Your teeth will be gone and you'll have a trick knee.
Our rockers will rock, and we'll sit, you and me
Remembering Grandmama, poetry and tea.

GRANDPA ED'S LESSONS

Mary Lou called to the troops playing down by the barn, "Dinner is ready. Wash up and come to the table." The food was plentiful and simple and the children ate with gusto. To minimize the task of washing dishes, the meal was served on paper plates. The Missus appreciated the help her daughters provided in meal preparation but cautioned, "You girls must not get into lazy habits like using paper plates. Please use my new set of dishes!"

In years past, after the field workers ate meals, the Missus had worked so hard to prepare, the men said, "Thank you, ma'am," and left the table. The modern mamas demanded help from the eaters. Each child helped clear the table of dirty dishes, put items back in the refrigerator and took turns drying the dishes.

Evenings were always lively. Children were dirty and sweaty from hours of outside play, so they all had to take baths. The old tub often held four of them at one time. When the grandsons grew older, Dan and Mr. Ed took them over to the pond where they could skinny dip and splash each other while cleaning off the dirt and sweat.

No one was in a hurry to get to bed. During the twilight hours the grown-ups sat in lawn chairs and watched the children run around the lawn chasing fireflies. Later, children rested on the cot's old covers the Missus saved to be used as lawn blankets. As children looked at the night sky Mr. Ed. pointed out the Big Dipper, the constellations and visible planets. Hank was overheard bragging to his cousins, "Our grandpa understands about everything in this world and can even tell about the stars in the heavens!"

In the middle of the summer, it was nearing midnight before the air was cool enough to go inside for the night. Finding a comfortable place to rest was a challenge. The grown-ups got the beds, the smallest two got the cribs, and the others made do with sleeping bags and old blankets. Each of the children tried to be the one who captured the old cot for his sleeping site.

Mr. Ed and the Missus created a perfect haven for their grandchildren. The Missus had filled the freezer with cinnamon rolls and other baked goods. She collected treasures like shiny rocks and butterfly wings and saved an assortment of nets and containers needed for catching and containing insects. She bought crayons and paper and saved pictures from calendars and magazines. A day or two before the children's arrival, she went to the library and checked out books she could read to the little ones when they were too tired to follow the long steps of their grandfather.

Mr. Ed claimed he did nothing special for the grandchildren. In truth, he was waiting for the opportunity to play a part in molding their characters. The grandchildren, who adored their grandpa, were a perfect audience. They hung onto every word he said, and he said a lot. He often expounded his thoughts about the world and how to live in it. Even though he never used the term "environmentalist," day after day he demonstrated to the small ones following his steps around the farm how they should take care of land and animals.

He preached honesty and complained to his young listeners that one of the biggest things wrong with this country was that politicians did not stand by what they promised. He stated seriously, "The behaviors of people on this earth seems to be getting worse rather than better. It's going to be difficult for each of you. Just remember who you are and what you believe in. You don't have to follow the crowd."

Religious beliefs were not to be left to chance. Mr. Ed thought his grandkids should be familiar with Bible stories. With his audience sitting around him he often pulled out his old Bible and shared thoughts about his favorite passages. Jimmy spoke for all the grandchildren when he commented, "I've heard the stories before, but they are so much more interesting the way that grandpa tells them."

Mr. Ed believed that his grandchildren should understand and adhere to a work ethic. As soon as they climbed out of their cars when visiting the farm, they would hear their grandfather say, "Now get your old clothes on. We are going to the garden and weed before it gets dark." Or, "The garden is filled with ripe vegetables. We need to pick them today. Your grandma wants to prepare them for the freezer when they are at their ripest."

A large wagon was hitched to the tractor. He called to the children, "Hop aboard. We're going to take a ride to the South Forty." Once there, children joined their grandfather in open combat with the thistles threatening to take over the field.

When the weather was rainy, Mr. Ed requested that the children be his work companions in the garage. He claimed he needed their help greasing and repairing equipment. Mr. Ed. always had a collection of broken furniture, tools, and toys. He taught the children names and uses of tools and how to fix broken parts. He insisted, "If it can be fixed, there's no need to keep buying new stuff."

In keeping with the concept of upkeep, Mr. Ed decided the children needed to learn how to paint. He gave each of his grandchildren a brush then invited each to dip into paint cans. The old shed down by the creek was their canvas. It wasn't long before one side resembled a rainbow.

The Missus and mothers gave up on keeping clothes clean and neat. A dresser in the east upstairs bedroom held a collection of old clothes. These items of apparel were meant to get dirty and greasy and have splotches of unusual colors.

The two oldest grandchildren constantly competed to be the best and first. Eight-year-old Casey had just returned to the farm after spending several years in Germany. The first thing she demonstrated to her cousin Jimmy was how easily she could shimmy up the clothesline pole. Jimmy tried to follow her example but his feet barely left the ground.

Jimmy was only eleven when his grandpa took him out to the hay field. He said, "Son, here's how you start this truck, and you press your foot on that peddle for the brakes. The only other thing you have to do is maneuver the truck around the hay bales." Within a day Jimmy considered himself an expert driver.

Mr. Ed was very aware that Casey was irritated and jealous. On her next visit he suggested, "Casey, you are getting long legs. Would you like to learn how to drive the tractor?" Casey gave her cousin a sneering smile indicating, "This time I won!"

Mr. Ed wasn't beyond using competition between his grandchildren for his own advantage. He gave Jimmy and Casey hoes and challenged, "Let me see which one of you is the best at hoeing the garden rows." Or, "I'm looking at the minute hand on my watch. We'll have a contest to see who can pick the most blackberries in fifteen minutes."

Casey had something in common with her great aunt, Mr. Ed's older sister Alicia. Each of them had been the only girl in a covey of boys. The aunt defended herself by becoming a constant tattle-tale who was delighted when her brothers were punished. Casey never went whining and crying to her elders about her cousins and brothers. She could easily out-talk and out-smart all of them. Mr. Ed. chuckled to himself, "Unless I miss my guess, that girl will grow up to become a first-class lawyer!"

Casey developed a skin problem. Her chest was covered with a rash caused by poison ivy. Her mother could not understand why the infection was so bad in that area but not on her arms. Turns out the children were pretending to be movie stars. Casey, in order to be a more perfect Marilyn Monroe, had stuffed her blouse with leaves and some of them were from a poison ivy vine.

MAN'S BEST FRIEND

The grandchildren weren't the only ones having extended visits to the farm. Over the years, several canines also found the farm to be a perfect home. Mary Lou and her husband bought a beautiful white and black Border collie as a playmate for their sons. Their yard in the city had no fence, so each time Silver was allowed outside the house, she disappeared. Sometimes it took hours before the dog was located. Finally, the decision was made to transfer Silver to the farm where she would be allowed to roam freely. It wasn't long before Silver was once again having problems. Responding to the instinct of her breed, she felt it her duty to herd the cars coming down the road. Also, within a few months, she was the proud mother of five puppies.

Mr. Ed decided that Silver needed a different home. The farm which provided a new home for the wandering dog had several sheep. Silver's instinct of herding would make her useful to her new master.

All of her puppies, except one, were given away to friends. Mr. Ed named the only remaining animal Zeek. This fine animal became Mr. Ed's constant companion and never left his side. When Mr. Ed was working in the garden, Zeek stood watching out for rodents trying to invade the area. During the long days Mr. Ed worked in the fields, Zeek could be found patiently waiting for him in the shade of the wagon or nearby tree. Each time the wagon was hitched to the tractor, Zeek jumped on for the ride. Zeek was even known to accompany his master into town where Mr. Ed displayed him to men shopping at the grain elevator. Mr. Ed would proudly state: "I swear to you this is the best dog I've ever had. He knows everything I say and think. I've never had a better friend!"

Prince was a special companion of Jane's family. He guarded the toddlers playing in an enclosed yard and made sure he was in the midst of joyful romps the children had with their dad when he returned home from work each evening. He always regarded Jane as his special mistress and often came to her side for a head pat or tummy scratch.

At night, he assumed the duty of looking after sleeping children. Every hour or two he would tour the bedrooms. Each child received a nose nudge. When they moved or groaned, he was assured that they were fine. One night, as he was acting as a nursemaid, he seemed to be aware that Hank was feverish and restless. At Jane's bedside he barked loudly until she asked, "What's wrong, Prince?" He moved to the bedroom door then insisted she follow him up to the bed of the sick child.

Jane's husband was again assigned overseas duty. This time the family would have to stay several months in an apartment in France. It would not provide a suitable space for a large active boxer. The only solution was to have Prince remain on the farm while they lived in another country.

Prince liked the farm. He was a fine friend to Mr. Ed and felt it his duty to keep the barnyard cats in their proper place, but his heart was with his young family now in Germany. The old dog often sat out under the maple tree watching the road. That was where he was two years later when he noticed a familiar red station wagon coming over the hill. He watched a minute then barked with anticipation as the car drove into the driveway. When the car door opened and Jane stepped out of the car, he yelped a welcome then collapsed with a heart attack!

THE ORPHAN TRAIN RETURNS

During summer vacations on the farm, the cousins spent long hours in adventurous imaginative play. The large lawn was the arena for chasing and wrestling. The dark corners of the sheds, hayloft, and stalls in the barn were perfect hiding places for fugitives. A favorite game was to reenact Civil War battles between the North and South. The only problem was it was also a war between girls and boys. Since the second girl was only a toddler, she was not much of a soldier. Casey was a fierce competitor, but in the end, the South, represented by the regiment of boys, always won.

Like their parents before them, the children were natural snoops. One day, while playing in the attic, they found the files holding stories and poems Jane had written in high school. The younger children were fascinated as Casey and Jimmy read poems about a calf named Billy, the kittens, the dogs, the national pig, and other animals that once lived on the farm. It is no surprise they were spellbound when listening to Jane's play about the Orphan Train traveling through the Midwest.

That evening the children stated to the adults. "We want to put on a play for all of you. Come in the parlor and watch our performance."

The children formed a train line and chugged around the room. Whenever the pretend train stopped, one child would step forward and tell a sad story about being an orphan from New York City. The plea was always, "Will you take me to be your child?" Those in the audience responded quickly by holding out their arms.

Casey and Jimmy represented the brother and sister, Pauline and Jerome. All the others were cuddled with parents and they were the only ones who continued to chug around the room. When their pretend train stopped each pleaded, "Will someone please take both of us to your home? We need to be together."

Grandpa Ed stepped up to the platform. Using a gruff voice asked, "The wife and I have a house full of young children. Would the two of you be willing to help with the babies and with work around the farm?"

Jimmy, as Jerome, answered, "Yes Sir. I am big and strong for my age and I really like to work with horses. You will find me a good worker."

Casey, as Pauline, pleaded her value, "I see your wife is holding a baby. I love babies and can be of help in taking care of him. I also notice that your older children are fussy, and the sister is punching her brothers. On the long train ride through the Midwest, I read stories and played games with the younger ones who were restless. I can be a lot of help to your wife."

The play ended as Mr. Ed representing his father stated, "The two of you can come and live with us on our farm. We will treat you like our own. You will get schooling, have plenty to eat and even get new clothes."

COUSINS

Hank became an ardent baseball fan when still quite small. Grandpa teased him by asking, "How come you don't choose the Kansas City Royals as your favorite team?" Hank never wavered in his loyalty to his chosen team. To signify he was a devoted fan of the Baltimore Orioles, he proudly wore their orange cap night and day. Unfortunately, he lost the cap somewhere on the farm. Every nook and cranny was checked to no avail. Uncle Dan commented, "Well, your aunt lost a bra several years ago down by the creek. Maybe an old bullfrog stole your hat just like he did that bra!" The hat turned up a year later when Mr. Ed noticed a cow chewing on it. In all likelihood it fell off Hank's head while he was playing in the hayloft.

The children loved exploring in the woods and liked climbing the rocky slopes on the south side of the creek In addition to fishing and swimming in the creek, they collected rocks, frogs, and tadpoles. Box turtles found along the dusty road were brought back to the yard and treated as honored guests who would reside in a cardboard box home. The turtles were even fed strawberries from grandmother's garden. A few garden snakes were snared and assigned to be pets but had to be released after Mary Lou pitched a fit.

Each child had a favorite collection, so there often was bartering and trading for their favorite object. Jimmy, perhaps because his dad was an entomologist, was fascinated with insects. His cousins were aware of his interest and were most helpful in finding bugs for his collection. Hank found a huge beetle. He pretended he wanted to keep it but was secretly delighted that Jimmy was actually willing to give up his weekly allowance of fifty cents to become the proud owner of the dead bug.

When Jimmy was only five, his mama gave him a large plastic container to hold insects he caught with his new net. A few days later he filled the container with angry bees he had collected in the garden. As he opened the lid, the bees instantly buzzed around his head and arms. Two painful stings helped him to be more selective when collecting critters.

Jimmy's next discovery in the garden was a male and female praying mantis linked together in the act of procreation. Jimmy carefully lifted the twig and attached insects and placed them in a container. He had visions of this being the start of a happy insect family. Nature is not kind. The next morning tears started rolling when he looked into the carton. The female had eaten everything but her partner's legs!

Roger, Jimmy's brother, had a jar filled with pennies by the time he was four. The young child observed that his older brother never saved a dime. He suggested, "Jimmy, if you will find me a jar, I'll take care of your pennies." The plan worked. When Jimmy wanted some of his own money, Roger demanded, "Why do you need it?" If Jimmy failed to provide a good answer, Roger would refuse to open the jar. After the pennies started accumulating, Roger had another suggestion, "Since I am saving you so much money, you owe me a fee for being your banker." Mr. Ed chuckled, "Even at a very early age children seem to give indications of their future professions. Roger is sure to go into the business of taking care of finances for other people."

Three-year old Paul had followed his grandfather around the entire day. He was exhausted by twilight. As he had his bath, the Missus said to his mama, "I think Paul should go to bed with the chickens tonight." As soon as his pajamas were on, little Paul headed out for the chicken house. He assumed grandma wanted him to sleep perched on a rafter just like the chickens!

Fishing was an obsession with grandpa, the fathers, and grandchildren. There were occasions when the boat was hitched to the car for an outing to a nearby lake. Most of the time they fished in one of the three ponds on the farm that Mr. Ed had stocked with fish.

As soon as the daily work was completed, the children helped Mr. Ed dig for worms in the rich black soil in the cattle pen or would use nets provided by the Missus to catch flying bugs in the garden. With poles over their shoulders, the children followed their grandpa to the old watering hole. They would stay at the pond until dark and usually came home with a mess of fish that could be served for lunch the following day.

All the ponds had fish, but the favorite fishing site was the one inhabited by the famous bass, Old Fighter. Mr. Ed and the children knew of his existence because

he had been snagged several times. Thus far, the clever fish had always managed to break the fishing line then dive for safety.

Seven-year-old Roger was delighted to be the only grandson fishing with grandpa one Saturday afternoon. He made statements like, "Old Fighter is just around the corner Grandpa." Or, "Old Fighter is mighty hungry. He can't wait to take a bite of the worm on my line." Roger soon had the shock of his life. Old Fighter did take a bite and this time got snagged. It took a lot of work pulling him to shore, but Mr. Ed. and Roger came home with a fish weighing eleven pounds!

On a hot summer afternoon, Mr. Ed and the Missus were sitting on lawn chairs under their favorite maple tree. Surrounding them in the grass was a circle of children and grandchildren. Mr. Ed. looked at the Missus and said, "Didn't I tell you that this would happen? The circle of life has unfolded. We have wonderful children who like to spend time with us and grandchildren who agree that our farm is a little bit of heaven."

It is obvious, Mr. Ed, with willing help from his wife, was successful in helping to mold the personalities and interests of his grandchildren. Mr. Ed was devoted to his wife and willing to lavish both time and love on his children. All of his children and grandchildren followed the examples of his teaching. Mr. Ed considered the Kansas farm a piece of paradise and his family agreed. Dan and his family were constant visitors and others came as often as possible.

Mr. Ed was never at a loss for words. Like their grandfather, most of the grandchildren never missed the opportunity either. The cot was amused. It was noted that when sitting at the kitchen table, all so busy talking that, occasionally, comments of others were not heard.

Many events repeated the past. Like the great-grandfather, Hank and his wife added two orphans from Russia to their growing family. Even though their lives are whirlwinds of responsibilities raising three children, Roger and his wife enjoyed quiet moments of working together to complete crossword puzzles. The Bible stories told and retold by Mr. Ed also made lasting impressions. There was a sense of Mr. Ed's presence in a tiny white country church on Palm Sunday. Family members filed into two pews then listened to Paul deliver a beautiful sermon.

Mr. Ed wisely guessed the probable professions of his grandchildren. Casey became a lawyer, and Roger is managing millions belonging to others. Several of the grandchildren, following the professional aspirations Mr. Ed had when a young man, became engineers.

Each grandchild, if asked, would probably state, "My grandfather was the one who had the greatest influence on my life."

Chapter 22

THE BURIED TREASURE

Mr. Ed, the Missus, and I would have the house alone for months at a time. Then summer would come and all the children and grandchildren found their way back to the farm. I enjoyed several years of holding a whole covey of Mr. Ed's young squirmy grandchildren. Just when they were getting long legged and so big that only one at a time could enjoy my soft mattress, we were blessed with two beautiful new babies.

The Sociable Cot

THOSE LEFT BEHIND

Dan's youngest son was named after him. Fortunately, he did not have to suffer the nickname tagged to his father's name and the only one using endearing terms such as Sweet Danny and Little Dan was his grandmother. The fourth child in Jane's family was called Madeline. As her two older brothers and sister gazed lovingly at the tiny baby girl in the cradle, they immediately started calling her Mattie.

Mattie and Danny enjoyed total devotion from family members. The adults stated that every child in the family was precious, but these two were perfection. In many ways Mattie resembled her mother. However, instead of golden curls needing constant care, Mattie had soft, wavy, light brown hair. Danny had a sturdy little body and a quick smile. He was a picture of his dad in many ways but had flaming red hair like his mama.

Fortunately, the other children were not overwhelmed with jealously toward these young siblings. They were old enough to understand the joy the babies brought to their parents and were contributors of the constant love and patience displayed toward the little ones.

Mattie and Little Dan, in spite of all the affection and attention they received, were not spoiled. Both possessed loving carefree personalities and willingly returned the affection paid to them by their relatives.

When Mattie and Danny were around six years of age, the other members of the family failed to respect the fact that they were no longer babies. A special outing was planned which included only the older children. Margie and Danny had to remain home with only the Missus and their mothers. To say the least, they were outraged!

The morning of the outing did not start well for Mattie and Little Dan. They crawled out of their beds at least an hour later than the others and were so sleepy that little attention was paid to the flutter of actions by their siblings and cousins.

The reason for their laziness was due to staying awake until a very late hour the previous night. After supper, their grandmother had provided two of their favorite treats, sugar cookies and peach ice cream. They finished a second helping then hurried out to the lawn where the others were playing "keep away" with a large ball. Instead of telling the two they were too little to play, the ball was frequently thrown their way.

After the world was finally in full darkness, the Missus spread several old cot covers on the soft grass. All the children rushed to claim a spot, preferably close to Grandpa Ed. The night sky was brightly lit with glowing stars. Each set of eyes tried to be the first to sight a shooting star skidding through the heavens.

Grandpa Ed was prepared to provide another lecture about the stars. This time he explained how the ship captains utilized the position of stars in the sky to navigate across the oceans. The only problem with the story he was telling about naval history was there were several long pauses and no ending. The day and been a long one. Grandpa Ed finally closed his eyes and started snoring.

The oldest grandchildren, Jimmy, Casey and Hank, took over the entertainment by telling add-on ghost stories. When one kid paused in the development of a plot, the next took up the story. Each tried to add even more blood and gore. The creative additions delighted everyone else, but the two little ones were thoroughly frightened. The horrors of the stories made it difficult for them to relax. Even when their mamas had tucked them in comfortable beds for the night, they had trouble getting to sleep.

Danny and Mattie were finally awakened the next morning because of the shouts and laughter of the older children. After a quick visit to the little room behind the kitchen, they joined their grandfather on the cot for a short cat nap on the cot. Their senses were alerted by the smell of fresh cinnamon rolls being removed from the oven. They quickly jumped off the cot and ran for the table. Just as they were ready to claim a roll for their breakfast, Jimmy and Hank, now teenagers with tremendous appetites and long hollow legs, snatched the last of the rolls. Mattie and Danny had to settle for oatmeal, Cheerios and milk.

After finishing breakfast, the two, still dressed in pajamas, lounged on the living room sofa and watched two favorite television programs, Captain Kangaroo and Mr. Rogers. They failed to notice that the older children were combing unruly hair, brushing teeth, and changing into clean clothes.

Their ears perked up to their surroundings when they heard Jane say, "Everyone have a good time." Then Aunt Mary Lou yelled from the sidewalk, "Don't wait up for us. We won't come back until after the fireworks."

Mattie wailed, "Mommy, what's happening? Where is everyone going? Why aren't we going with them?"

Jane explained the situation to her young daughter and nephew. "Grandpa, Uncle Danny and Aunt Mary Lou are taking the older children to the county fair. They will be gone all day and half the night. We felt like the trip would be too tiring for two of you."

Danny had tears in his eyes. "I can't believe my daddy would leave without me!"

The mothers and the Missus tried to comfort two very unhappy children. The two small ones were not one bit interested in helping grandma bake cookies, rejected Carol's suggestion that they pick flowers and even refused to make a trip to the barn with Jane to see the new batch of kittens.

The two sad and dejected children retreated to the mulberry tree at the corner of the yard. The tree was small and ignored by the older children. Perhaps that is why it became a special place where the little ones could go when they wanted to be alone. At the tender age of three, Danny and Mattie had easily pulled themselves up to the lowest limbs. At that time Mattie stated, "When I grow up, I'm going to marry my daddy. I love him bestest in the whole world."

Danny gave a nod when he heard Mattie's wish. His mother was so special he would probably marry her. The following year, when they were four, he suggested, "Our mommies and daddies love each other and shouldn't be separated." He thought a minute then decided, "We could marry each other. When Grandpa Ed is too old and weary to take care of the garden and feed the chickens, we will do the chores."

Now, with the accumulation of six years of wisdom, they did not consider any thoughts about a future together. Instead, they spent their time lashing out anger and disgust because their family was treating them like babies.

Mattie reflected. "Casey taught me to tie my shoes. Hank realized how smart I was and helped me learn math tables through five. This summer Paul helped me read his old first grade books. How can they think I am too little to take along when they go on an interesting adventure?"

Little Dan whined, "My daddy always takes me fishing with him. He brags about how grown up I am because I can stay with him all day in the boat. If I can sit all day in his stupid boat, then I could walk around the fair grounds."

Their thoughts turned to their unconcerned aunt. "Aunt Mary Lou teaches kindergarten and claims she knows all about kids who are five and six. She should have known we were big enough to enjoy the fair. Why didn't she ask us to come with them?"

Even Grandpa Ed received a portion of their wrath. "Grandpa didn't even leave the extra car so our moms could take us to the swimming pool this afternoon. Instead, he took the old car and told Jimmy he could drive the other one!"

SEARCHING FOR CLUES

The Missus watched as her youngest grandchildren abandoned the sanctuary of the mulberry tree and slowly dragged their feet back toward the house. They certainly looked rejected and disgusted. She thought, "I need to think of something they can do which will lift their spirits." She knew her little ones would display no interest in the games and stories usually appealing to them. After thinking for a few minutes, she smiled and said to herself, "This will spark their interest!" What the Missus had remembered was listening to Mr. Ed and his sister Alicia as they discussed a treasure buried somewhere on the farm

She called to the dejected grandchildren, "Come over here and sit on your grandmother's lap. I want tell you about something the two of you can do that the other children don't even know about." The Missus gave each of them a kiss on the cheek before explaining further, "I've been told there's a buried treasure here on the farm. Why don't you ask your mamas if they'll help search for the treasure?"

As she listened to her mother's words, Jane vaguely recalled hearing about the treasure as a young child. For some reason, she and her inquisitive older sister had never attempted to discover any of the clues. Searching for the buried treasure would divert the children from their misery. She smiled in anticipation. The search would be as much fun for her and Carol as it would be for the children.

The Missus continued, "I remember that Grandpa Ed told me the first clue is hidden in the oldest book in the house."

Mattie and Danny raced to the bookshelf holding the worn picture books once belonging to the oldest children, Casey and Jimmy. As the years had passed the stories had been reread countless times to younger children in the family.

Jane smiled and advised, "I think your Grandmama is thinking of a book that would be even older than Grandpa Ed."

Carol looked at her small son and added, "Do you remember one rainy day last year when we explored the attic?" We found a stack of old books and picture albums in a trunk. Let's start there."

It was always an adventure to climb up in the attic. The house was now so old that the narrow stairs leading up to the high room squeaked and groaned even under the light footsteps of the small children. Years had added an accumulation of narrow slits in the walls. Dim bands of light filtered through the slits and provided the light needed to find their way into the attic. Jane noticed the many spider webs but decided to ignore them. She was relieved that, for the time being, the frightening mice were not scampering near her feet.

Mattie and Danny had heard the story about the witch who once lived in the attic and believed every word. Mattie and Danny cautiously looked around at the odds and ends of broken furniture. They agreed with their mamas that the witch had probably decided to find a more suitable abode in some other attic.

After their eyes became accustomed to the dim light, they identified the large trunk sitting in a corner. Carol switched on a flashlight and beamed it at the trunk. Jane carefully opened the lid and found it filled with smelling musty books. Danny examined each of the books as they were lifted out of the trunk before he decided, "This old Bible looks like the oldest of all. Maybe it will lead us to the treasure."

Jane carefully cracked the Bible open to the cover page. It was filled with a long list of names. She suggested, "I bet these are signatures of our grandfathers."

Mattie and Dan could both read. With only a little help from their mothers, they read the names William, George, William, Richard and Edward."

The children stared at the last signature. Mattie exclaimed, "I know that writing! That's the way Grandpa signs his name."

Danny thought a minute then added "When my daddy gets old and lives in this house, I bet he will add the name Dan to the list."

Mattie thought the Bible was interesting, but was anxious to continue with the treasure hunt. "Mama, see if you can find something which will give clues about the treasure."

Jane slowly turned the yellowed pages. Stuck between the old and new testaments she found a small envelope. She carefully lifted the tab and read the message aloud.

"Grandchildren of the future,
Do you seek the family treasure?
If this is what you truly seek
Take a stroll through the pasture to yonder creek.
Stand in the area above where the stream shifts to a hard right
Look up and note landmarks in your sight.
Shift your gaze to rocks on the nearby hillside.
See the overhanging cliffs the deep ravine seems to divide.
Climb toward the South Forty, see the overhang rock so big
Then three feet below and to the left of the rock you should dig."

The mothers had a difficult time keeping up with the small adventurers as they ran toward the creek. Danny dashed far ahead of the others. The site indicated by the message would be easy for him to find. He and his daddy often fished for perch in the stream. Earlier this summer he and his brother, Greg, had gone swimming in the deep pool located at the curve of the creek.

After arriving at the designated site, the explorers looked toward the South Forty. The cliff loomed above them on the other side of the creek but no overhanging rock was seen. Mattie and Danny were discouraged. Maybe the hunt was over before it ever really started.

Jane gazed at the cliff for a few minutes and recalled, "When I was a little girl there was a large overhanging rock about where we are looking. See that big flat rock about halfway down the hill? I bet it fell from above."

Carol suggested, "Why don't we climb up the cliff? Maybe, when a little closer, we can identify where the rock was lodged."

As the explorers carefully climbed up the hillside Mattie grew cautious. "Maybe we shouldn't be here. Aunt Mary Lou says there are snakes around these rocks."

Jane shook her head. "Don't pay attention to your silly aunt when she is talking about snakes. She even thinks that long sticks in the grass could be snakes. Aunt Carol and I are here to protect you. We will watch out for any suspicious critters." As they continued the climb, the only moving creatures seen were grasshoppers, bees and a toad.

After arriving at the top of the cliff, it was apparent where the rock had once stood. Jane carefully stepped off the distance directed in the message. Danny and Mattie started digging in the soft soil with the garden trowels borrowed from Grandpa's shed.

Each time a trowel hit something hard, it turned out to be a small rock. Just as the children were getting discouraged, a ping sound was heard as Danny's trowel hit something hard. Both children gleefully dug deeper into the soil until a green jar was exposed. Carol carefully twisted off the lid and pulled a yellowed note out of the jar. She slowly read the message suggesting the next place to search.

Do you think this adventure to the hillside was for naught?
Nay, it's the roots of the family that you have sought.
Look around at all the treasurers you see,
Pastures, the fields, the large white house, and yonder trees.
Retrace your steps to the beloved home
There in its east side, through the dirt you will comb.
You'll stand on the porch but where is the spot?

Eight steps to the right and you'll be on the dot.
Are the spirea bushes still in a line?
Under the third one another clue you will find.

Carol rolled up the note, squeezed it back into the jar then tightly screwed the lid back in place. Danny placed the jar in the hole then carefully covered it with soft dirt. This clue, like the one found in the Bible, would remain where it was found. Perhaps someone from a future generation would once again search for the family treasure.

Danny, the fearless leader anxious to search for the next clue, ignored his mother's caution, "Danny, be careful!" Due to his haste when rushing down the cliff he suffered a bad fall. There was a bump on his head, scrapes on his hands, and blood gushing from the cut on his knee. His injuries made it difficult to walk so Jane and Carol took turns carrying him.

The Missus noticed the slow advance of the four as they headed toward the farmhouse and knew there had been an accident. She rushed out to meet the slow-moving troop. Danny's crying had been reduced to whimpers. When he noticed his grandmother running to meet them, he once again turned on the shrieks and howls. His grandmother gently reassured the small child that he was in good hands. Even though he weighed nearly fifty pounds, she insisted on carrying him the rest of the way to the house. Once inside the kitchen she gently placed him on the cot. After cleaning his wounds, and added a soothing salve. The cut on his wounded knee felt much better when covered with a Mickey Mouse band-aid and the goose egg on his forehead no longer throbbed so much after Grandmother provided him an ice cube wrapped in soft cloth.

The Missus said, "Perhaps you need to take a break before continuing the treasure hunt. While you were gone, I made soup using the vegetables your grandpa brought in from the garden." She added, "I also baked something which you will enjoy."

Mattie took a deep sniff. "Danny, Grandma made blueberry muffins! They will make your hurts go away."

The soup and muffins quickly revived Danny's spirits. The children were once again feeling fine, but their mamas were exhausted. Jane and Carol suggested it would be a good idea for everyone to take an afternoon nap. The children nixed the idea. "We need to keep up the hunt. It's important that we find the treasure before the others return home."

Danny and Mattie had difficulty following the next set of directions. They went to the steps leading off the east porch but turned left instead of right. Eight steps put them near the large maple tree not mentioned in the message.

Danny's mother said to her small son, "Think a minute, Danny. When you write, which hand holds that pencil? Maybe you should head in that direction."

Thanks to her reminder, Danny changed directions and carefully took eight steps. Even though he went in the right direction, the site didn't seem right. He was barely past the first spirea bush.

His mother had another suggestion. "Danny, take daddy steps instead of kid steps."

Danny took eight long strides and ended up exactly where the note said, in front of the third spirea bush.

Once again, the two children used their trowels for digging. This time they did not hit rocks but the task was difficult because the soil was dry and hard. It was several minutes before they once again heard the ping, an indication that glass had been tapped.

You will find the treasure near the garden
Under the bush that each spring is laden
With purple blossoms and an aroma so sweet
If you dig toward the sunset, you're in for a treat.

Jane gazed at the lilac bush and realized that the container holding the treasure would be difficult to find. The lilac bush was far larger than it was when she was a little girl and must have been only a small bush when Aunt Alicia was the explorer. Digging up the treasure would require more than small garden trowels. She searched the shed and found clippers large enough to cut away leaves and branches and a sharp spade to use for digging deep into the soil. The lilac bush was in for a drastic trimming.

The Missus, who avoided the sunshine like a plague, could not clearly observe the activity without going outside. She donned the old scarecrow outfit including sunglasses, a large hat, the old long-sleeved shirt and gloves. She joined the children where they stood watching mamas dig. It was obvious Jane and Carol did not enjoy the heavy manual labor. Their faces were red and puffy and sweat ran down their noses. Both were complaining about the blisters appearing on the palms of their hands.

OPENING THE TRUNK

Success finally came when they heard a dull *plunk*. Spirits once again soared. The mothers ignored the blisters and kept digging until a brass trunk was revealed. As the trunk was pulled from the ground, Mattie danced in excitement. "I bet this trunk is filled with jewels and gold, and we'll be rich!"

The Missus smiled, "This family was never rich in that way. If your great Aunt Alicia once dug up a treasure of jewels and coins, you can be assured she would not have reburied the trunk."

The condition of the trunk was surprising. The brass was a dark dingy color but had its original shape. Unfortunately, the hinges sealing the trunk were rusty so it was impossible to lift the lid. Another trip was made to Mr. Ed's tool shed. The claw hammer was chosen as the best tool to gently pry open the lid.

All the viewers gasped as the contents were revealed. Instead of jewels and coins, it contained an odd assortment of articles. It took Jane only a moment to determine the value of the items. She gasped, "Now we can believe all the stories Uncle Jack and Grandpa Ed told us about the family history." Jane's eyes filled with tears. She had always been fascinated about stories of the past. Even though she had wanted to believe what her father and uncle said, she recognized that both tended to stretch the truth.

The search party carefully inspected each item in the trunk. Carol recalled hearing stories about a great grandfather of the past named William who traveled from England to the new land of opportunity. "This old pro-tractor and bent compass must have been used when he helped to survey downtown Chicago."

Danny found an old tin cup filled with crumbled leaves. He sniffed the leaves then guessed the historical value. "These leaves smell like tobacco. The grandpa who fought in the Civil War probably used that bent cup for coffee, and I bet the leaves are some of the tobacco sent to the farm by his friend who lived in Kentucky."

"Look at this black purse. Don't you think it looks a little like a doctor's kit?" Jane carefully untied its strings and examined the contents inside. It contained a small magnifying glass, tweezers, knife, thread, a needle and sev-eral vials. Inside the vials were dried seeds and herbs. "I was sure Uncle Jack was making up the story about Ruth, the grandmother who was an herbal doctor. This is proof that she existed."

Mattie held up a bell and what looked like strands of horsehair. "These are funny items to find in a treasure box. Can you imagine who owned them?"

Danny quickly guessed, "Even though those look like hair from a horse I bet they were clipped from the mane of the pet mule Grandpa talks about. He is always telling us stories about Anamule."

Jane added, "Do you remember how the ladies did not like it when Anamule was around the house? Maybe this bell was put around her neck so they could keep track of her whereabouts. If they heard her near the garden or flowers, they probably ran out the door and shooed her away."

The next two items also puzzled the children. One was a lace handker-chief decorated with tiny flowers in the corner. It still smelled like lavender. The other item was a pitch pipe. Jane immediately identified the owners of these items. "I remember my grandmother holding me when I was about your age. She always smelled like lavender so this hankie must have been hers." She blew into the pitch pipe. It was rusty but still made a distinct sound. "My grandmother and grandfather were known for their beautiful voices. Maybe the pipe was used to get a proper pitch before they started singing a duet."

The Missus picked up a pink hair bow, a lock of brown hair and a locket. She opened the locket and gazed at a lovely young girl. "This is a picture of Aunt Alicia when she was about ten years old. She was the last one to search and find the family treasure."

Jane challenged the children. "Now that we have found the treasures, it is our responsibility to add to it before replacing it in the ground. Do you think we could find special items which will remind future generations about Grandpa Ed and Grandma?"

Everyone raced back to the house in search of new treasurers. Mr. Ed had purchased a new knife last week. His discarded old knife with only one broken blade would make a great addition to the treasure box. He was always using that knife for whittling wood, pealing fruit, or prying open nuts.

Mattie noticed his dirty overalls hanging on the porch. She searched the pockets and found a small card with a picture of Jesus on one side and the Lord's Prayer on the other. "Grandpa always carries a Jesus card like this in his pocket. Let's add this one to the trunk."

Mattie decided to sit on the old cot and think about other treasures to add. Her eyes lit up with a new idea. "Mama, can we add a pillow from the cot? This old cot has always been part of the family so it should be represented with a treasure."

Jane responded, "That's a good idea but the trunk is small. There just isn't room for the pillow."

"I know something that can be added which will represent the old cot." Mattie searched through the photographs recently taken by her sister with her new camera. The print Mattie selected was tilted and blurred but represented the family's affection for the old piece of furniture. Grandpa was asleep on the old cot with Mattie and Danny cuddled next to him.

Jane looked at the Missus. "Mama, I noticed that you have extra quilt block sets in your sewing basket. Please let us put a section in the trunk. You will always be remembered for your beautiful quilts."

Carol had an additional idea for a contribution representing the Missus. "Last week Mary Jane helped the children make bookmarks. Dried flowers from your garden were placed between sheets of clear contact paper. When we think of you, we always think of your love of flowers. A floral bookmark would be a perfect addition."

THE APPROACHING STORM

Jane and Carol were in no hurry to cover the chest with dirt but the Missus had other ideas. "Have you two forgotten that in Kansas it's a good idea to always watch the sky? Look to the west. Do you see those dark clouds? The storm coming this way looks like it will be a downpour. It may even produce ground lightning and hail." The Missus frowned then added, "It's a little late in the season, but we've had tornadoes in August."

The mothers looked at the sky and agreed with the assessment made by the Missus. Treasures were quickly placed in the trunk and the trunk returned to the hole. After it was covered with dirt, wheat straw was scattered over the loose soil. Meanwhile, the Missus pulled clothes off the line then hurriedly shut the doors to the barn, sheds and chicken house.

Mattie and Danny found the approaching storm exciting. They danced and whirled in circles then held out their arms and raced through the yard as gusts of wind whipped at their backs.

The Missus expressed her concern, "We need to get inside the house as quickly as possible. You might get hurt by something flying in the wind."

Quick preparations for the coming storm were completed. The TV was unplugged and the iron put away. The Missus cautioned, "Don't use the telephone. During strong storms the electricity hops right out of the speaker."

Jane raced up the stairs when she remembered that all of the windows on the second floor were open. Seconds after she closed the last window, she heard her mother yell from the bottom of the steps, "Get downstairs this instant. Feel the heavy air and quietness outside? There may indeed be a tornado in this storm."

319

The Missus had been through hundreds of storms in Kansas and was always cautious. Jane remembered the many times she had been carried down to the cellar as a small child and wondered if her mother was going to insist that they retreat to that dingy dark space under the house.

The Missus ordered, "There isn't time to go to the cellar. Mattie and Danny, crawl in the space under the stairs. Your mamas and I will stay in the hallway with you. We won't have to worry about flying glass in here because there's only one window and it faces away from the wind."

Seconds later, the angry storm swooped over the house. A roaring rumble, similar to the sound of a freight train, passed overhead. The next sound was the *plunk* of heavy raindrops hitting the tin roof of the porch. The storm noise became even louder when tiny beads of hail replaced raindrops. It seemed to the five that they stayed huddled in the hallway for hours, but in actual time, only a few minutes had elapsed.

The Missus peeked out the hallway window and decided, "It will be safe for us to go into the kitchen now. A tornado probably passed overhead, but I don't think it hit the ground."

Mattie and Danny were frightened and not too sure they wanted to leave their stairwell cave. The Missus reassured them. "When your parents were small, they huddled on the old cot during the storm. That will be a safe place for you to stay until the storm has passed."

The storm continued to rage, pelting the area with heavy rain as well as asserting its power with wind, thunder, and flashes of lightning. Trees bent back and forth and some limbs lightly touched the ground. A bucket sitting by the porch door was pushed over by the wind. It made a plunk, plunk, plunk sound as it was pushed down the walkway. There was an intense bolt of lightning which made the adults and children shriek and jump. Immediately following the lightening flash, the thunder grumbled and lights went out. The Missus, who never cussed, was driven to say, "Darn! That lightning strike hit the electric transformer out by the road. We'll probably be without electricity at least until tomorrow."

The worst of the storm finally seemed to be over. The Missus again looked out the windows and noted that the lawn was covered with broken tree limbs and large balls of hail. Puddles of water were everywhere.

Jane commented, "This storm is what my husband calls a toad strangler."

The Missus was worried. "The storm came from a westerly direction and Springville would have been in its path. I hope Ed saw to it that everyone found shelter!

ADVENTURES AT THE FAIR GROUND

About an hour later two muddy cars drove into the barnyard and nine wet soggy bodies stumbled out of the doors.

Roger, the budding meteorologist, was the only one who displayed any enthusiasm about the weather. "Wow, did you ever see such a storm? I thought we were going to be blown away!"

The fairgoers changed into dry clothes than gathered in the kitchen to tell about their experiences. Greg, Danny's older brother, started the tale by saying, "This was a disaster from start to finish."

Casey felt it her duty to share the problem caused by Jimmy. She had been a bit put out because Grandpa allowed Jimmy to drive the car instead of her, so she was anxious to tattle about his inefficiency. "You all have heard Jimmy state how skilled he is when driving the old truck around the hay bales in the field. Well, he found driving on a road more of a challenge. Up the road about two miles he took a curve too sharply and ended up in the ditch. Grandpa, Uncle Danny, and Jimmy had to push the car while Aunt Mary Lou backed it onto the road." She smiled with satisfaction, "Grandpa won't let Jimmy drive on the road again until he has improved a bit."

Paul took up the story. "Aunt Mary Lou kept up a running dialog about all the attractions and rides we would enjoy at the fair. She still remembers the excitement felt when riding on the Ferris wheel when she was a young girl."

Greg added, "Grandpa listened to her then reminded us that he had been to nearly seventy county fairs and had never tried the Ferris wheel or any other ride. He told us that today would be no different. He attended the fair to talk about farming matters with friends and see the animals."

Jimmy continued, "Grandpa Ed suggested that, since it was already late in the morning, we should first stroll and look at the farm exhibits, eat a late lunch, listen to the band concert then move on to the Midway to enjoy rides. Some of us, mainly Mom, were not too excited about this schedule, but Grandpa was boss."

Every child had something to add to the story. Roger said, "Grandpa seems to know every farmer in Logan County. He stopped to chat with everyone he met. Grandpa also took us from pen to pen to observe fat pigs, angry steers, and lazy sheep." By the way the other children rolled their eyes and pinched their noses, it was evident that, even though they liked animals, these city kids found the inspection of dozens of animals boring.

Uncle Dan laughed with the children. "Hank expressed a wish for all of us."

Hank nodded his head and agreed. "Yep, I told grandpa we were starved and needed to amble over to the food tent."

Aunt Mary Lou continued, "Evidently everyone else at the fair had the same idea. It took almost an hour before the line brought us to the food table. Mom, you watch your grandchildren eat so you can visualize how the kids piled their plates full of hot dogs, hamburgers, pickles and chips. We were so thirsty that we drank three large pitchers of ice tea."

Mary Lou again turned to the Missus. "Mama, you and Daddy have an uncanny understanding of the weather. While we were eating Daddy sensed the change of atmosphere. Dad commented about the stillness, heat, and thought the sky was a funny color."

Casey started laughing. "After we finished eating, we walked by the band stand. We listened to a hog caller and a hillbilly band. An announcer then asked if anyone in the audience would like to come up to the stage and preform. Wouldn't you know! Aunt Mary Lou remembered that she used to sing with a group with a ridiculous name, Sunflower Sweeties. Jimmy and I had to hold on to her. We would have died of embarrassment if she had walked up on that stage to screech a cowboy song. She might have even offered to play the guitar!"

Grandpa, never one to keep quiet, had to tell a bit more about the adventure. "Each one of my grandchildren had money in his pocket, and it was evident they planned to spend every penny at the Midway. Jimmy paid fifty cents for the privilege of shooting the air gun at moving ducks. He hit all three and won a fuzzy duck he thought would make a nice gift for Mattie. The other children pitched pennies but had no luck at all. Meanwhile, my daughter looked for high places just like she did when young. She kept urging the children to finish their games, so they could ride on the Ferris wheel."

Uncle Dan described the coming storm. "The wind was picking up momentum. Lady's hats, paper cups, and an assortment of fair litter whirred through the air. Just when we approached the Ferris wheel the first strike of lightening flashed across the sky."

Roger had great pride in his grandfather's ability to forecast the weather. "Grandpa told us to forget the rides! He suggested we run as fast as we could to the cattle barn since it was the only building in the area. We made it inside just before the sky opened up. It was kind of scary. We could hear sounds of people shouting to each other to run for cover, heard some tent poles break and knew from low moos and squeals that the animals were frightened."

Casey shook her head then continued with an observation. "The cattle barn was awful. It smelled like cow manure and was dark and hot. There were lots of sweating people crammed in the space with us. We stood there packed like sardines and listened to the storm raging outside. All of us were scared to death."

Paul continued, "There was an awesome bolt of lightning then thunder so loud it made the building shake. Uncle Dan told Aunt Mary Lou that she was very lucky not to be on the Ferris wheel. Since it was the highest structure around if she had been on it, she would have been fried!"

Hank related, "The storm seemed to go on for hours. Before long, Grandpa Ed got restless. He said he hoped the Missus was watching the sky because the storm was heading in the direction of the farm. As soon as the winds died down and the lightening seemed to ease, Grandpa suggested we run to the cars and drive home. He didn't want Grandma to be worrying about us."

Jimmy said, "It seemed like the car was parked a mile away from the cattle barn. We all were soaked as we ran through the downpour. " He turned to his small cousin. "Mattie, the fuzzy duck I won for you was destroyed by the rain."

The saga about the disastrous day at the county fair was drawing to a close. They all stopped talking when the Missus presented them with a large platter of blueberry muffins and a pitcher of lemonade.

The older children had been aware that Danny and Mattie were probably disappointed that they were not included in the trip to the county fair. They wondered why the youngest children now seemed so gleeful and smug. Casey said to them, "The fair wasn't that much fun and the only fireworks we saw were high in the sky. Still, I guess it was better than staying here all day."

Mattie and Danny had been sitting on the cot, patiently waiting for the right moment to tell their story. Now was the time. "No, we had a wonderful adventure. Do you want to hear about the treasure buried here on the farm?"

Chapter 23

THE GOLDEN YEARS

There seems to be an opinion that old folks feel unwell, sit around all day, and have very little fun. Mr. Ed, during his senior years, exemplified that this assumption is incorrect. He continued to enjoy each day and his energy surpassed even that of his young grandsons. Mr. Ed did not sit around on any old chair. When he felt a need to rest he came to me.

An Energy Enhancement Mechanism, the Cot

THE YEARS ROLL ALONG

The old house was in need of a new coat of paint. Mr. Ed did not fiddle around. If a job needed to be done, he would do it! Mr. Ed ignored the fact that he was now eighty-one years old. Age didn't matter that much. Last year when only eighty, he had painted the entire barn by himself. Mr. Ed was on the extension ladder painting the eastern side of the house when he noticed his daughters standing on the lawn below him. They had tears in their eyes and were saying a prayer for their dad. He yelled to the sobbing sisters, "Now you girls stop your fretting. I'm just fine. Remember, up here I'm a little closer to the angels!"

Except for a bad knee, occasionally greased down with WD-40, Mr. Ed enjoyed good health during his senior years. When people asked him how he kept so young, he would respond. "There are several reasons. I keep busy and don't think about my aches and pains. The other reason is I have that old cot. When my bones are feeling tired, I go rest on it, and in no time, I feel a lot better."

Mr. Ed never retired from farming. Instead, he adjusted the work to what he could easily manage. The milk cows and chickens were no longer around. The beautiful glossy ebony Angus cattle still grazed in the pastures but a second cousin took care of them. The same cousin also planted and harvested the crops. Of course, Mr. Ed. was always available to supervise.

Mr. Ed did not give up his garden. The lush black soil, tended with skillful care by Mr. Ed, produced an abundance of vegetables. The Missus canned a little, froze a lot and gave away bushel baskets of goodies to nieces and friends. Still the vegetables kept coming. The Missus suggested, "Ed, why don't you put the extra vegetables in the back of the truck? If you set up a stand by the filling station, I bet some folks might want to buy our corn, zucchini, tomatoes, and green beans."

Mr. Ed had a great time displaying the produce and visiting with everyone who stopped at the station. He talked to a couple from California on their way to visit their daughter in Illinois. As they were leaving, he suggested, "The crop of green beans was outstanding because the rains came just at the right time. Why don't you take along some to give your daughter?"

He enjoyed discussing the weather with a man from Texas and gave him all of the zucchini. About an hour later, he helped a young man on the way to his wedding fix a tire. He insisted the new bride would appreciate some fresh red tomatoes and corn.

When Mr. Ed finally came home that evening, he gleefully announced, "All the vegetables are gone." The only trouble was he had given them all away and didn't collect a dime!

Jane's husband gave Mr. Ed an old set of golf clubs. Mr. Ed thought the game was hilarious. He was quite good for someone who had never had lessons. He swung the driver like a baseball bat and somehow made the ball fly straight and far. The years of playing croquet on the lush green lawn at the farm gave him a sense of how hard to tap the putter. The balls were easily guided into the tiny holes. Those playing with him, who professed to be skilled at the game, shook their head in disbelief that his score was often better than theirs.

Mr. Ed accompanied two of his grandsons and a couple of their friends out for a day of golf. After nine holes the teenaged boys were exhausted. Mr. Ed, who walked four miles each day checking the electric fence back at the farm, was not one bit tired. He suggested, "Boys, it is only two o'clock. Let's play at least another nine holes." After returning home, the boys professed to their parents, "We will never go golfing with Grandpa again! He has too much energy!"

Jimmy was serious about obtaining the Eagle rank in Boy Scouts. His troop was very active in developing outdoor skills and many of his merit badges were earned in this manner. Jimmy enthusiastically participated in frequent weekend trips to mountains in Georgia and Tennessee where the boys engaged in climbing and survival training. His grandfather just happened to be visiting in Georgia on a weekend when Jimmy and his troop were scheduled to go on an outing featuring where they would practice repelling off the side of a mountain.

Jimmy, with the approval of his scout leader, invited his grandfather to go along.

Mary Lou was skeptical. "Dad, you will have to hike several miles to get to the mountain."

"Honey, walking never hurt anyone. I still walk several miles each day back at the farm."

"But Dad, you will have to eat the food that Jimmy cooks over the small camp fire."

"Honey, I eat your cooking so surely I can chew the stuff your son cooks!"

"There is one other problem, Dad. The boys only have sleeping bags. Won't it be difficult for you sleeping in one on the hard ground?"

"Mary Lou, I have been sleeping on that old cot for close to a century. Sleeping on the ground shouldn't be a problem."

Mr. Ed satisfied his daughter's reservations, and accepted the invitation to go along with the troop. He had a great time with the boys. He was able to keep up with them on their hike up the mountain, slept soundly on the hard tent floor, ate poorly cooked food, and told bathroom jokes which made the boys blush.

When the troop returned home late Sunday evening Mary Lou asked, "Did you enjoy the experience, Dad?"

He replied, "It was great until I looked up at the steep mountain cliff and saw my grandson dangling upside down. Only a small rope kept him from plunging fifty feet!"

THE FIX-IT MAN

Mr. Ed had always enjoyed the role of handyman. In his senior years, he improved his skills and could make old furniture look new. He spent one entire winter taking off the varnish on the old buffet. By the time he completed the restoration project, the buffet was a valuable piece of antique furniture. His skillful hands transformed the rickety old workbench sitting on the porch into a stately oak table.

The Missus was very pleased, and had it carried into the parlor. There it was put to good use displaying the treasured vase once belonging to her mother and multiple pictures of grandchildren. Mr. Ed eventually refinished almost every old piece of furniture in the house, including the beds, the chests and even the cot. He took the rust off its springs and frame then painted all of the metal with a coat of black paint. When the Missus noticed the cot's updated look, she contributed to its appearance by making it a new paisley print cover.

Mr. Ed spent a winter refinishing the kitchen chairs. First, he stripped off the dull green paint. After sanding the wood, he added stain, then varnish. He completed the task by weaving perfect cane seats for each.

Jane, who loved old furniture, would go to antique stores and garage sales looking for chairs for her dad to refinish. The pieces he restored eventually filled her kitchen and dining room.

An antique dealer visited Jane's home. His eyes fell on the lovely chest and vanity. He was most impressed with the quality of refinishing techniques used by her father.

Jane talked to her dad on the telephone later that evening. "Dad, Mr. Jervoski thinks you could make a fortune refinishing furniture. He went on and on about the chairs you caned."

Mr. Ed shook his head as he replied, "If I had to refinish furniture for a living it wouldn't be so much fun."

THE 60ᵀᴴ WEDDING ANNIVERSARY

The telephone's three rings woke Mr. Ed from his nap on the cot. Mary Lou greeted him by gushing, "Dad, Jane and I have been thinking about how lovely Kansas is in September."

He agreed. "It sure is, Honey. We've had plenty of rain this year, and the crops look good. Sunflowers are always pretty in the fall. However, this year I think they are the prettiest we've ever seen. Your mama has some in the garden which must be over fifteen feet tall."

Mary Lou continued, "I miss you and Mom and want to see the farm. I have decided to take a few days off from teaching next week to fly back to see you."

Mr. Ed frowned, "Honey, we are always pleased when you come back. Since you were in Mexico most of your summer's vacation, you didn't get to pick gooseberries or enjoy seeing the pretty flowers your mama planted. However, this is a most unusual time for you to come. Won't it be difficult to leave the classroom so early in the school year?"

"Don't worry about it, Dad. I have several days of personal leave available." Mary Lou shared, "Jane is coming too. She said she is really looking forward to going on long walks to the South Forty, and she wants to collect flowers and leaves to use in dry arrangements."

Before completing the telephone conversation, Mary Lou commented, "Oh, Dad, I almost forgot something. Tell Mom that I am bringing back a twelve-pound present you will both love."

Mr. Ed was suspicious. Something special was going on. Mary Lou never tried to leave the kindergarten classroom at the start of a new school year, and it was absolutely foolish to make the expensive plane trip for just a long weekend.

Mr. Ed pulled the calendar off the wall and studied the month of September. He grinned and said to himself, "So this is why our girls, who live in distant Georgia, picked this particular time to fly back to Kansas!" At the end of the following week, he and the Missus would celebrate their 60th wedding anniversary.

After solving that puzzle, he pondered over the secret of the gift weighing twelve pounds. He grinned when he remembered that years ago, he had given the girls a record player that weighed about that amount. That surely wasn't what she was bringing because Dan had given them a new phonograph for Christmas.

He looked up and grinned as the Missus slowly approached the kitchen.

Ed said, "Honey, I had the most interesting telephone call. Jane and Mary Lou are planning to come back here at the end of next week. Why do you suppose they are coming?"

The Missus smiled. "The girls always loved early fall when the air is cooler and our fields are filled with yellow. When they called last week I told them about the sunflowers in our garden. Maybe they are coming back to see the lovely landscape."

Mr. Ed grinned but said nothing. It was obvious that his wife had no inkling as to why the daughters were making the air trip back home. The anniversary party would be a wonderful surprise for her.

Mr. Ed continued by sharing with his wife more of the telephone conversation. "Mary Lou is bringing us a twelve-pound gift. Can you think of anything we need that weighs twelve pounds?"

The Missus responded, "Whether we need it or not won't bother the girls. I'd guess it would be a trunk for you to refinish if Jane was picking out the present. Mary Lou probably has in mind some kitchen appliance we don't need."

The Missus smiled. "The last time the girls were home, they said that we desperately needed a microwave. Wouldn't that weigh about twelve pounds?"

Mr. Ed agreed. "I'll bet that's the surprise. Do you suppose a new gadget like that would be difficult for us to operate?"

The following Thursday afternoon Mr. Ed was taking his after the lunch siesta on the cot when Danny's car arrived in the driveway. Dan had taken the day off to meet the airplane then bring his sisters, Jimmy's wife, and the special surprise to the farm.

Mary Lou tiptoed into the kitchen and stood by the cot. This time she placed a tiny pink bundle weighing twelve pounds in her daddy's arms. "Wake up, Daddy. It's about time for you to meet your first great granddaughter."

Mr. Ed had tears in his eyes as he looked at the perfect baby. The circle had once again repeated itself and seemed to be getting better each time.

Mr. Ed had very little sleep on his cot once the girls arrived. The blasted telephone kept ringing off the wall both night and day. All the aunts, cousins, and friends had important messages for Jane or Mary Lou.

Mr. Ed was not fooled by the telephone conversations. He knew grandiose plans were being made for a party celebrating their anniversary. He pretended to be sleeping. Even though his hearing was slipping, he could hear enough to know what was going on.

The Missus was almost deaf and barely heard the telephone's three long jingles. The limited hearing was only a part of the reason why she ignored the phone. She was much more interested in watching and fondling her new great granddaughter.

On Saturday the girls dressed in their best clothes and were ready to leave the house about eleven in the morning. Just before shutting the door

Jane said, "Mom and Dad, please change into your nice clothes. I think some of your friends want to see you this afternoon over at the church."

At two in the afternoon, a polished 1927 black Ford sedan arrived at the farm gate. A cousin and her husband had generously offered to chauffeur Mr. Ed and Missus to the church in their antique car. The arrival at the churchyard of the old car was spectacular. The waiting crowd included family members, neighbors, and special friends.

Mr. Ed, looking handsome dressed in a new dark blue suit, stepped out of the back seat and saluted to the crowd. He then gently and graciously helped his lovely bride, the Missus, as she too slowly stepped out of the ancient car. He took her arm and gallantly led her past those whose lives were richer because of their association with these two special people.

A short religious ceremony was held in honor of Mr. Ed and the Missus. The old couple did not renew their vows but nodded their heads when the minister stated they had never forgotten the words promised sixty years before. He related how they always worked together as a team and always put the welfare of the other ahead of anything else.

A feast was held in the fellowship hall after the ceremony. Everyone had a wonderful time and the twelve-pound baby didn't seem to mind as she was constantly passed from arm to arm.

Chapter 24

MISSUS, I'M WAITING FOR YOU

*Mr. Ed and the Missus had several more good years together
after their 60th Wedding Anniversary. Their quality of life
was good even though their steps were slower. They continued
to enjoy meeting with their friends at the old church for a
prayer meeting and supper one Sunday evening each month.
Sometime during each week, either they went to see Dan's
family or Dan's family came to the farm. Mr. Ed no longer
tried to make the long drive to Georgia. Instead, he purchased*

affordable senior citizen airline tickets so he and the Missus could visit their daughters at least twice a year.

The Loving Cot

SLOWING STEPS

M r. Ed and the Missus made a practice of visiting Western Kansas in late June or early July when the wheat fields were a golden glow. Dan recognized the regret he heard in his dad's voice, "I'm getting too old to drive that far each summer, and even if I could, your mother doesn't feel like going with me."

Dan had a great idea. He was able to arrange for one of his pilot friends to take Mr. Ed on a flight over the wheat fields.

It was a glorious day when Mr. Ed made the airplane journey. The sky was a perfect blue and there was not a cloud in sight. Mr. Ed, who knew the geography of Kansas backward and forward, enjoyed identifying the towns and communities as the small plane flew over them. After he identified Dodge City, the pilot swooped down over a palatial ranch that had once belonged to Mr. Ed's distant cousin, Wild John. Mr. Ed grinned and shook his head at the thought of how fate changes over time for each person. A few years after Wild John had visited the farm so many years ago, oil was discovered on his spread. Drilling for oil and harvesting huge wheat fields resulted in Wild John becoming a very wealthy landowner.

Mr. Ed was awed by the sea of wheat fields seen from high in the air. It looked like an endless ocean of gold. When he returned home, his first comment to the Missus was, "God surely loves his people. He gave us a beautiful sight of waving golden wheat which will later be harvested to provide food for the masses."

THE LAST DAYS

Mr. Ed, the Missus and the old cot had grown old together. The cot had a lot in common with Sir Lancelot of the Round Table. Like Sir Lancelot, its devotion was to his master, but his affection for the master's chosen one. There were so many times when the cot wished there was some way it could demonstrate to the Missus how much the special caring she gave it for many long years was appreciated.

In the cot's opinion the Missus was just as pretty as she was when he first met her as a new bride. She was still petite and neat as a pin. Her hair was no longer bobbed but was curled with a gentle perm. Would you believe it? In spite of being in her mid-eighties there were only a few gray hairs on her head!

The Missus had been nearly deaf for quite some time now. Rather than admit to an inability to hear, she nodded her head to Mr. Ed's constant rambling about what would be good for the world and how their children and grandchildren could better manage their lives.

Cataracts had dimmed her eyesight. Before this happened and her fingers grew stiff from arthritis, she had completed a quilt for each family member. These quilts were so perfect that, rather than for daytime use, they were displayed on a quilting rack or on a guest room bed.

The Missus continued to provide simple meals for Mr. Ed and anyone who happened to appear when it was time to eat. The children gave her a microwave oven as a Christmas present, but she claimed the food did not taste as good as when she cooked using her old pots and pans. The microwave sat unused on the counter except when Mr. Ed fancied a bowl of popcorn or needed his coffee reheated.

The upstairs rooms were unused and shut off but the Missus continued to keep the downstairs areas spotless. She still considered the cot a mess and was always straightening his covers and puffing up his pillows.

The Missus frowned and said, "Edward, I've been telling you for over sixty years, that old cot is a disgrace. The sides won't stay up, the frame needs painting again, and the mattress is a mass of lumps. Why don't we have Dan take it to the dump and replace it with a nice recliner? You sure enjoyed the Lazy Boy at Jane's last summer!"

Mr. Ed grinned and gave the cot a pat. "This old cot suits me just fine! These lumps in the mattress are a perfect fit for my body."

Mr. Ed and the cot had been together for almost ninety years. The cot watched him grow from a toddler into manhood, endured the abuses of his children, loved his grandchildren and enjoyed having the privilege of holding two of his great grandchildren. Never once did it shirk its duty of providing Mr. Ed rest and relaxation.

Mr. Ed never lost interest in the world around him. He enjoyed watching television and listening to the radio each day. His eyesight remained keen so he constantly read newspapers, magazines and books. It was not unusual for him to remain on the cot and read throughout the night.

Even though Dan did the heavy garden work, like turning the soil and cultivating, Mr. Ed still worked almost daily planting, weeding, or harvesting the vegetables.

Mr. Ed did have times when he felt mean and aggressive. He would get on his tractor and drive to the South Forty where he continued his war on the thistles. That weed truly was a thorn in his side.

The crisp early December day had been busy. Mr. Ed took the Missus into town for her weekly visit to the beauty parlor where she had her hair shampooed and set. While she was getting all prettied up, he picked up some groceries and visited with his friends at the garage.

Once home, he was feeling a bit tired and decided to take a quiet rest on the cot. Just as he was settling into a nice nap, he heard Miss Tilly, the golden cat, scratching the screen door. Miss Tilly was insistent. It was time for her dinner!

Mr. Ed put on his coat and walked slowly to the garage to get the food for the demanding animal. He wondered why he felt so dizzy. A few minutes later, as he bent over to put food in Tilly's dish, the excruciating pain in his head made him reel then fall.

The Missus sensed rather than heard his moan. She put on her old slippers and sweater, slammed the kitchen and porch door, and tottered to the garage. Even though the garage was dim and unlit her eyes found the crumpled body near the car. She rushed to his side, "Edward, Edward, please answer me." In response her husband rolled his eyes, gestured with his hands but made no sound.

The Missus tugged and pulled but found it impossible to move his body. She commanded, "Stay where you are." She rushed into the kitchen, grabbed a pillow and quilt cover off the cot then ran faster than she had in years back to the garage. After trying to make her husband comfortable, she again rushed to the house and called a neighbor to help.

Mr. Ed was always described as an easy-going, amiable man. After the stroke, his last days were spent in direct contrast to this personality. He was mean spirited, refused to follow the directions of doctors and nurses and acted as though the family members taking their turn at his side were a nuisance.

Each family member tried to make him comfortable. Jane, the nurse, straightened his sheets, placed a cloth on his forehead, and gently pushed a flavored lemon stick between his dry lips. Mary Lou kept up a constant chatter even though her father's eyes remained closed. The Missus spent endless hours at his side. She held his hand and rubbed his arm but never said a word.

Roger happened to be taking his turn when his grandfather's eyes opened and focused on his grandson. Roger fished into his pocket and brought out several coins. He asked, "Grandpa, how much do I need to get a couple of beers somewhere around this joint?" Slowly, with the fingers on his right hand, he correctly pointed to the correct change.

The paralysis did not improve, and Ed grew weaker. Dan noticed that his father's movable fingers were pointing upward. He gently asked, "Dad, are you telling me you're ready for that trip to heaven?" Dan later stated that his dad seemed pleased to be understood.

In a few short days the family once again flocked back to the farmhouse. All the available beds and sofas were filled. Each and every person quickly expressed a willingness to sleep in Mr. Ed.'s favorite resting place, the old cot.

A wake was held the evening before the funeral. The barnyard filled with so many cars that a distant cousin had to assume the role of parking attendant. Inside the house, food was abundant. The ladies aid members had been aware of Mr. Ed's impending death and had menus prepared well ahead of the wake.

Rose's youngest daughter assumed the responsibility of deciding how to arrange the overflow of food in the crowded space. Flossie and her close friend, Miss Simmons, were among the first to arrive. Flossie was directed to place her plastic pail filled with potato salad on the table while Miss Simons uncovered her spicy pumpkin bread and set up a card table on the porch to hold desserts. Danielle, still beautiful but with a silver cap of short curls, was greeted by the tearful Missus. As they hugged the Missus looked at the contribution Danielle was providing. She sighed, "You remembered that chocolate cake was Ed's favorite dessert!"

Allison did not bother bringing food. She knew there would be enough food to feed an army so instead brought paper plates, napkins, tissues and toilet paper. To bring a smile to sad faces, she even brought an old Sears catalog to be displayed in the Sweet Pea House.

Allison smiled, "What wonderful hours were spent in this kitchen. She hugged the Missus. "You served delicious meals and always had cookies for Sunflower Sweeties to nibble on at our stay overs. This room still exudes a feeling of warmth and comfort.

She started to giggle when eyes roamed to the corner of the room. She went to it and bounced up and down a few times. "Mary Lou, didn't you suggest years ago that the old cot was talented in music and was capable of performing with the Sunflower Sweeties? It is ancient now, but bet squeaks and groans have been perfected."

The evening was filled with reminiscing stories of how Mr. Ed had enriched all their lives. There were so many present that, at first, no one recognized the quiet man operating a video camera. Danielle walked in from another room and exclaimed, "Roy, it that you?" Roy, the photographer who had roamed the earth and now lived in Europe. He had returned to pay respects to his former teacher and the family of a man who had always been his special friend.

THE COT GIVES COMFORT

The ritual of the funeral and burial were completed, the last of the guests had kissed the old woman's cheek. Her girls insisted, "Mama, you simply must come back to Georgia with us and stay during the cold winter months."

The Missus crossed her arms, shook her head. "No! No! No! Girls, this is my home and this is where I will stay."

Dan gave his mom a tight hug before suggesting, "Don't worry about Mom. I'll come by each day after work to check on her. On weekends, Carol or I will take her to the beauty parlor and grocery store. Whenever she wishes, we will take her up to our house to stay for a few days."

The following evening the Missus was alone in the big house. She was keenly aware of Mr. Ed's absence because he always filled the rooms with noise. If company wasn't around, he talked to his wife, the walls, and even the cot. In his off-key voice he sang parts of familiar songs, whistled tunes, or retold nutty stories. After reading a good book he always provided a synopsis of the story and an evaluation of the author's writing skill for the Missus. When he wasn't making noise himself, he clicked on the radio or television.

In contrast to her husband, the Missus was calm and quiet. Now that Mr. Ed was gone, the house had an eerie silence. It was so quiet that the sound of trucks shifting gears before climbing a distant hill and the whispering moan of the winter wind seeped through the walls. The only distinctive sound coming from inside the house was the ticking of the ancient clock hanging on the wall near the cot. It's a wonder it continued to tick. When teenagers, the girls had often sung, "My Grandfather's Clock," while doing dishes. Mary Lou once asked her sister, "Do you suppose that old clock on the wall will stop ticking when Daddy dies?"

The Missus was not one to cry over the loss of her mate. She and Mr. Ed were well aware that their days on this earth were numbered. Because of her frail health, she had always assumed that she would be the first to leave. She was a bit angry about not being present to enjoy seeing his entrance into heaven. Her mind's eye could easily visualize him tipping his straw hat to St. Peter then almost running through the golden gates. Once inside, he would greet Jack and his other siblings, parents, and friends of the past while he hugging Anamule's neck.

The Missus was restless. She quietly roamed throughout the house. She found the bedroom cold and the bed bumpy. She slipped on her old slippers and strolled into the living room but found the sofa and chairs very uncomfortable. It was not long before she wandered into the cozy kitchen. She immediately sat down in her old rocking chair but even it failed to help her relax.

The cot made a silent plea, "Come rest on me, Missus, I can give you comfort."

The Missus slowly walked over to the cot's side. She gazed at its appearance, before preforming the lifelong ritual of smoothing covers and puffing up pillows. Arthritic fingers slowly turned the radio knob until she heard a voice describing a K-State basketball game. The old lady shook off her slippers and housecoat and, for the first time in her long life, slipped quietly under the cot's covers.